DRAGON KINGDOM

of Wrenly

THE COLDFIRE CURSE

By Jordan Quinn

Illustrated by Ornella Greco at Glass House Graphics

LITTLE SIMON

New York   London   Toronto   Sydney   New Delhi

LITTLE SIMON
An imprint of Simon & Schuster Children's Publishing Division
1230 Avenue of the Americas, New York, New York 10020
First Little Simon edition February 2021
Copyright © 2021 by Simon & Schuster, Inc.
All rights reserved, including the right of reproduction in whole or in part in any form.
LITTLE SIMON is a registered trademark of Simon & Schuster, Inc., and associated colophon is a trademark of Simon & Schuster, Inc. For information about special discounts for bulk purchases, please contact Simon & Schuster Special Sales at 1-866-506-1949 or business@simonandschuster.com. The Simon & Schuster Speakers Bureau can bring authors to your live event. For more information or to book an event, contact the Simon & Schuster Speakers Bureau at 1-866-248-3049 or visit our website at www.simonspeakers.com.
Designed by Kayla Wasil
Text by Matthew J. Gilbert
GLASS HOUSE GRAPHICS Creative Services
Art and cover by ORNELLA GRECO
Colors by ORNELLA GRECO and GABRIELE CRACOLICI
Lettering by GIOVANNI SPATARO/Grafimated Cartoon
Supervision by SALVATORE DI MARCO/Grafimated Cartoon
Manufactured in China 1120 SCP
2 4 6 8 10 9 7 5 3 1
Library of Congress Cataloging-in-Publication Data
Names: Quinn, Jordan, author. | Glass House Graphics, illustrator.
Title: The coldfire curse / by Jordan Quinn ; illustrated by Glass House Graphics.
Description: First Little Simon edition. | New York : Little Simon, 2021. | Series: Dragon kingdom of Wrenly ; book 1 | Audience: Ages 6–9 | Audience: Grades 2–3 | Summary: "Ruskin, the pet dragon of the royal family of Wrenly, forms new friendships with the dragons of Crestwood and goes on exciting adventures"–Provided by publisher.
Identifiers: LCCN 2020024829 (print) | LCCN 2020024830 (eBook) | ISBN 9781534475007 (paperback) | ISBN 9781534475014 (hardcover) | ISBN 9781534475021 (eBook)
Subjects: LCSH: Graphic novels. | CYAC: Graphic novels. | Dragons–Fiction. | Fantasy.
Classification: LCC PZ7.7.Q55 Co 2021 (print) | LCC PZ7.7.Q55 (eBook) | DDC 741.5/973–dc23
LC record available at https://lccn.loc.gov/2020024829

Contents

Chapter 1

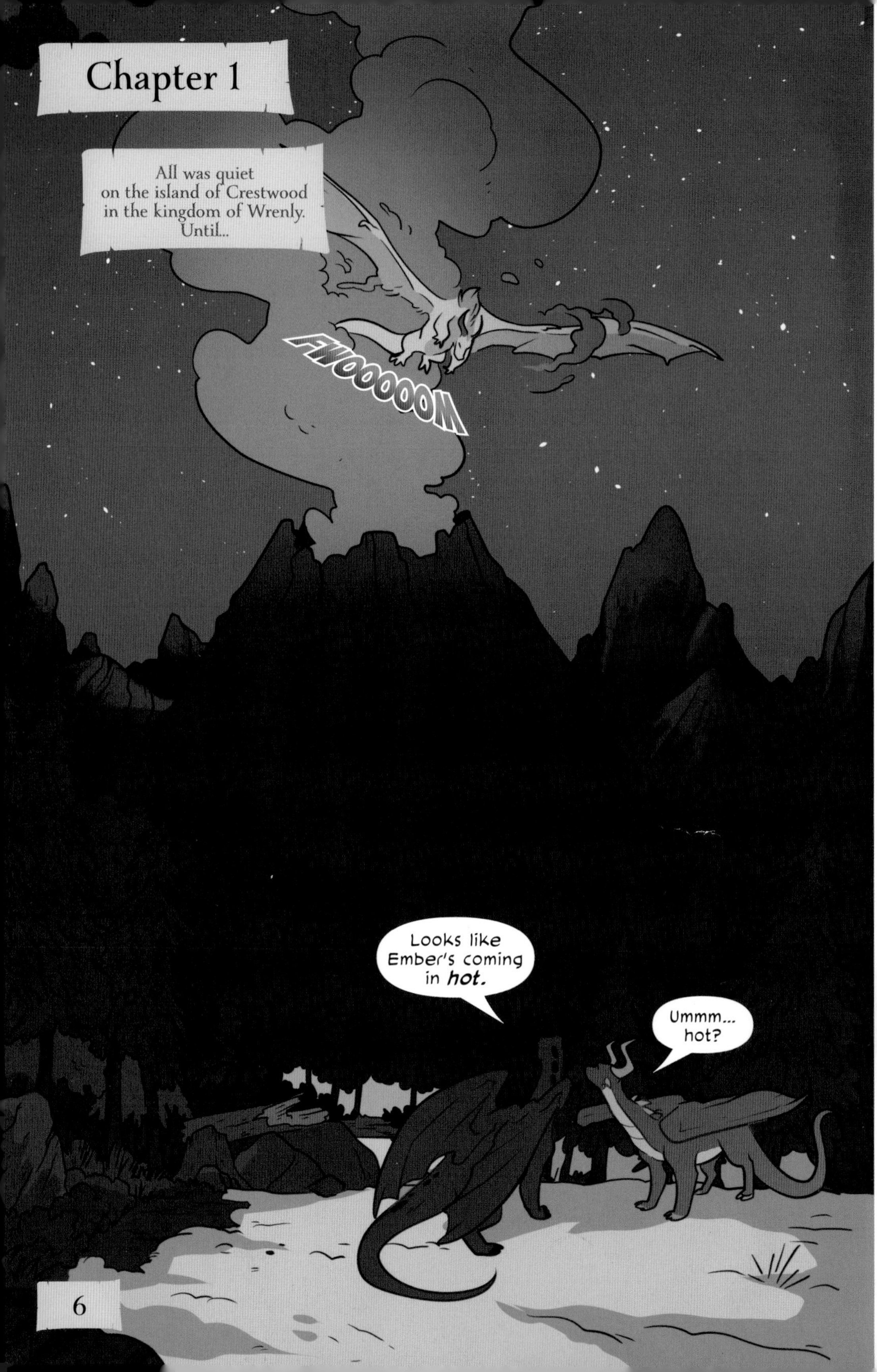
All was quiet on the island of Crestwood in the kingdom of Wrenly. Until...
FWOOOOOM
Looks like Ember's coming in *hot.*
Ummm... hot?

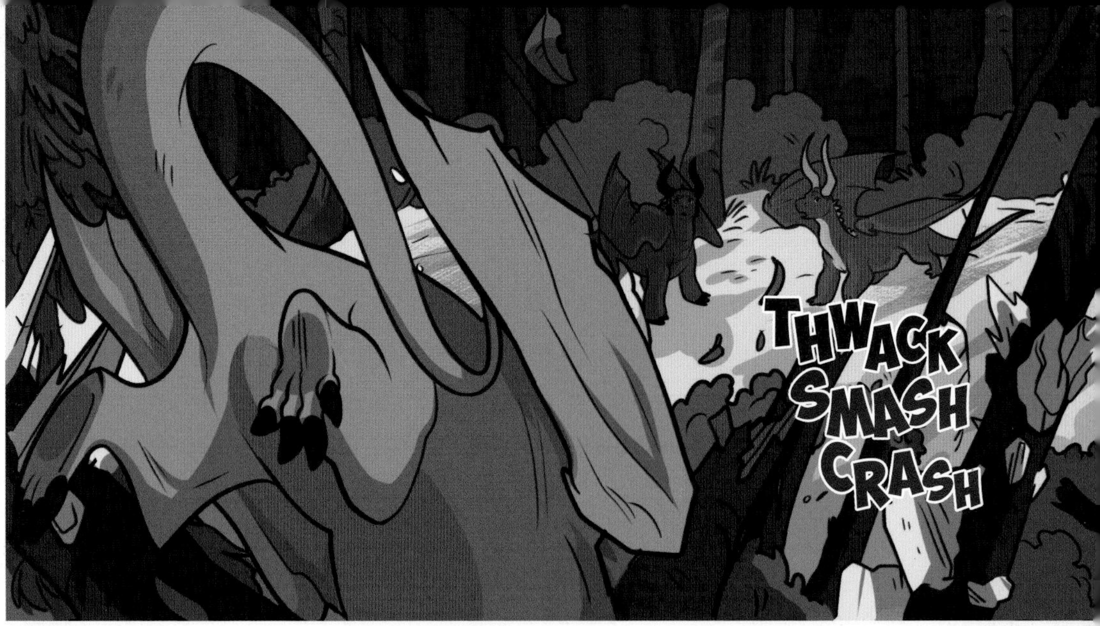
THWACK
SMASH
CRASH

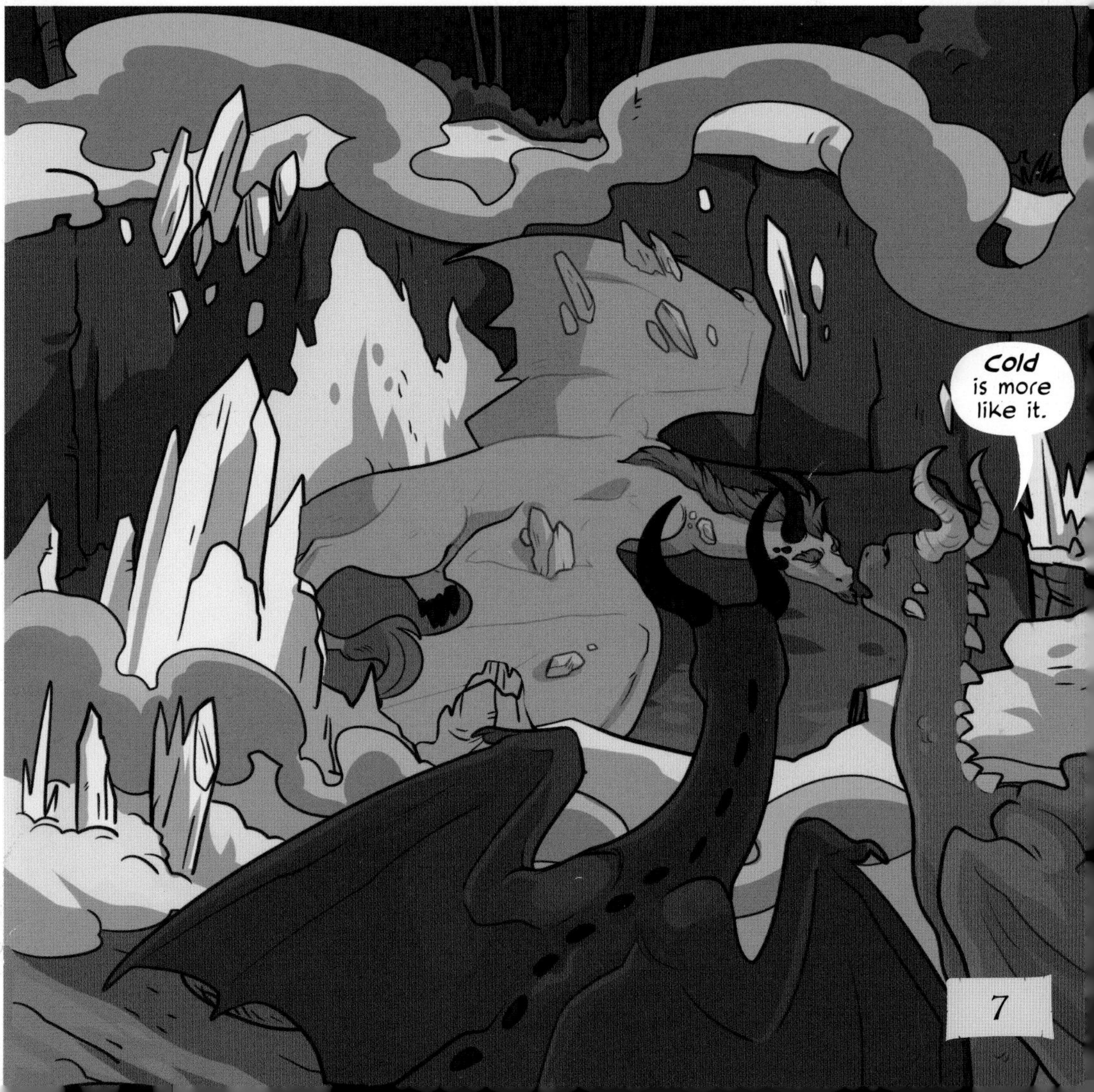
Cold is more like it.

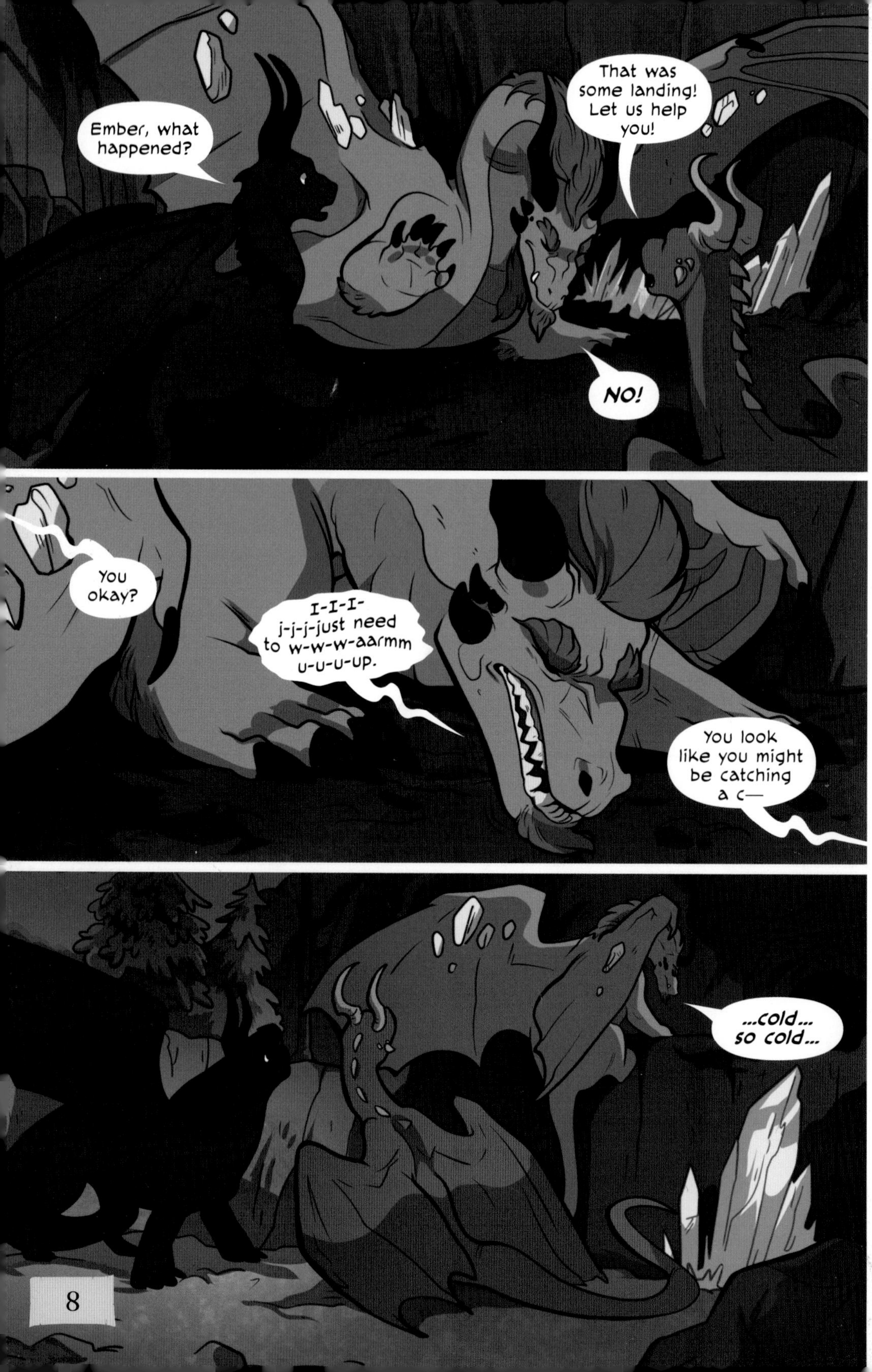

Ember, what happened?
That was some landing! Let us help you!
NO!
You okay?
I-I-I- j-j-j-just need to w-w-w-aarmm u-u-u-up.
You look like you might be catching a c—
...cold... so cold...

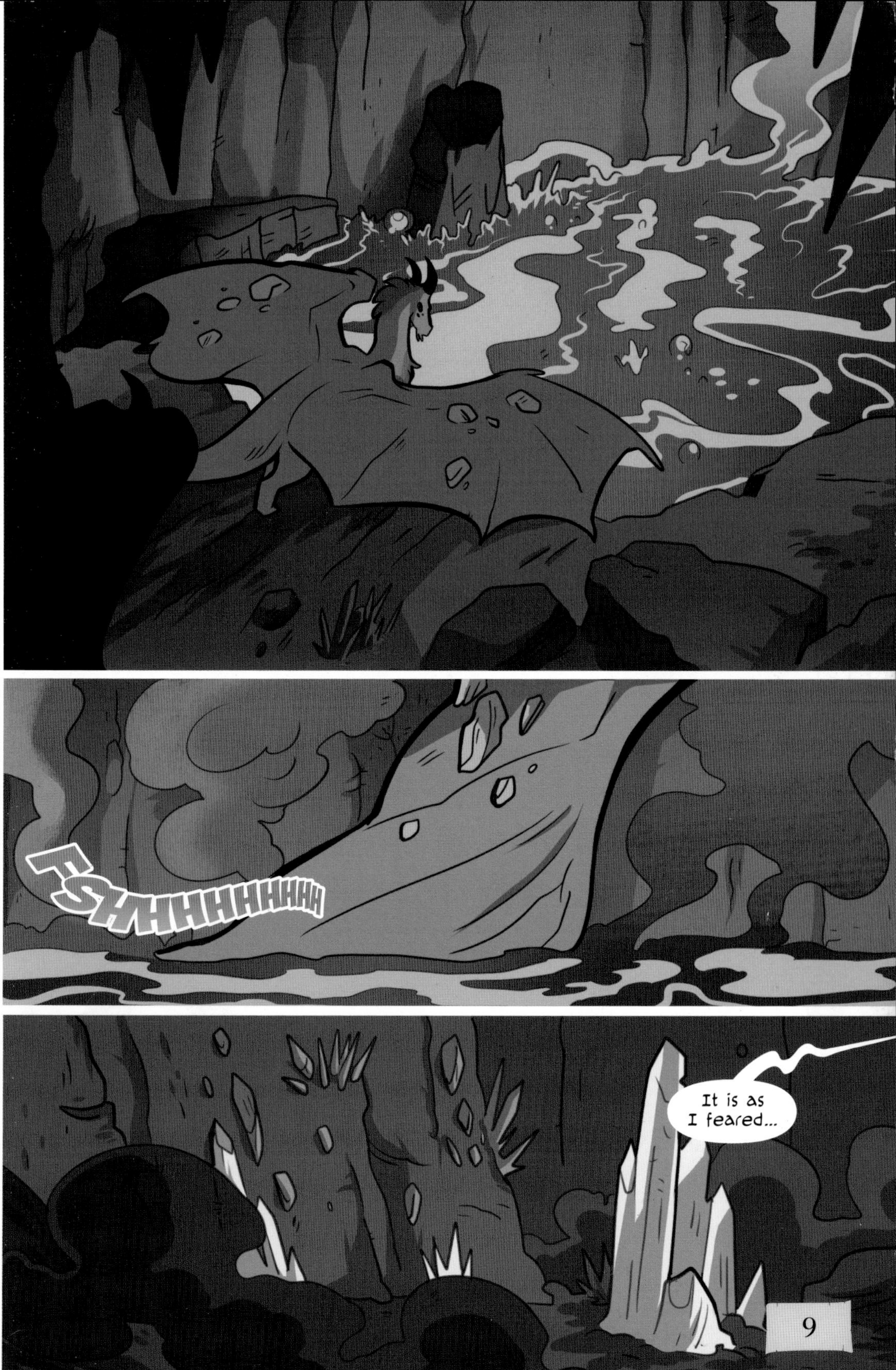
FSHHHHHHHHH
It is as I feared...

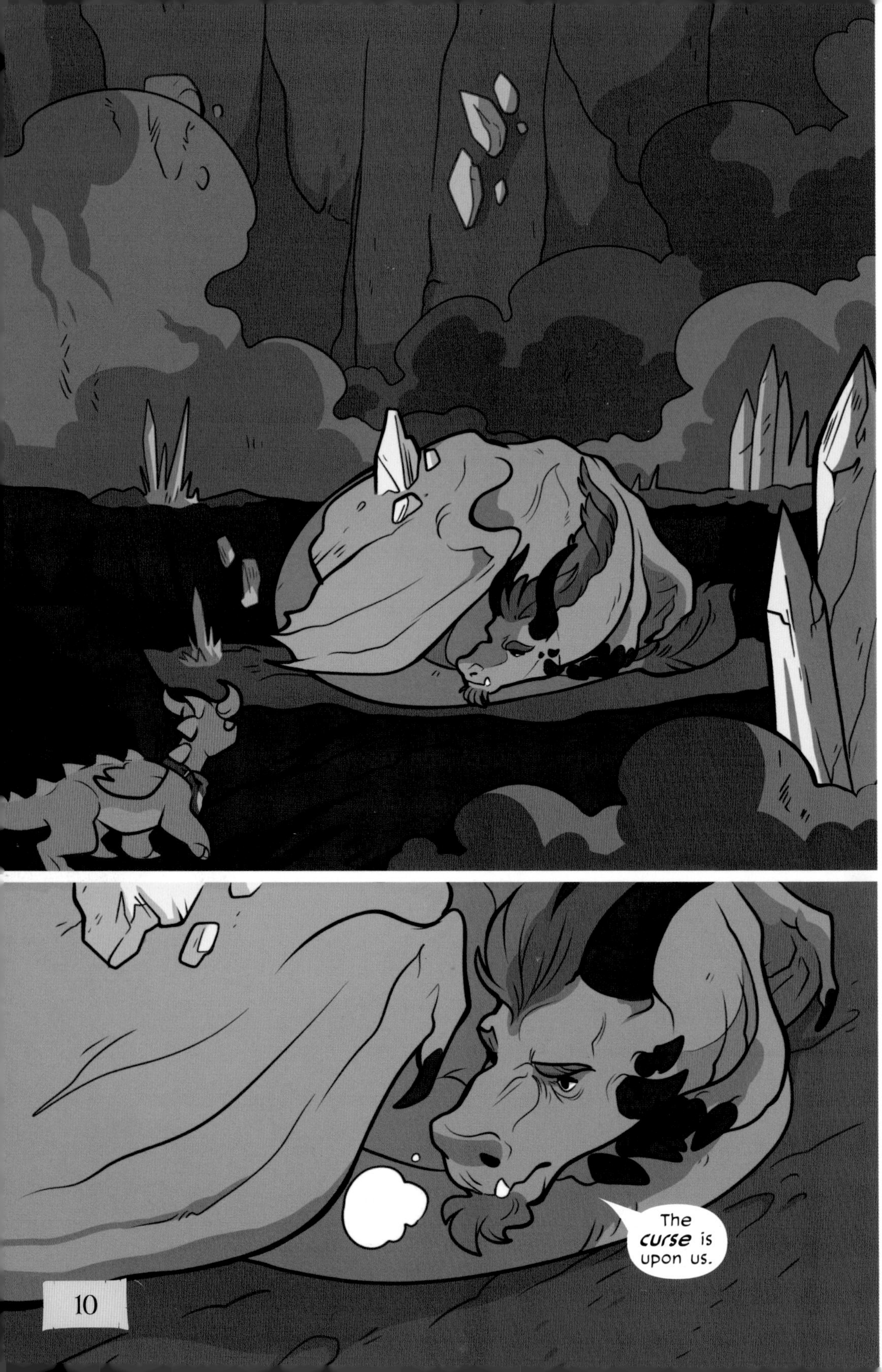
The
curse is
upon us.

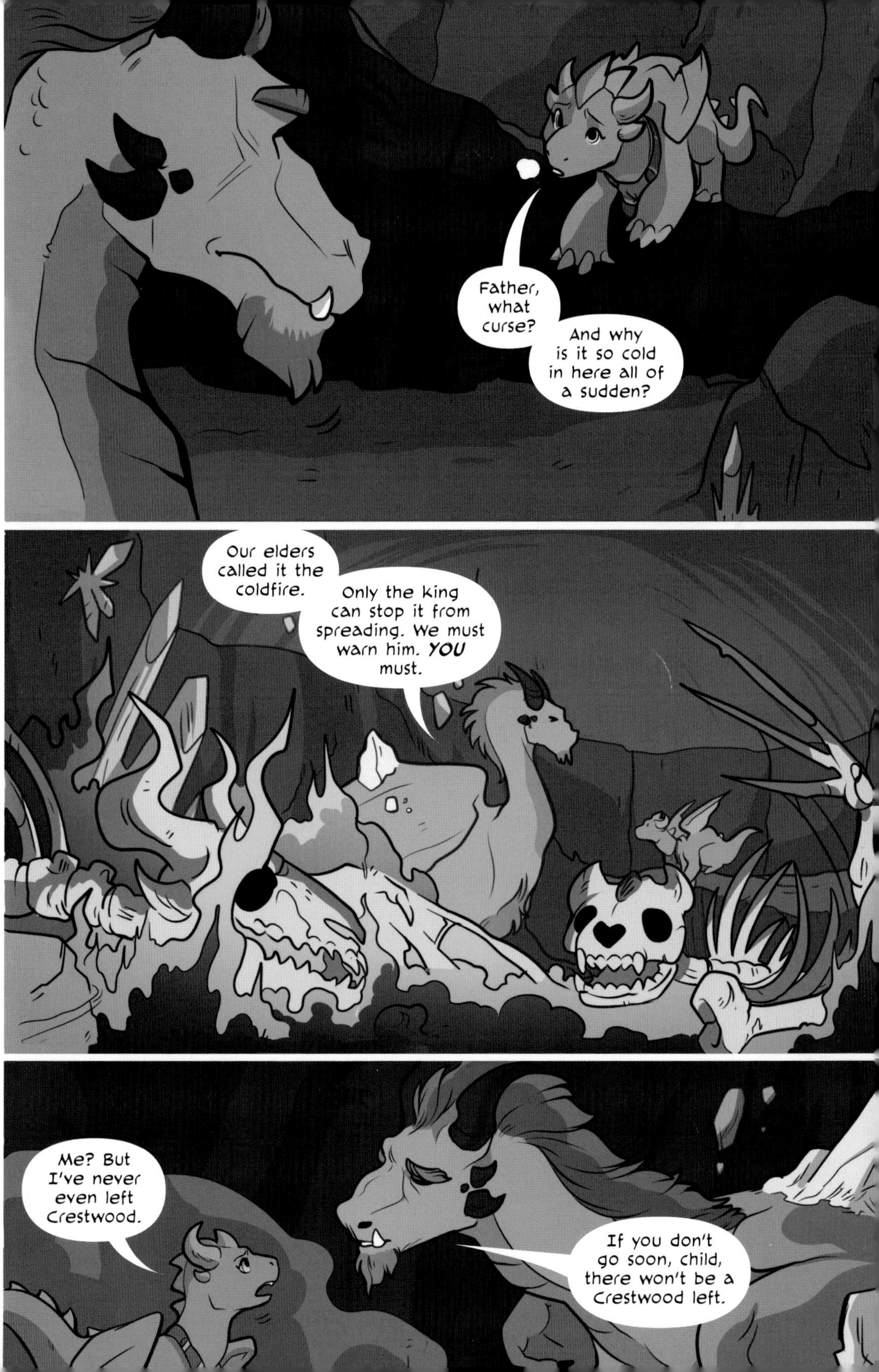
Father, what curse?
And why is it so cold in here all of a sudden?
Our elders called it the coldfire.
Only the king can stop it from spreading. We must warn him. YOU must.
Me? But I've never even left Crestwood.
If you don't go soon, child, there won't be a Crestwood left.

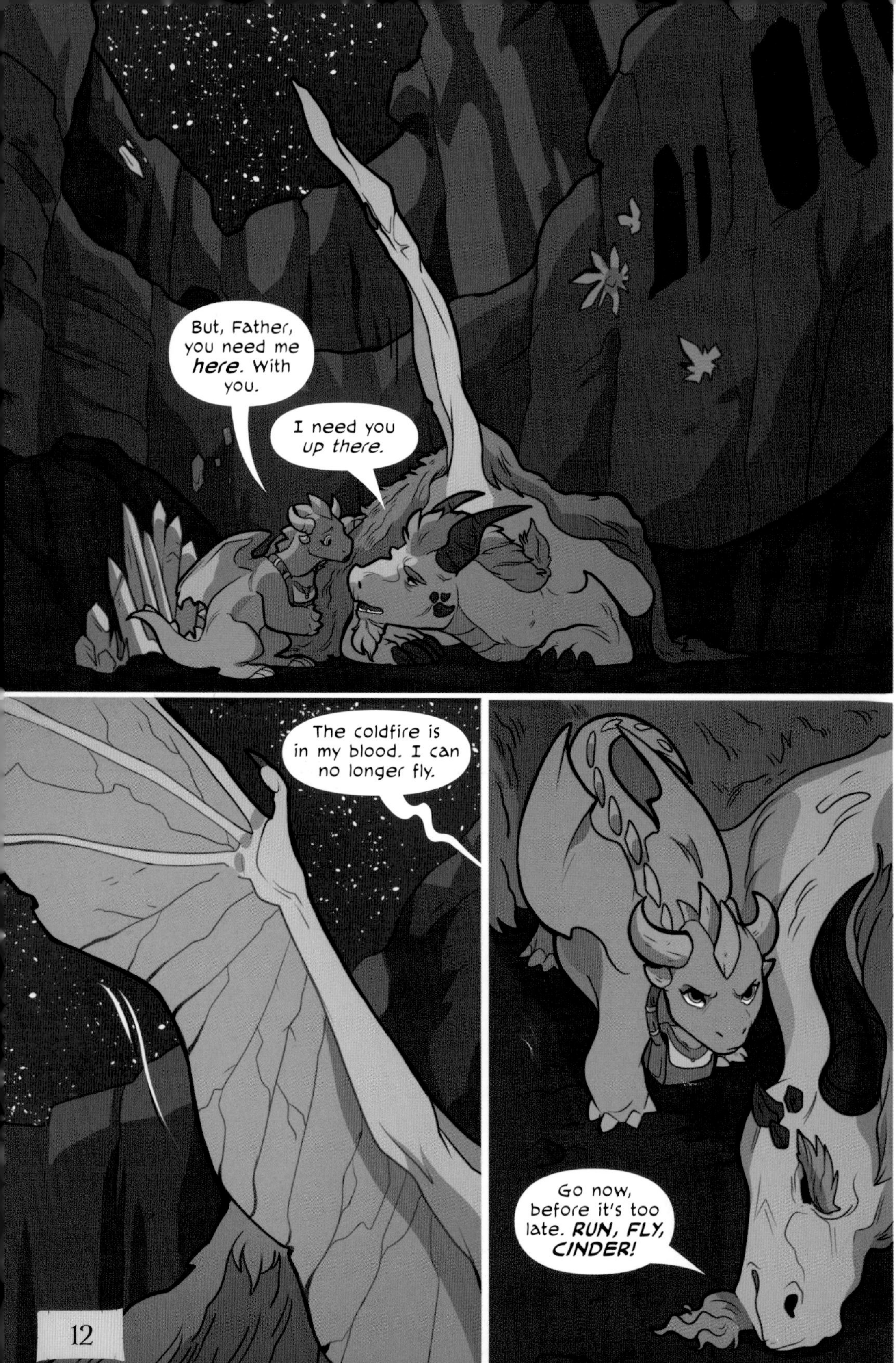
But, Father, you need me *here.* With you.
I need you *up there.*
The coldfire is in my blood. I can no longer fly.
Go now, before it's too late. ***RUN, FLY, CINDER!***

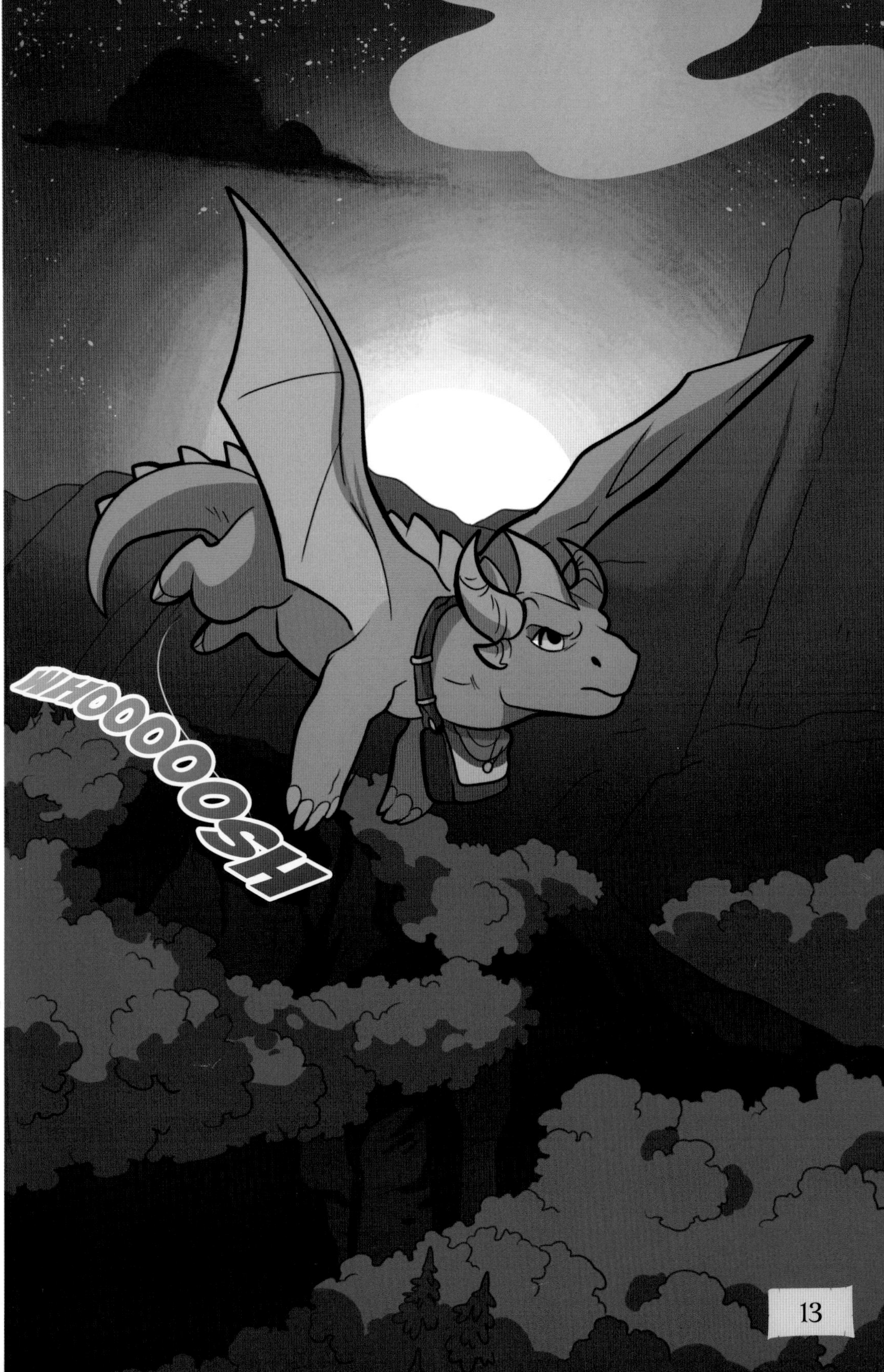
WHOOOOOOSH

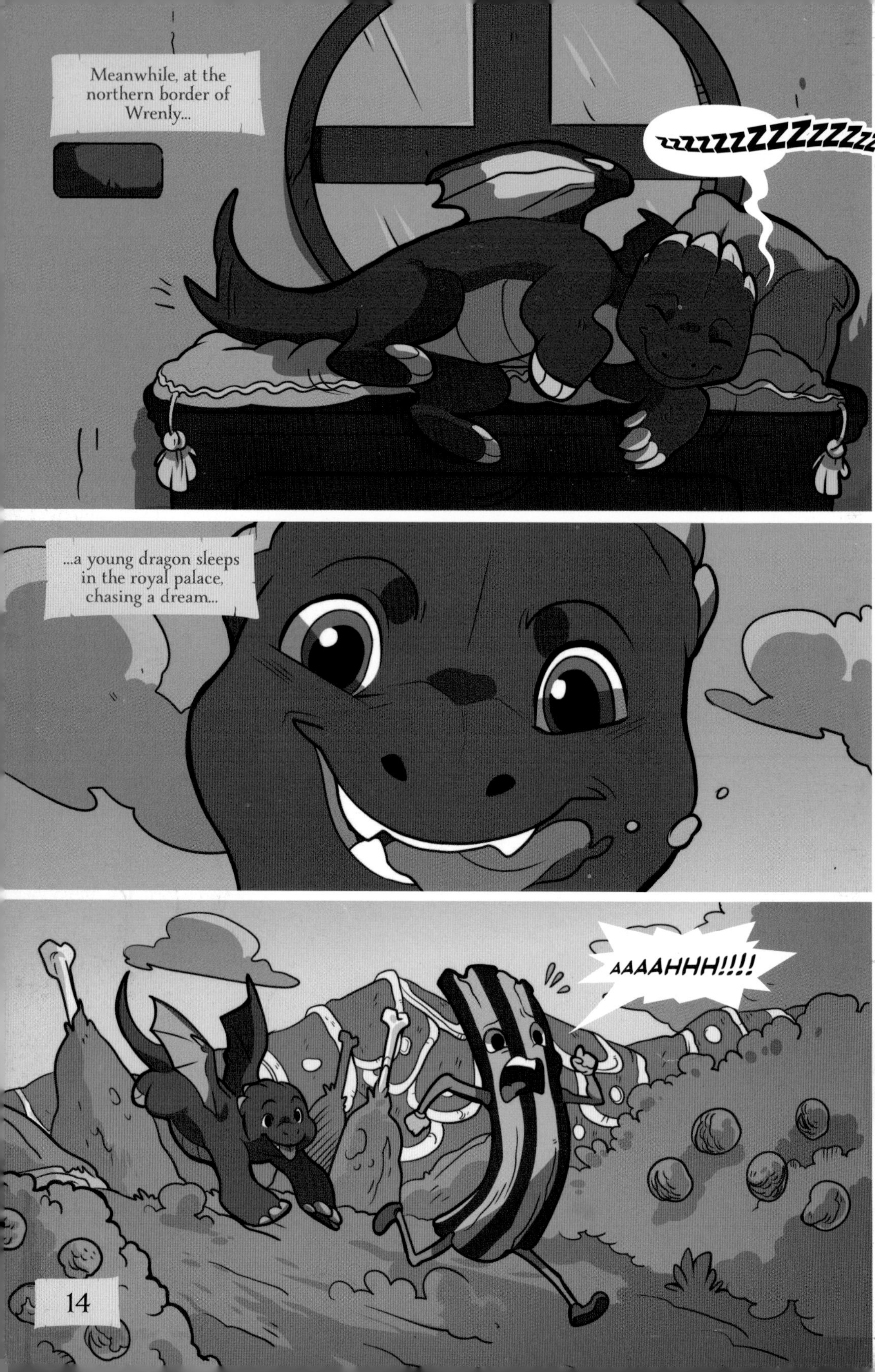

Meanwhile, at the northern border of Wrenly...
zzzzzzZZZZZzz
...a young dragon sleeps in the royal palace, chasing a dream...
AAAAHHH!!!!

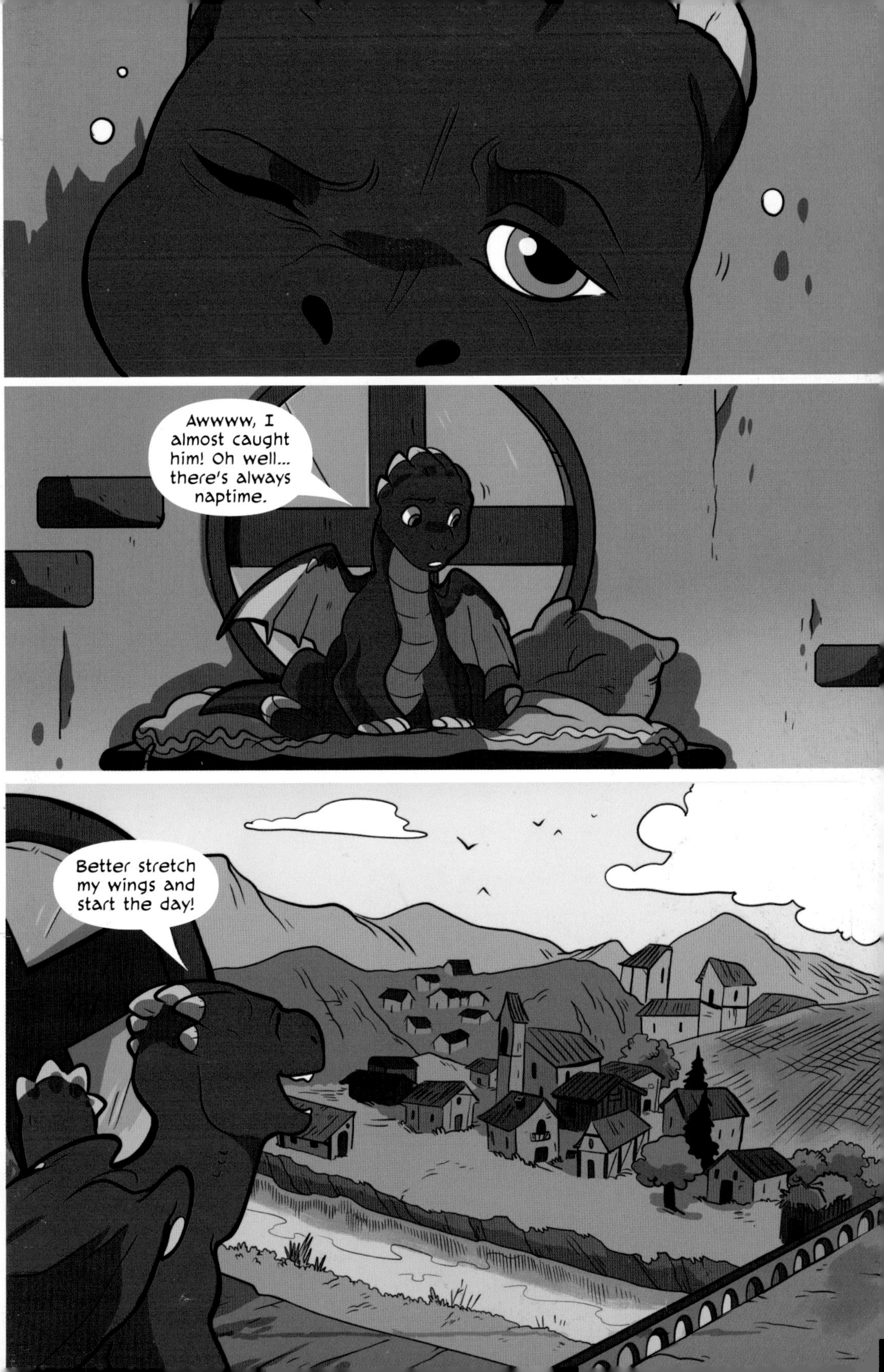
Awwww, I almost caught him! Oh well... there's always naptime.
Better stretch my wings and start the day!

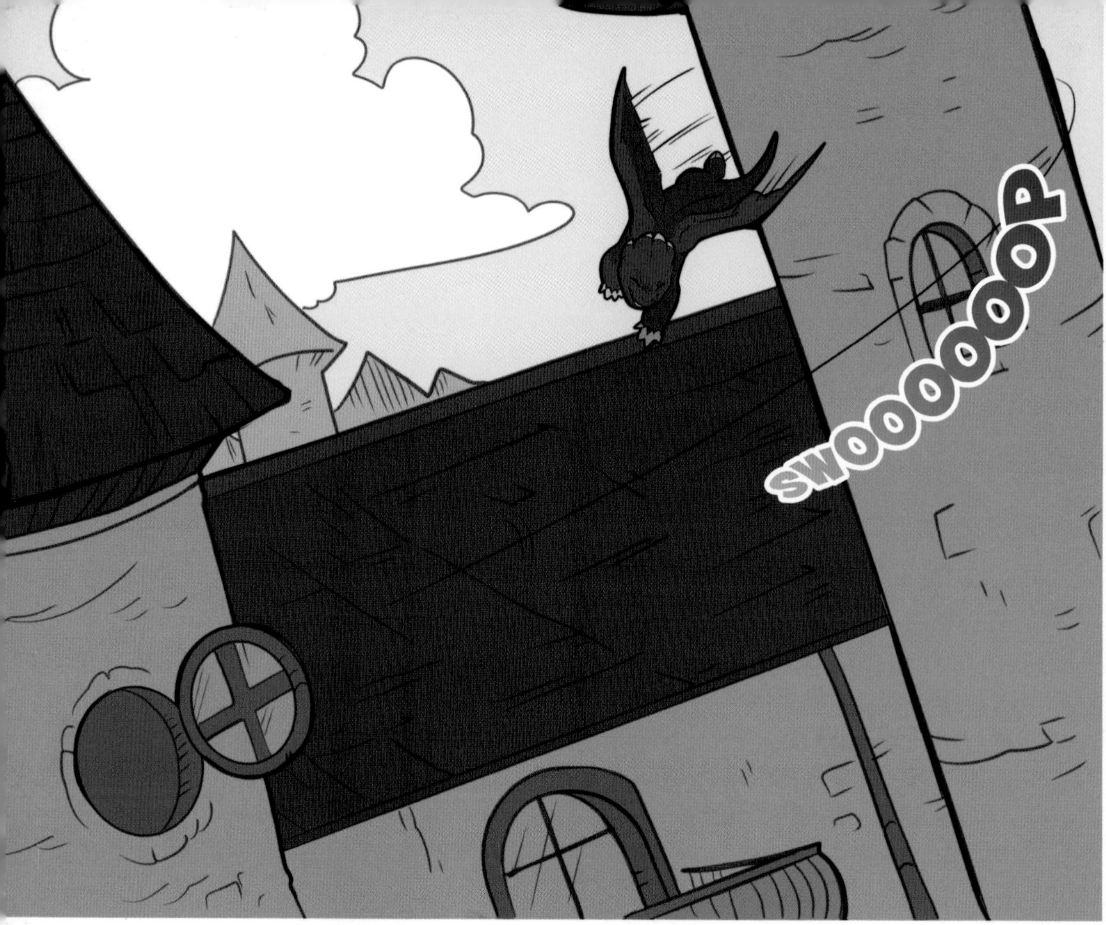
SWOOOOOOOP

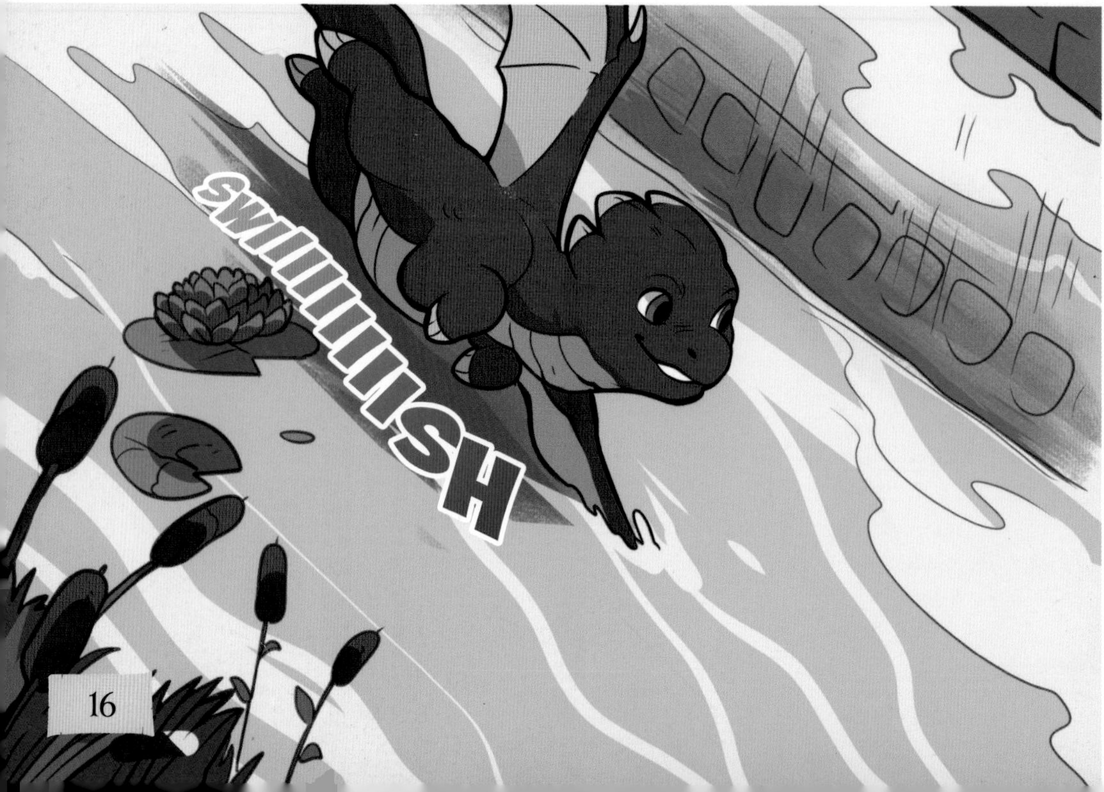
SWIIIIIIIISH

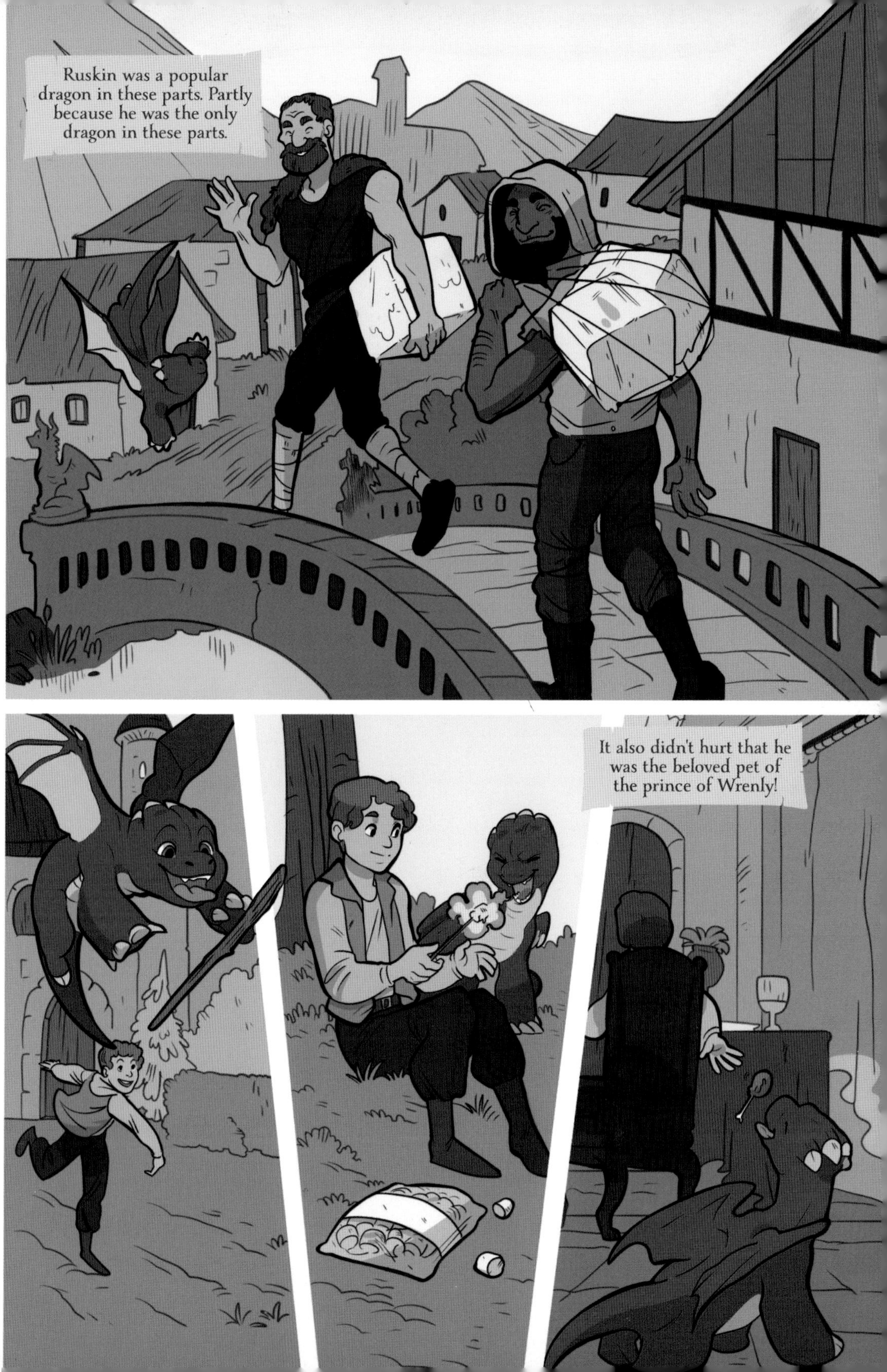
Ruskin was a popular dragon in these parts. Partly because he was the only dragon in these parts.
It also didn't hurt that he was the beloved pet of the prince of Wrenly!

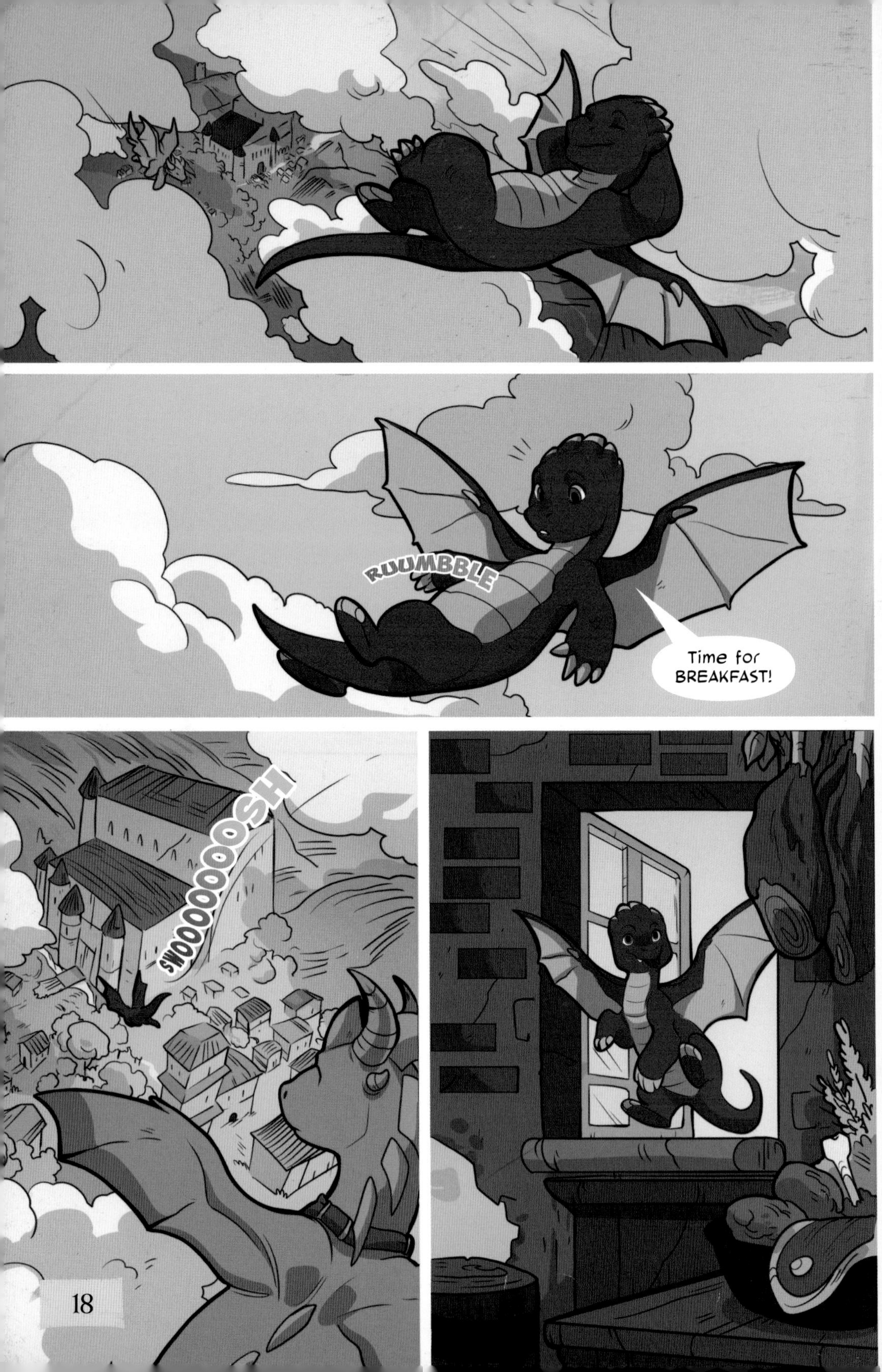
RUUMBBLE
Time for BREAKFAST!
SWOOOOOOOSH

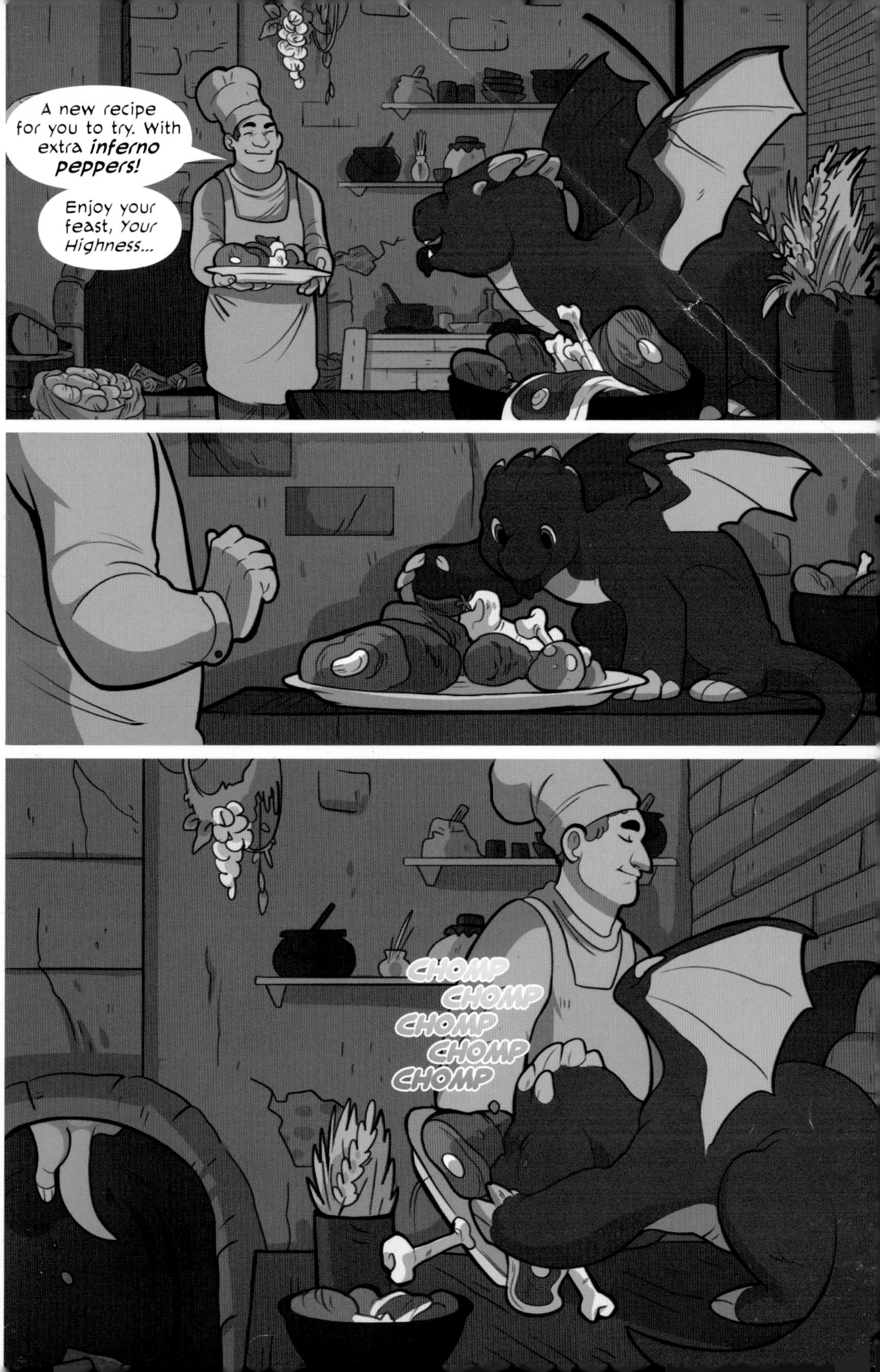
A new recipe for you to try. With extra *inferno peppers!*
Enjoy your feast, *Your Highness...*
CHOMP
CHOMP
CHOMP
CHOMP
CHOMP

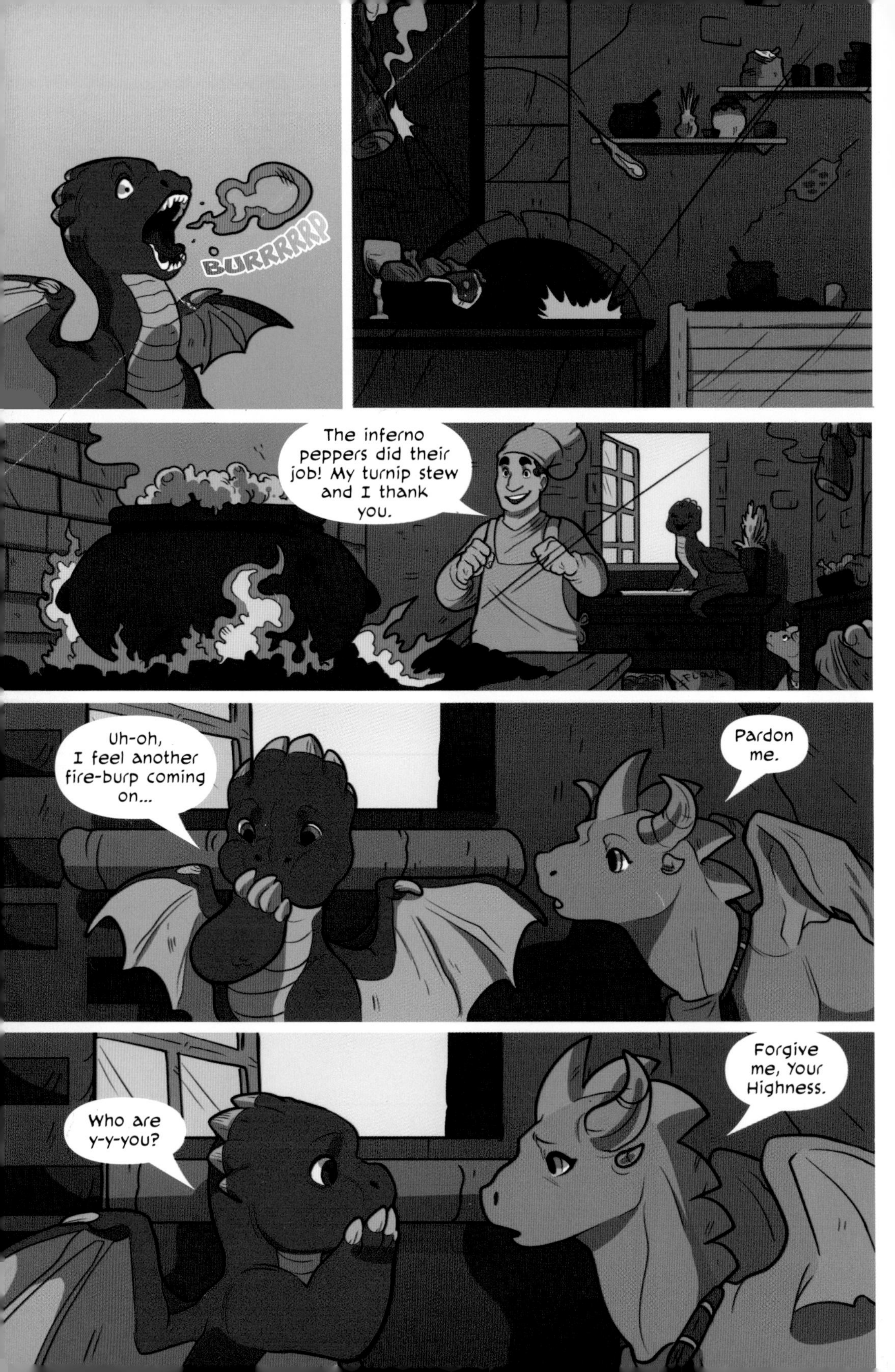
BURRRRRP
The inferno peppers did their job! My turnip stew and I thank you.
Uh-oh, I feel another fire-burp coming on...
Pardon me.
Who are y-y-you?
Forgive me, Your Highness.

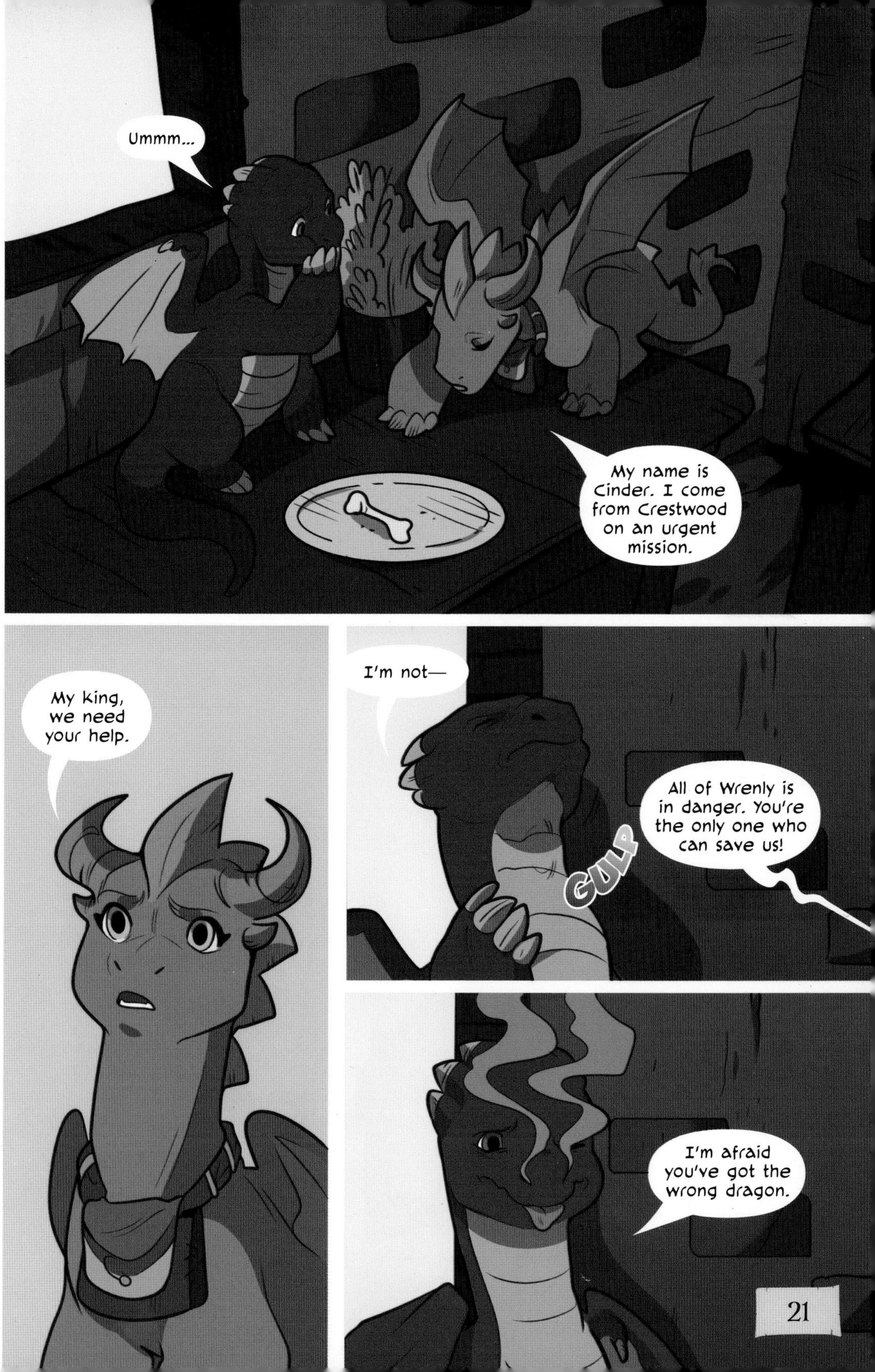
Ummm...
My name is Cinder. I come from Crestwood on an urgent mission.
My king, we need your help.
I'm not—
GULP
All of Wrenly is in danger. You're the only one who can save us!
I'm afraid you've got the wrong dragon.

Chapter 2

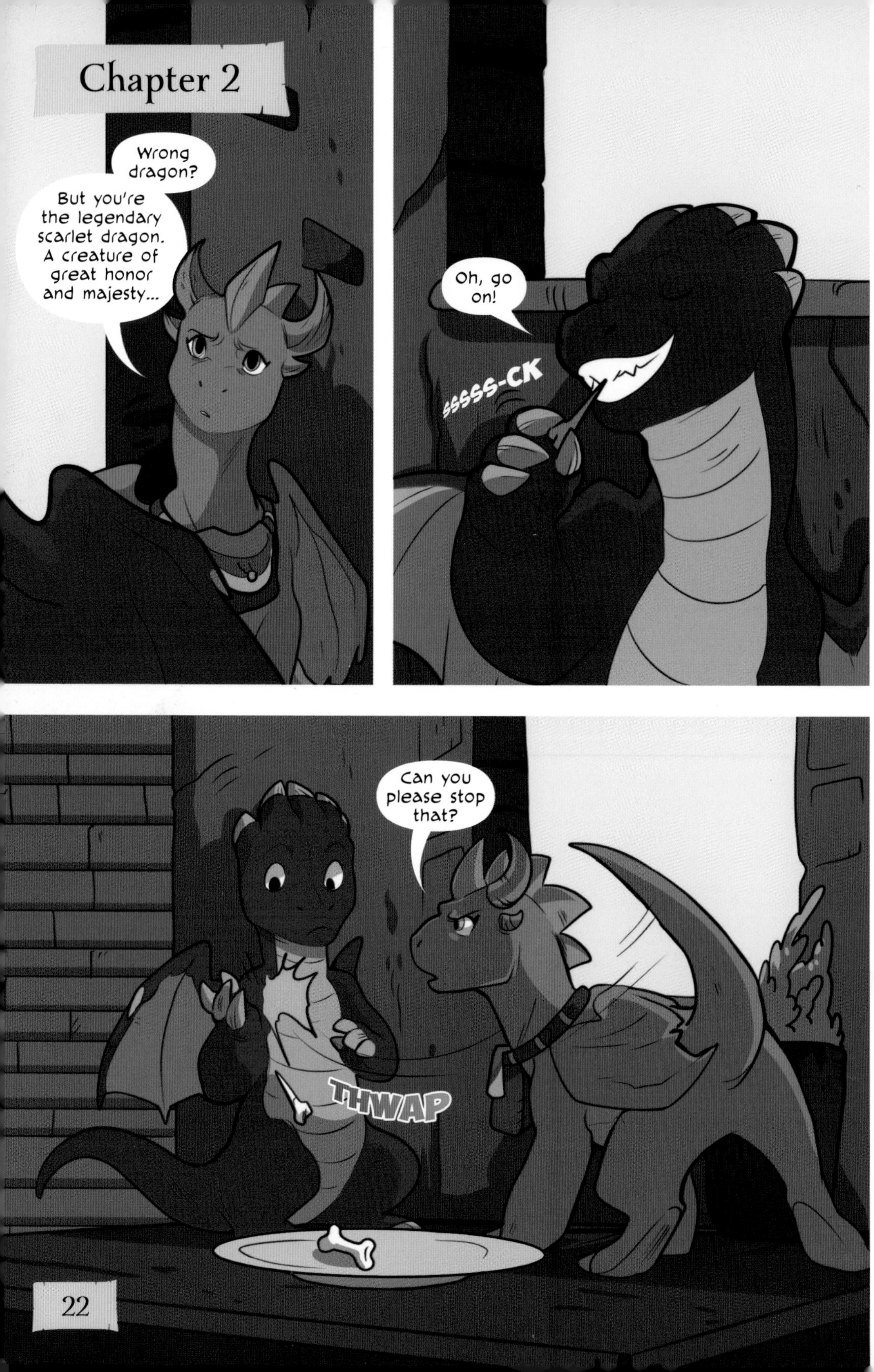
Wrong dragon?
But you're the legendary scarlet dragon. A creature of great honor and majesty...
Oh, go on!
SSSSS-CK
Can you please stop that?
THWAP

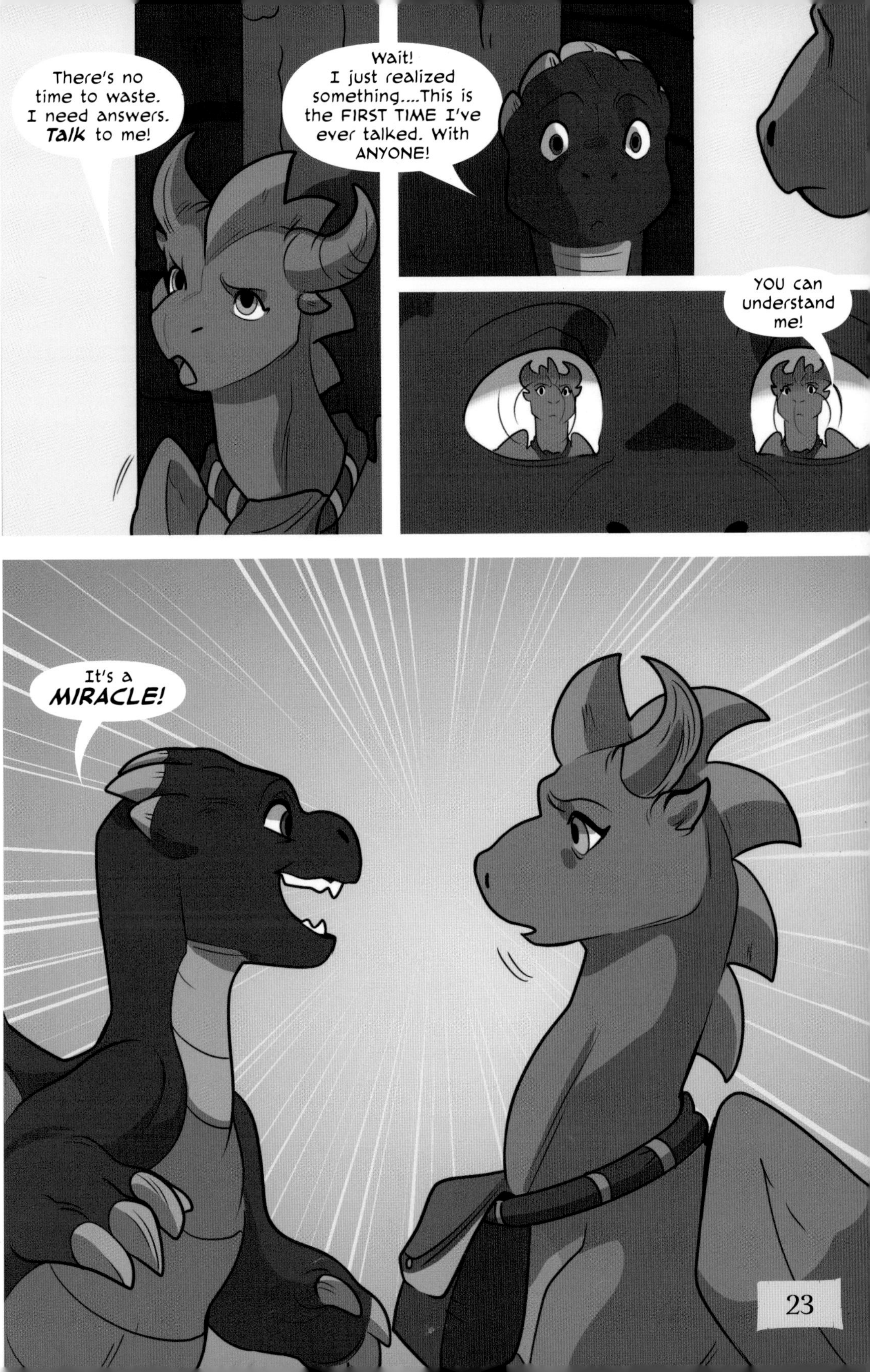
There's no time to waste. I need answers. *Talk* to me!
Wait! I just realized something....This is the FIRST TIME I've ever talked. With ANYONE!
YOU can understand me!
It's a *MIRACLE!*

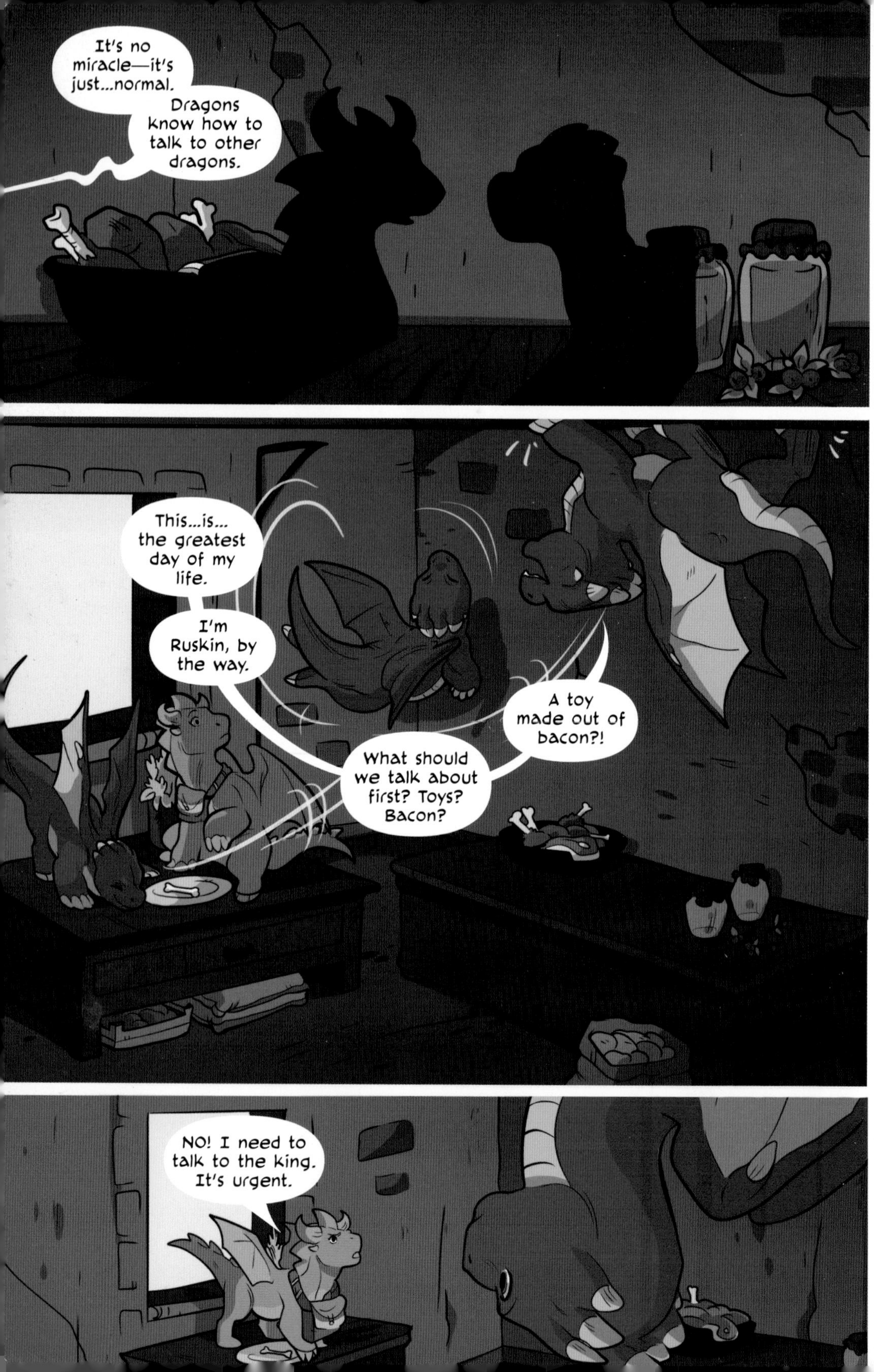
It's no miracle—it's just...normal.
Dragons know how to talk to other dragons.
This...is... the greatest day of my life.
I'm Ruskin, by the way.
What should we talk about first? Toys? Bacon?
A toy made out of bacon?!
NO! I need to talk to the king. It's urgent.

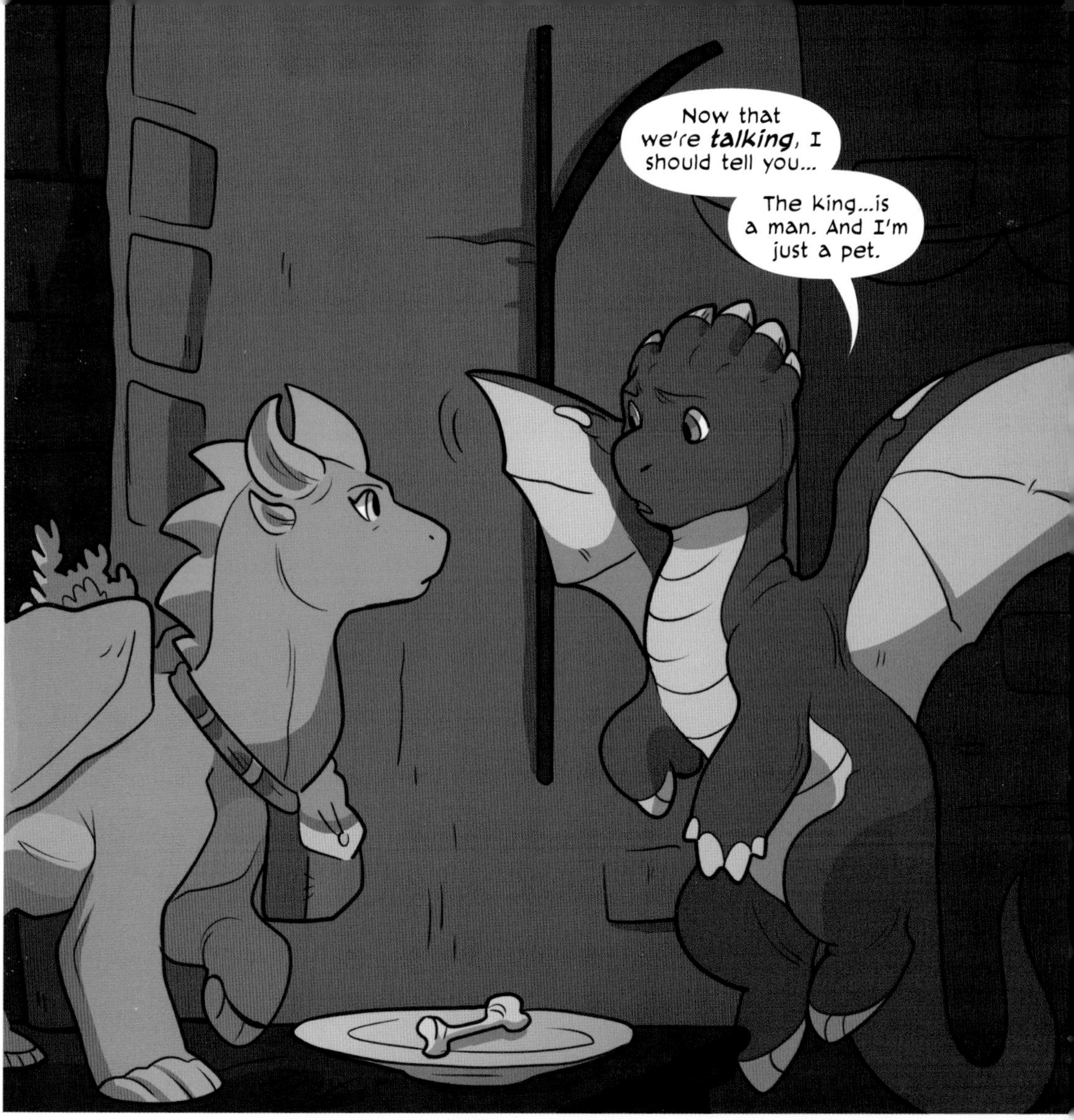
Now that we're *talking*, I should tell you...
The king...is a man. And I'm just a pet.

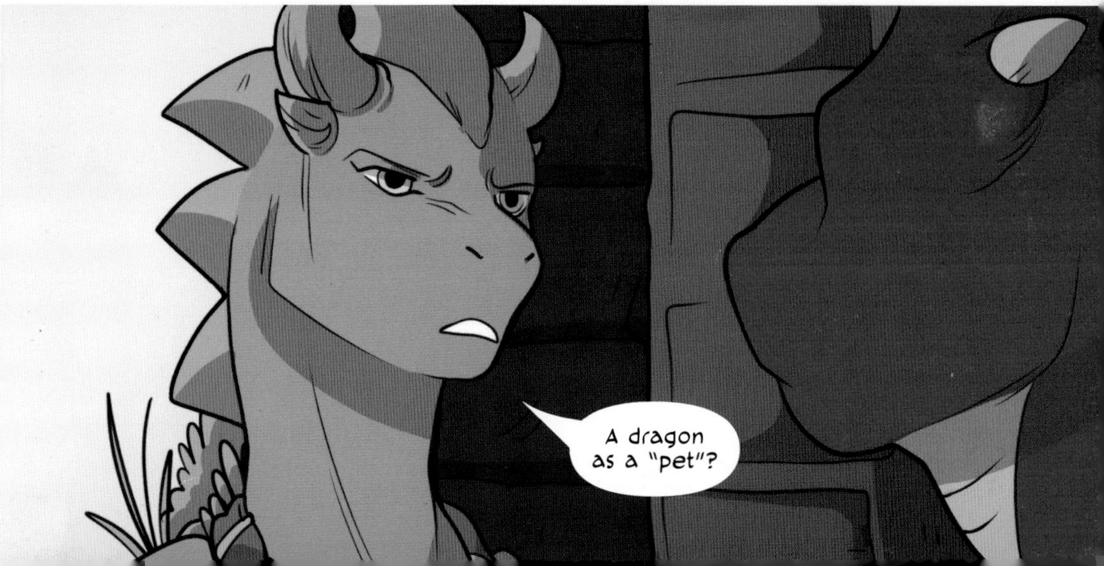
A dragon as a "pet"?

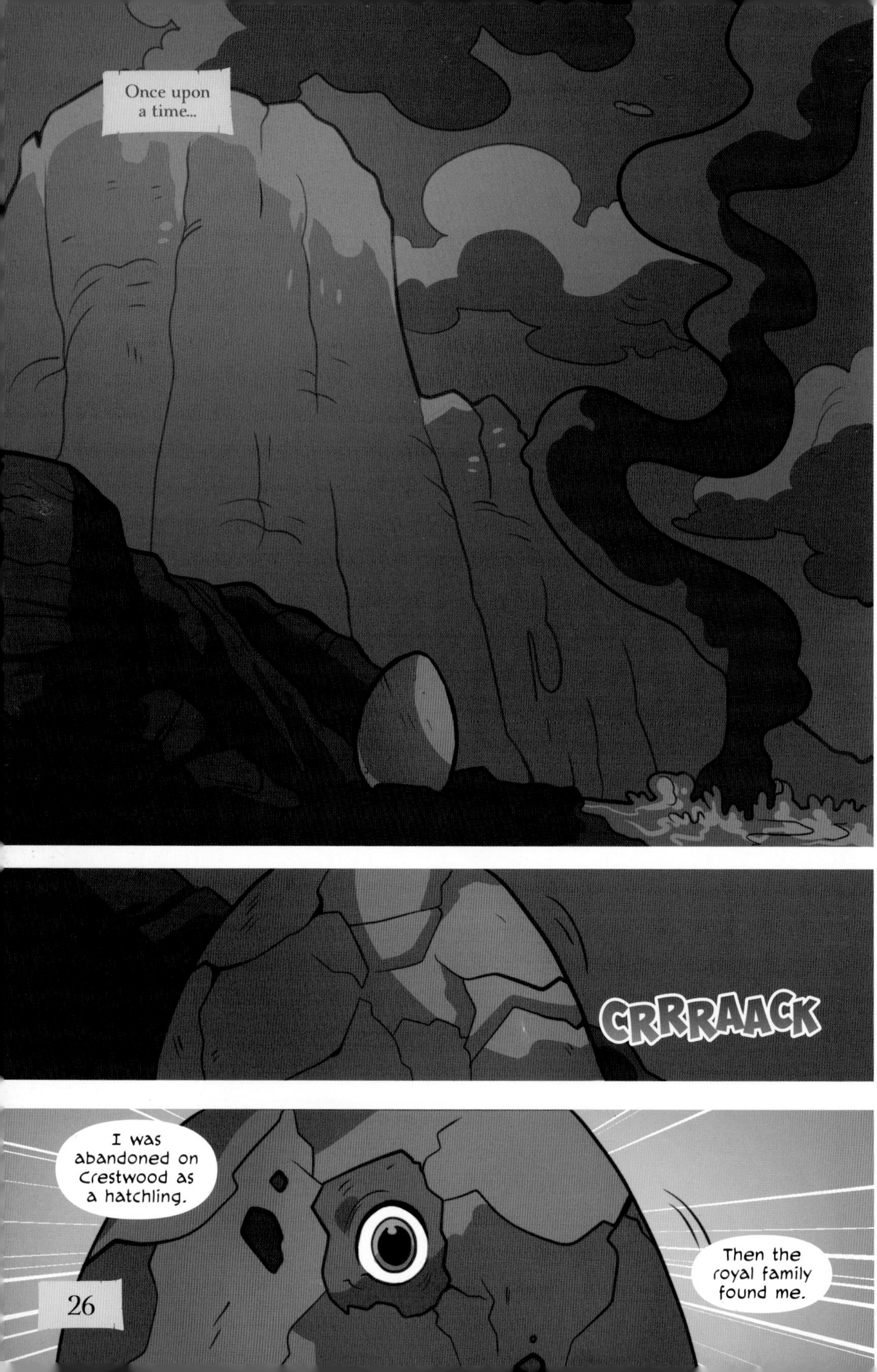
Once upon a time...
CRRRAACK
I was abandoned on Crestwood as a hatchling.
Then the royal family found me.

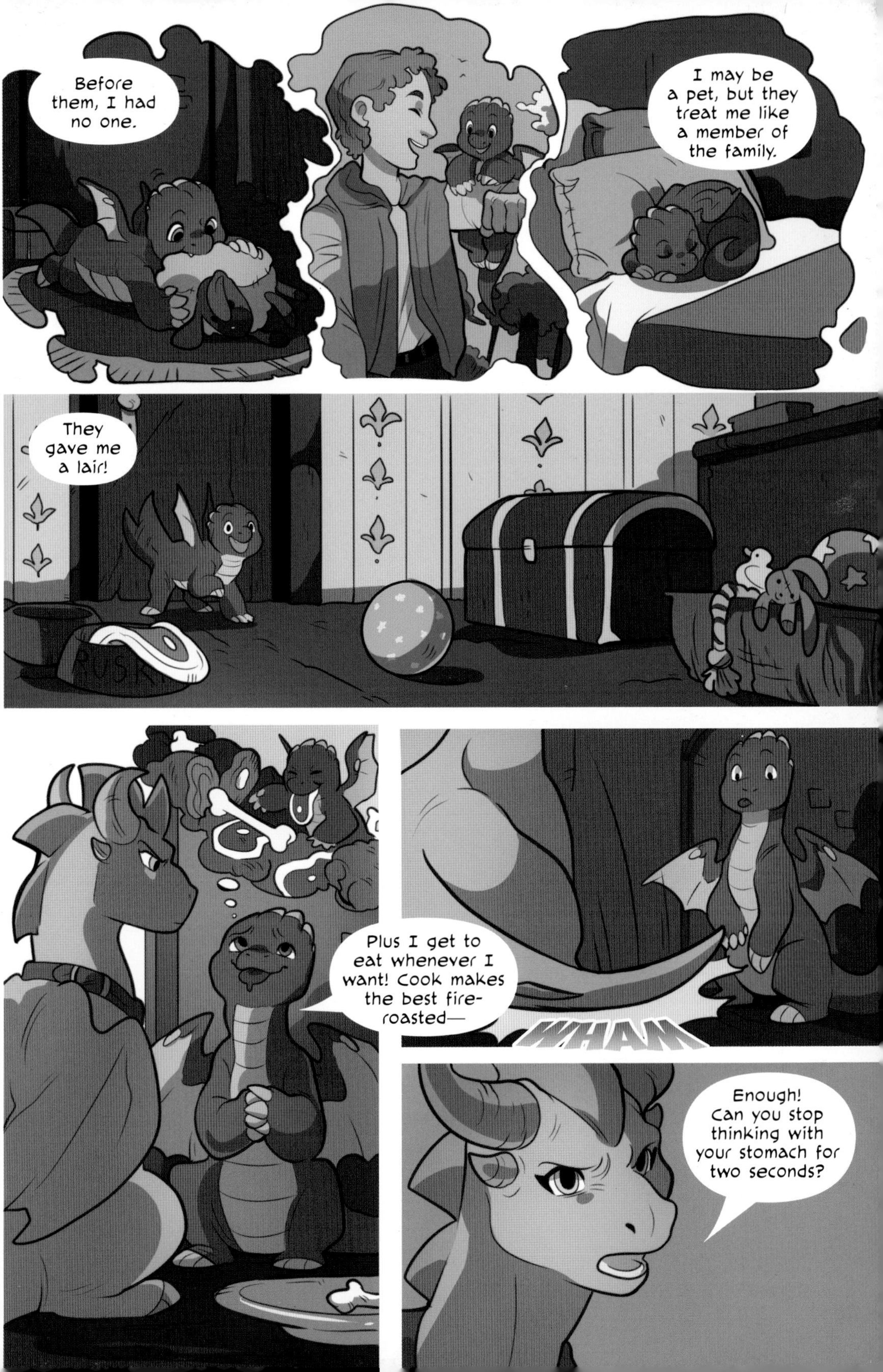

Before them, I had no one.
I may be a pet, but they treat me like a member of the family.
They gave me a lair!
RUSK
Plus I get to eat whenever I want! Cook makes the best fire-roasted—
WHAM
Enough! Can you stop thinking with your stomach for two seconds?

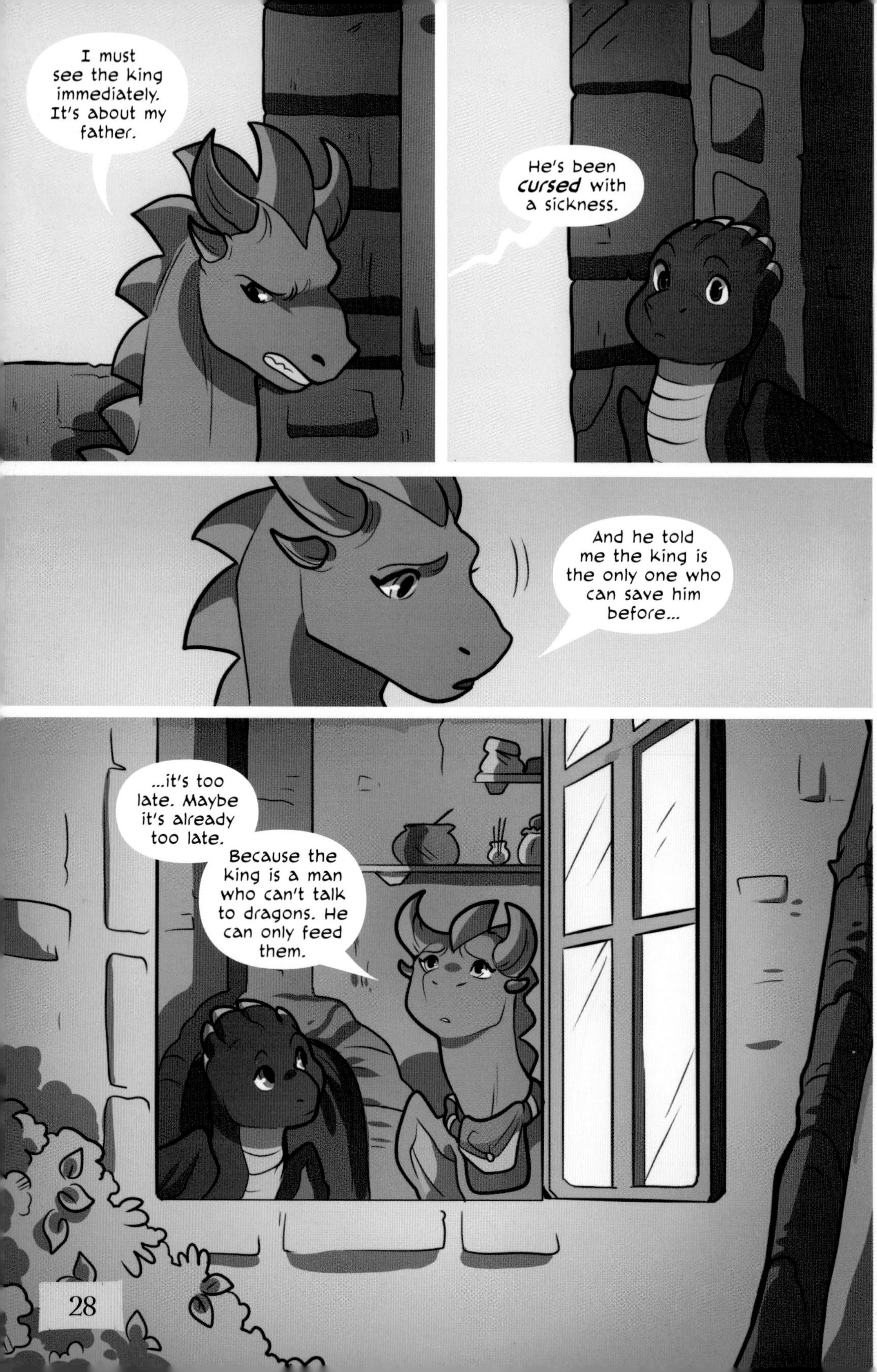

I must see the king immediately. It's about my father.
He's been *cursed* with a sickness.
And he told me the king is the only one who can save him before...
...it's too late. Maybe it's already too late.
Because the king is a man who can't talk to dragons. He can only feed them.

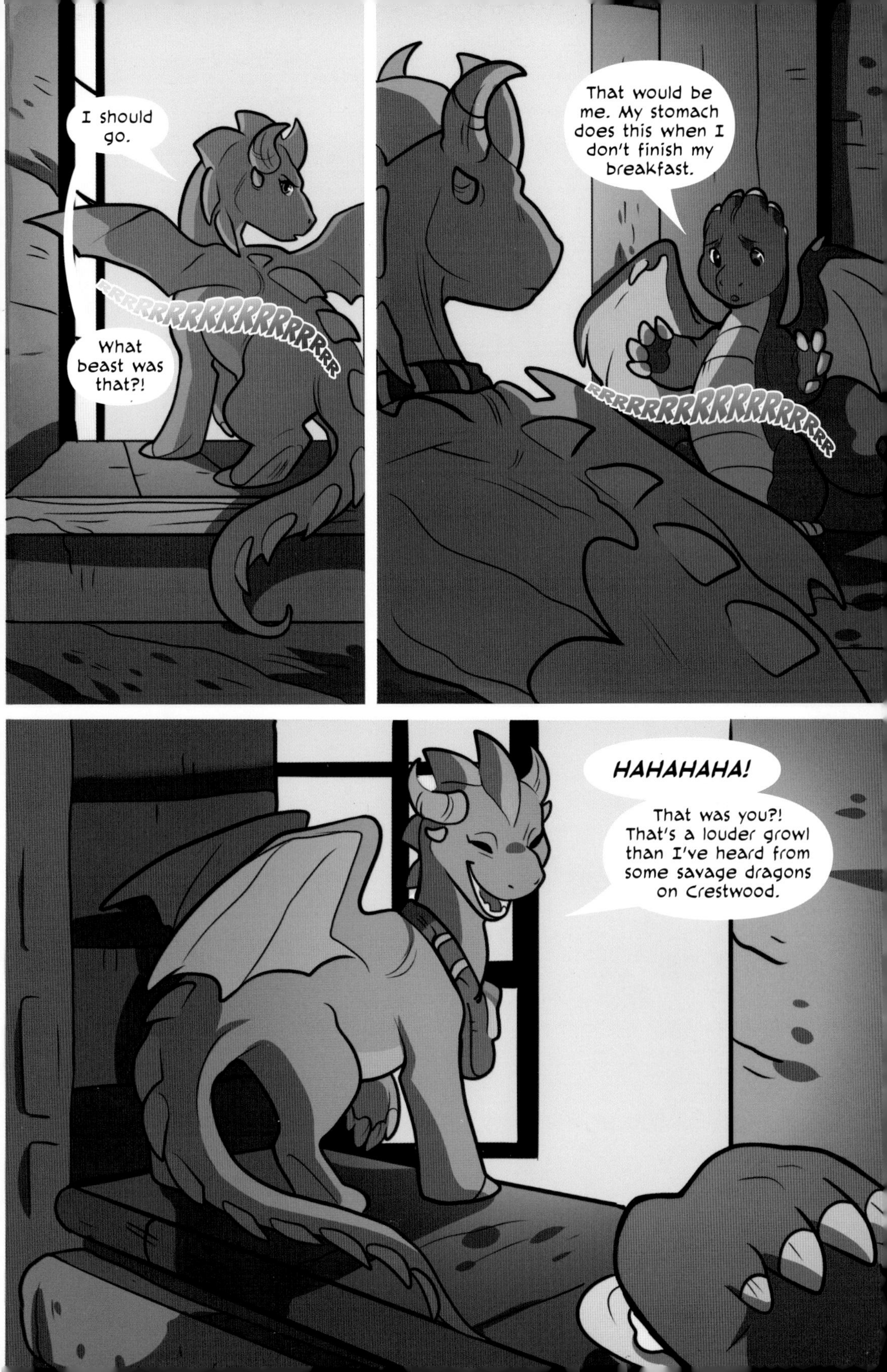
I should go.
RRRRRRRRRRRRRRRRRRRRRR
What beast was that?!
That would be me. My stomach does this when I don't finish my breakfast.
RRRRRRRRRRRRRRRRRRRRRR
HAHAHAHA!
That was you?! That's a louder growl than I've heard from some savage dragons on Crestwood.

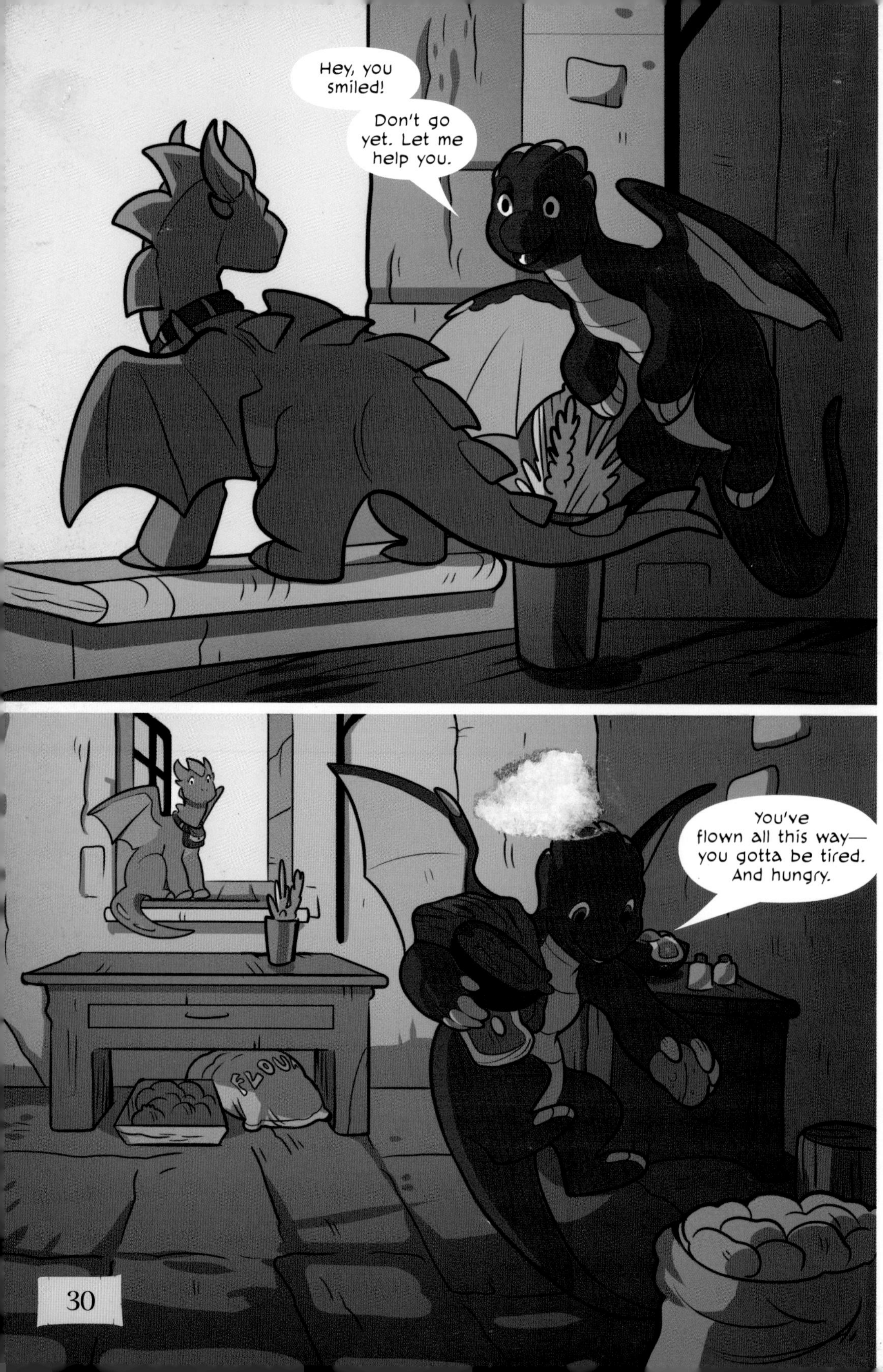
Hey, you smiled!
Don't go yet. Let me help you.
FLOU
You've flown all this way—you gotta be tired. And hungry.

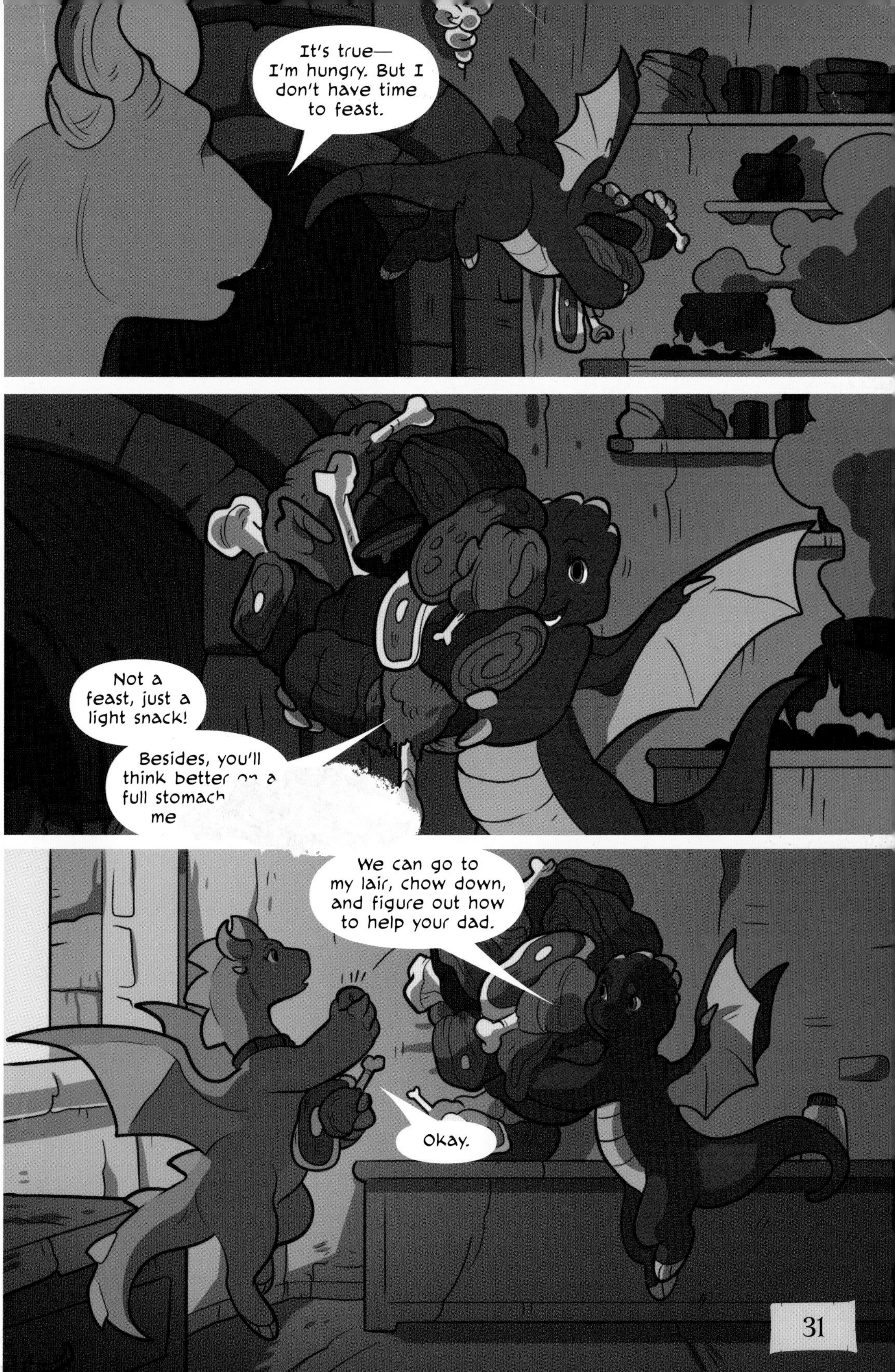
It's true— I'm hungry. But I don't have time to feast.
Not a feast, just a light snack!
Besides, you'll think better on a full stomach me
We can go to my lair, chow down, and figure out how to help your dad.
Okay.

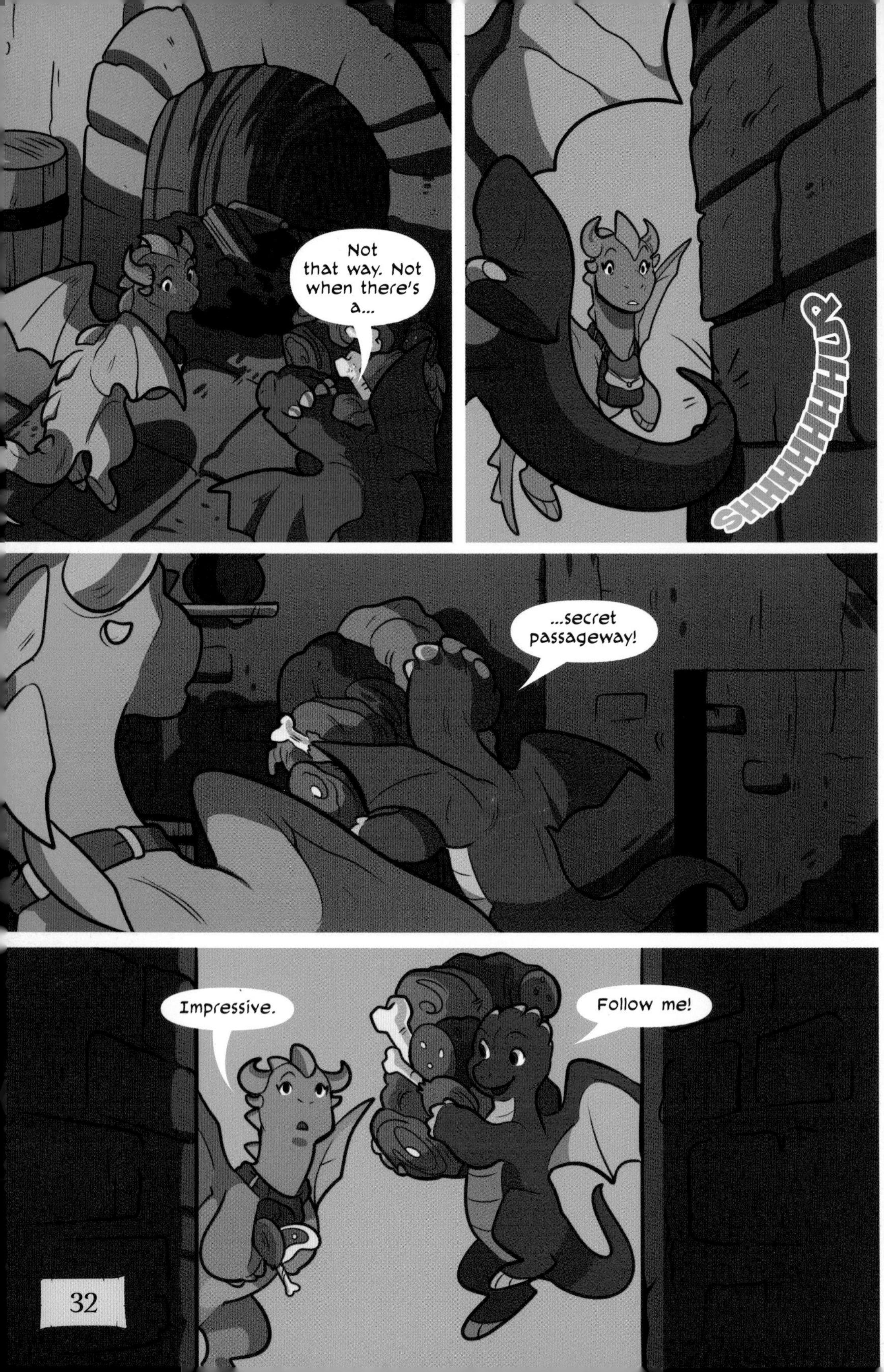
Not that way. Not when there's a...
SHHHHHHHHHHHH
...secret passageway!
Impressive.
Follow me!

Chapter 3

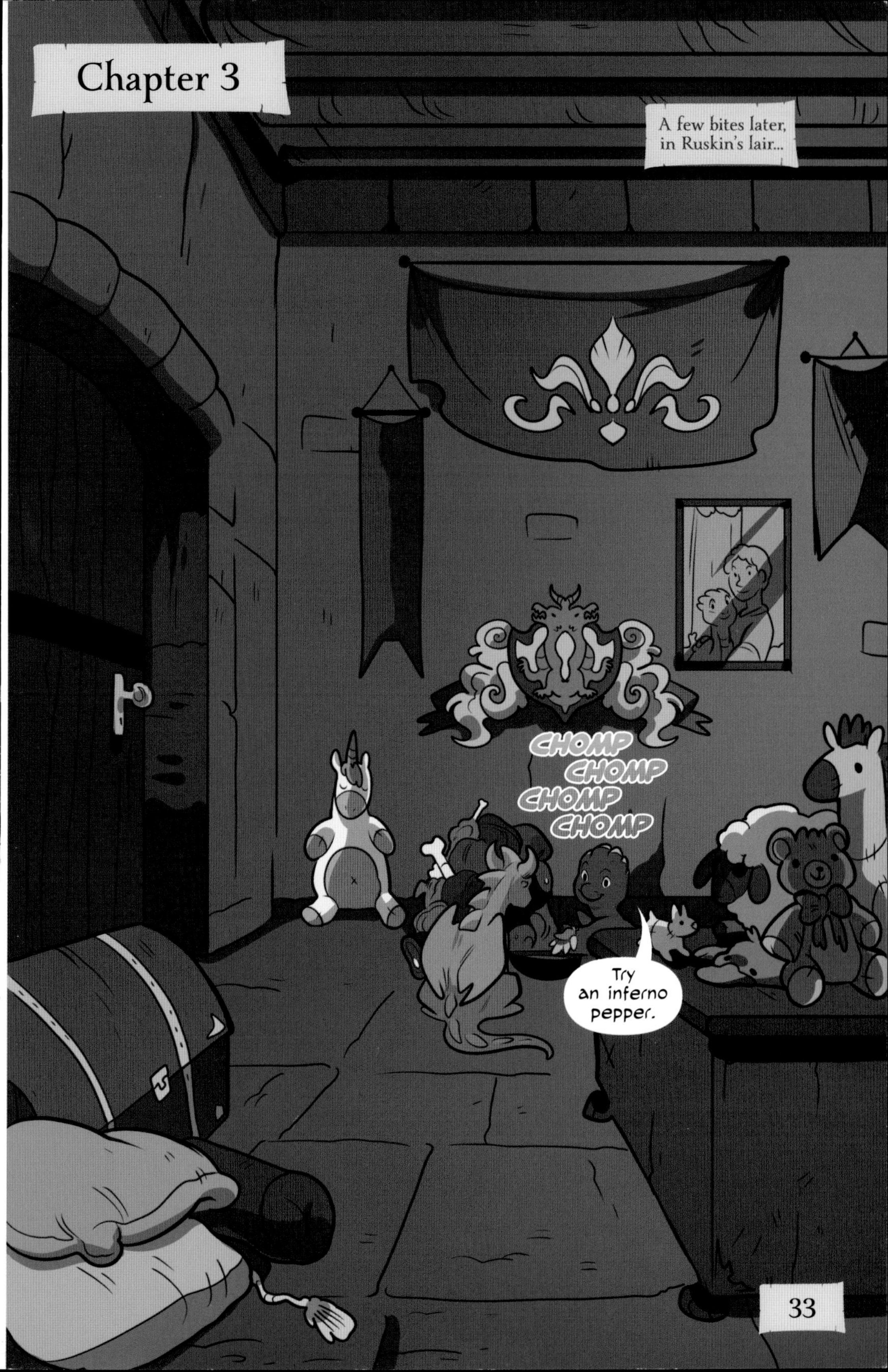

A few bites later, in Ruskin's lair...
CHOMP
CHOMP
CHOMP
CHOMP
Try an inferno pepper.

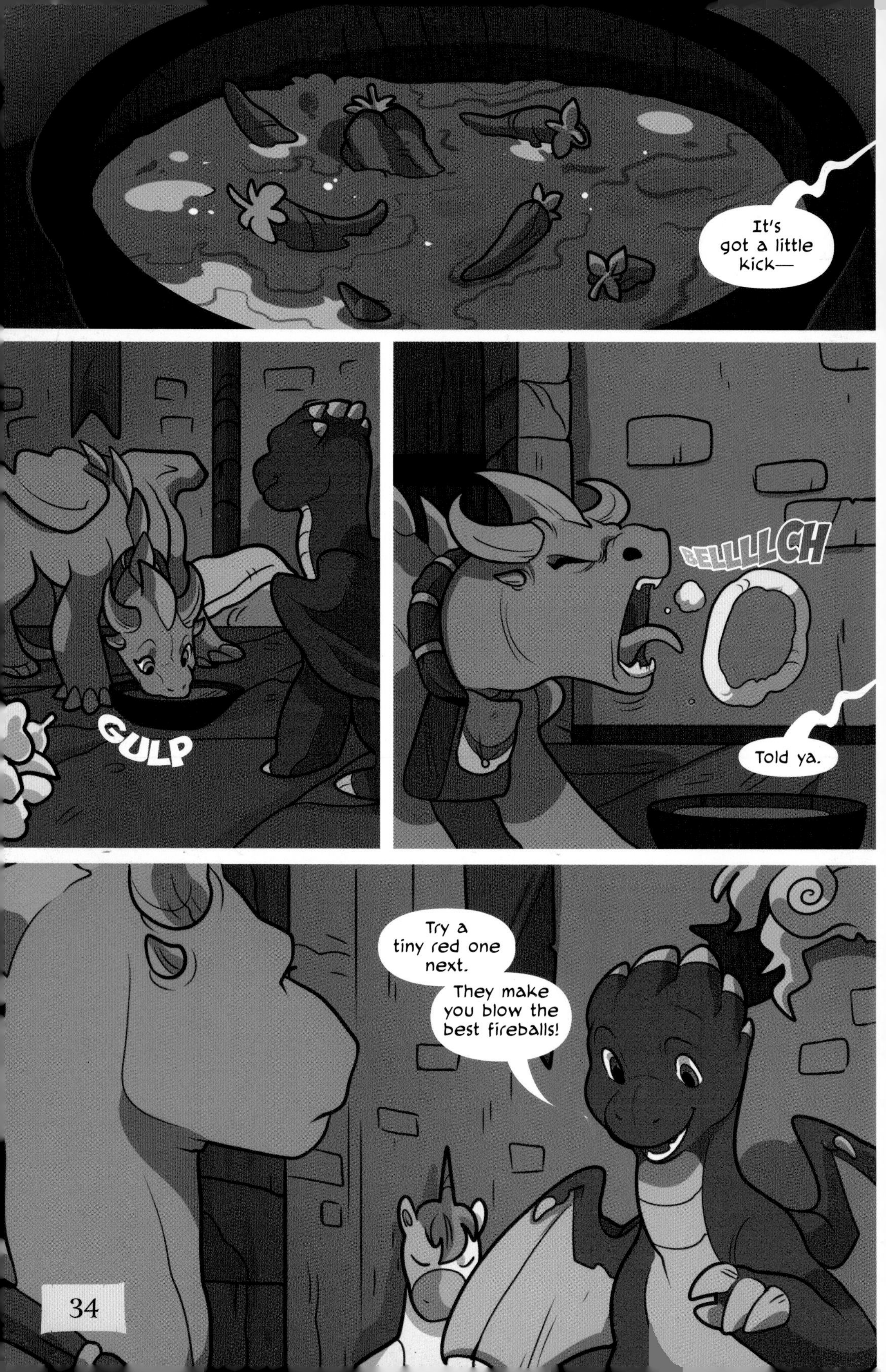

It's got a little kick—
GULP
BELLLLCH
Told ya.
Try a tiny red one next.
They make you blow the best fireballs!

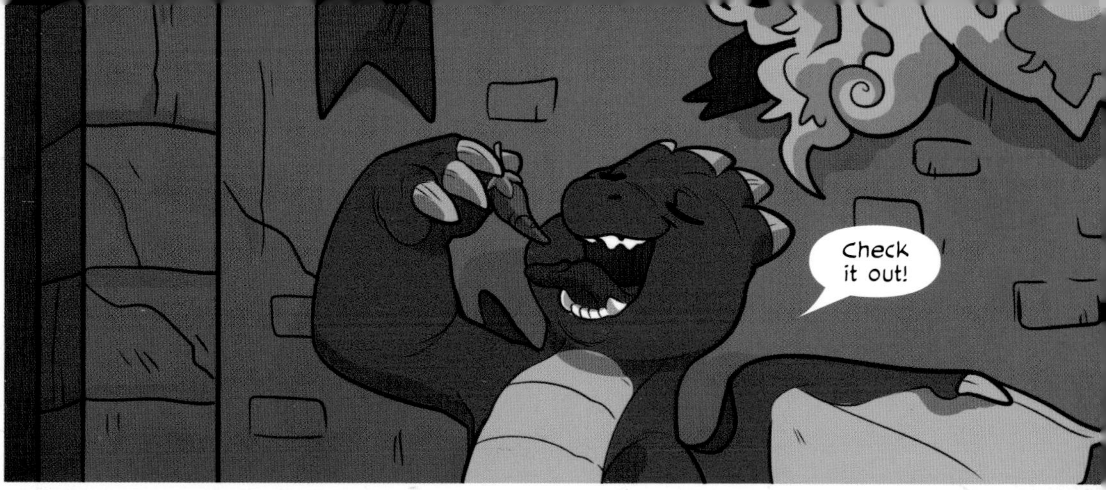
Check it out!

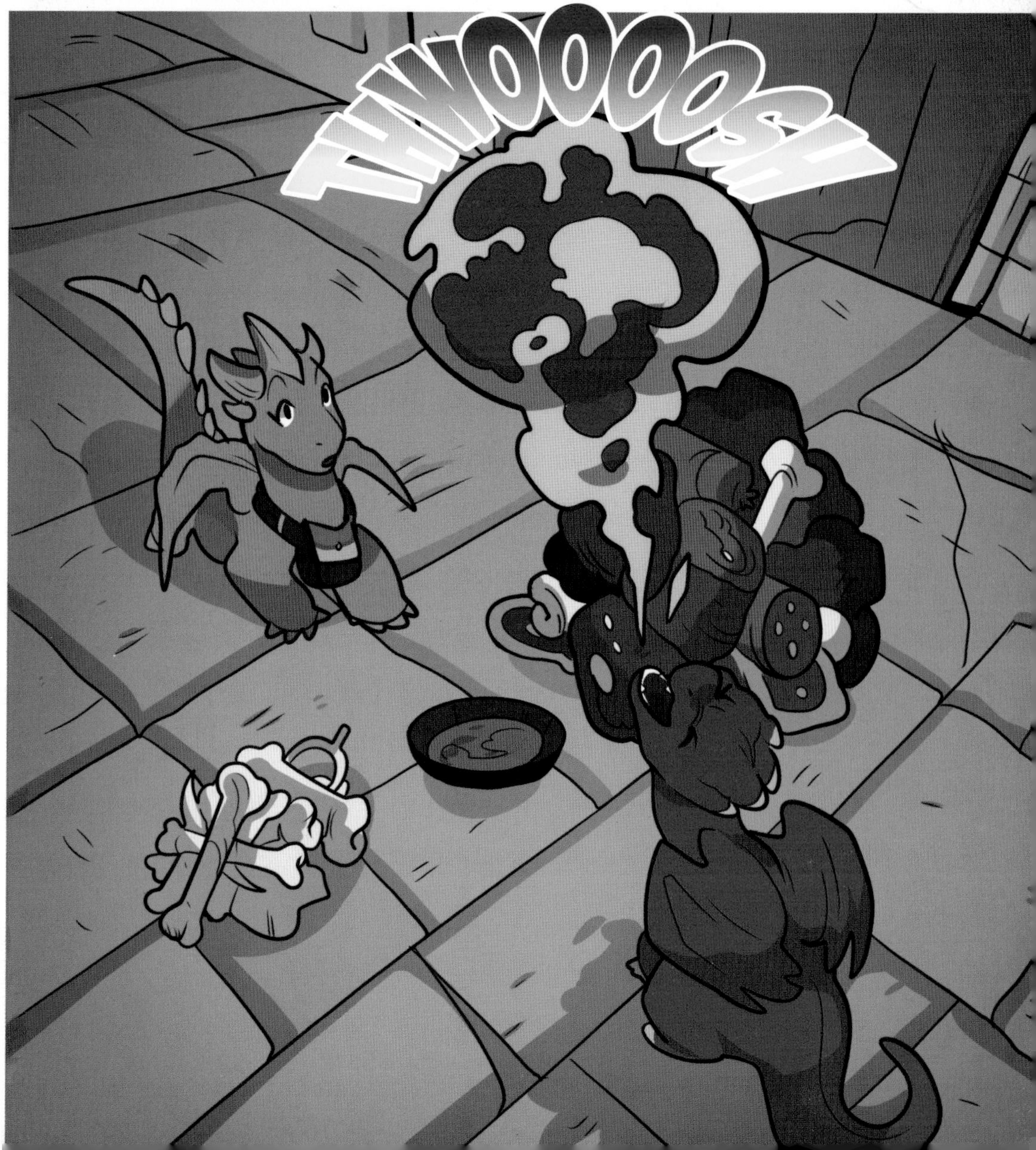
THWOOOOSH

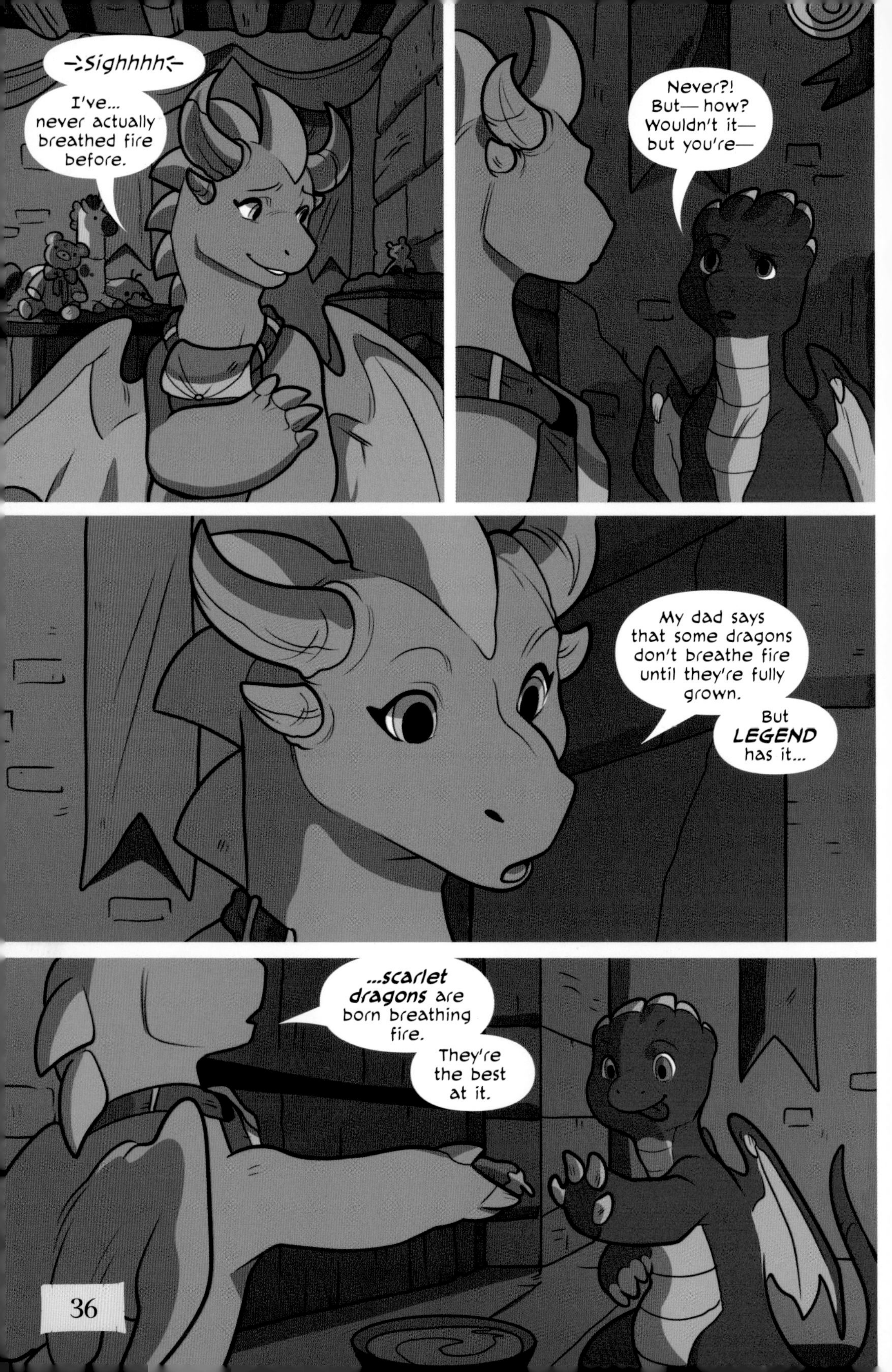

–>Sighhhh<–
I've... never actually breathed fire before.
Never?! But— how? Wouldn't it— but you're—
My dad says that some dragons don't breathe fire until they're fully grown.
But **LEGEND** has it...
...scarlet dragons are born breathing fire.
They're the best at it.

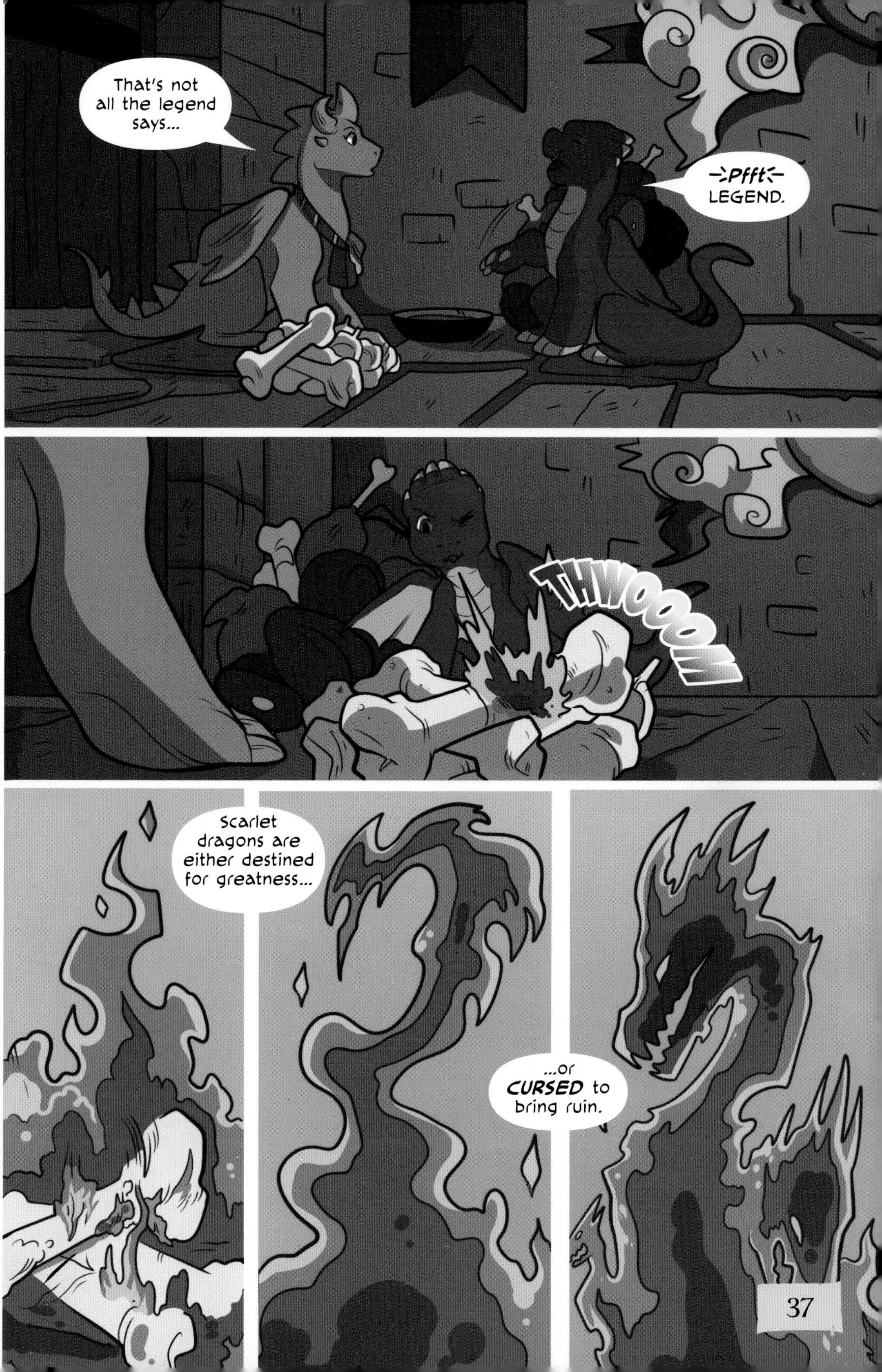
That's not all the legend says...
-Pfft- LEGEND.
THWOOOOM
Scarlet dragons are either destined for greatness...
...or CURSED to bring ruin.

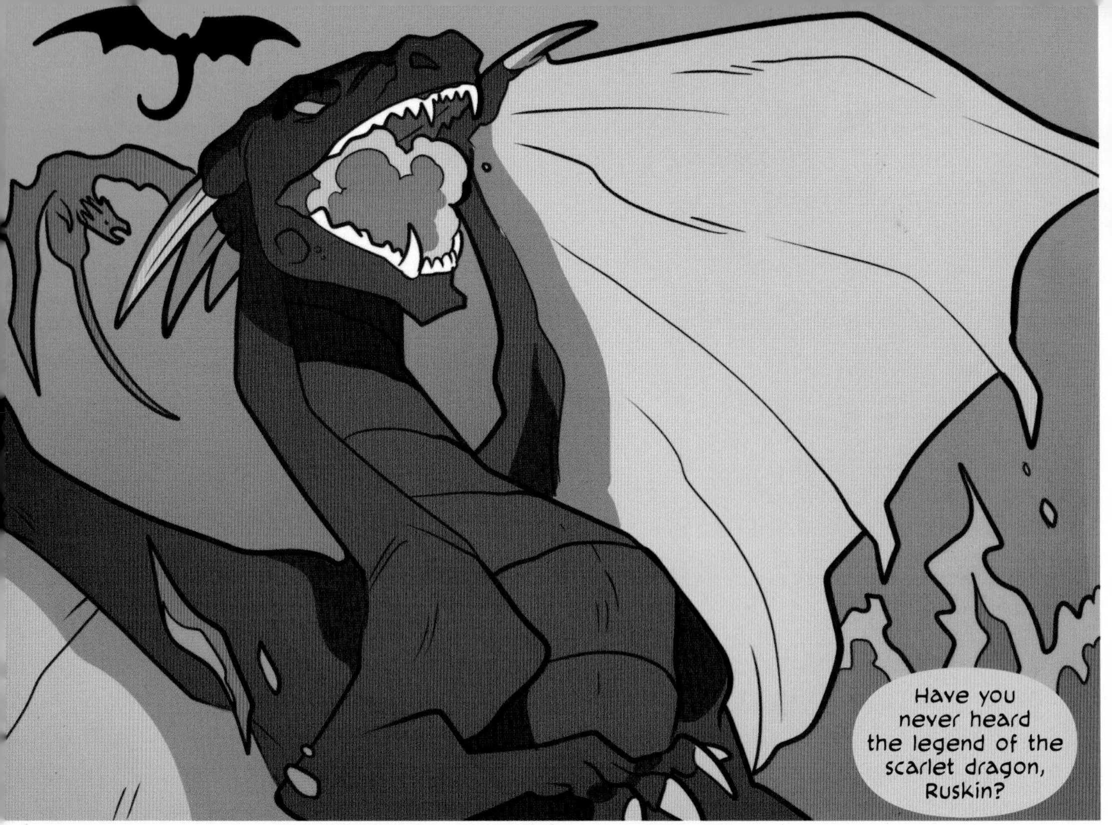
Have you never heard the legend of the scarlet dragon, Ruskin?

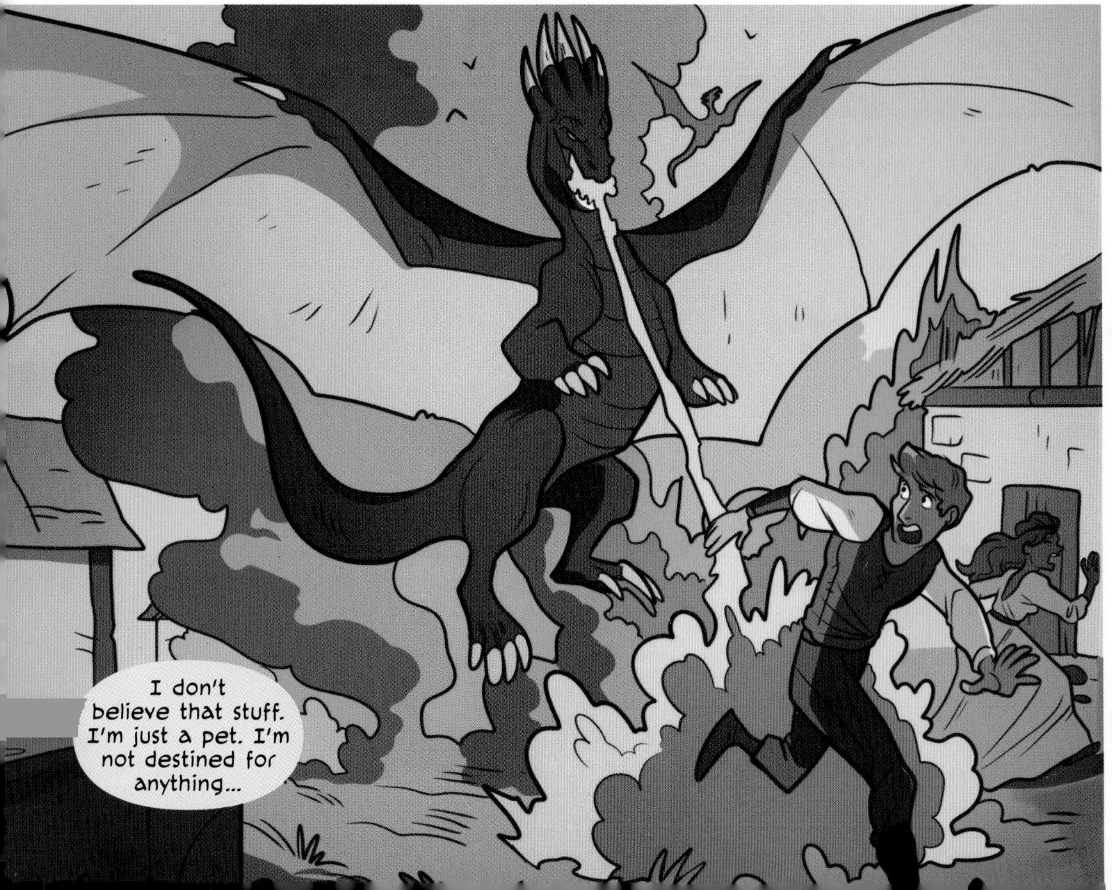
I don't believe that stuff. I'm just a pet. I'm not destined for anything...

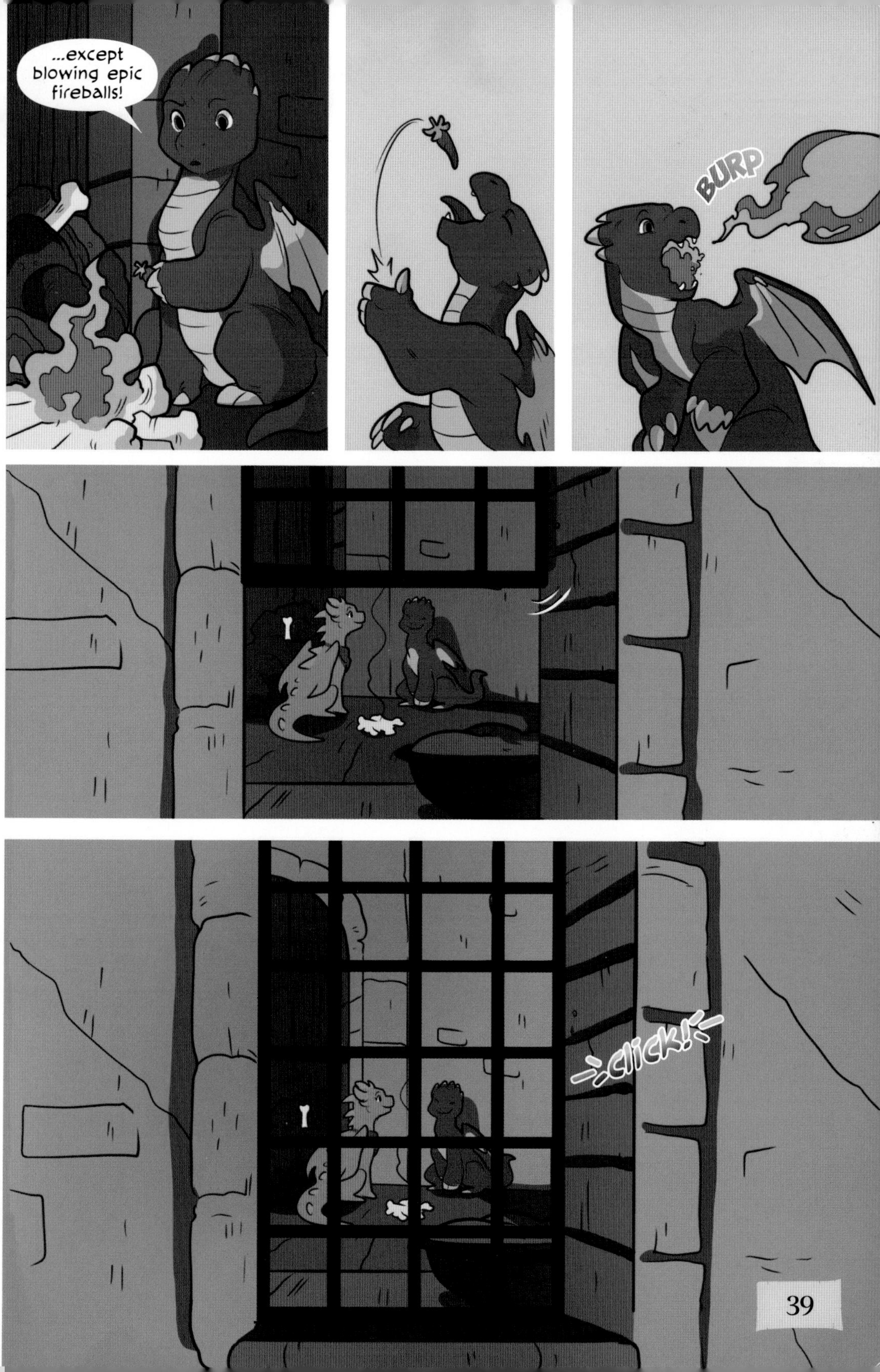
...except blowing epic fireballs!
BURP
-CLICK!-

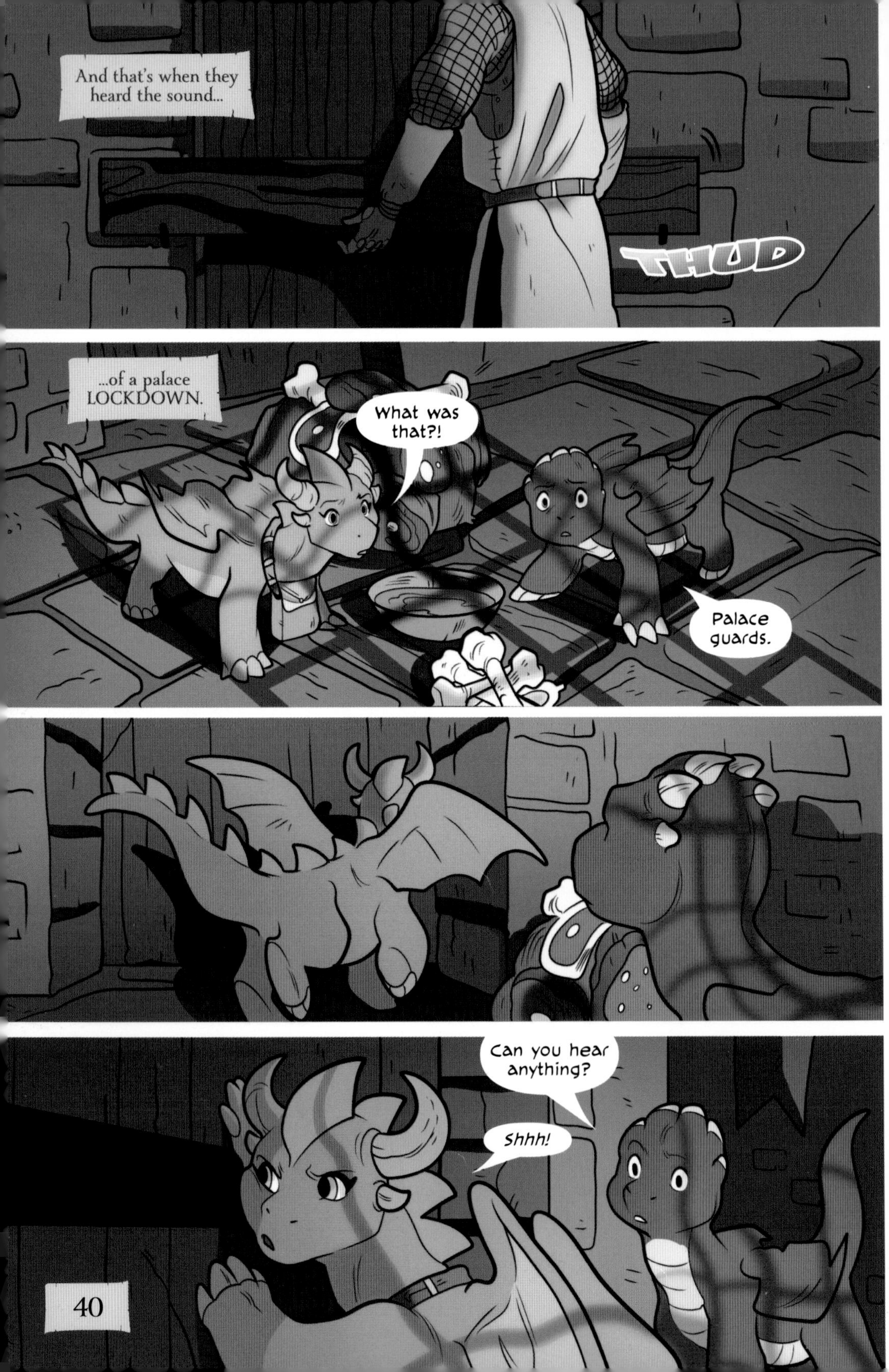

And that's when they heard the sound...
THUD
...of a palace LOCKDOWN.
What was that?!
Palace guards.
Can you hear anything?
Shhh!

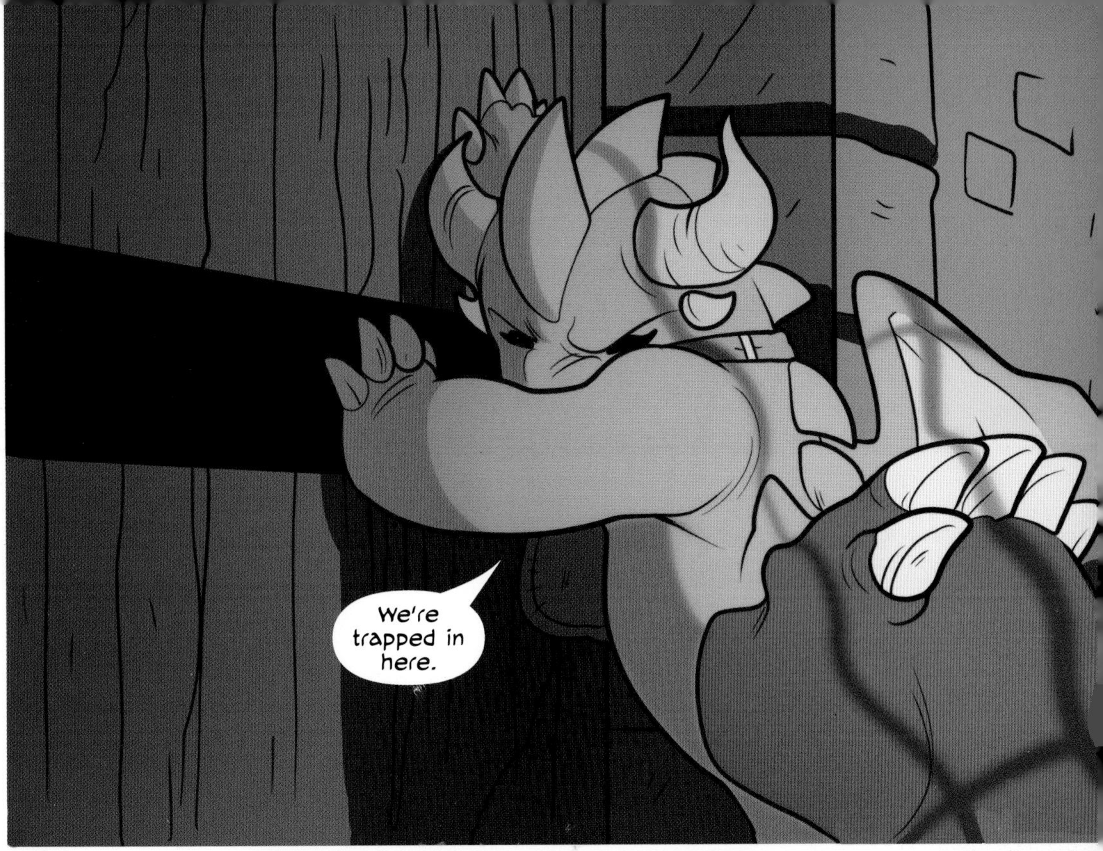
We're trapped in here.

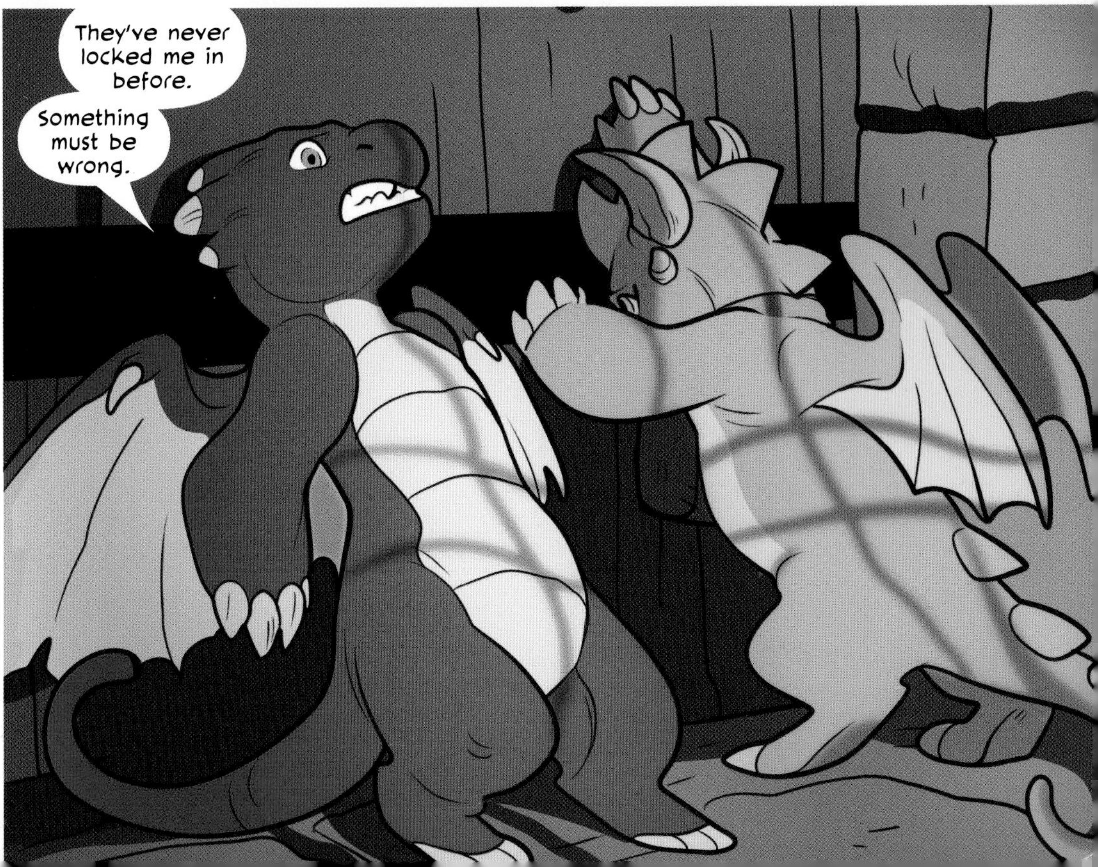
They've never locked me in before.
Something must be wrong.

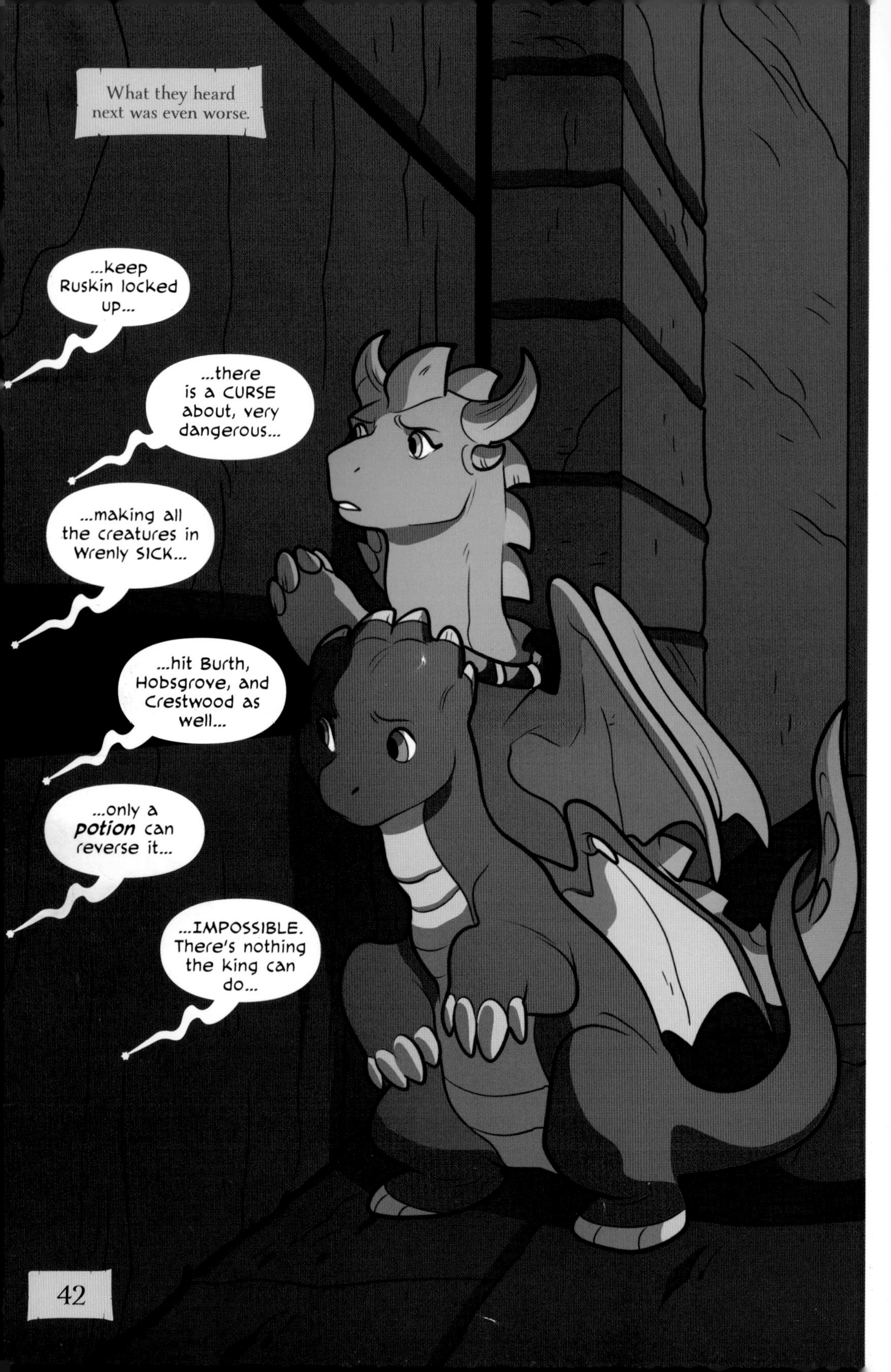

What they heard next was even worse.
...keep Ruskin locked up...
...there is a CURSE about, very dangerous...
...making all the creatures in Wrenly SICK...
...hit Burth, Hobsgrove, and Crestwood as well...
...only a *potion* can reverse it...
...IMPOSSIBLE. There's nothing the king can do...

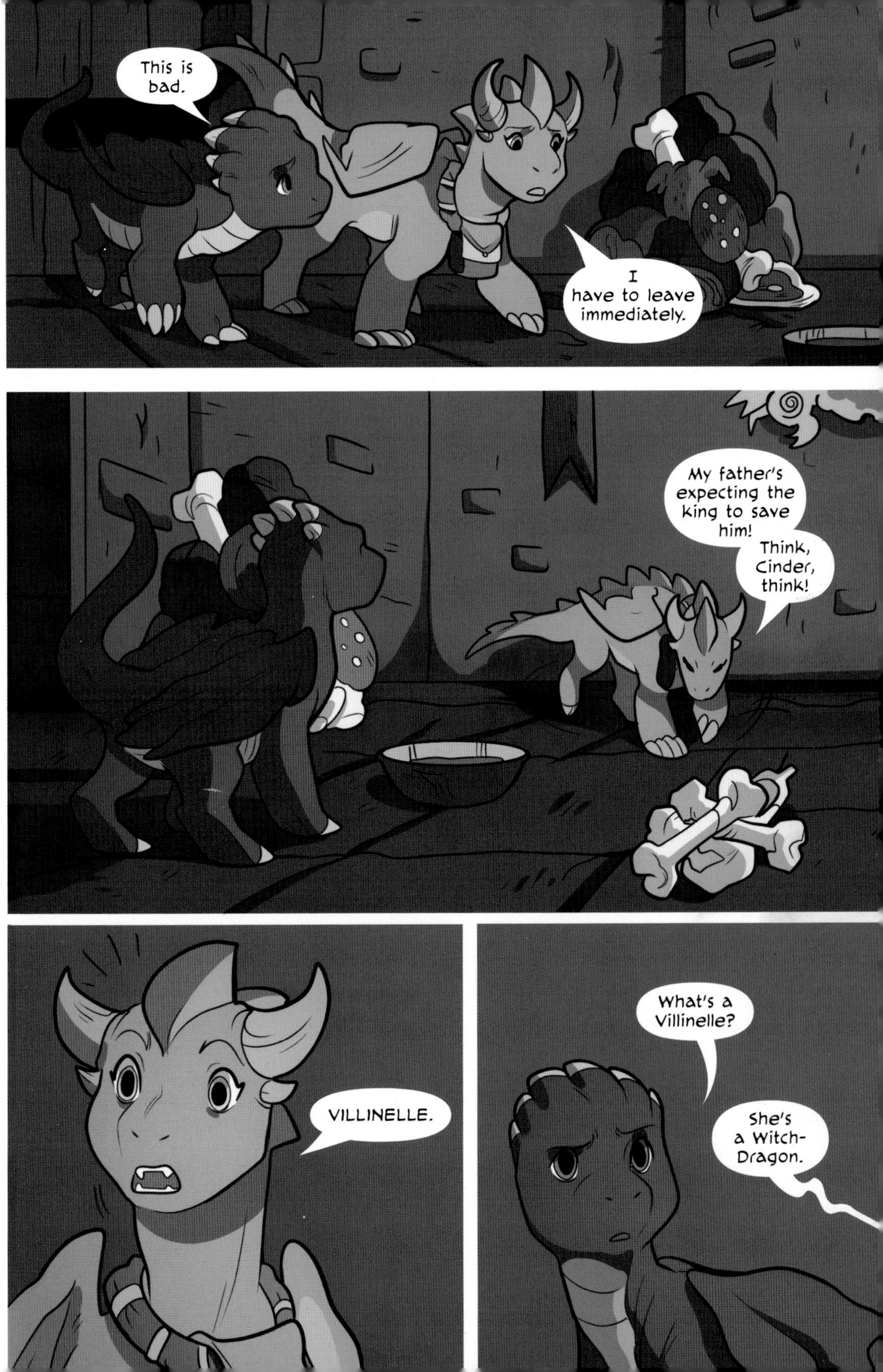
This is bad.
I have to leave immediately.
My father's expecting the king to save him!
Think, Cinder, think!
VILLINELLE.
What's a Villinelle?
She's a Witch-Dragon.

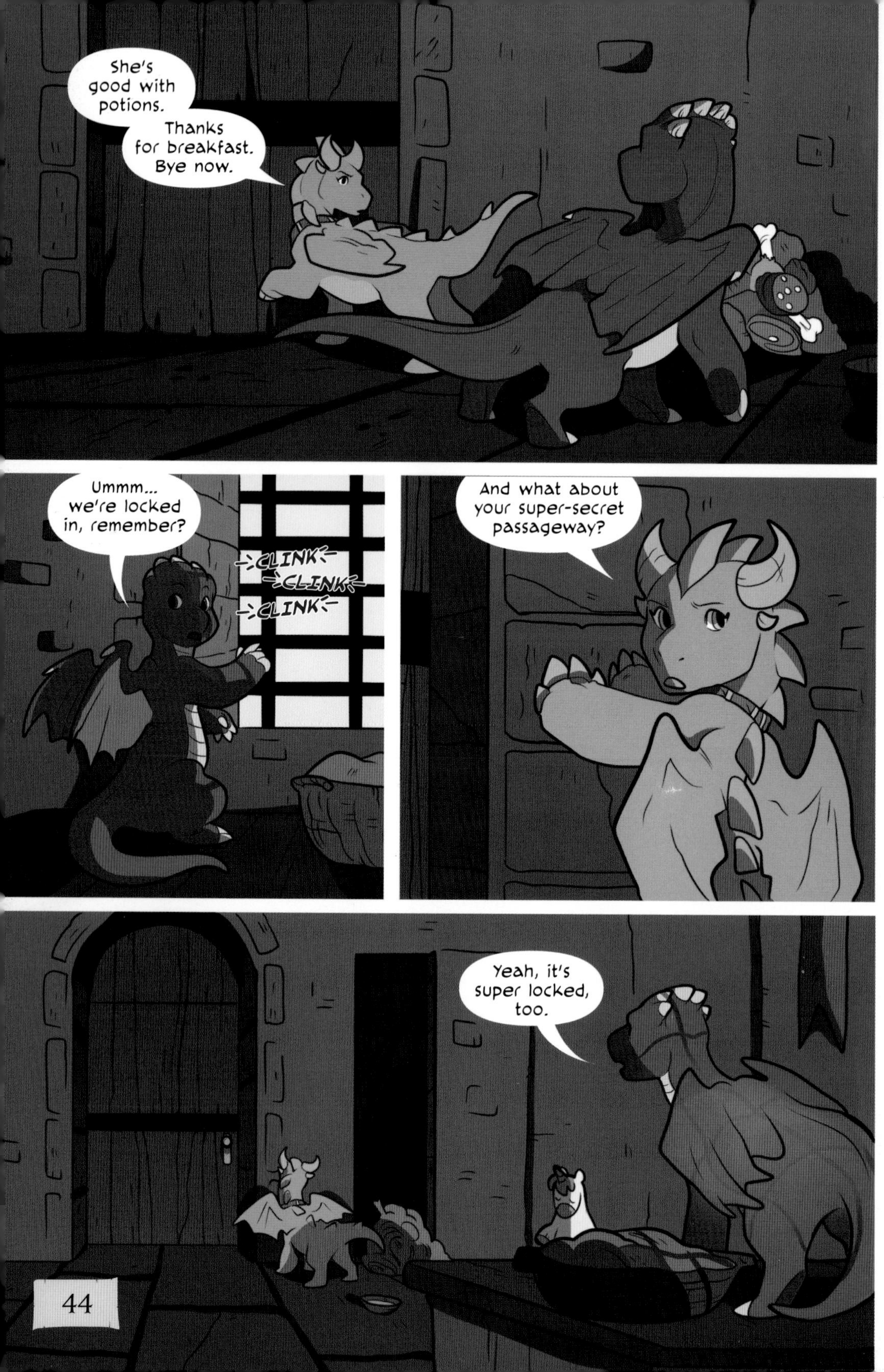

She's good with potions.
Thanks for breakfast. Bye now.
Ummm... we're locked in, remember?
CLINK
CLINK
CLINK
And what about your super-secret passageway?
Yeah, it's super locked, too.

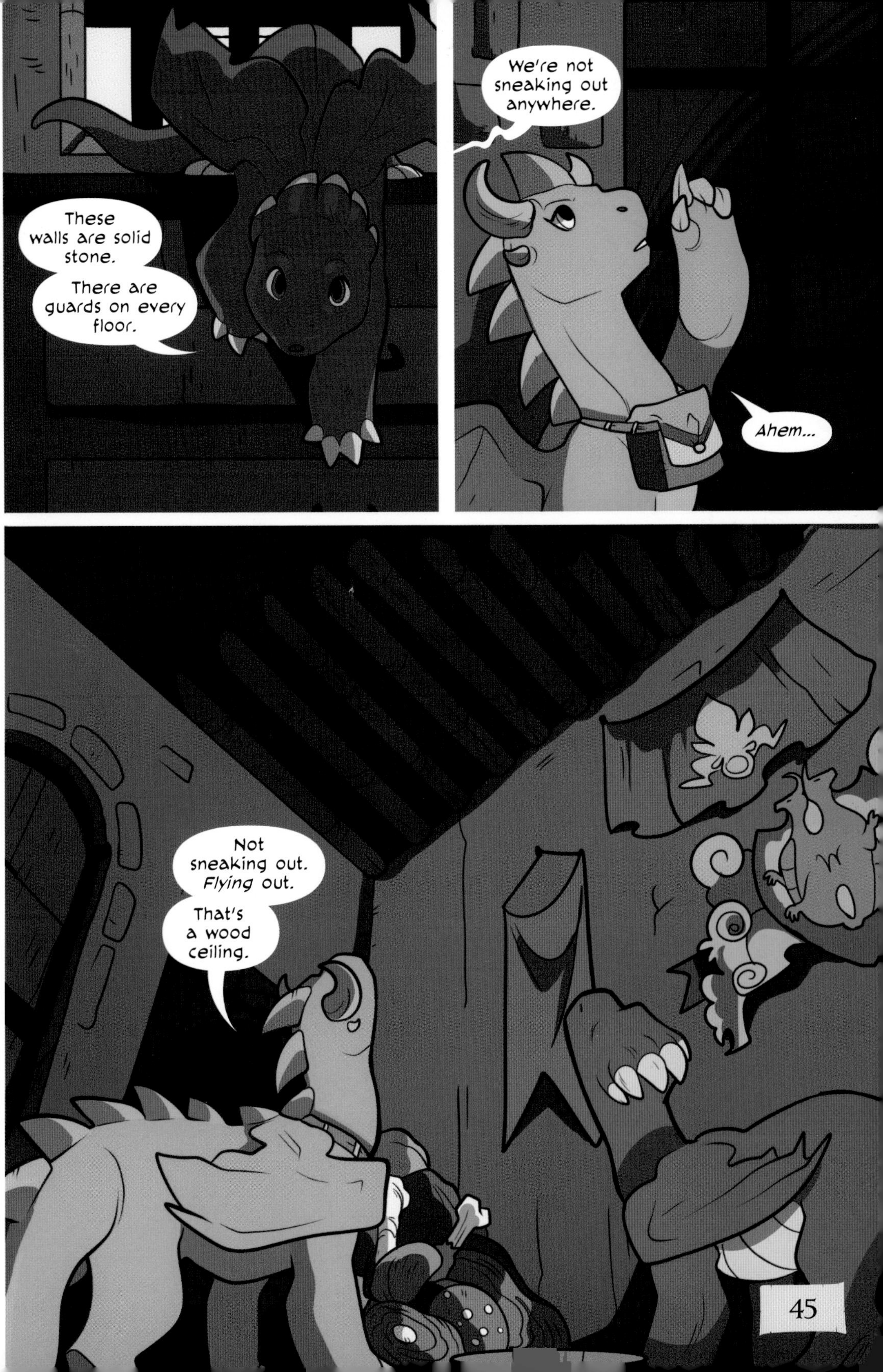
These walls are solid stone.
There are guards on every floor.
We're not sneaking out anywhere.
Ahem...
Not sneaking out. *Flying* out.
That's a wood ceiling.

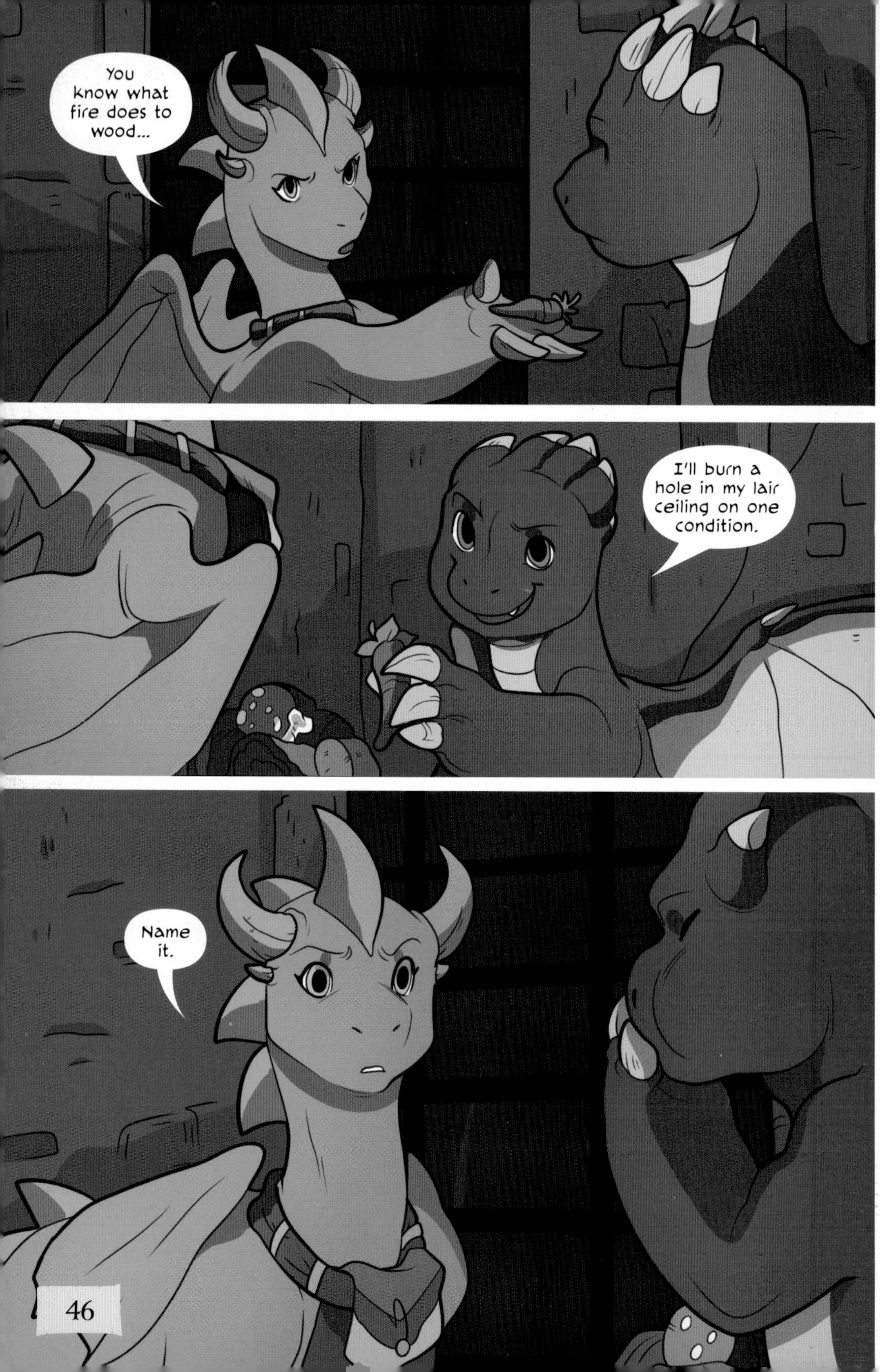
You know what fire does to wood...
I'll burn a hole in my lair ceiling on one condition.
Name it.

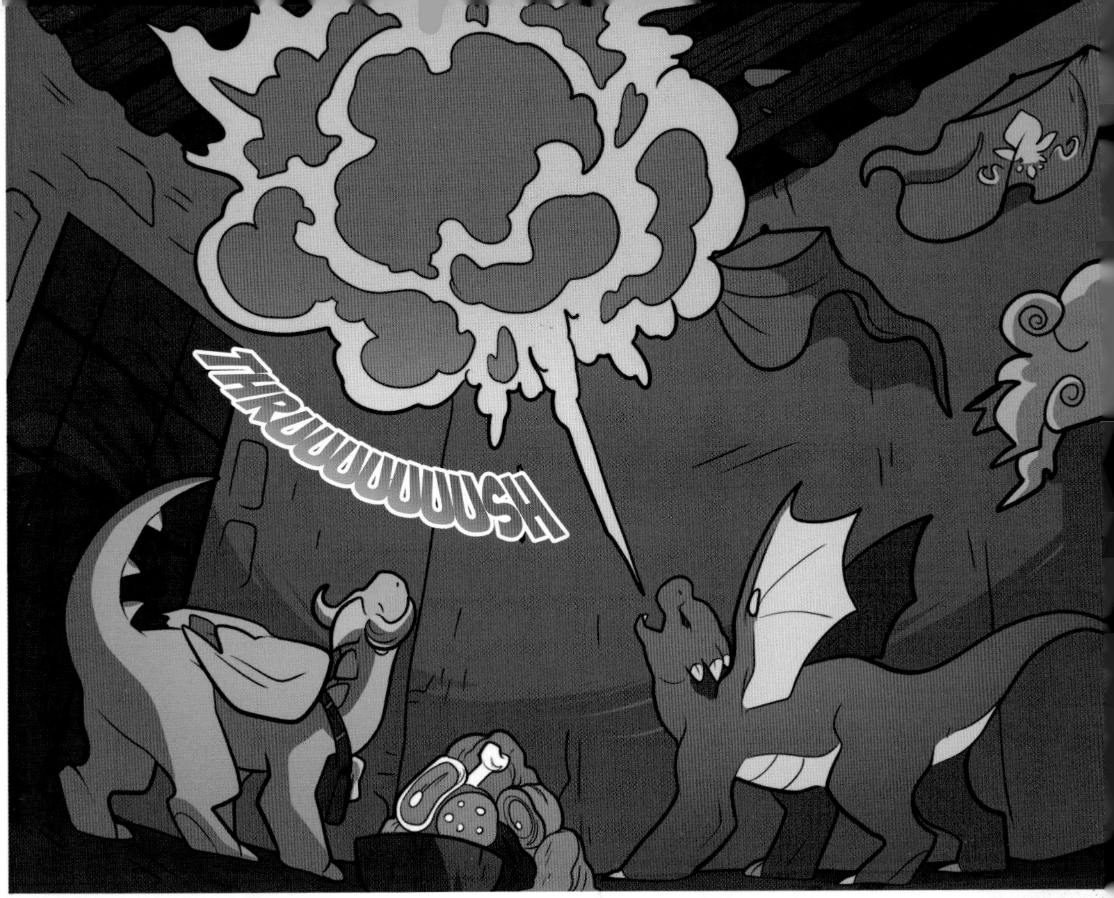
THRUUUUUUUSH

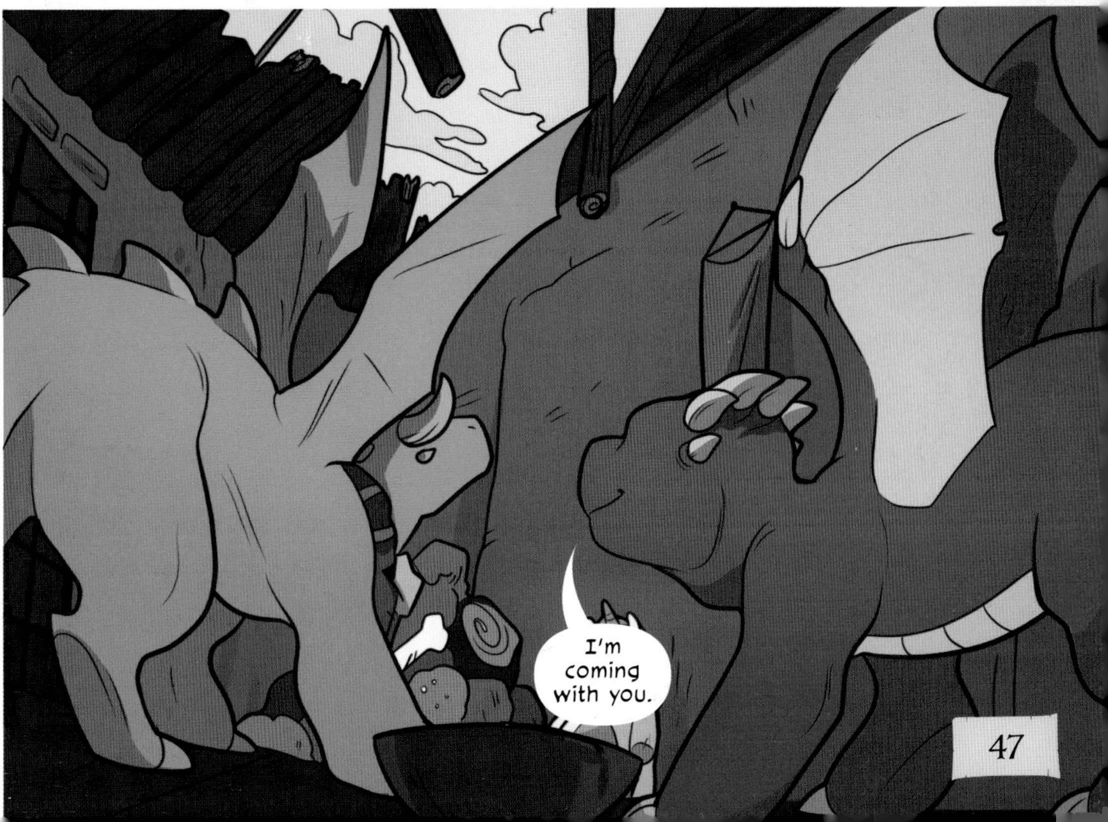
I'm coming with you.

Chapter 4

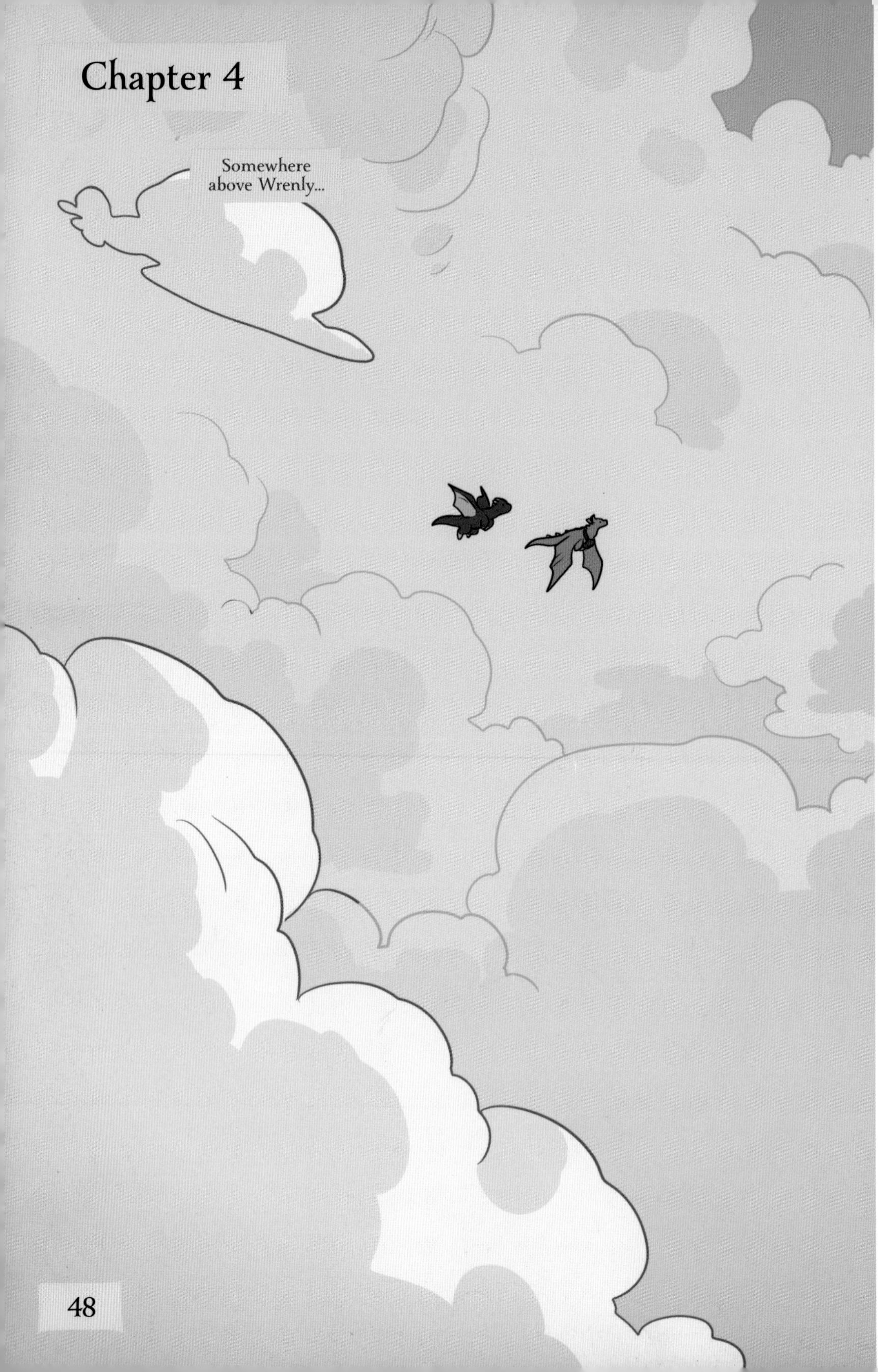
Somewhere above Wrenly...

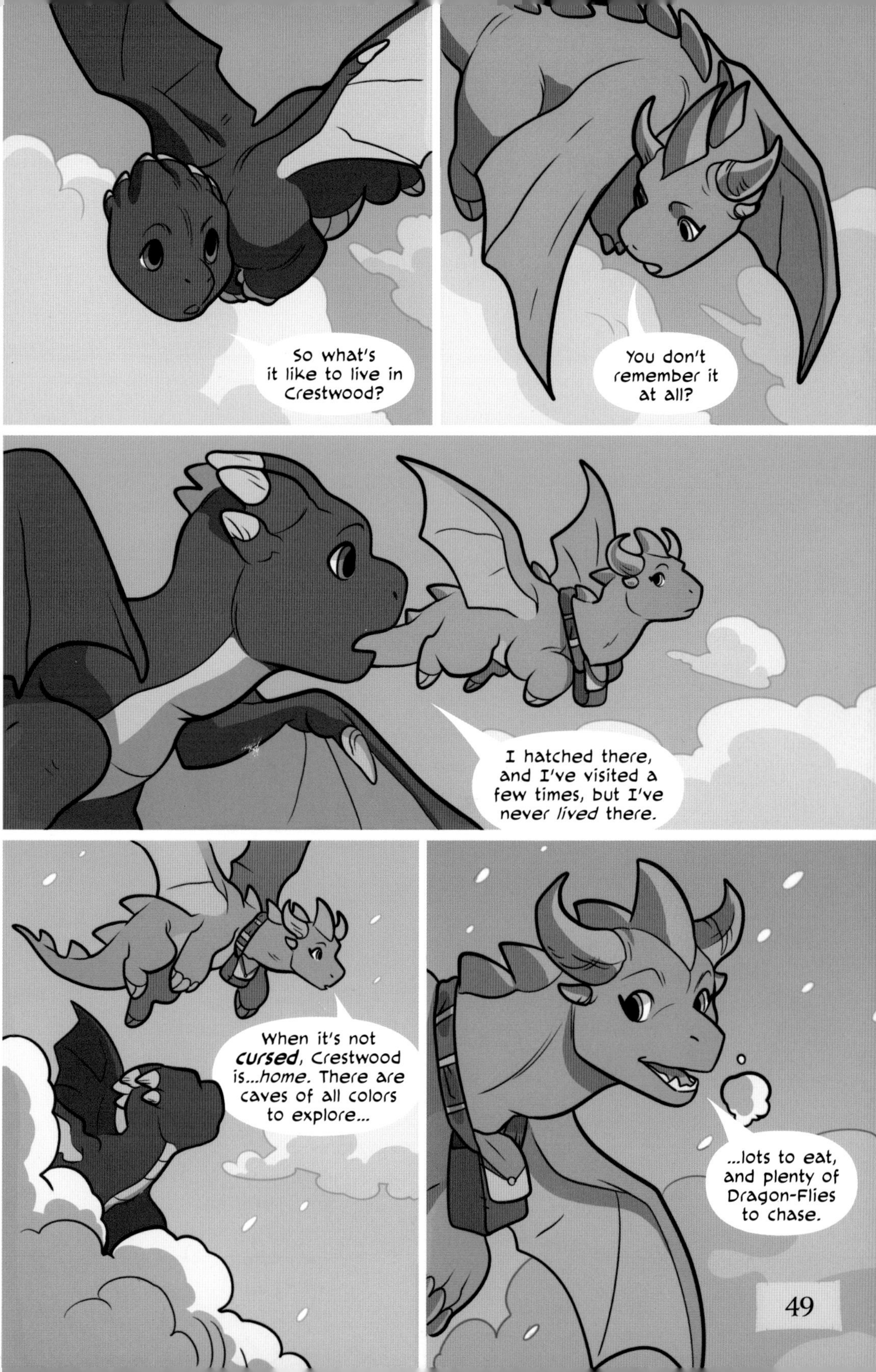
So what's it like to live in Crestwood?
You don't remember it at all?
I hatched there, and I've visited a few times, but I've never *lived* there.
When it's not ***cursed***, Crestwood is...*home.* There are caves of all colors to explore...
...lots to eat, and plenty of Dragon-Flies to chase.

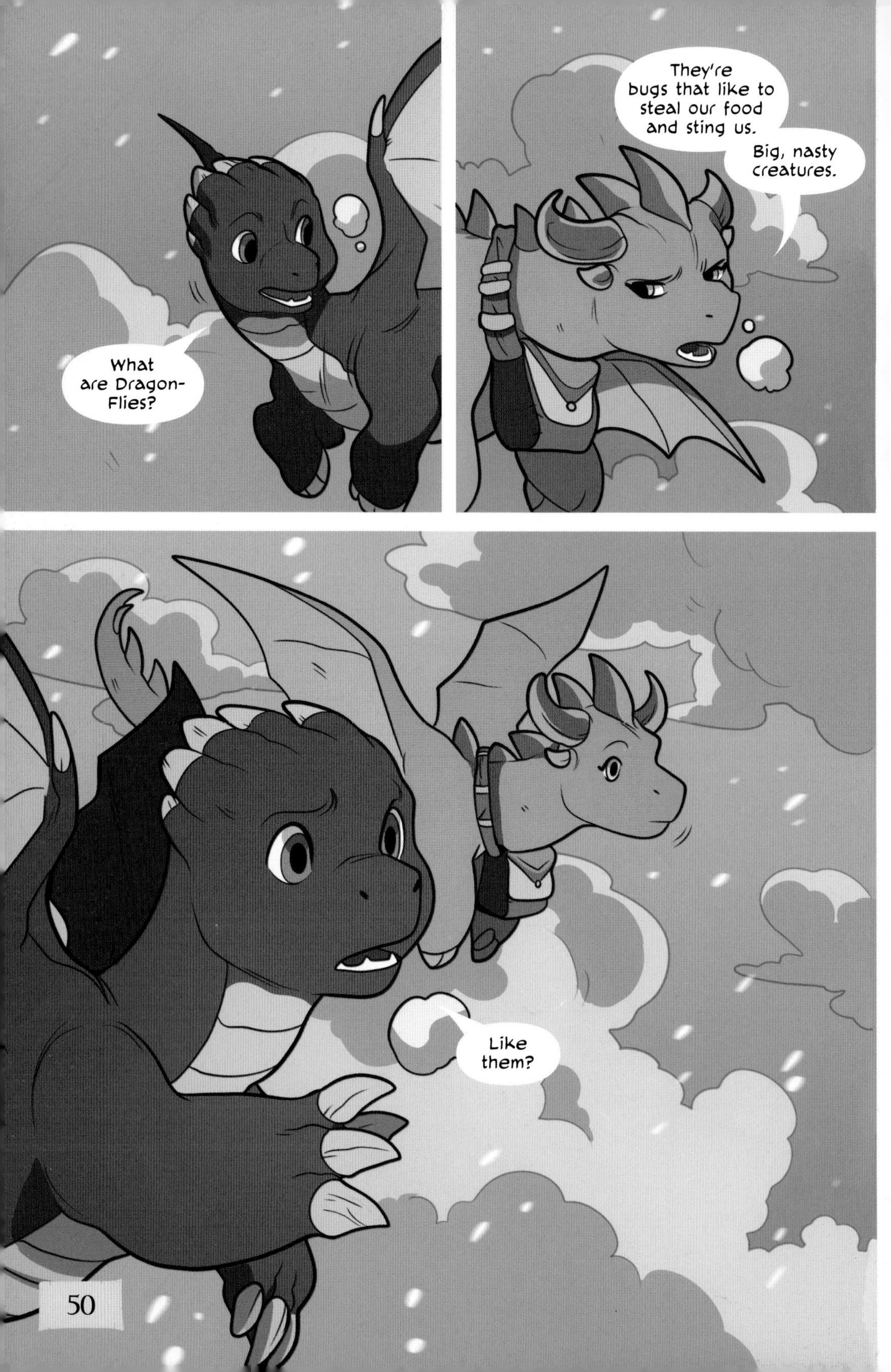
What are Dragon-Flies?
They're bugs that like to steal our food and sting us.
Big, nasty creatures.
Like them?

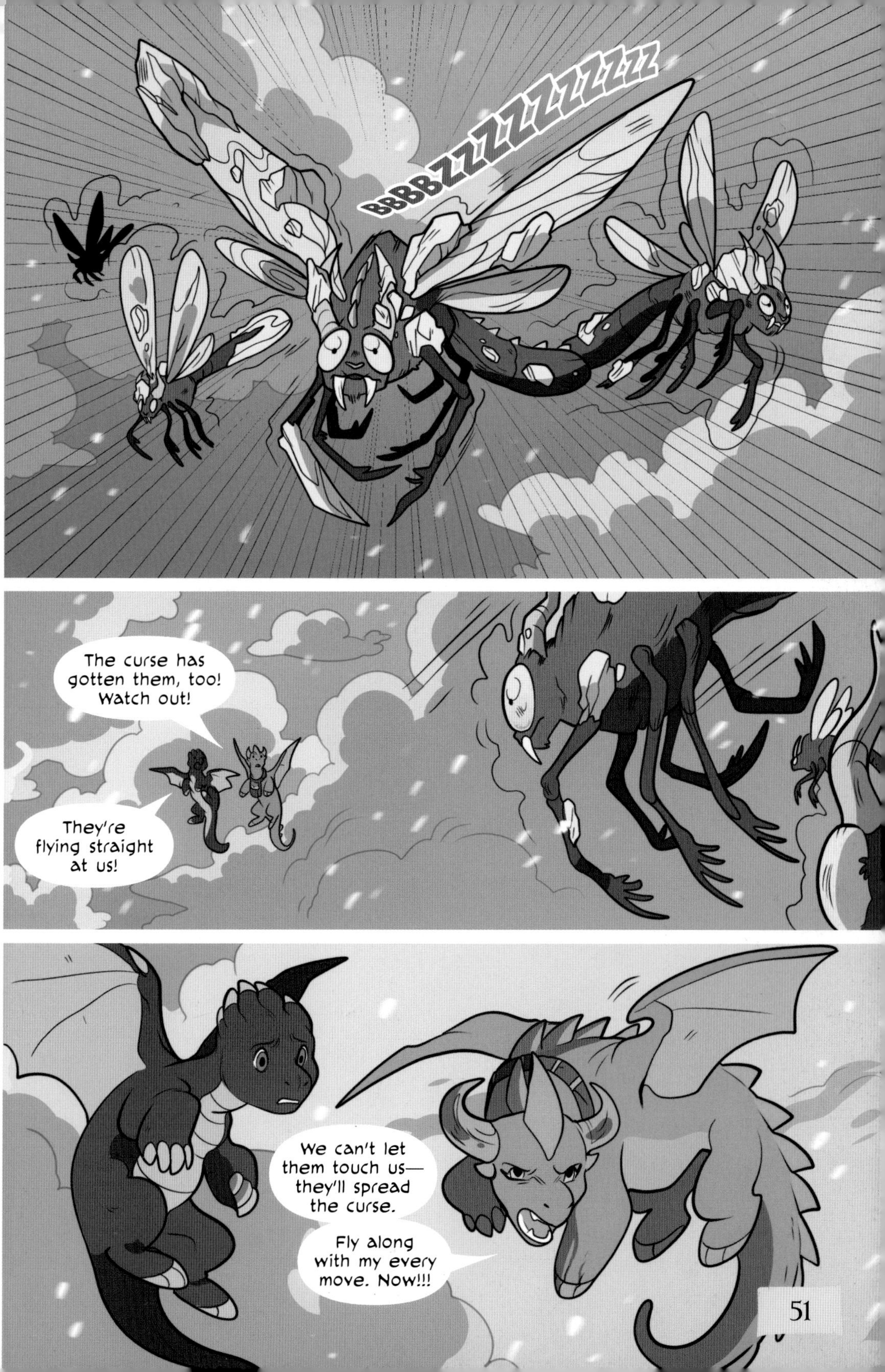
BBBBZZZZZZZZZZ
The curse has gotten them, too! Watch out!
They're flying straight at us!
We can't let them touch us—they'll spread the curse.
Fly along with my every move. Now!!!

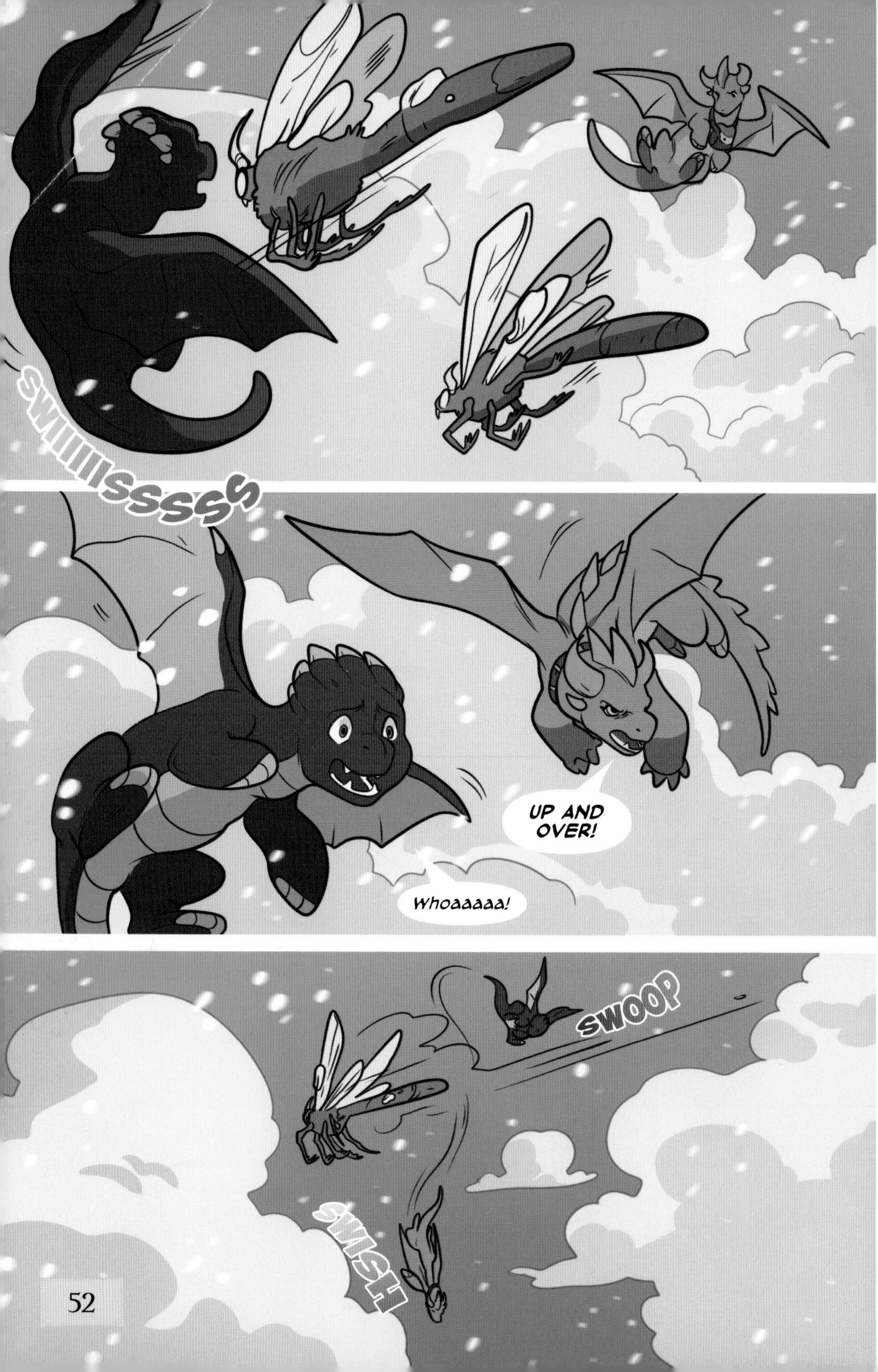
SWIIIIISSSSSS
UP AND OVER!
Whoaaaaa!
SWOOP
SWISH

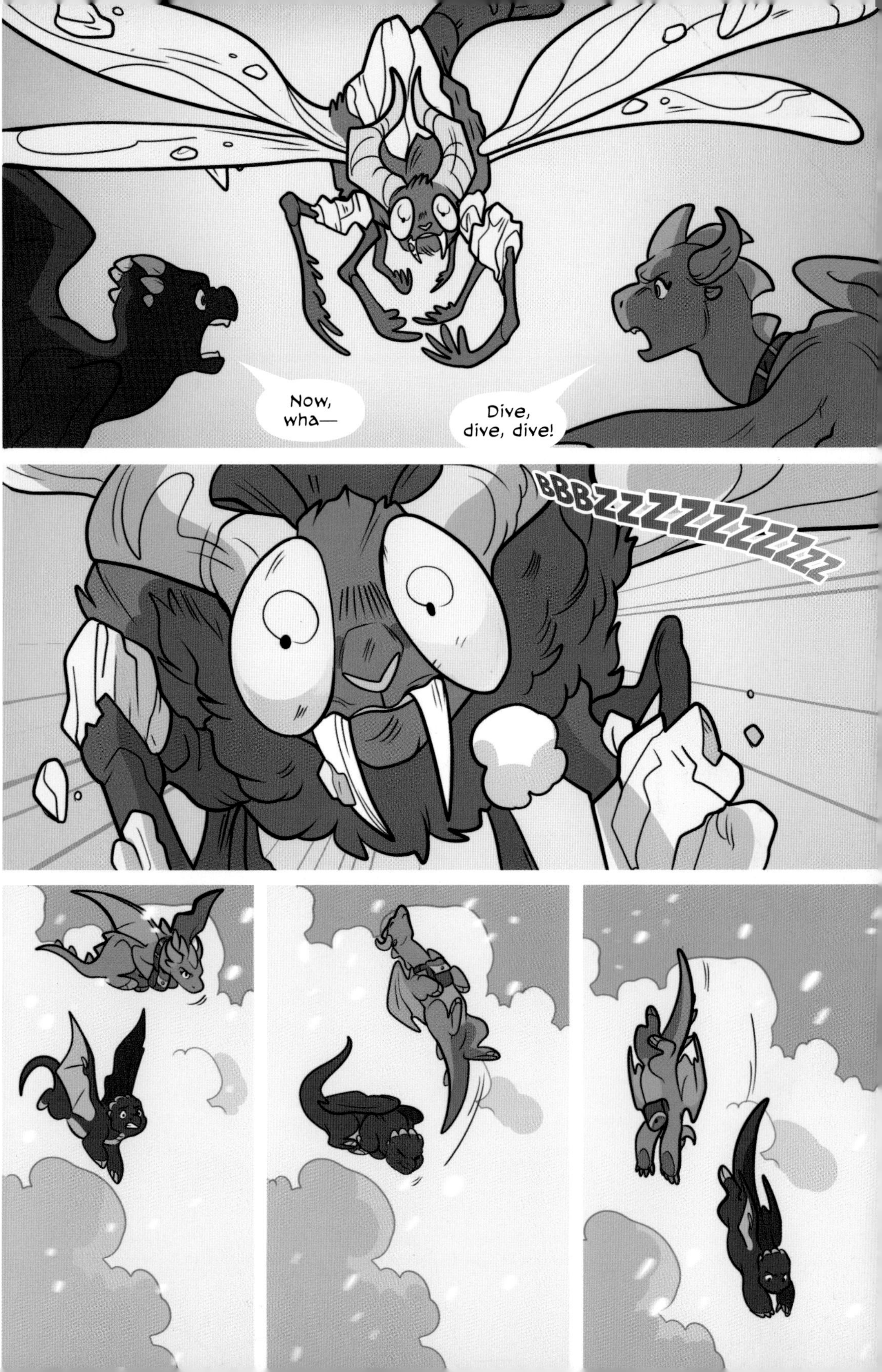
Now, wha—
Dive, dive, dive!
BBBZZZZZZZZZZ

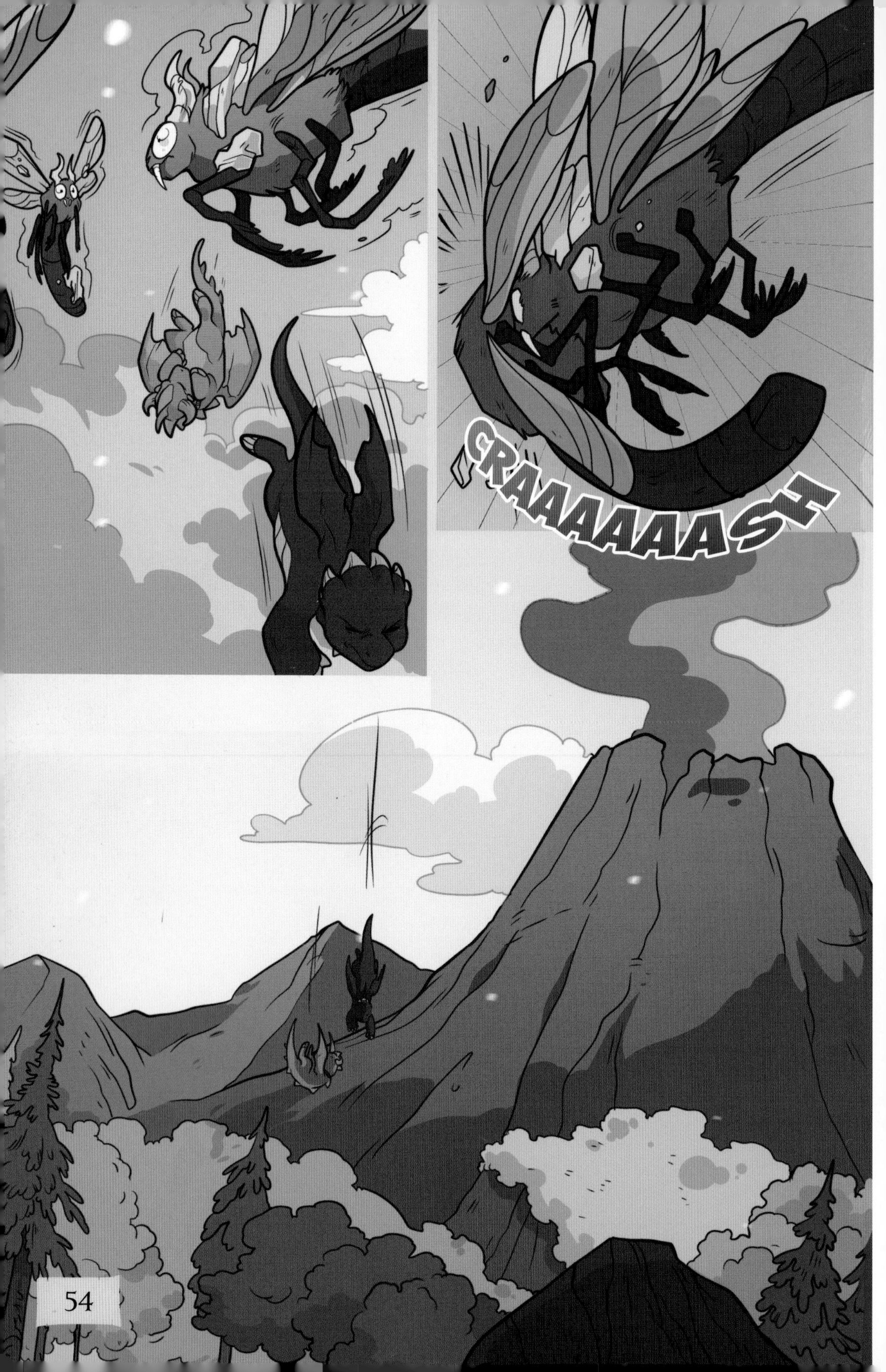
CRAAAAAAASH

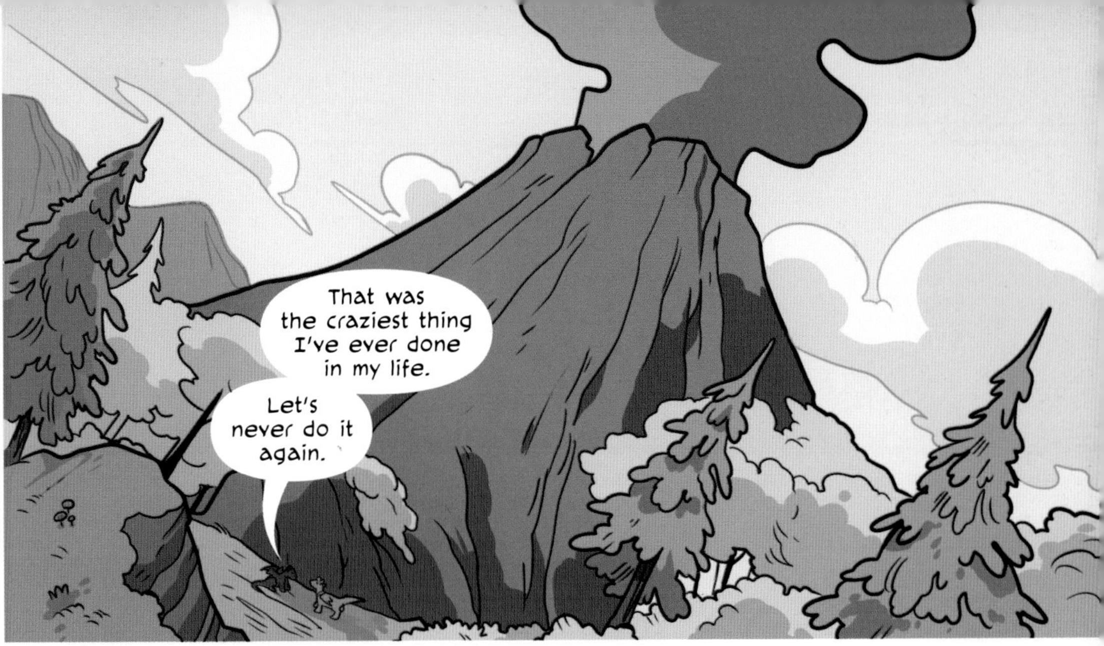
That was the craziest thing I've ever done in my life.
Let's never do it again.

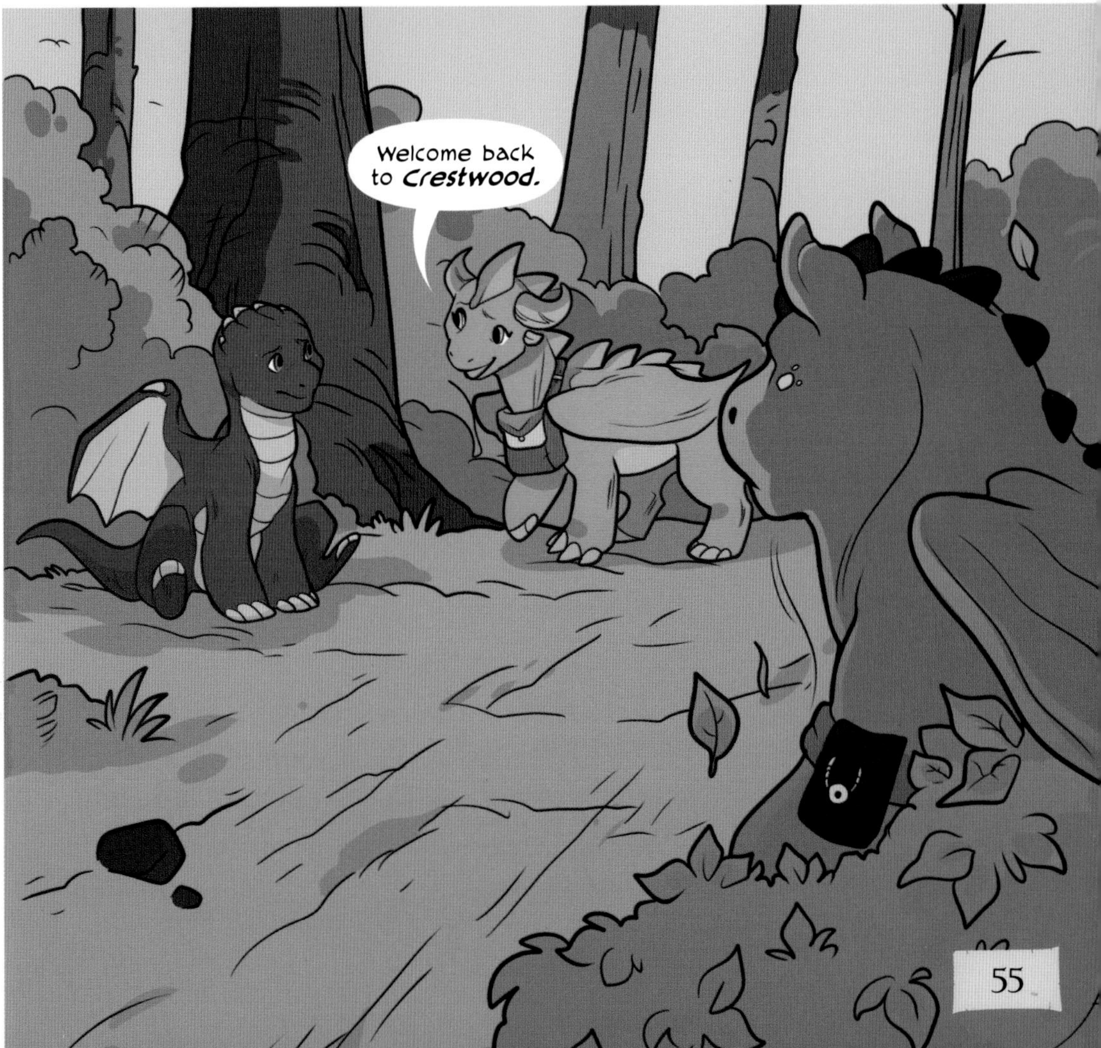
Welcome back to *Crestwood.*

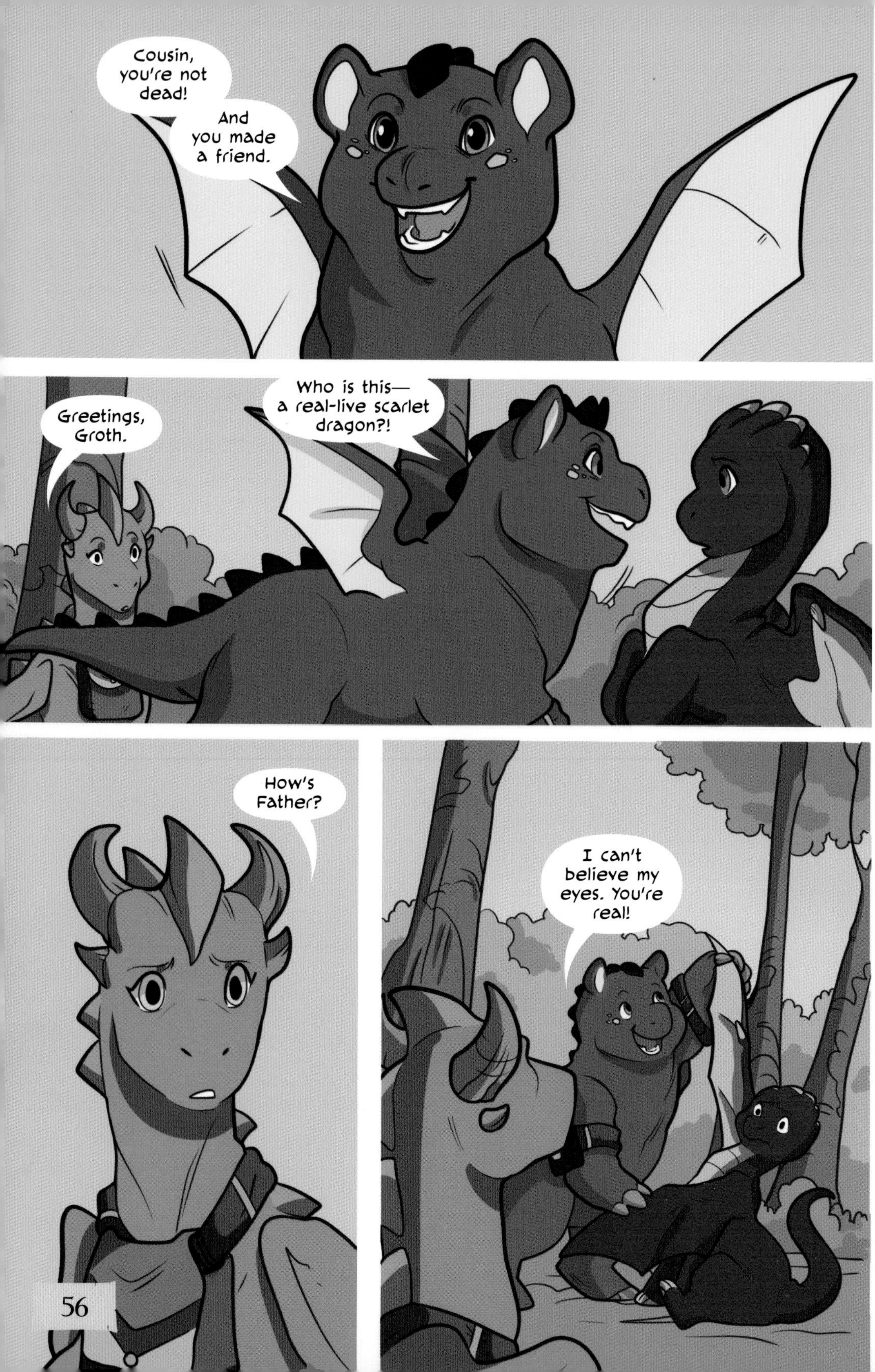
Cousin, you're not dead!
And you made a friend.
Greetings, Groth.
Who is this— a real-live scarlet dragon?!
How's Father?
I can't believe my eyes. You're real!

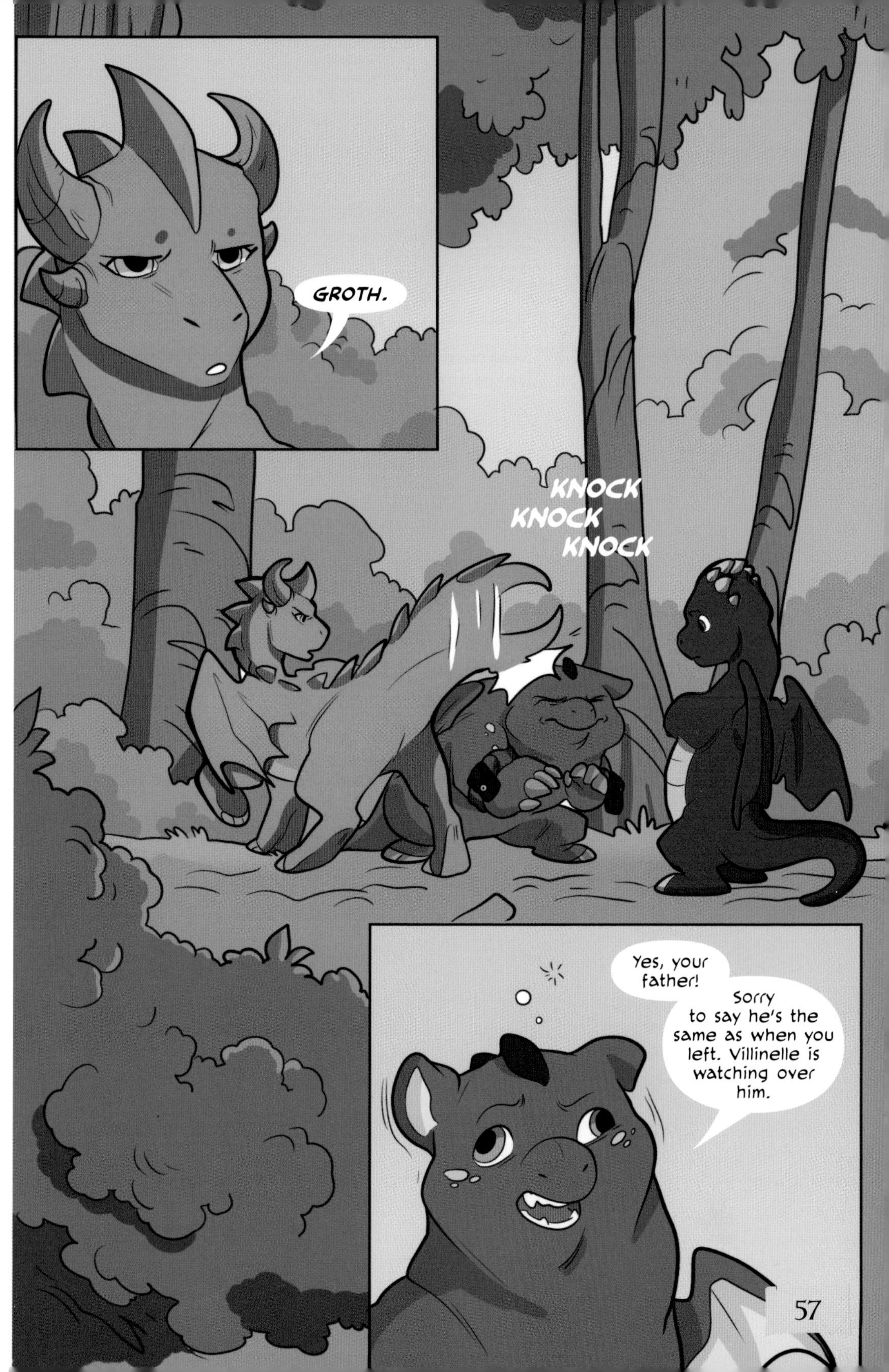
GROTH.
KNOCK
KNOCK
KNOCK
Yes, your father!
Sorry to say he's the same as when you left. Villinelle is watching over him.

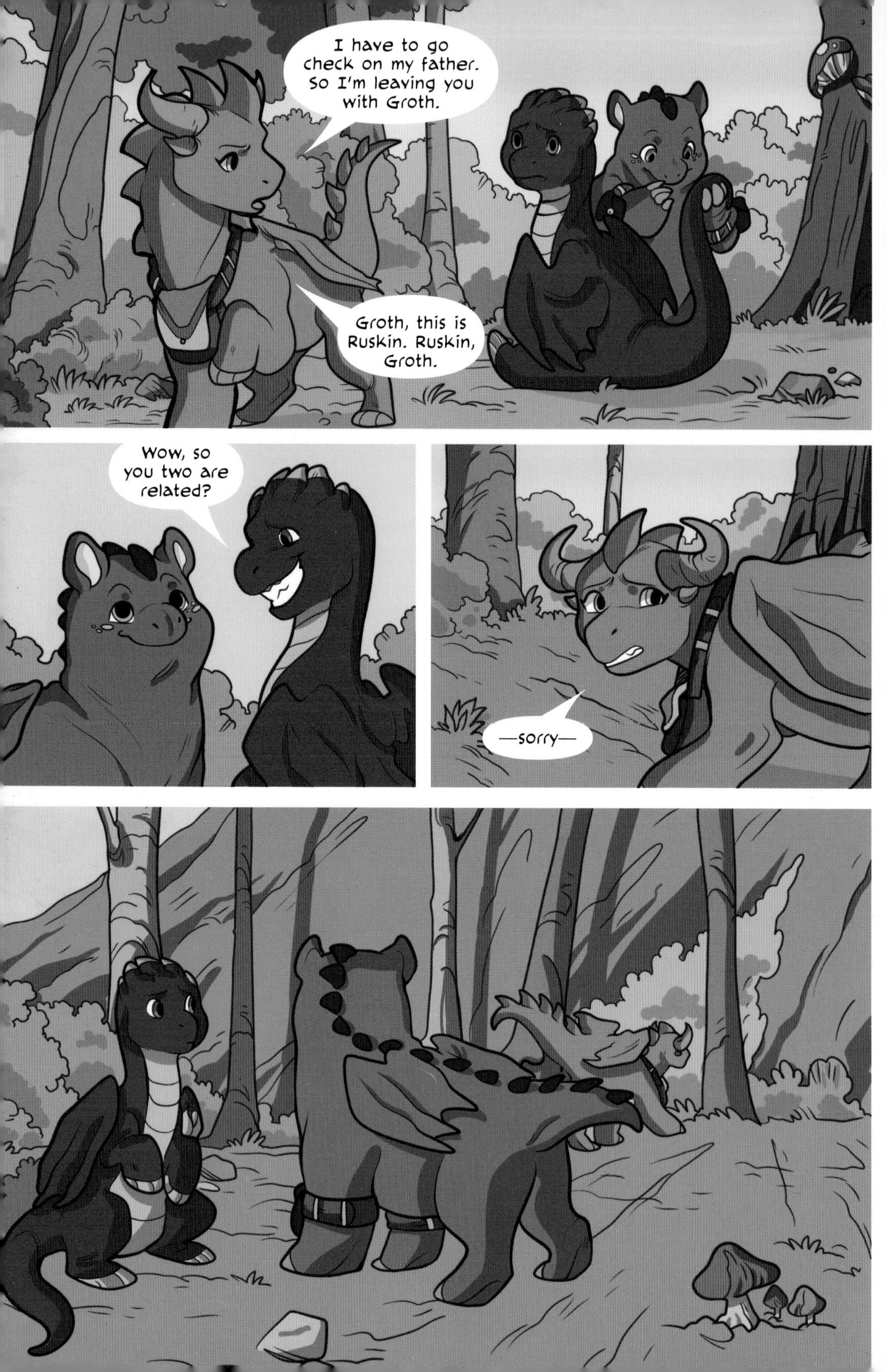
I have to go check on my father. So I'm leaving you with Groth.
Groth, this is Ruskin. Ruskin, Groth.
Wow, so you two are related?
—sorry—

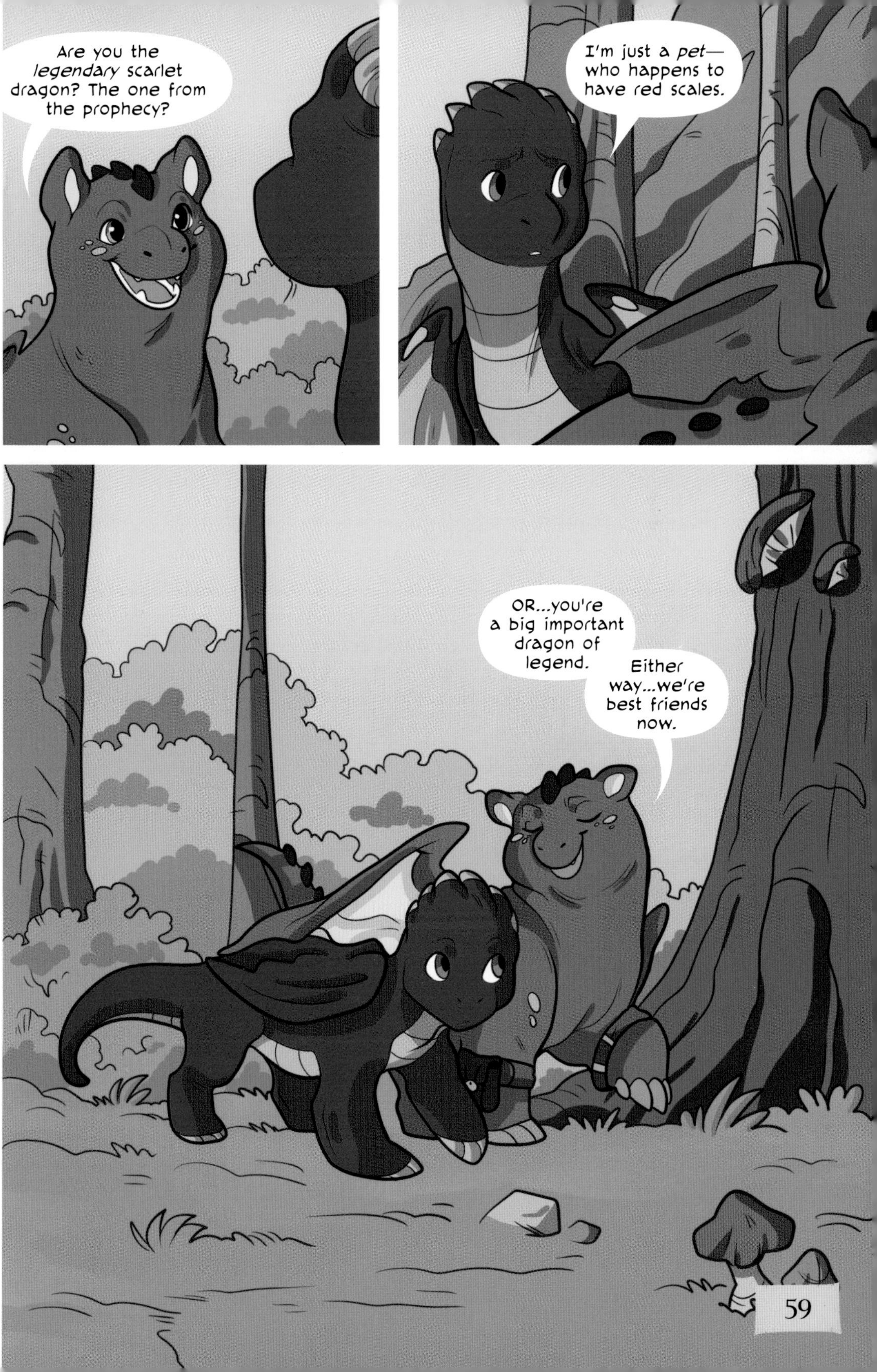
Are you the *legendary* scarlet dragon? The one from the prophecy?
I'm just a *pet*—who happens to have red scales.
OR...you're a big important dragon of legend.
Either way...we're best friends now.

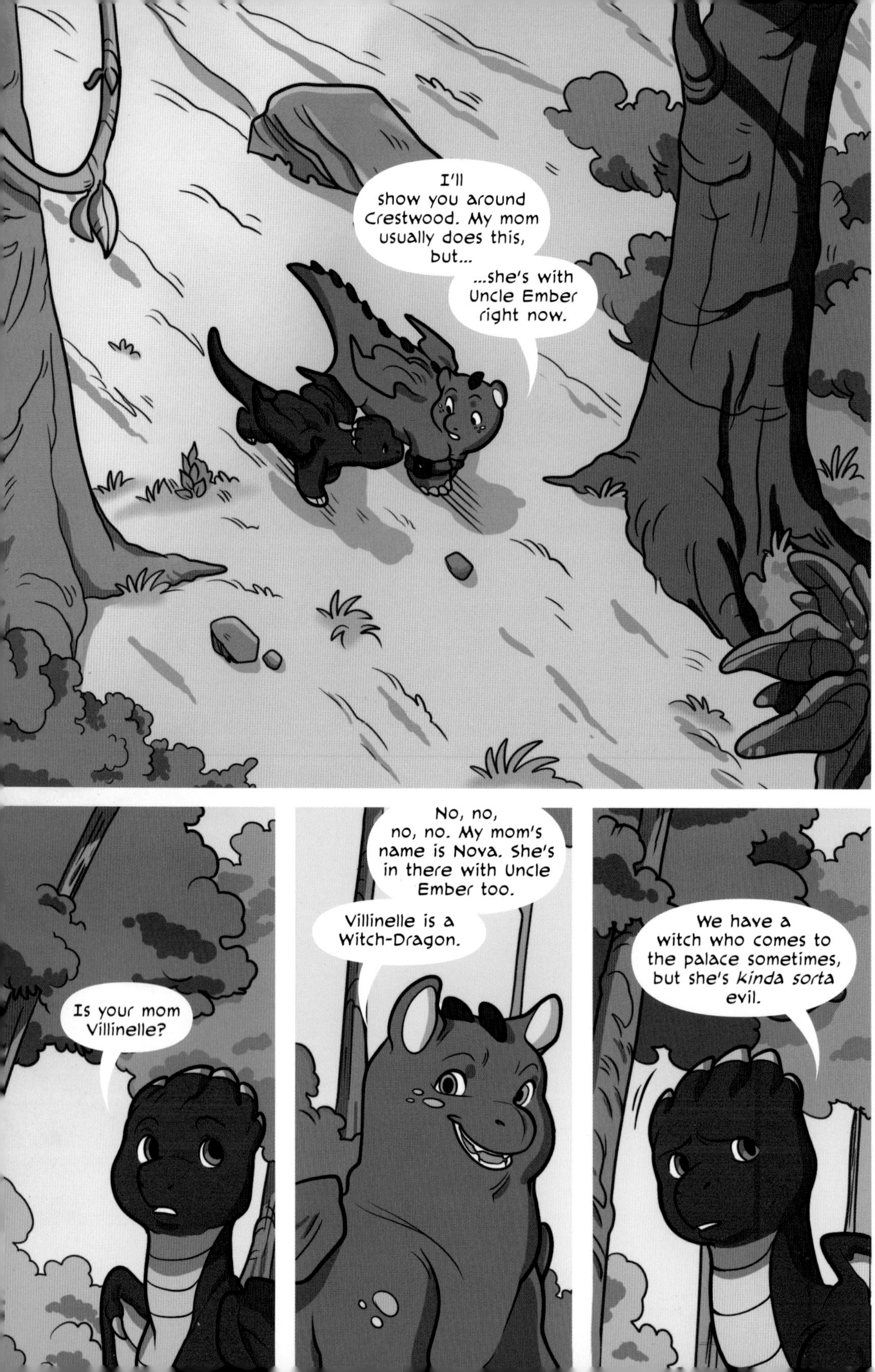
I'll show you around Crestwood. My mom usually does this, but...
...she's with Uncle Ember right now.
Is your mom Villinelle?
No, no, no, no. My mom's name is Nova. She's in there with Uncle Ember too.
Villinelle is a Witch-Dragon.
We have a witch who comes to the palace sometimes, but she's *kinda sorta* evil.

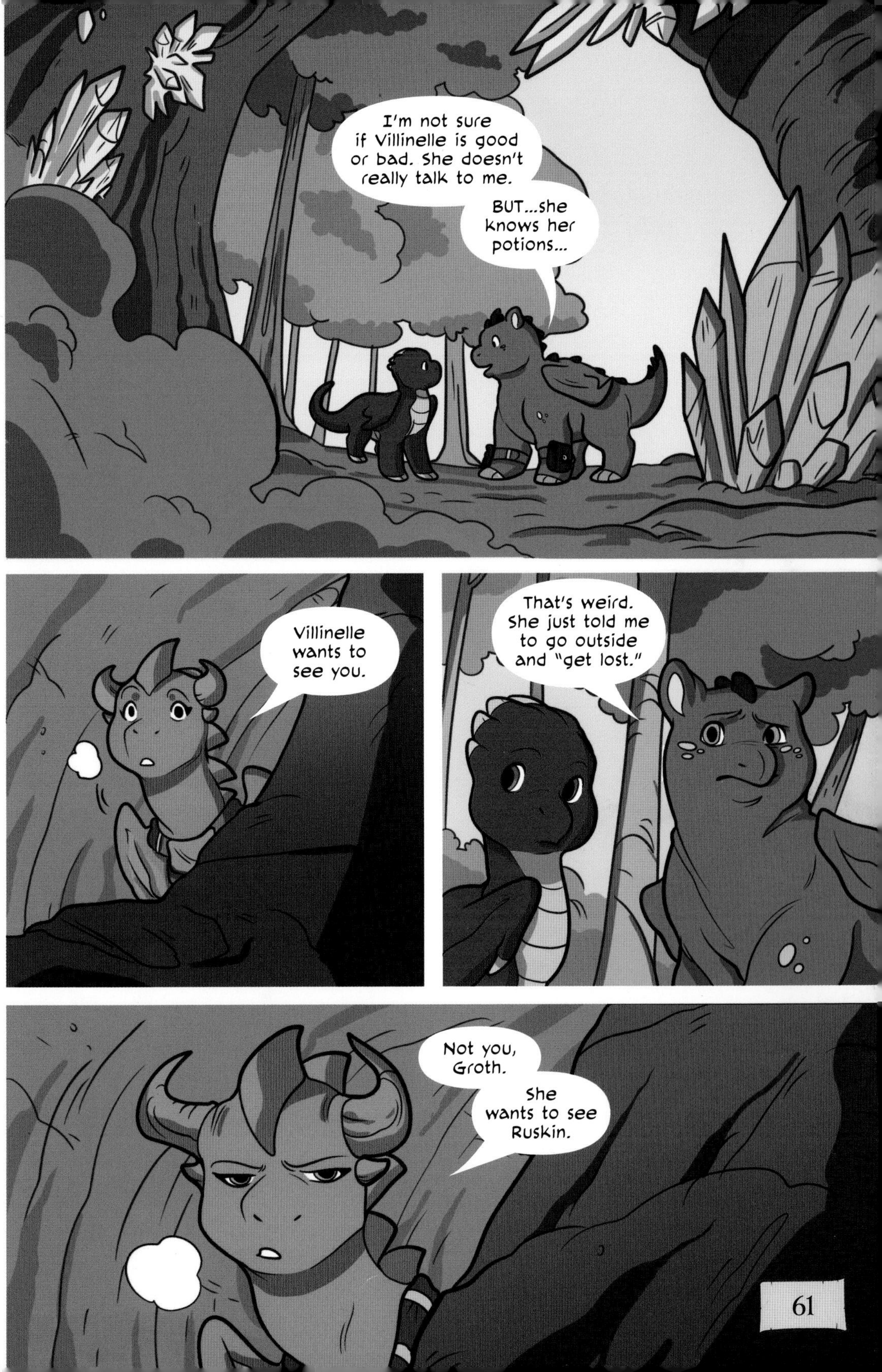
I'm not sure if Villinelle is good or bad. She doesn't really talk to me.
BUT...she knows her potions...
Villinelle wants to see you.
That's weird. She just told me to go outside and "get lost."
Not you, Groth.
She wants to see Ruskin.

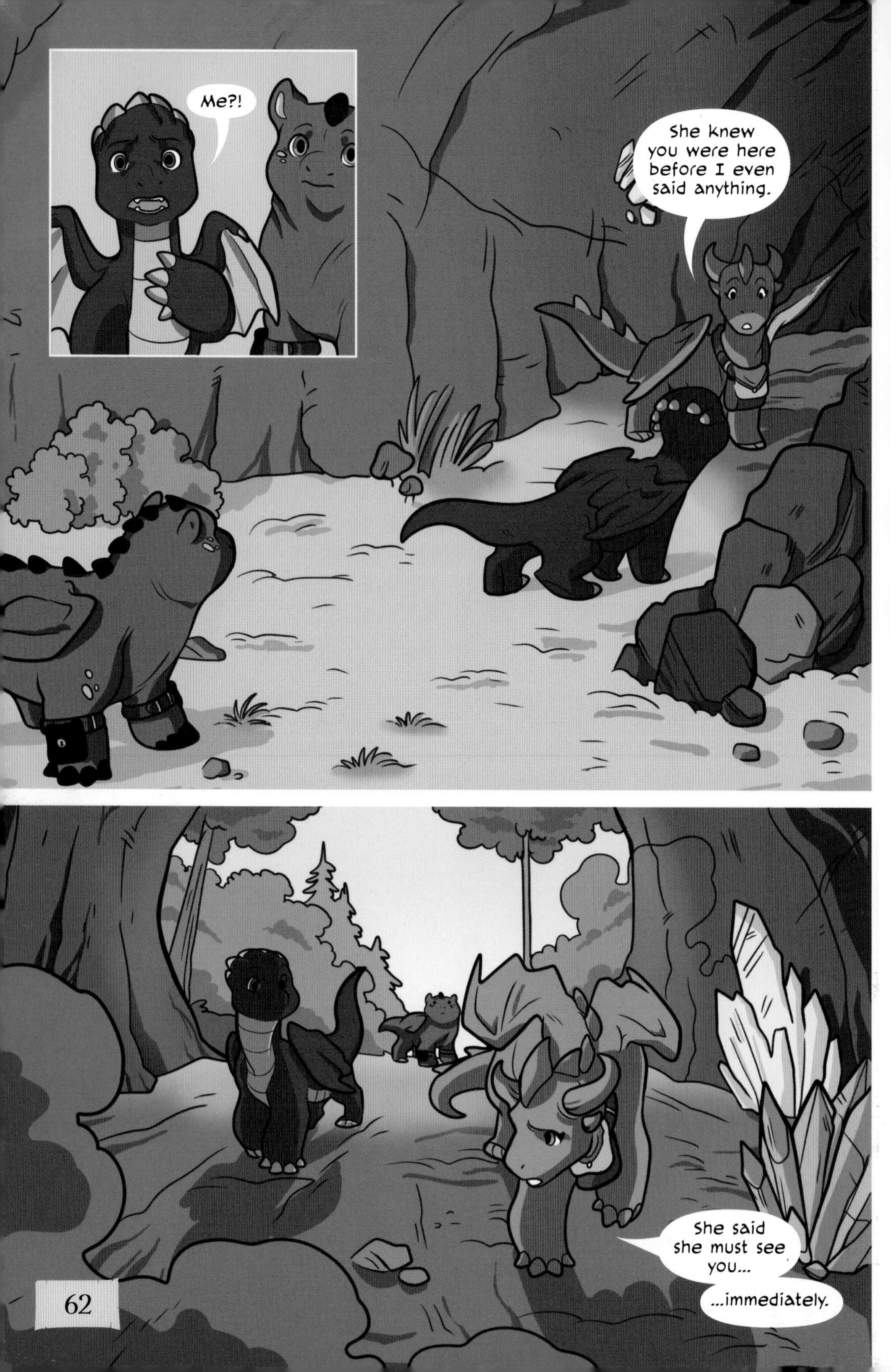
Me?!
She knew you were here before I even said anything.
She said she must see you...
...immediately.

Chapter 5

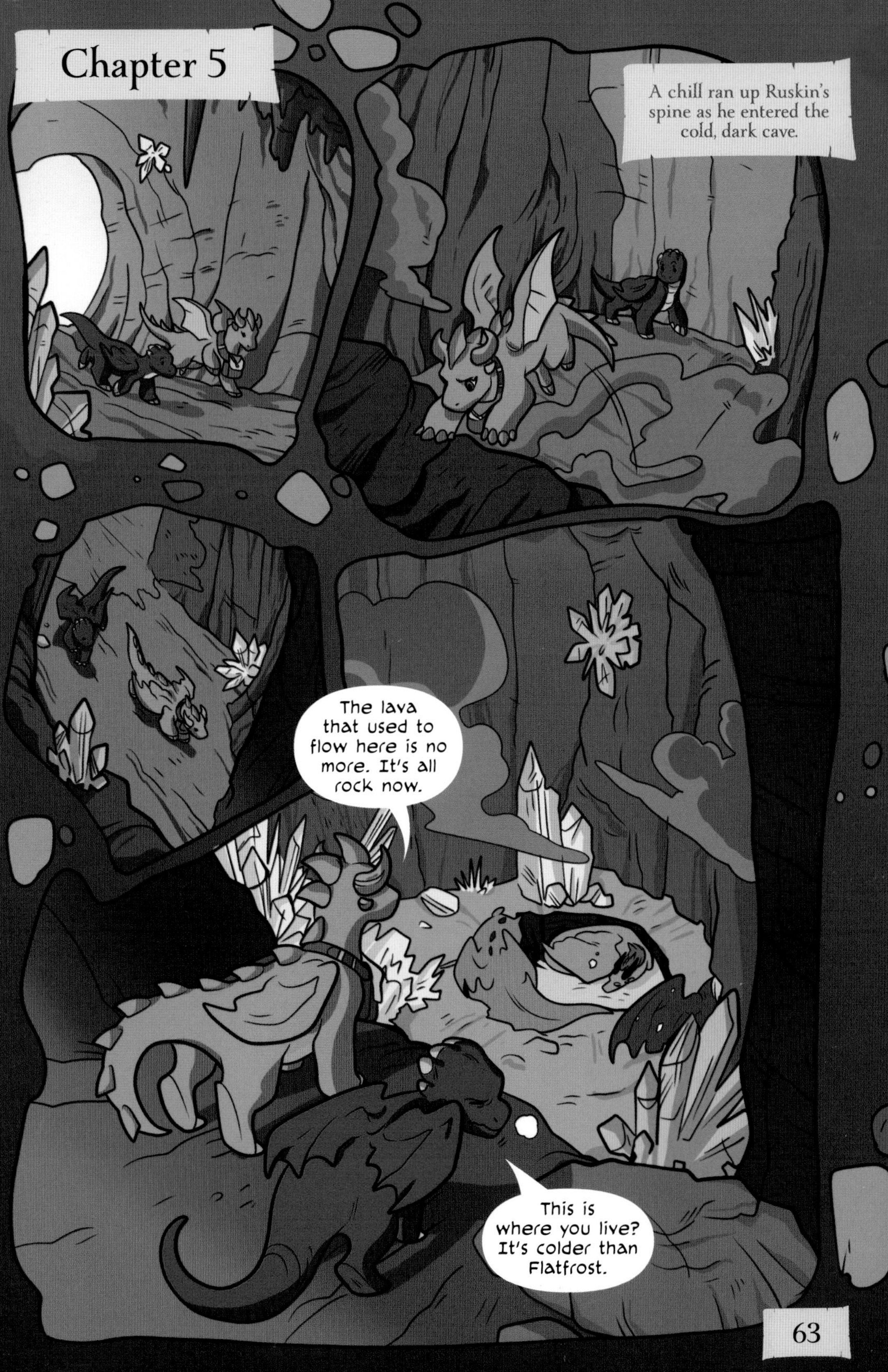
A chill ran up Ruskin's spine as he entered the cold, dark cave.
The lava that used to flow here is no more. It's all rock now.
This is where you live? It's colder than Flatfrost.

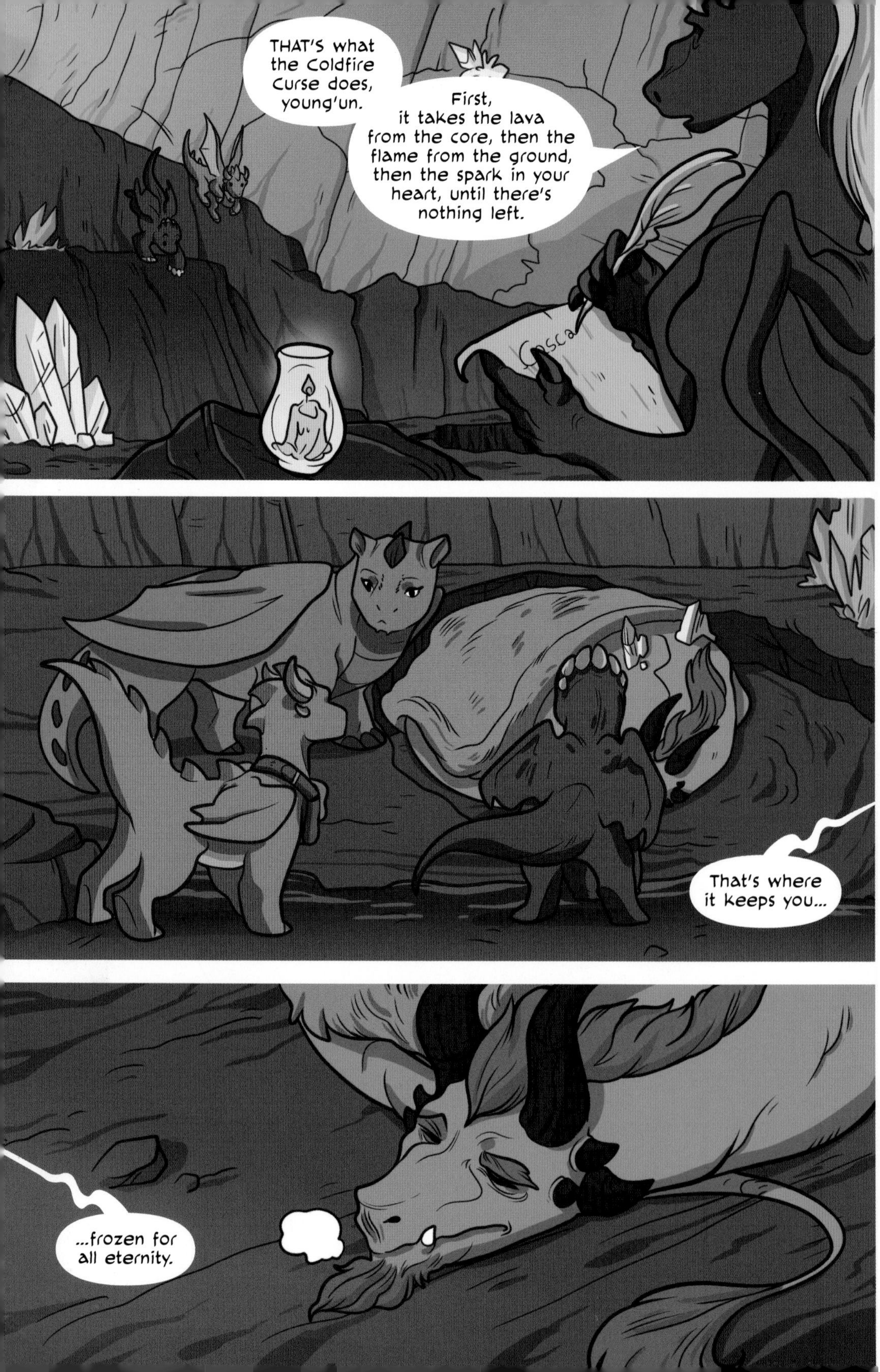
THAT'S what the Coldfire Curse does, young'un.
First, it takes the lava from the core, then the flame from the ground, then the spark in your heart, until there's nothing left.
That's where it keeps you...
...frozen for all eternity.

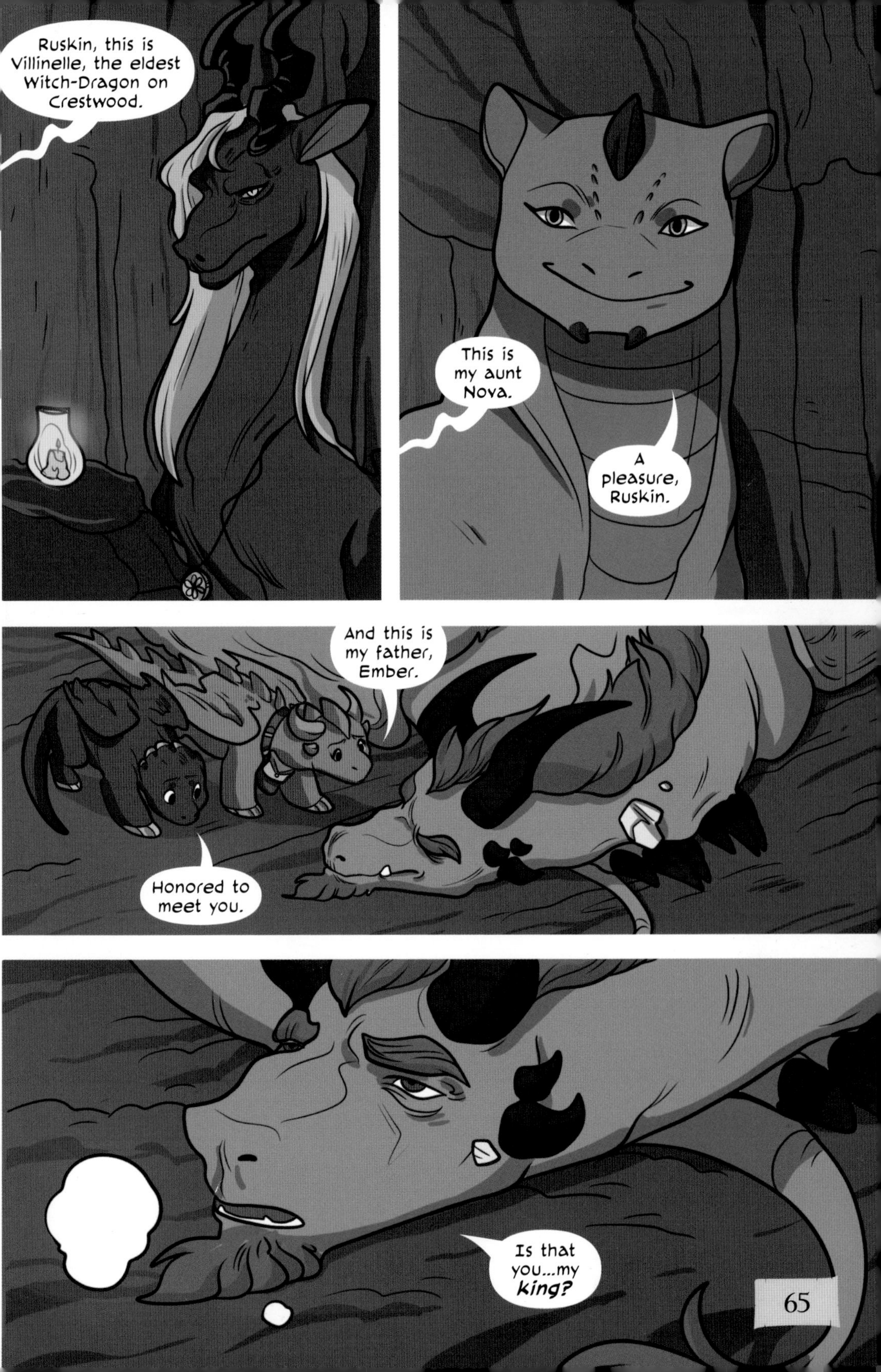

Ruskin, this is Villinelle, the eldest Witch-Dragon on Crestwood.
This is my aunt Nova.
A pleasure, Ruskin.
And this is my father, Ember.
Honored to meet you.
Is that you...my *king?*

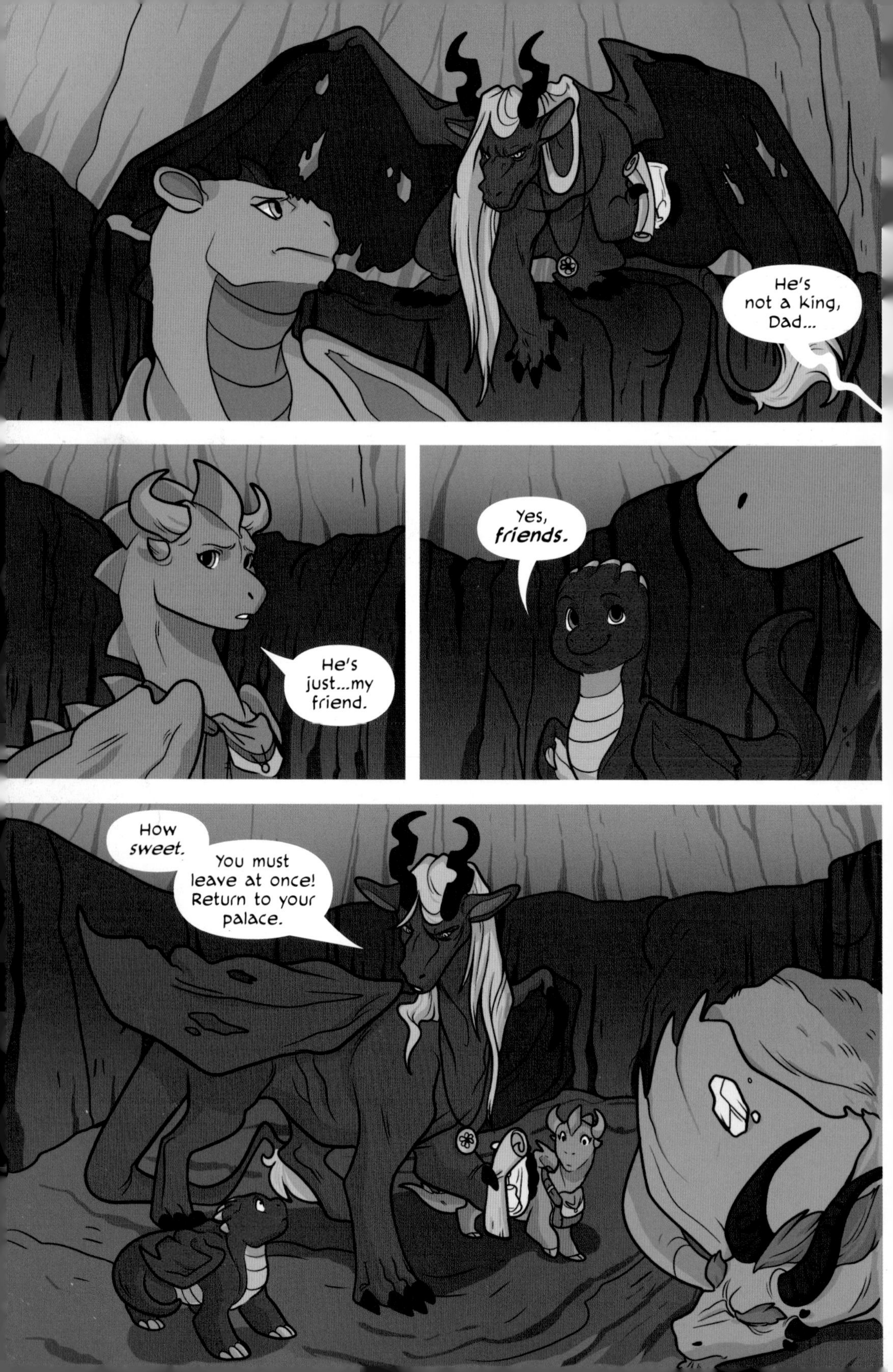
He's not a king, Dad...
He's just...my friend.
Yes, *friends.*
How *sweet.*
You must leave at once! Return to your palace.

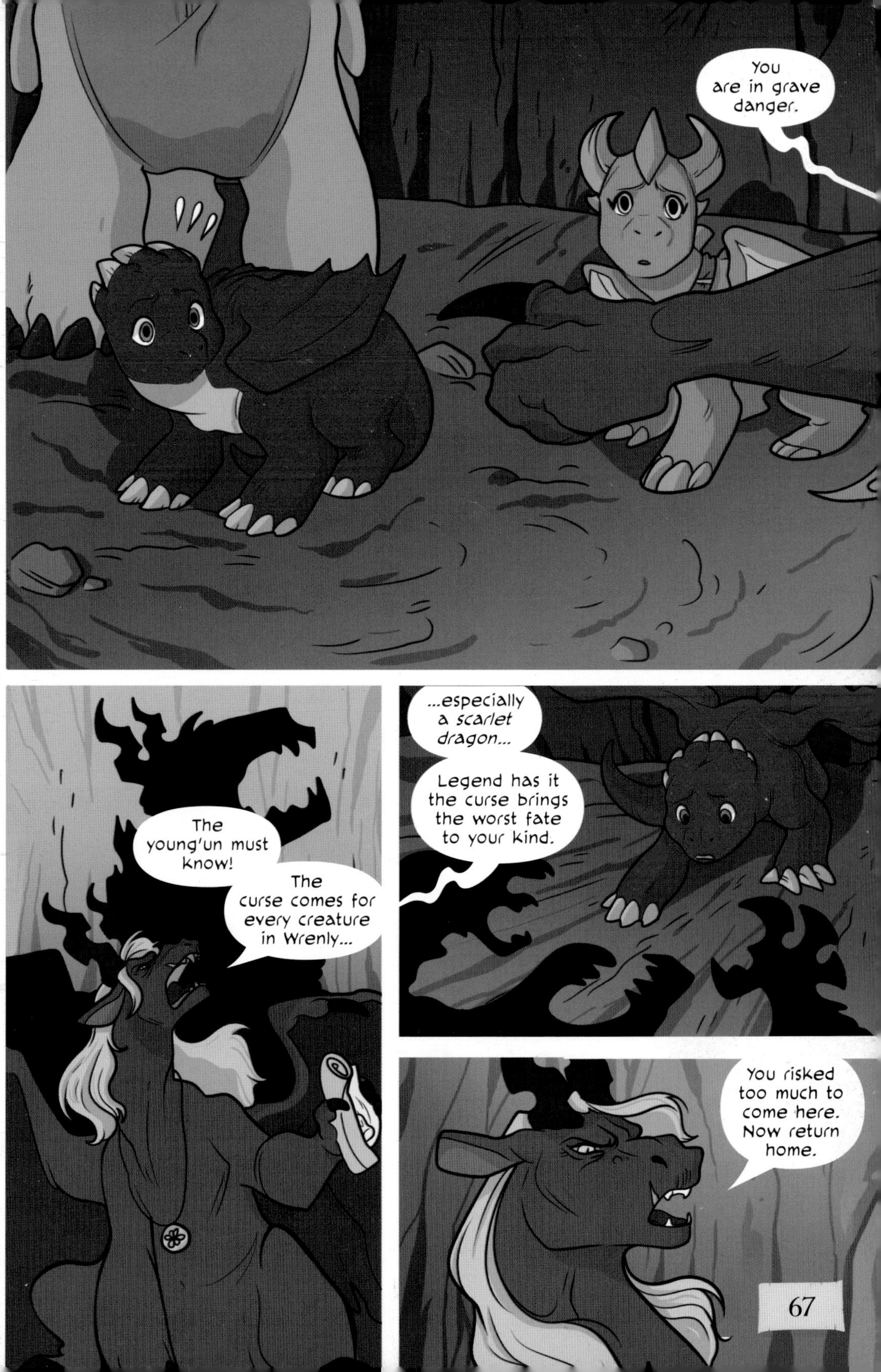
You are in grave danger.
The young'un must know!
The curse comes for every creature in Wrenly...
...especially a *scarlet* dragon...
Legend has it the curse brings the worst fate to your kind.
You risked too much to come here. Now return home.

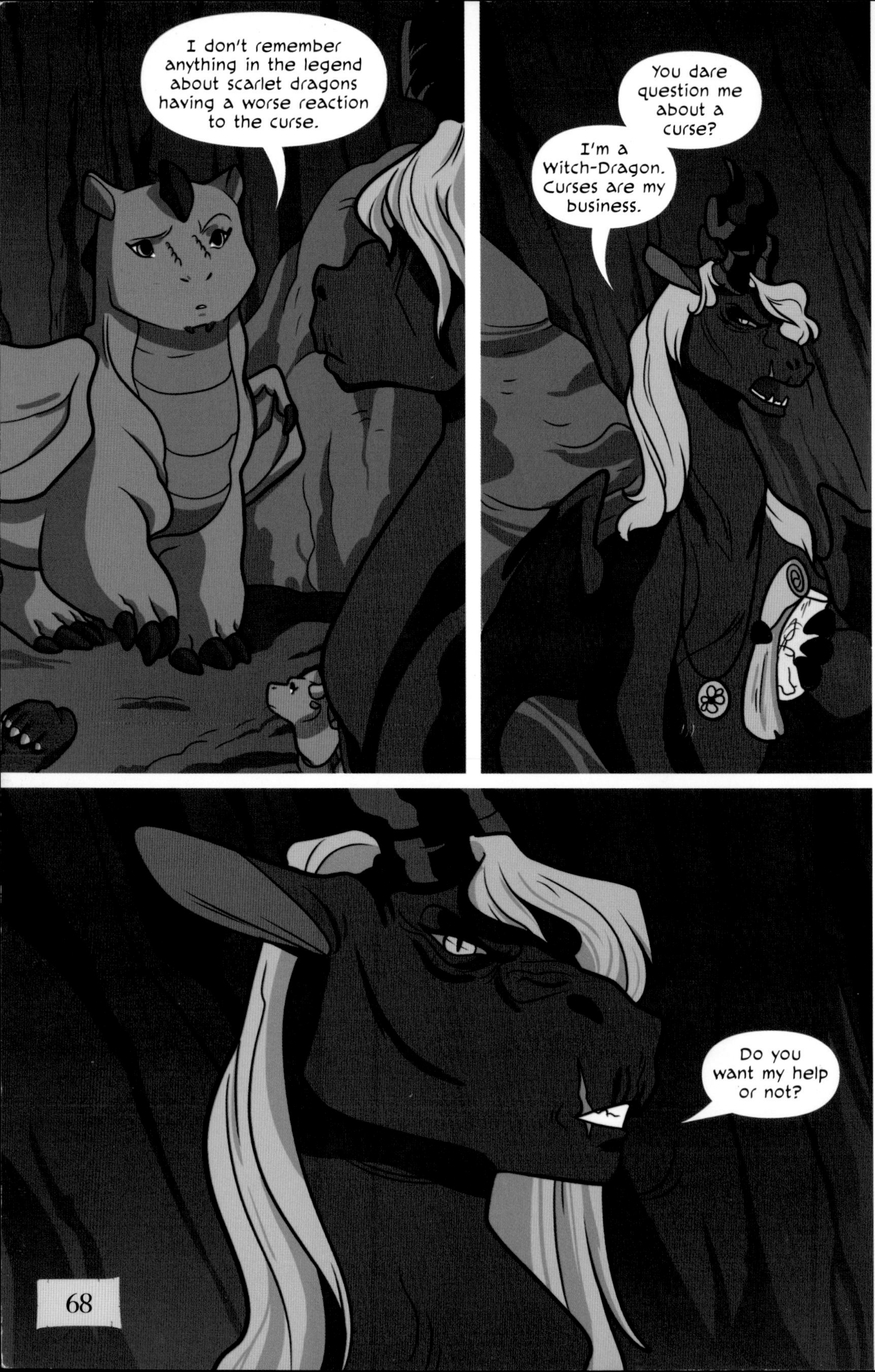
I don't remember anything in the legend about scarlet dragons having a worse reaction to the curse.
You dare question me about a curse?
I'm a Witch-Dragon. Curses are my business.
Do you want my help or not?

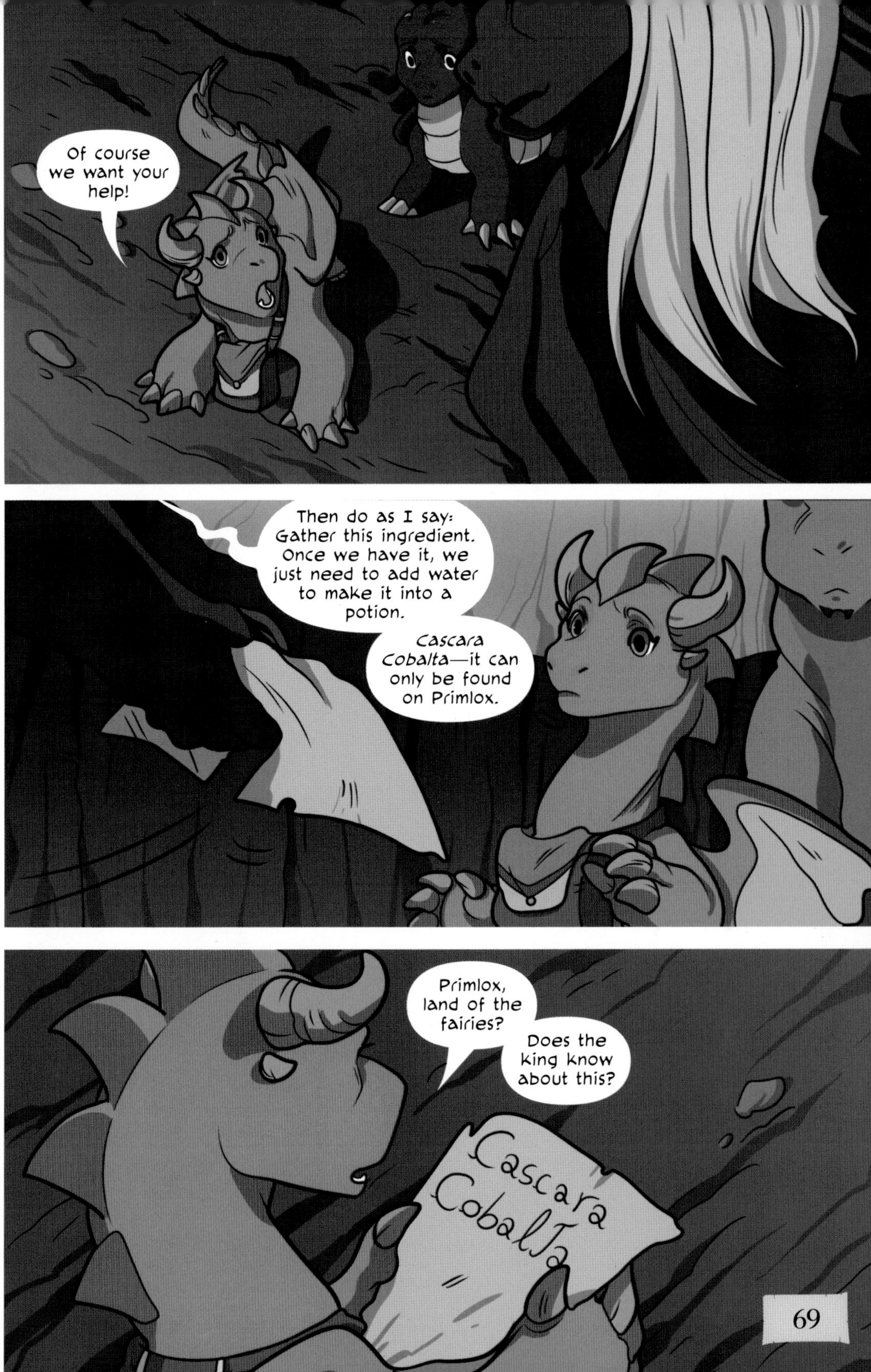

Of course we want your help!
Then do as I say: Gather this ingredient. Once we have it, we just need to add water to make it into a potion.
Cascara Cobalta—it can only be found on Primlox.
Primlox, land of the fairies?
Does the king know about this?
Cascara Cobalta

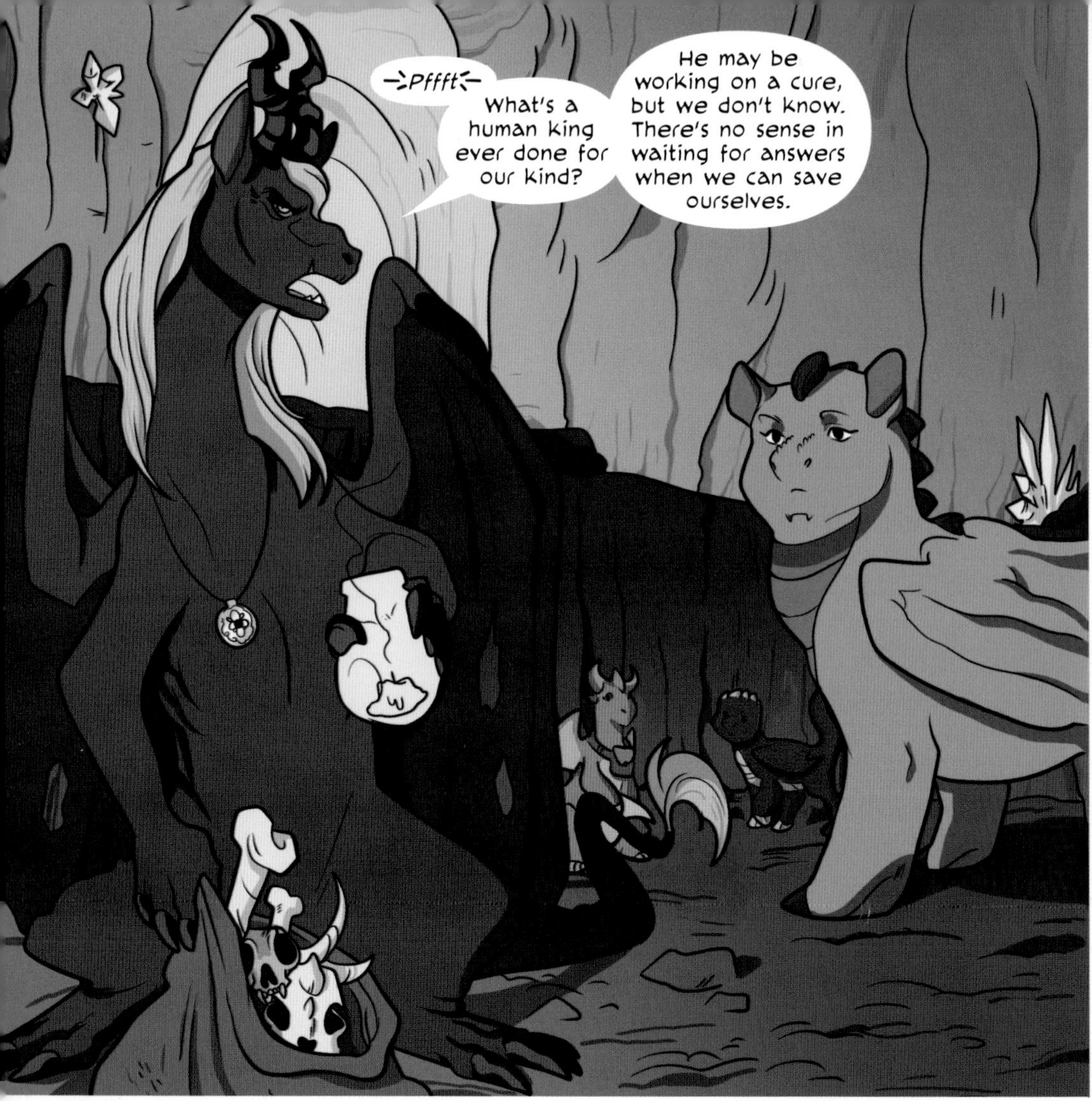

-Pffft-
What's a human king ever done for our kind?
He may be working on a cure, but we don't know. There's no sense in waiting for answers when we can save ourselves.

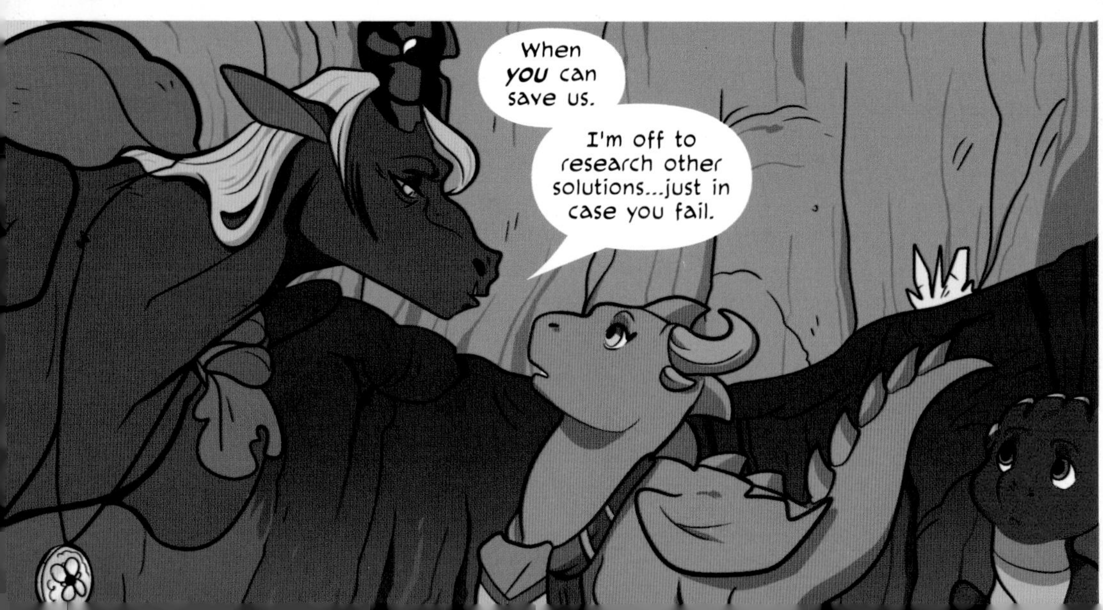

When *YOU* can save us.
I'm off to research other solutions...just in case you fail.

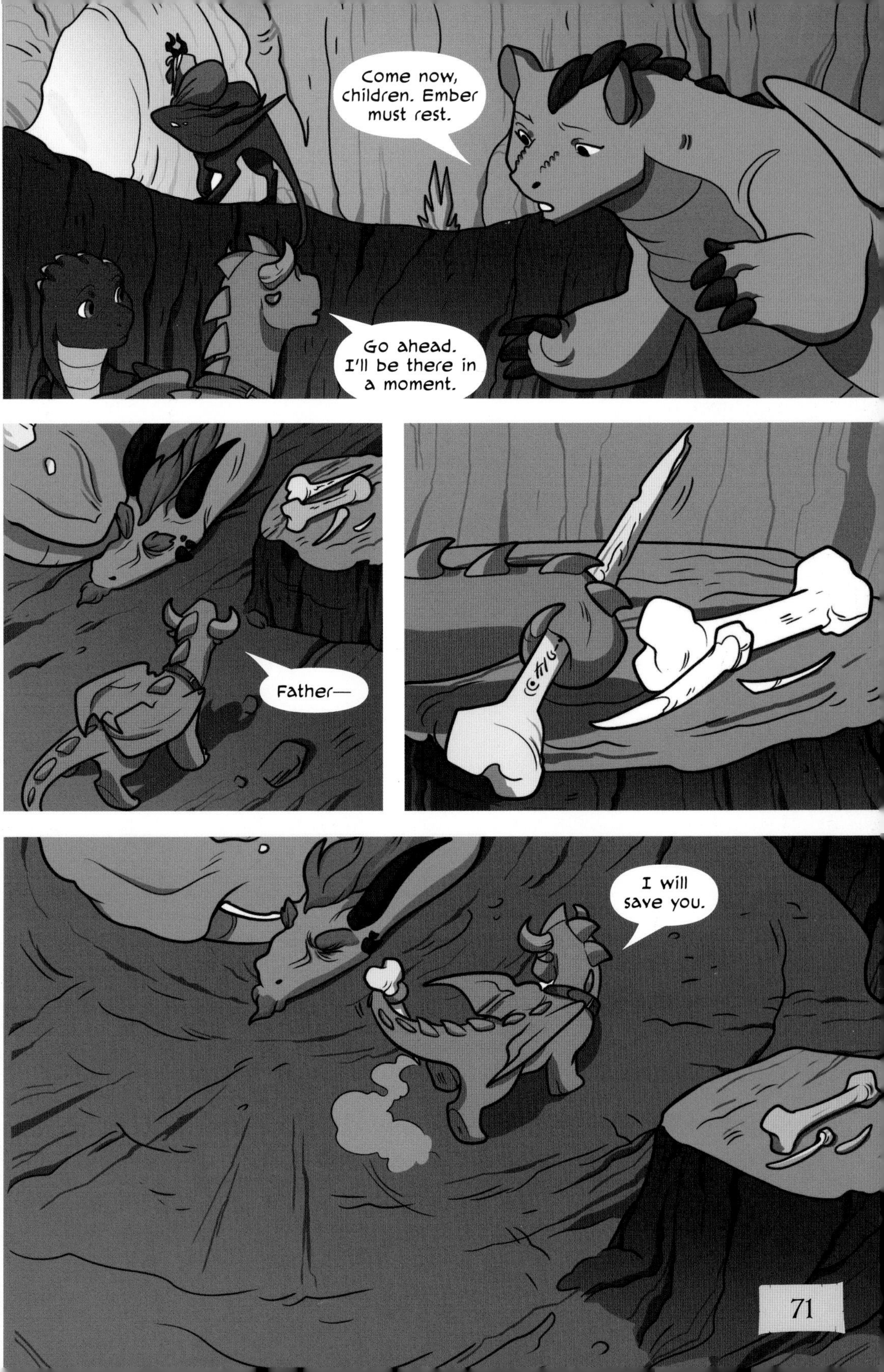
Come now, children. Ember must rest.
Go ahead. I'll be there in a moment.
Father—
I will save you.

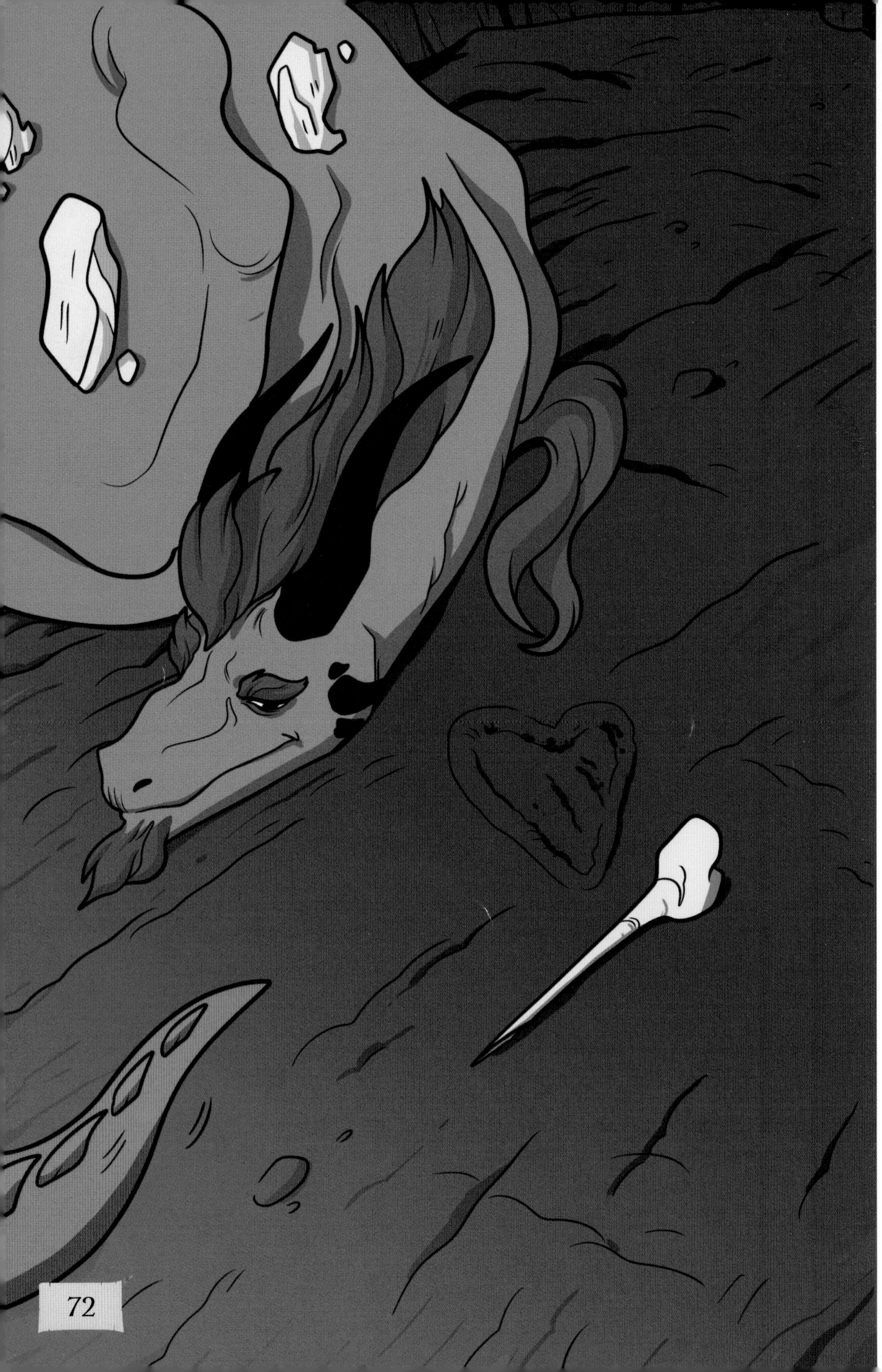

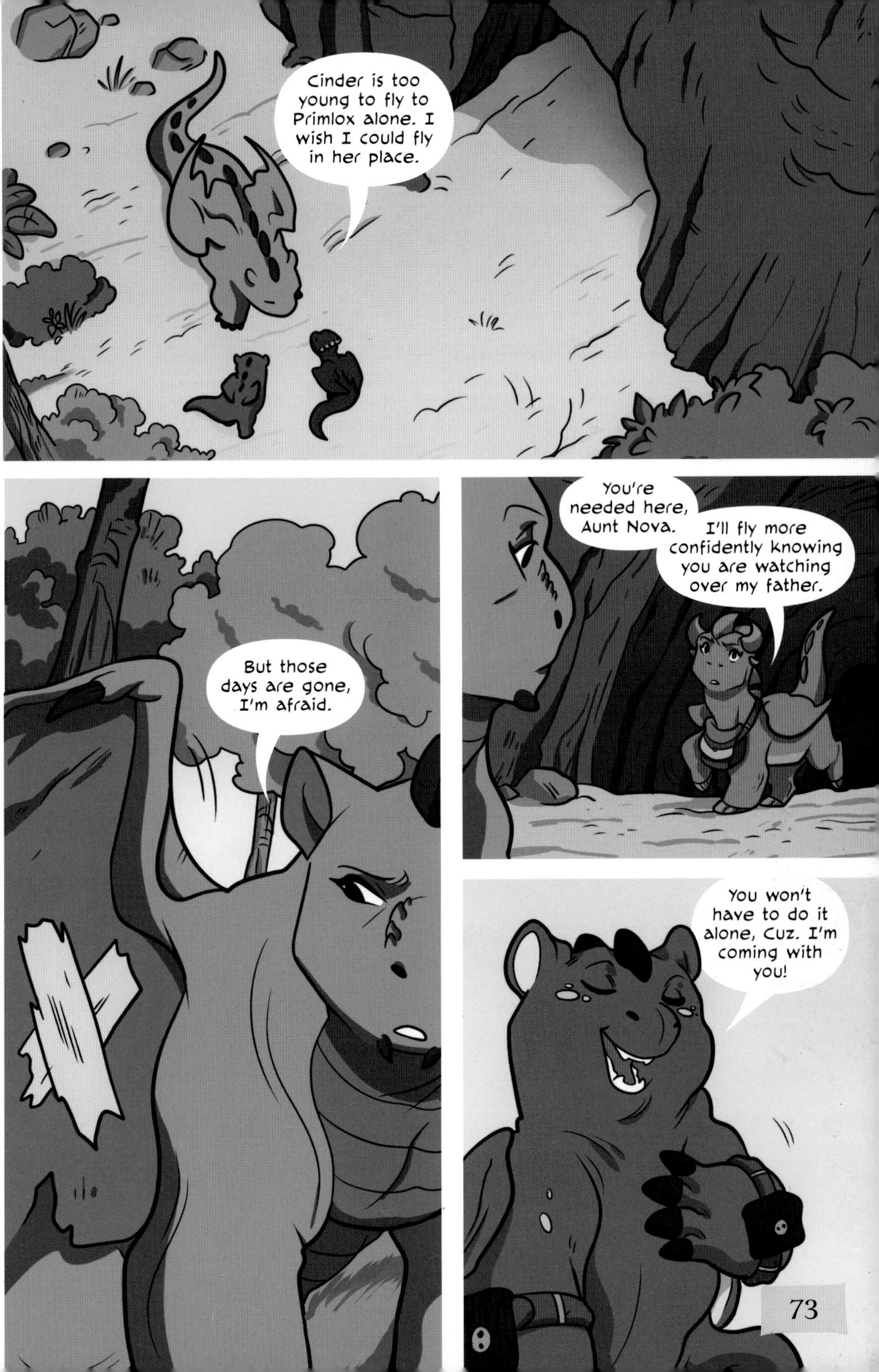
Cinder is too young to fly to Primlox alone. I wish I could fly in her place.
But those days are gone, I'm afraid.
You're needed here, Aunt Nova.
I'll fly more confidently knowing you are watching over my father.
You won't have to do it alone, Cuz. I'm coming with you!

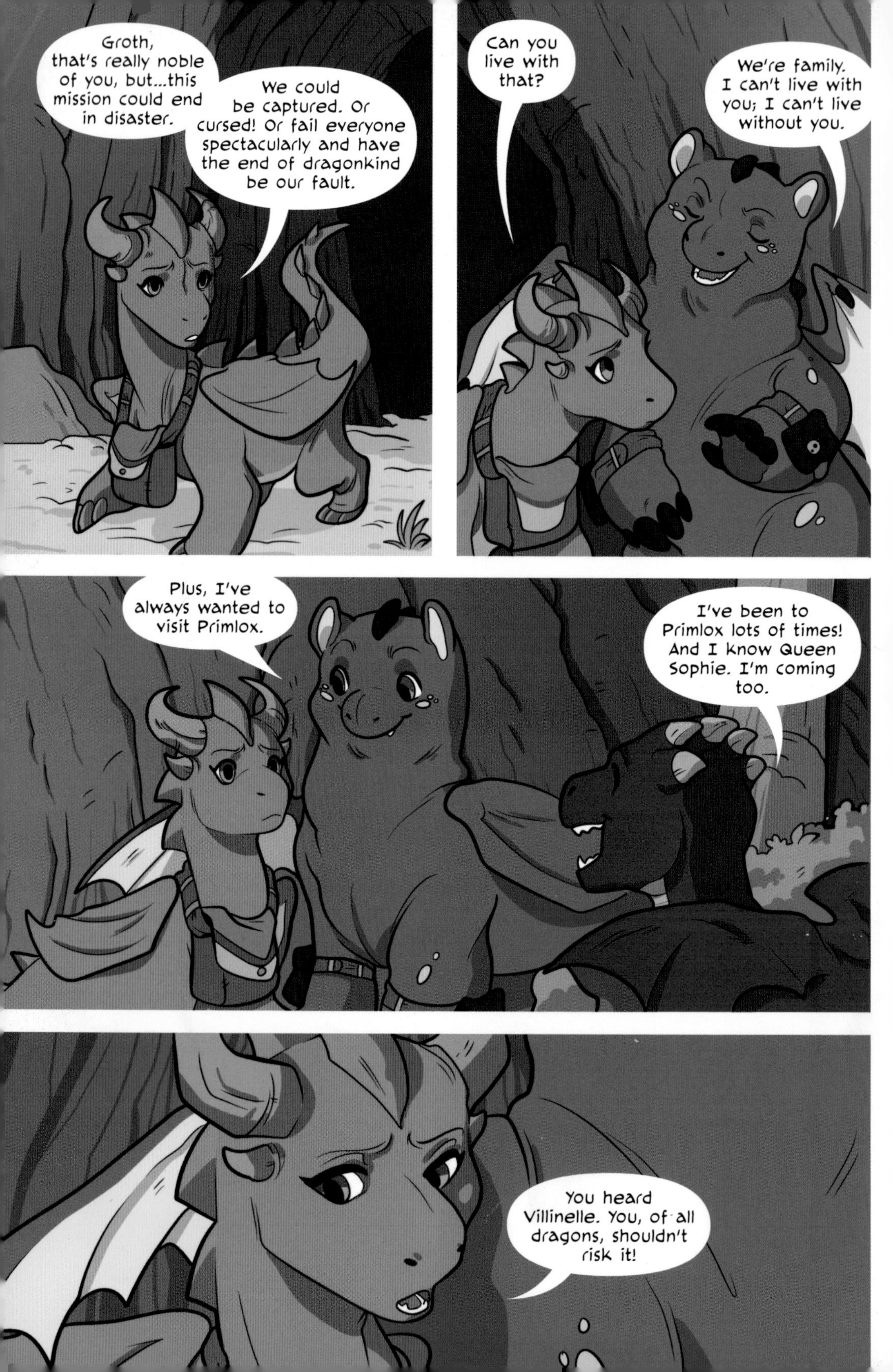
Groth, that's really noble of you, but...this mission could end in disaster.
We could be captured. Or cursed! Or fail everyone spectacularly and have the end of dragonkind be our fault.
Can you live with that?
We're family. I can't live with you; I can't live without you.
Plus, I've always wanted to visit Primlox.
I've been to Primlox lots of times! And I know Queen Sophie. I'm coming too.
You heard Villinelle. You, of all dragons, shouldn't risk it!

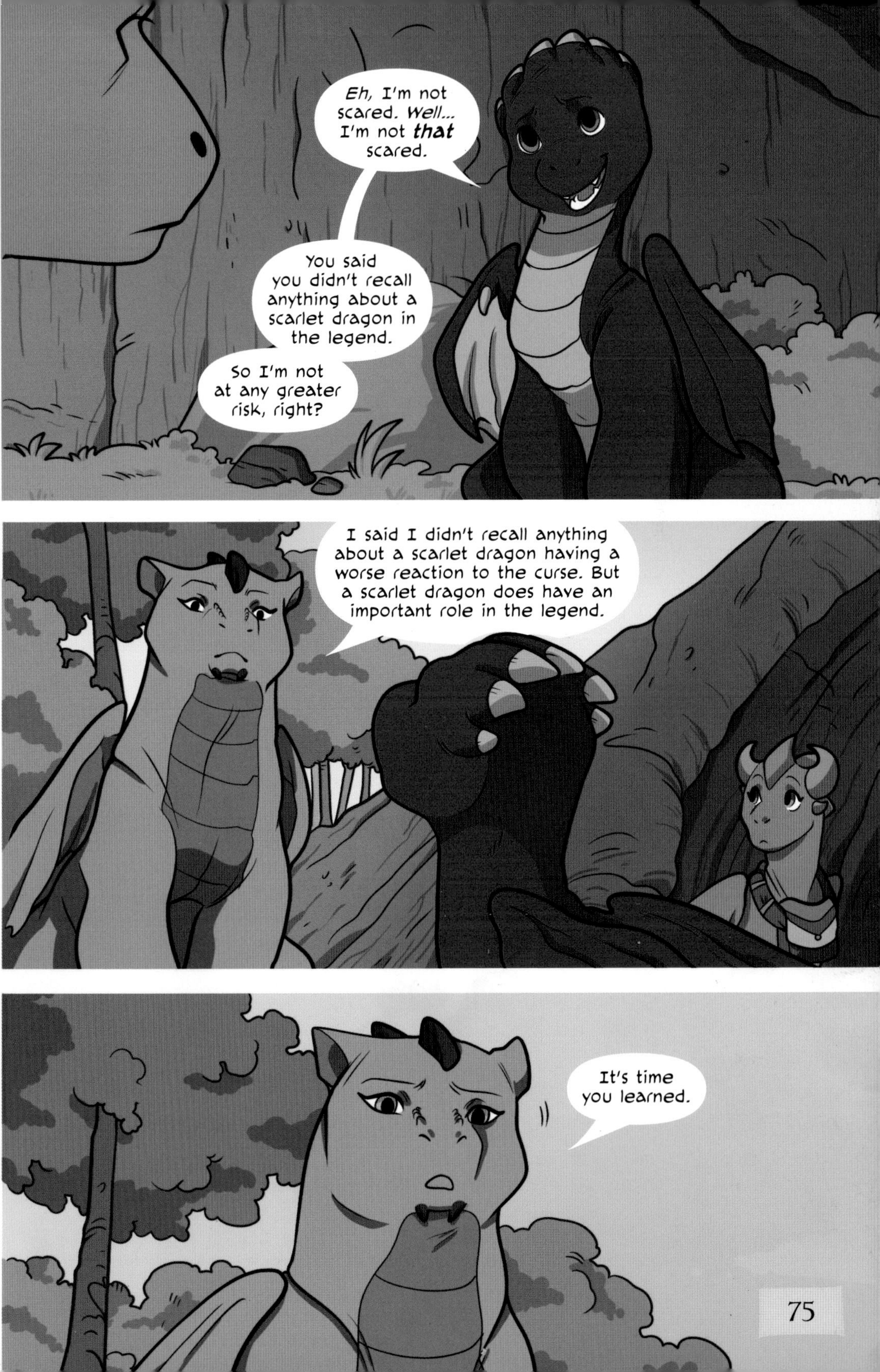

Eh, I'm not scared. Well... I'm not that scared.
You said you didn't recall anything about a scarlet dragon in the legend.
So I'm not at any greater risk, right?
I said I didn't recall anything about a scarlet dragon having a worse reaction to the curse. But a scarlet dragon does have an important role in the legend.
It's time you learned.

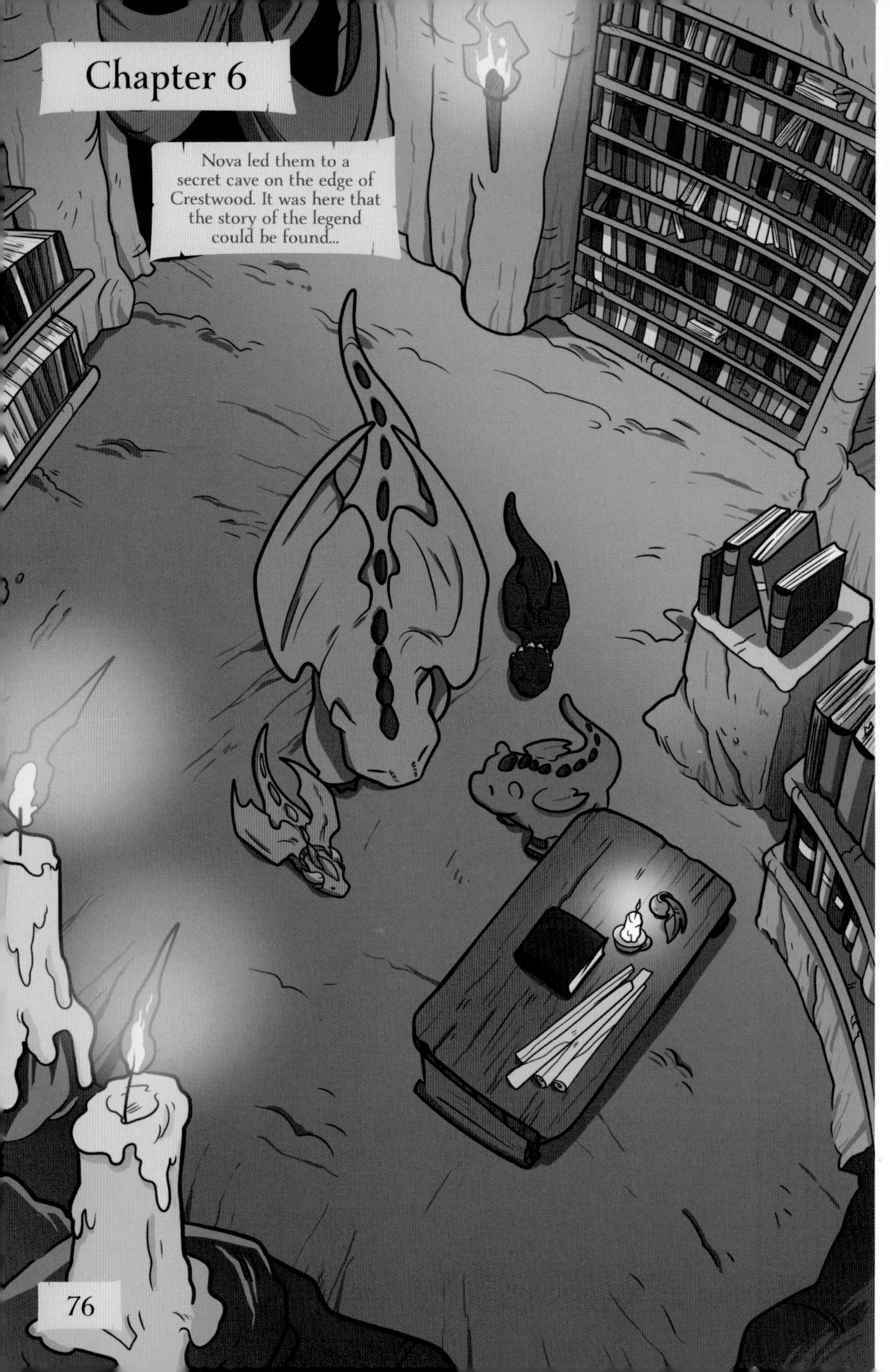
Chapter 6
Nova led them to a secret cave on the edge of Crestwood. It was here that the story of the legend could be found...

Story time, children...

Thousands of years ago, just as Wrenly was becoming a kingdom...

...Crestwood was led by a young king, a *dragon king...*

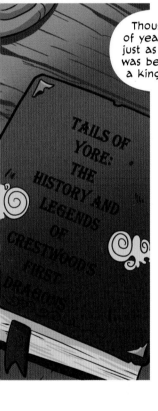

TAILS OF YORE: THE HISTORY AND LEGENDS OF CRESTWOOD'S FIRST DRAGONS

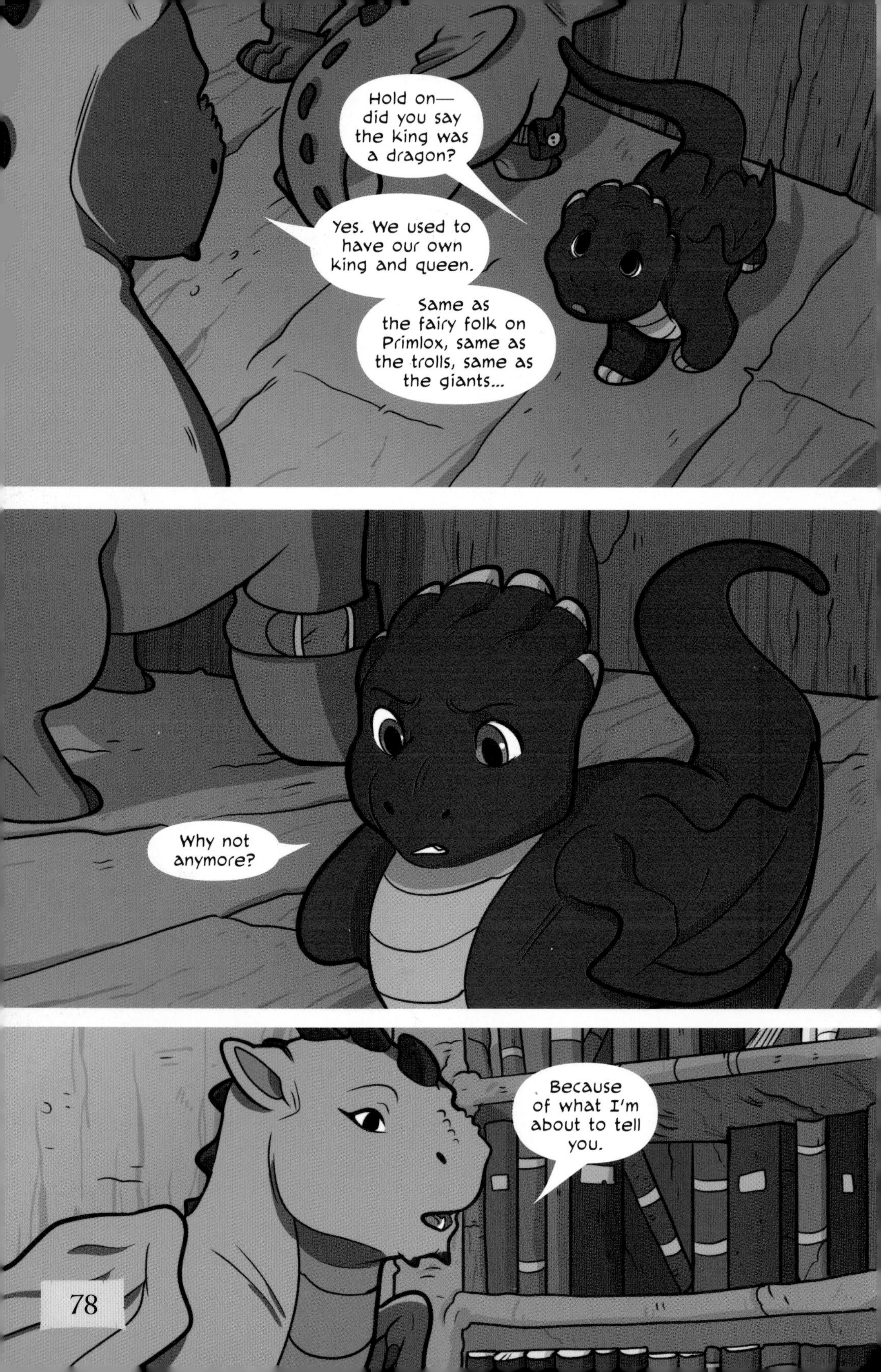

Hold on— did you say the king was a dragon?
Yes. We used to have our own king and queen.
Same as the fairy folk on Primlox, same as the trolls, same as the giants...
Why not anymore?
Because of what I'm about to tell you.

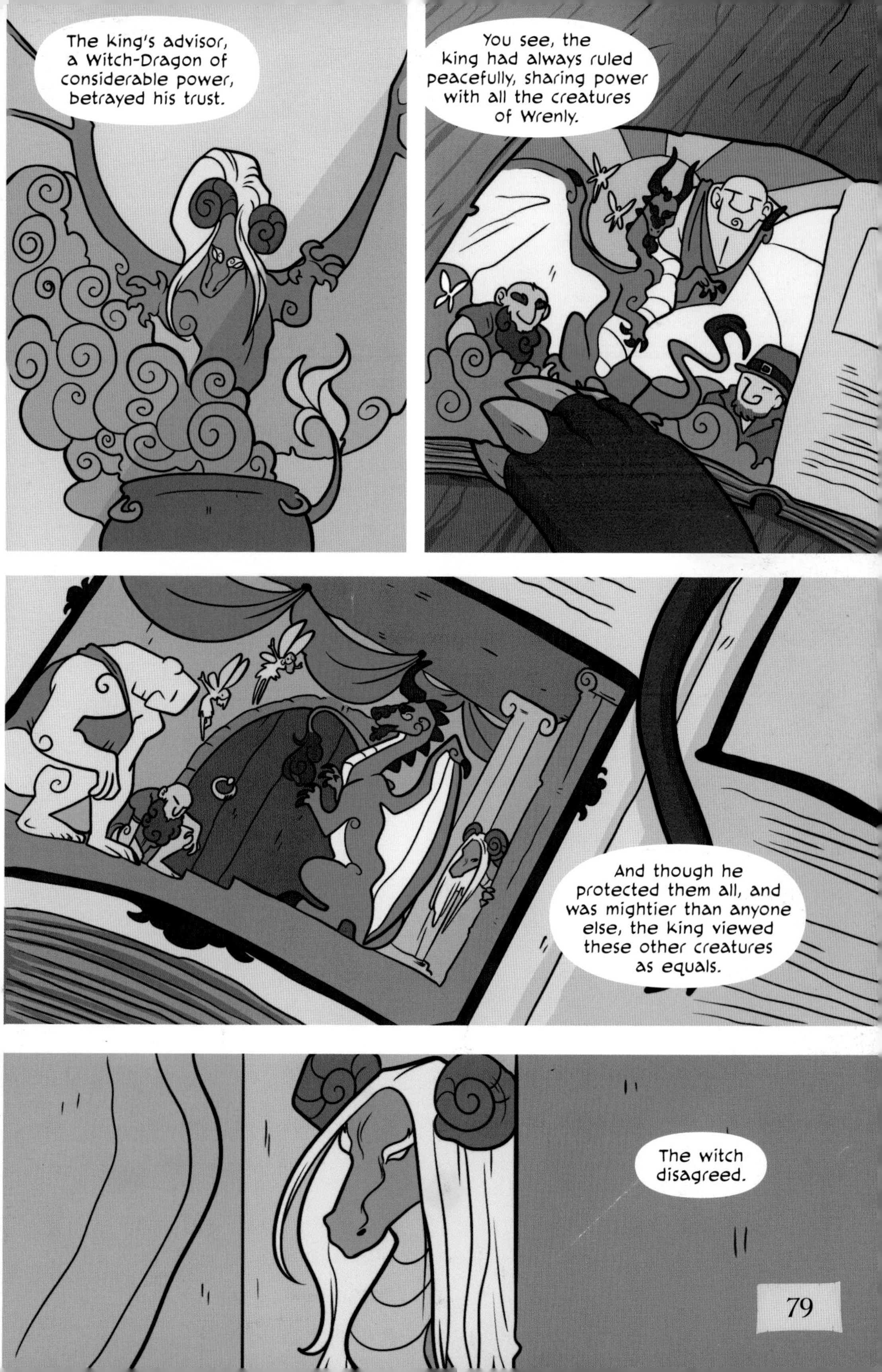
The king's advisor, a Witch-Dragon of considerable power, betrayed his trust.
You see, the king had always ruled peacefully, sharing power with all the creatures of Wrenly.
And though he protected them all, and was mightier than anyone else, the king viewed these other creatures as equals.
The witch disagreed.

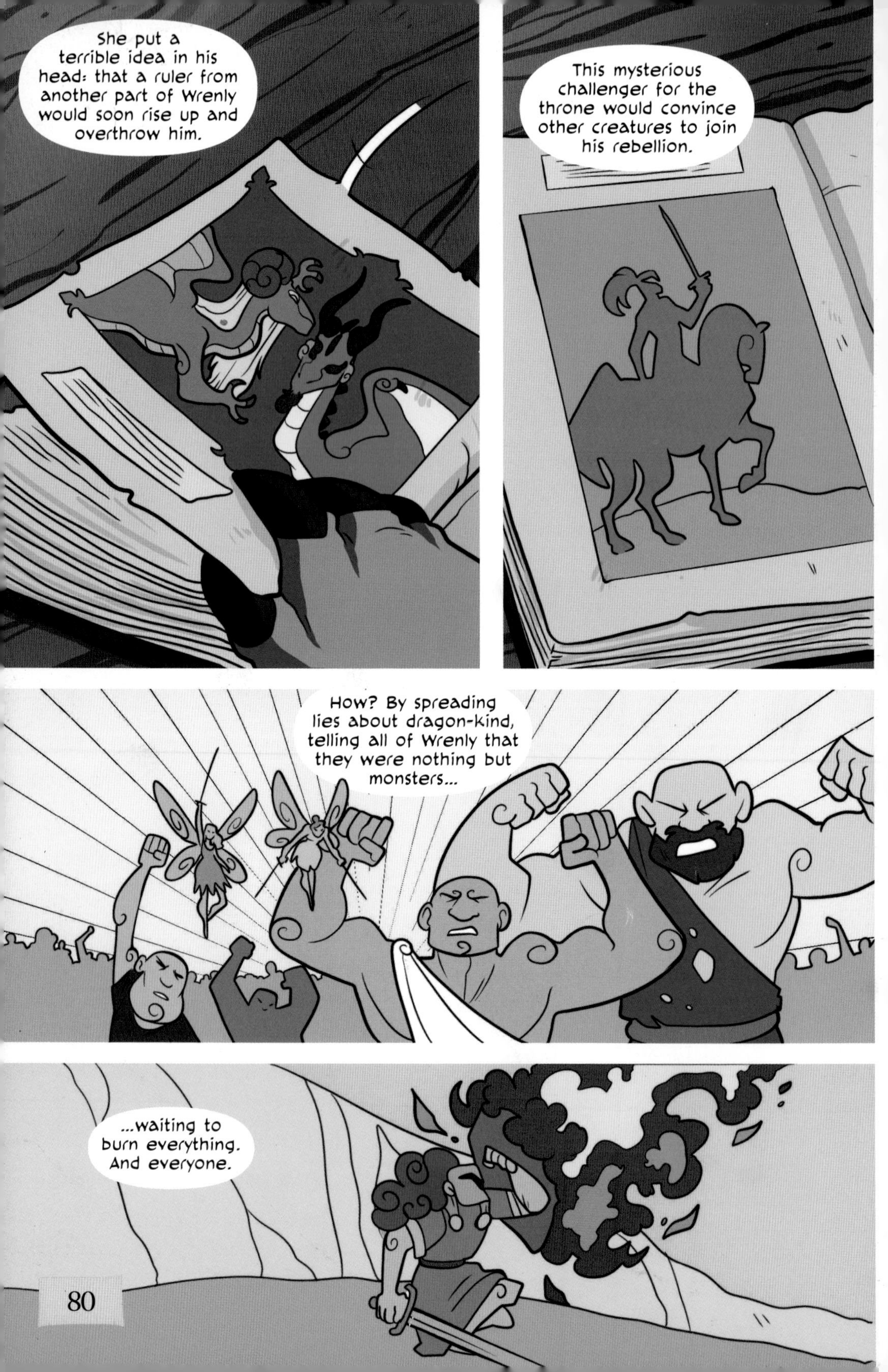
She put a terrible idea in his head: that a ruler from another part of Wrenly would soon rise up and overthrow him.
This mysterious challenger for the throne would convince other creatures to join his rebellion.
How? By spreading lies about dragon-kind, telling all of Wrenly that they were nothing but monsters...
...waiting to burn everything. And everyone.

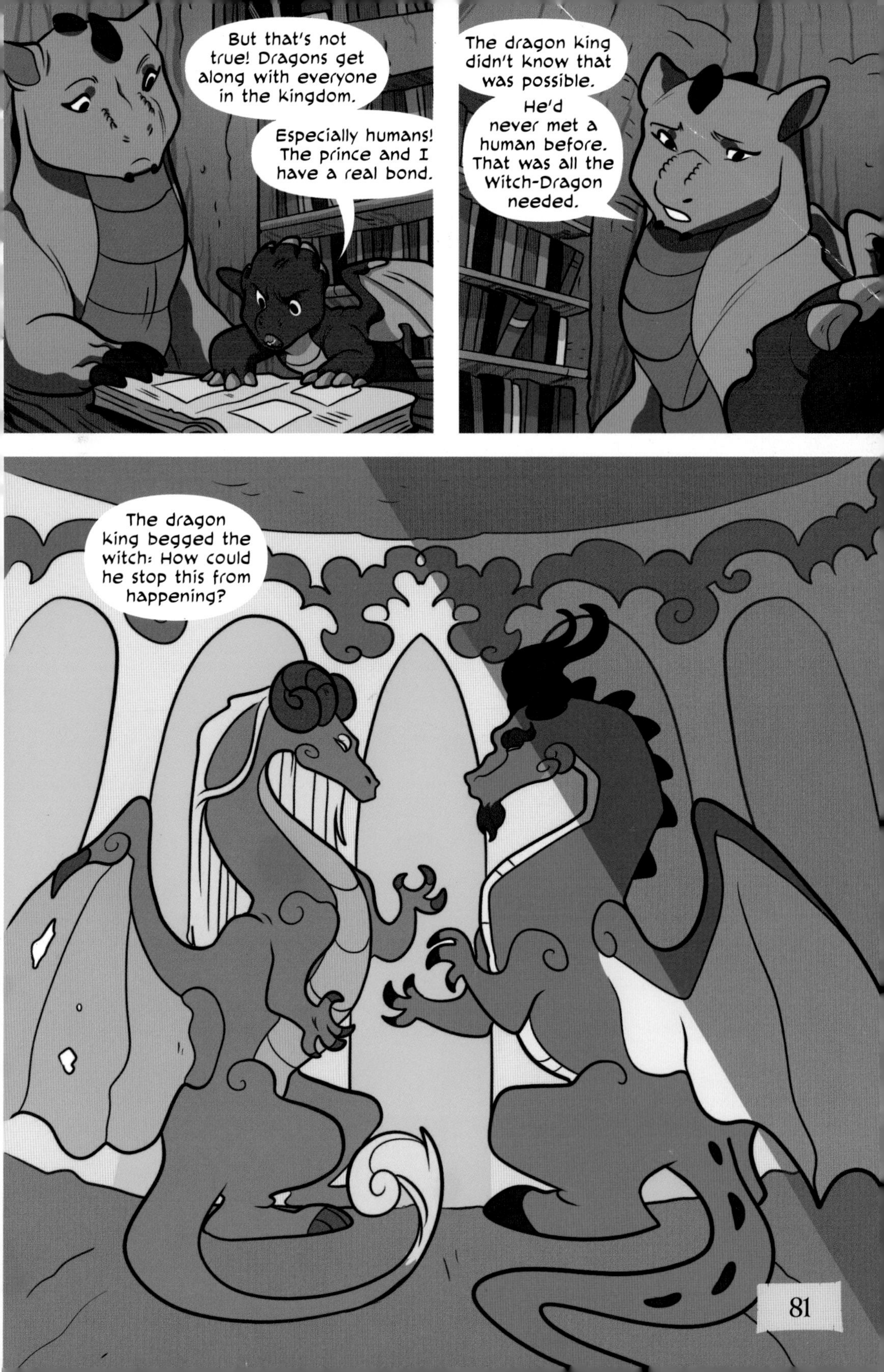
But that's not true! Dragons get along with everyone in the kingdom.
Especially humans! The prince and I have a real bond.
The dragon king didn't know that was possible.
He'd never met a human before. That was all the Witch-Dragon needed.
The dragon king begged the witch: How could he stop this from happening?

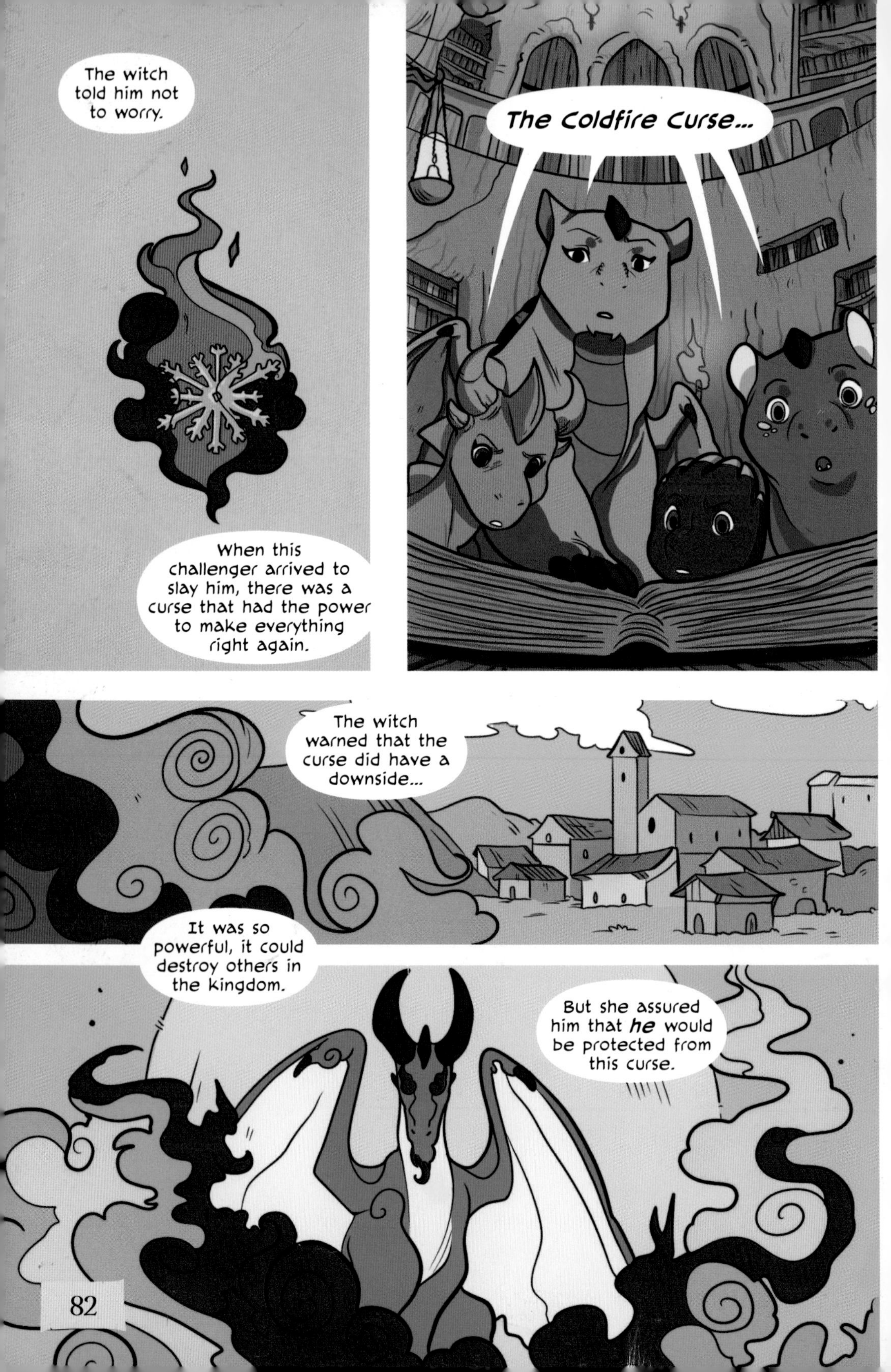
The witch told him not to worry.
The Coldfire Curse...
When this challenger arrived to slay him, there was a curse that had the power to make everything right again.
The witch warned that the curse did have a downside...
It was so powerful, it could destroy others in the kingdom.
But she assured him that *he* would be protected from this curse.

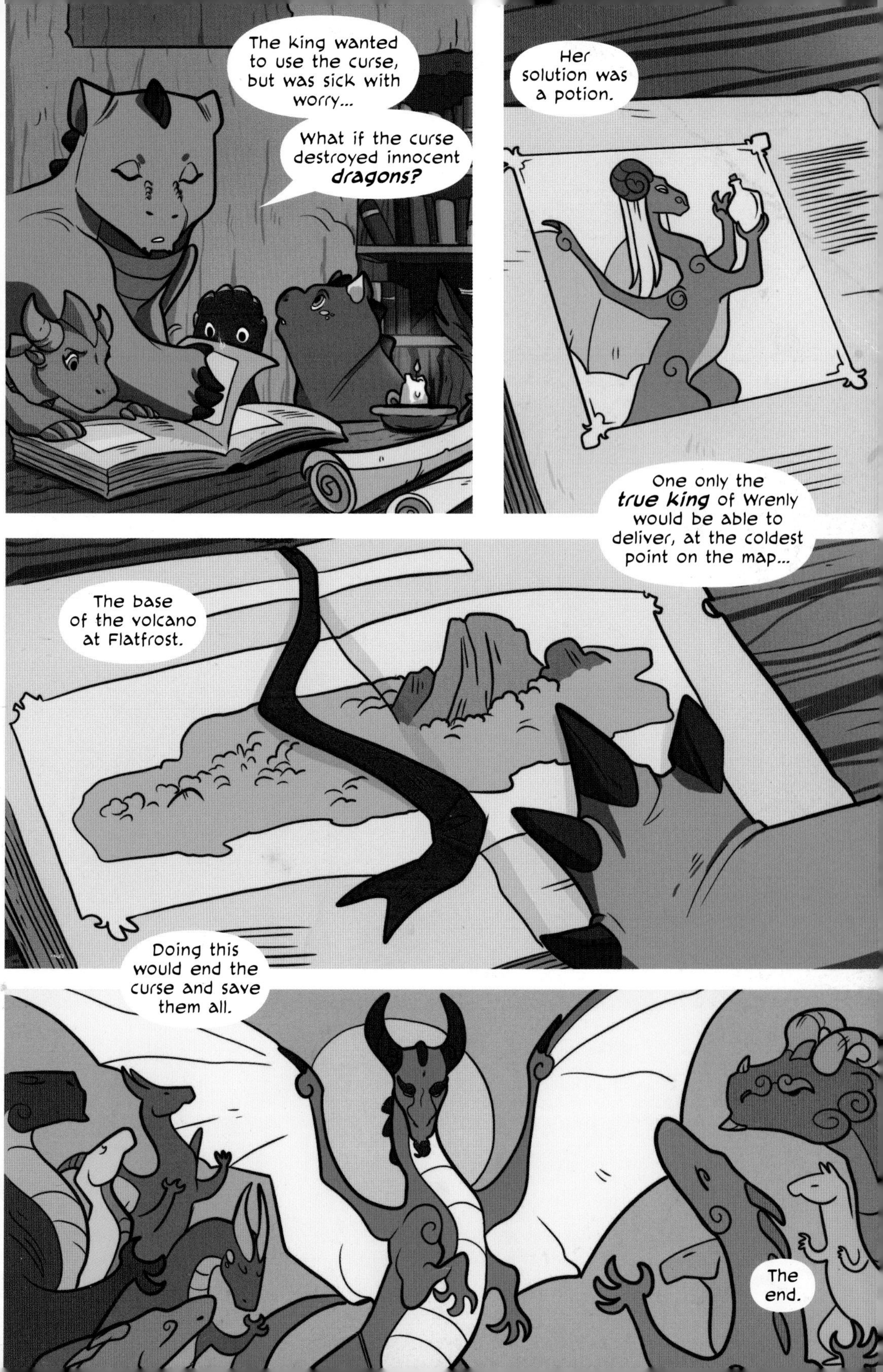
The king wanted to use the curse, but was sick with worry...
What if the curse destroyed innocent *dragons?*
Her solution was a potion.
One only the *true king* of Wrenly would be able to deliver, at the coldest point on the map...
The base of the volcano at Flatfrost.
Doing this would end the curse and save them all.
The end.

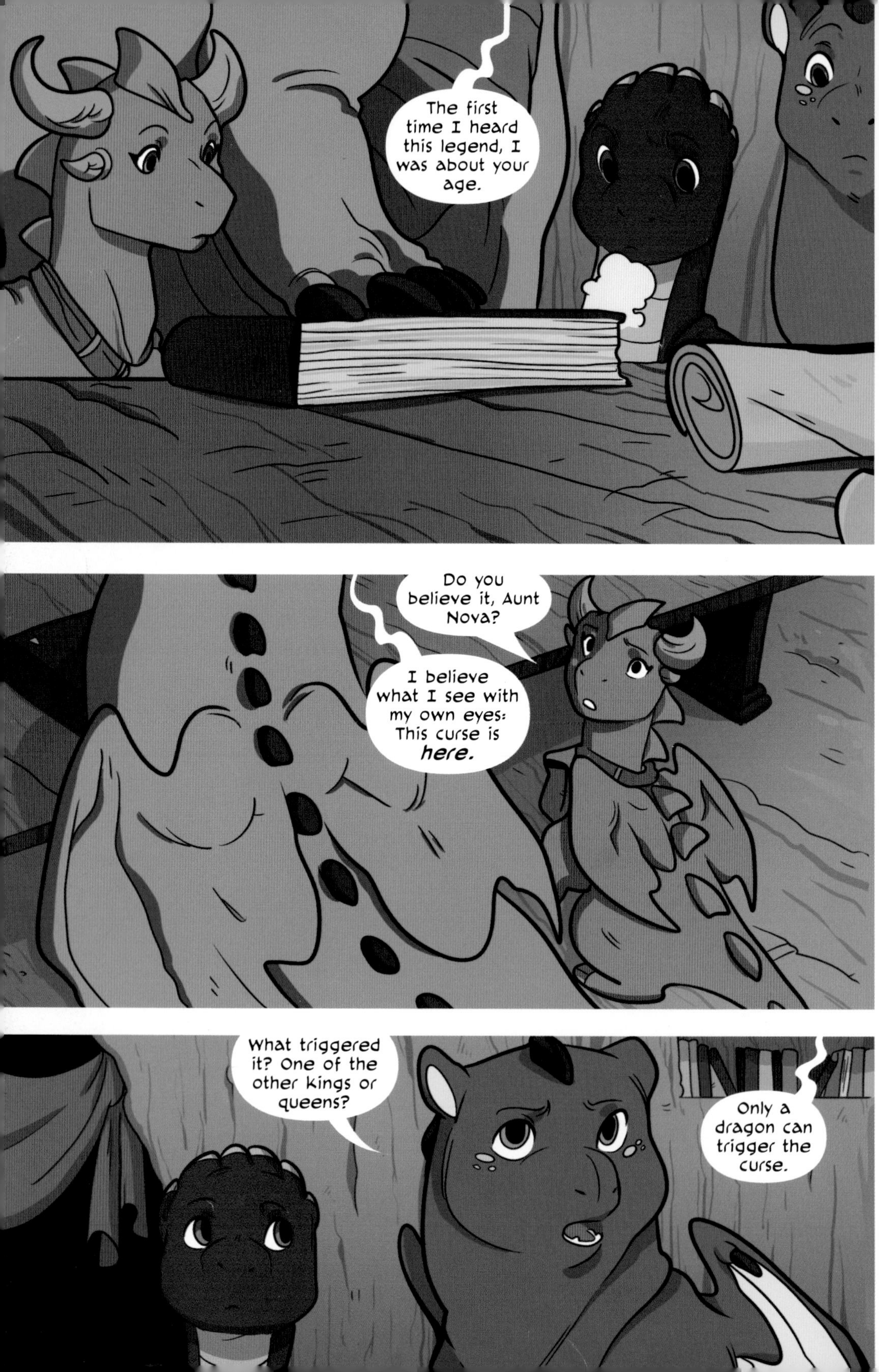
The first time I heard this legend, I was about your age.
Do you believe it, Aunt Nova?
I believe what I see with my own eyes: This curse is *here.*
What triggered it? One of the other kings or queens?
Only a dragon can trigger the curse.

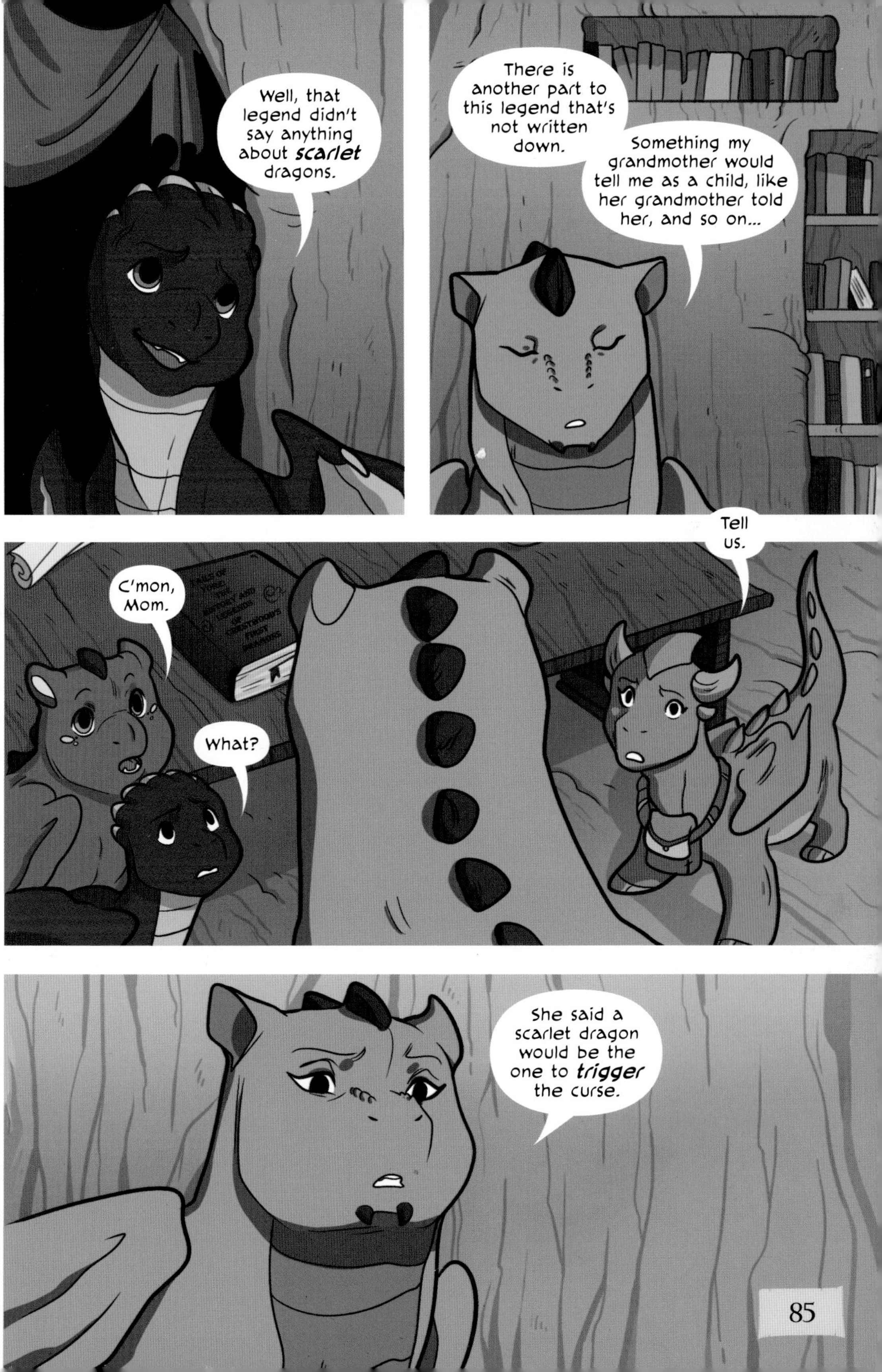
Well, that legend didn't say anything about ***scarlet*** dragons.
There is another part to this legend that's not written down.
Something my grandmother would tell me as a child, like her grandmother told her, and so on...
C'mon, Mom.
What?
Tell us.
She said a scarlet dragon would be the one to ***trigger*** the curse.

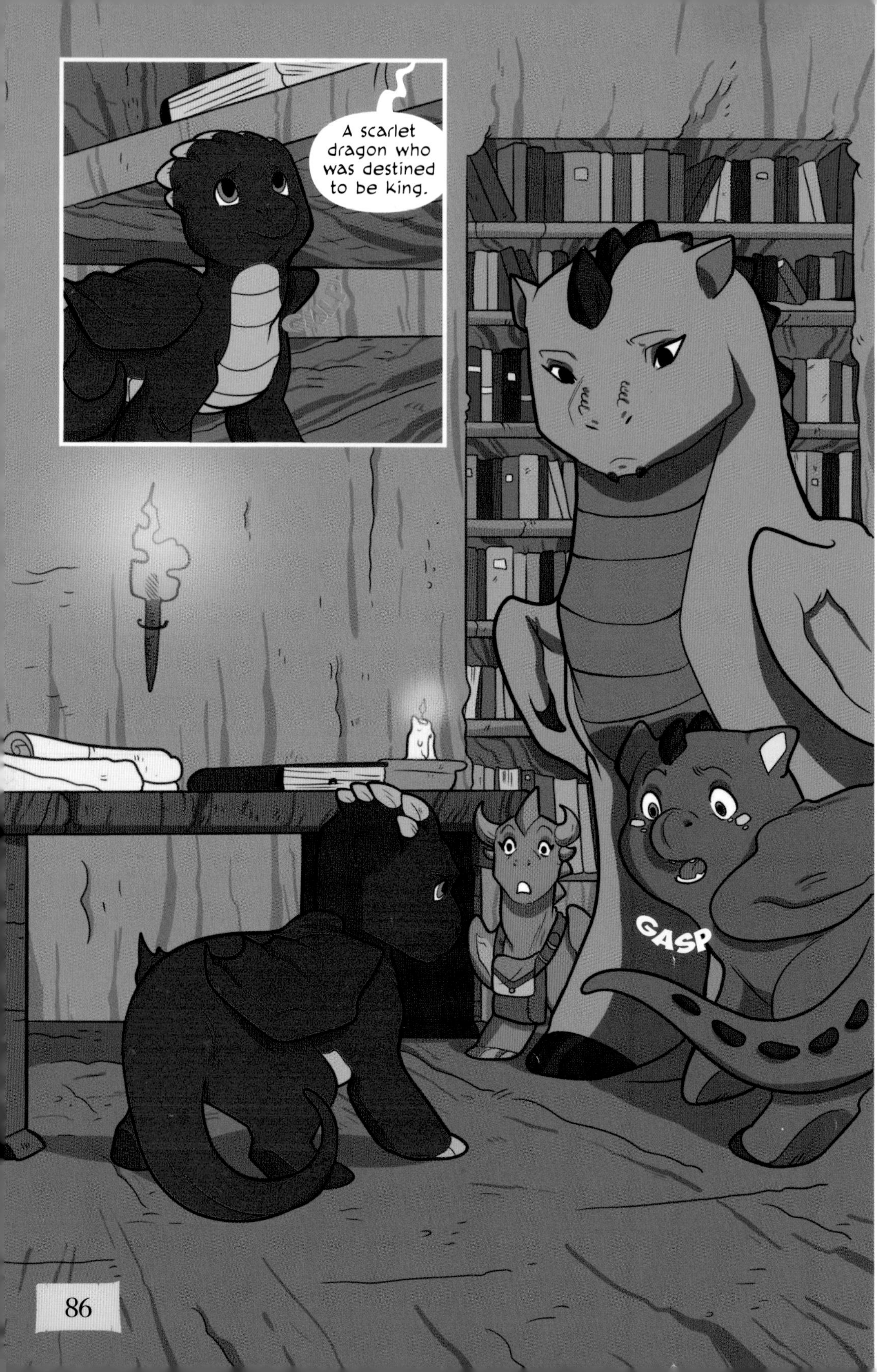
A scarlet dragon who was destined to be king.
GULP
GASP

Chapter 7

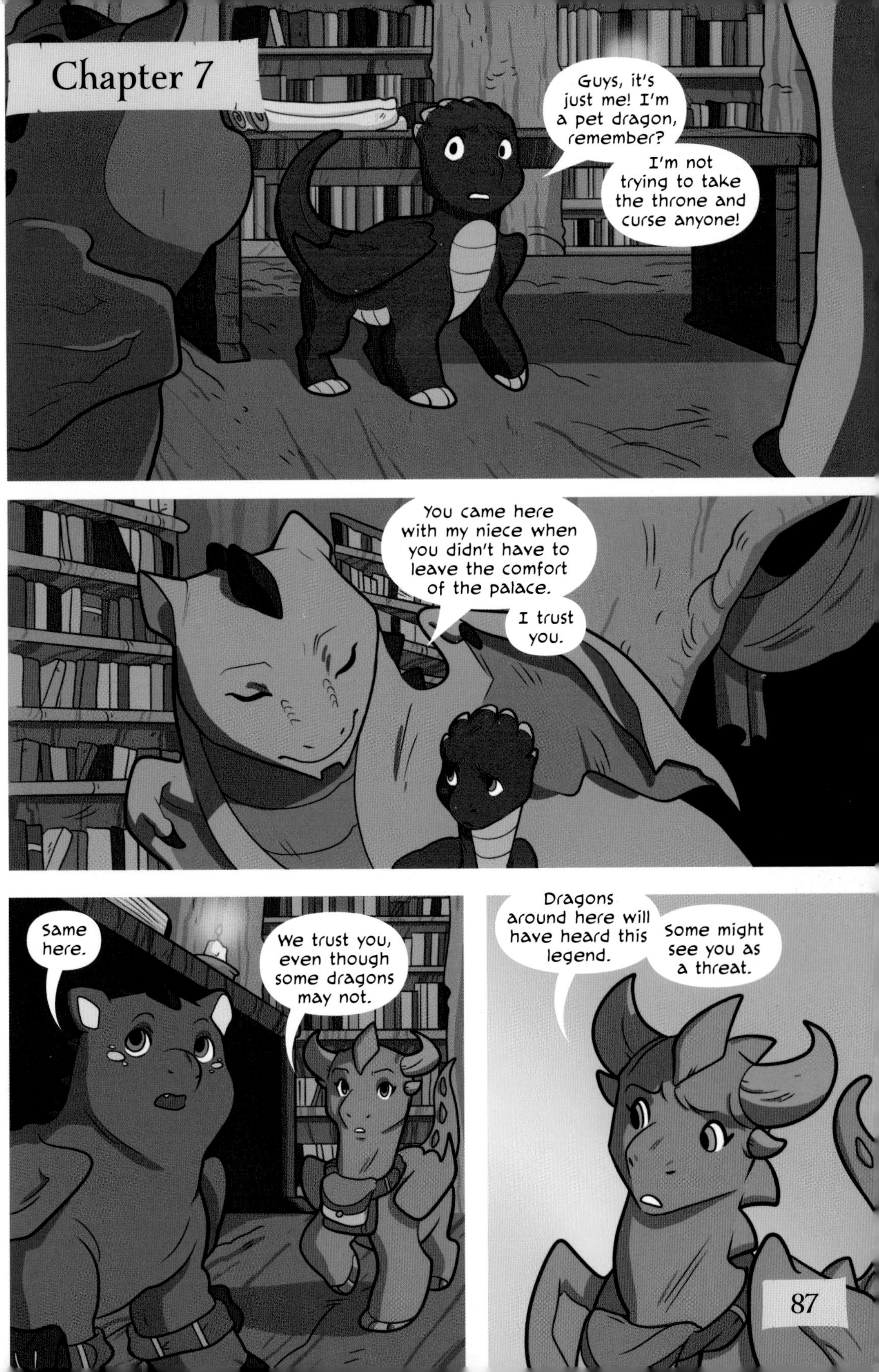

Guys, it's just me! I'm a pet dragon, remember?
I'm not trying to take the throne and curse anyone!
You came here with my niece when you didn't have to leave the comfort of the palace.
I trust you.
Same here.
We trust you, even though some dragons may not.
Dragons around here will have heard this legend.
Some might see you as a threat.

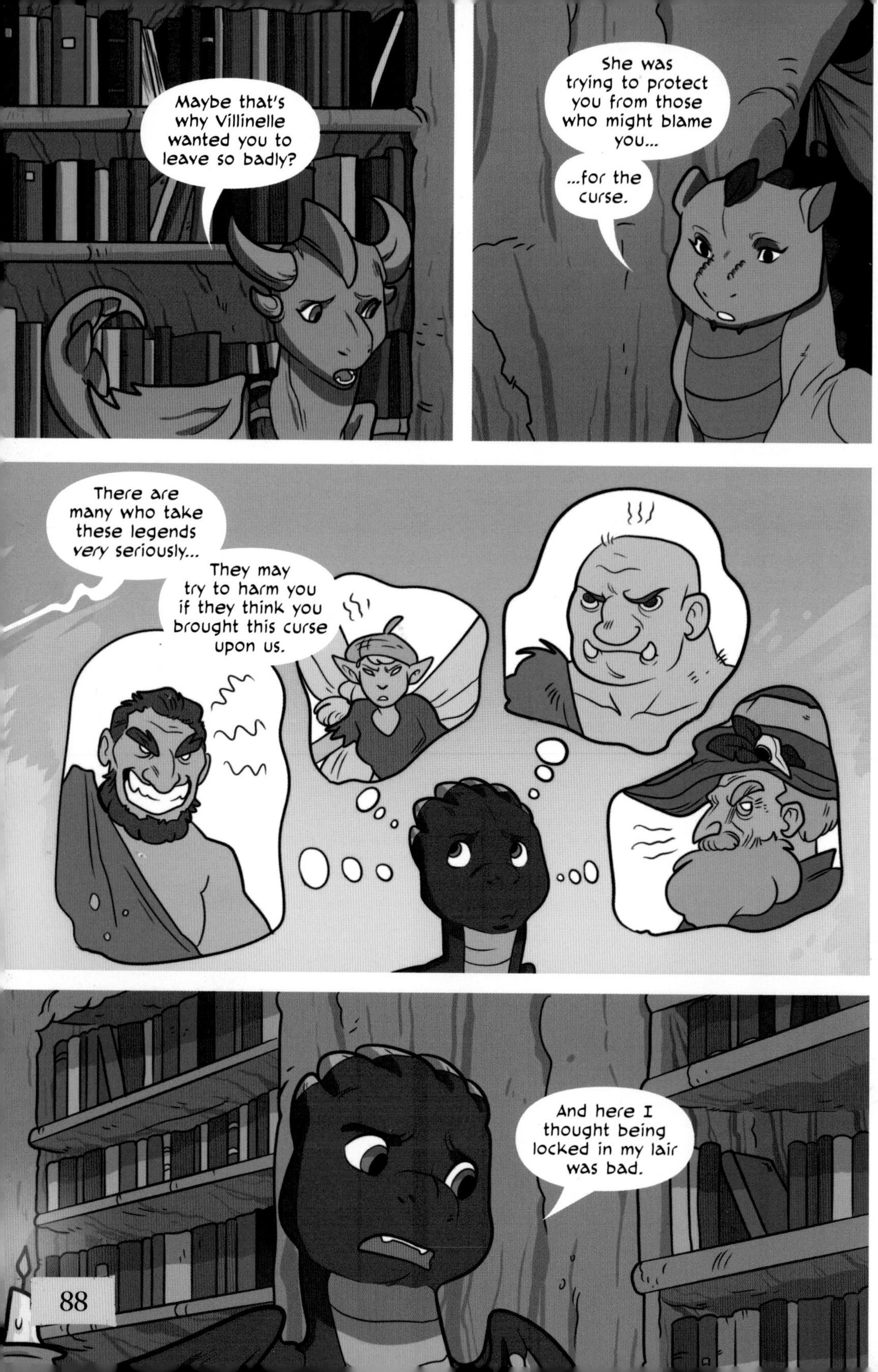
Maybe that's why Villinelle wanted you to leave so badly?
She was trying to protect you from those who might blame you...
...for the curse.
There are many who take these legends *very* seriously...
They may try to harm you if they think you brought this curse upon us.
And here I thought being locked in my lair was bad.

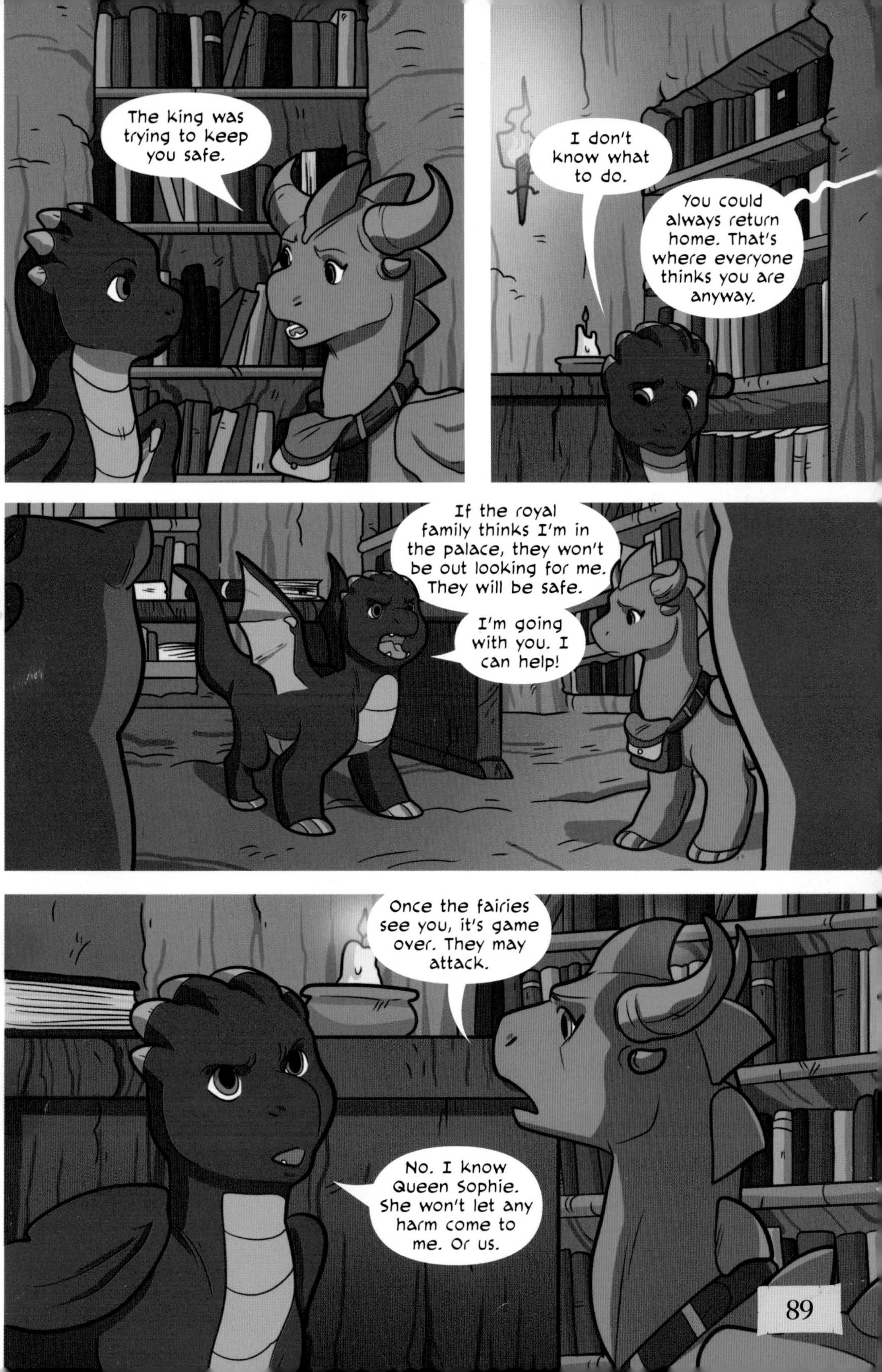
The king was trying to keep you safe.
I don't know what to do.
You could always return home. That's where everyone thinks you are anyway.
If the royal family thinks I'm in the palace, they won't be out looking for me. They will be safe.
I'm going with you. I can help!
Once the fairies see you, it's game over. They may attack.
No. I know Queen Sophie. She won't let any harm come to me. Or us.

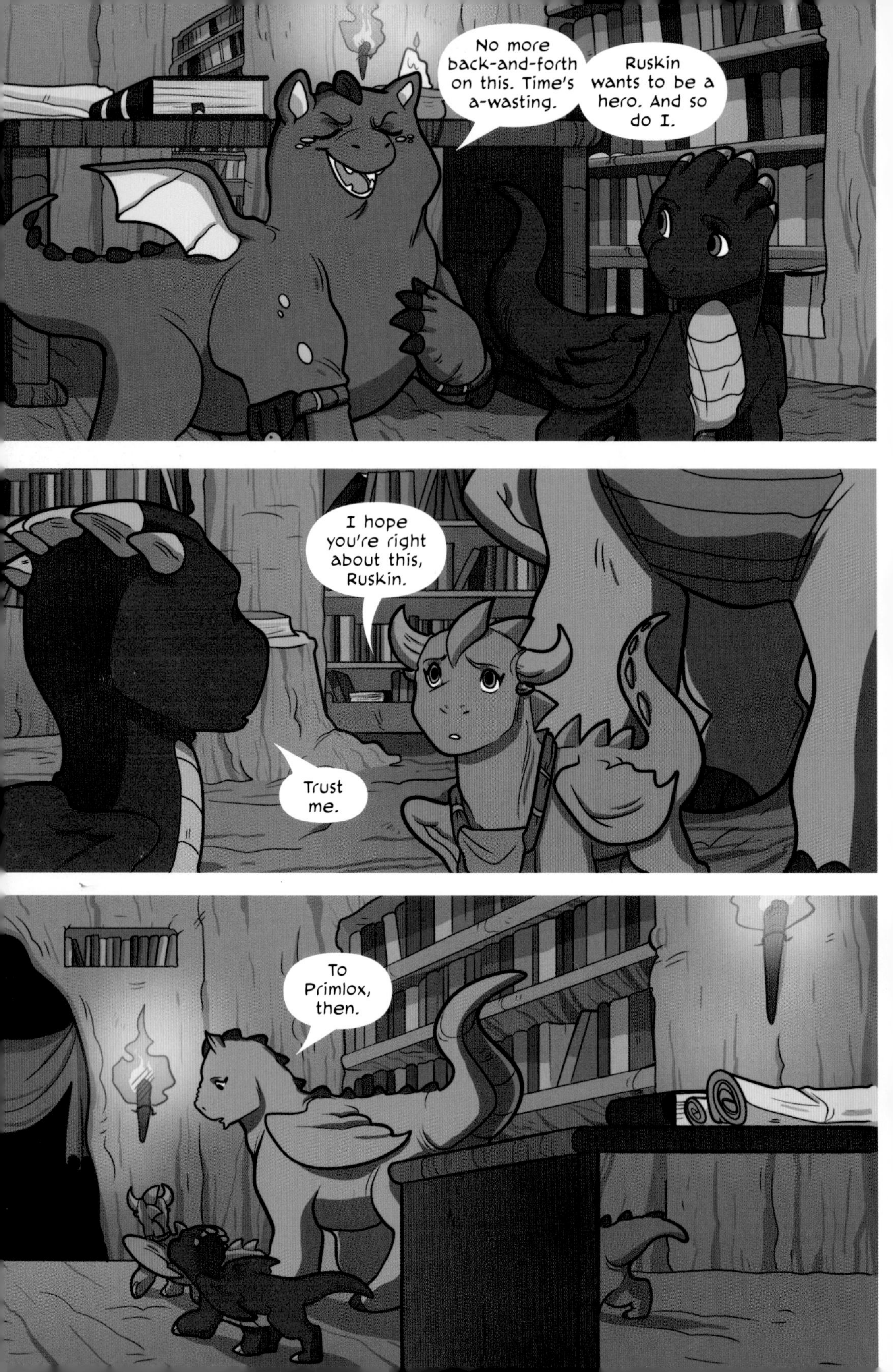

No more back-and-forth on this. Time's a-wasting.
Ruskin wants to be a hero. And so do I.
I hope you're right about this, Ruskin.
Trust me.
To Primlox, then.

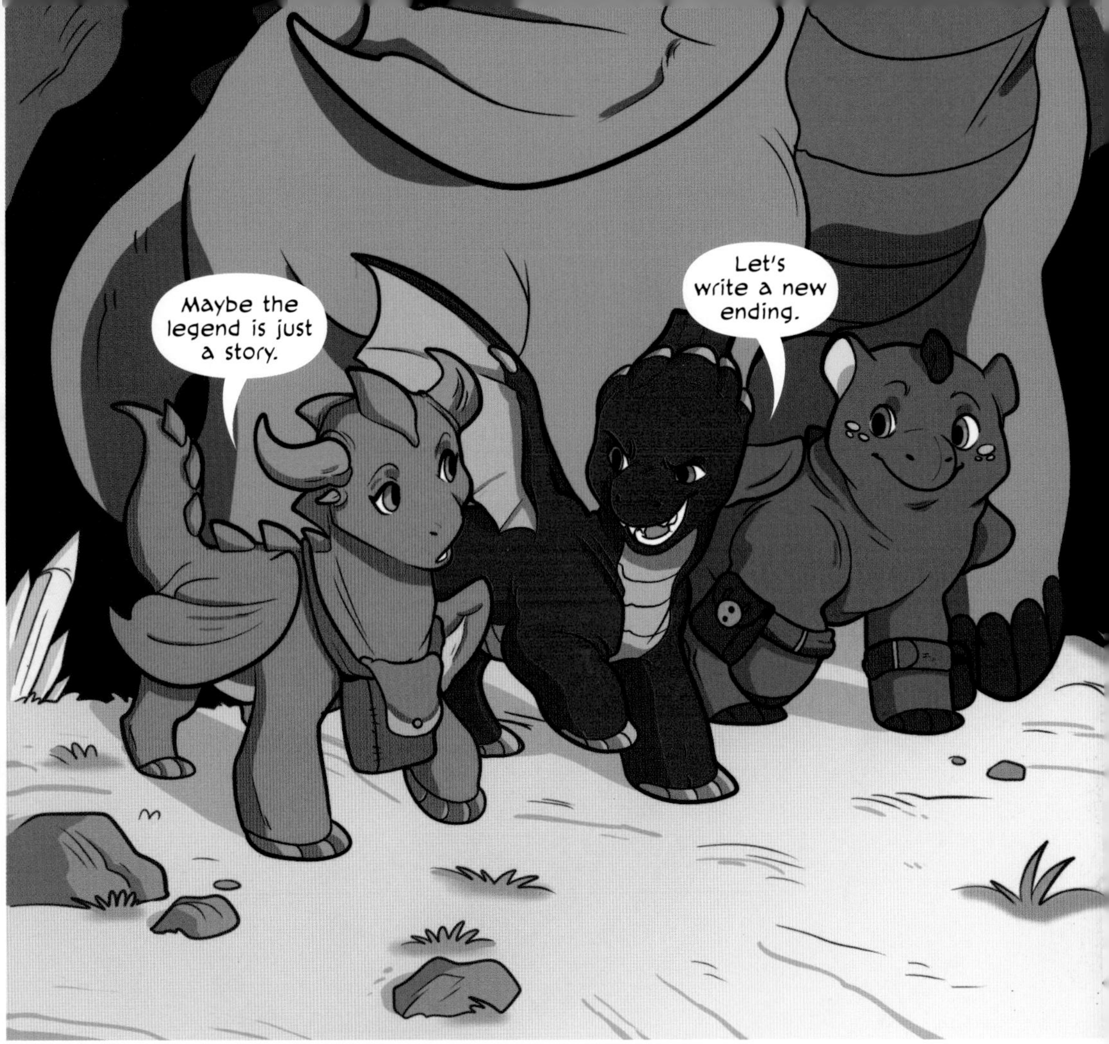
Maybe the legend is just a story.
Let's write a new ending.

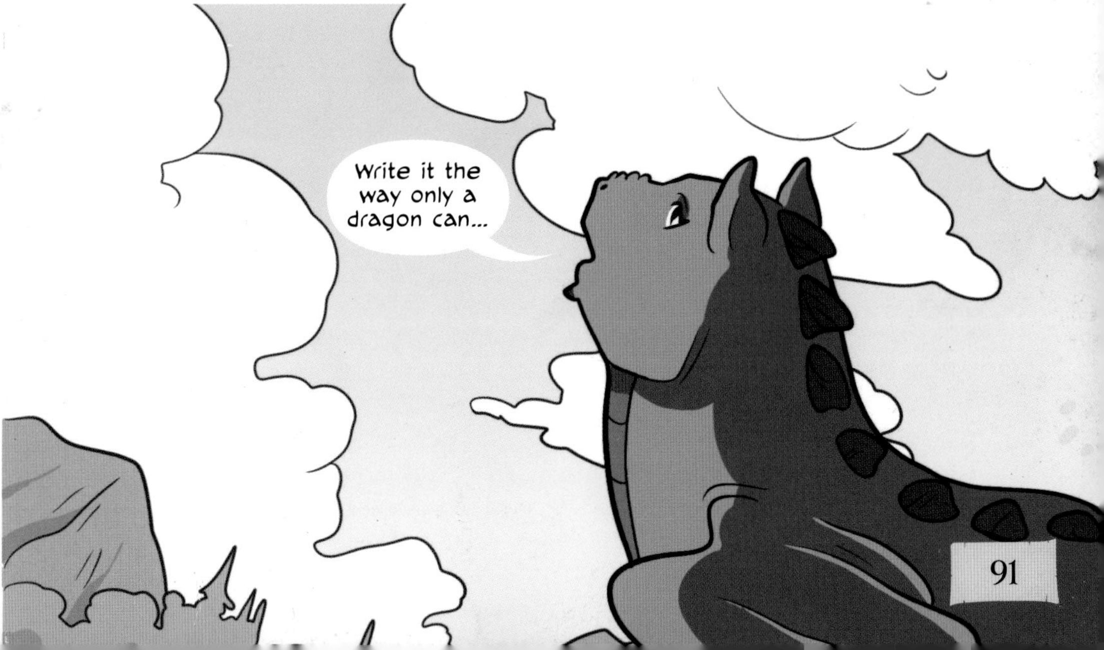
Write it the way only a dragon can...

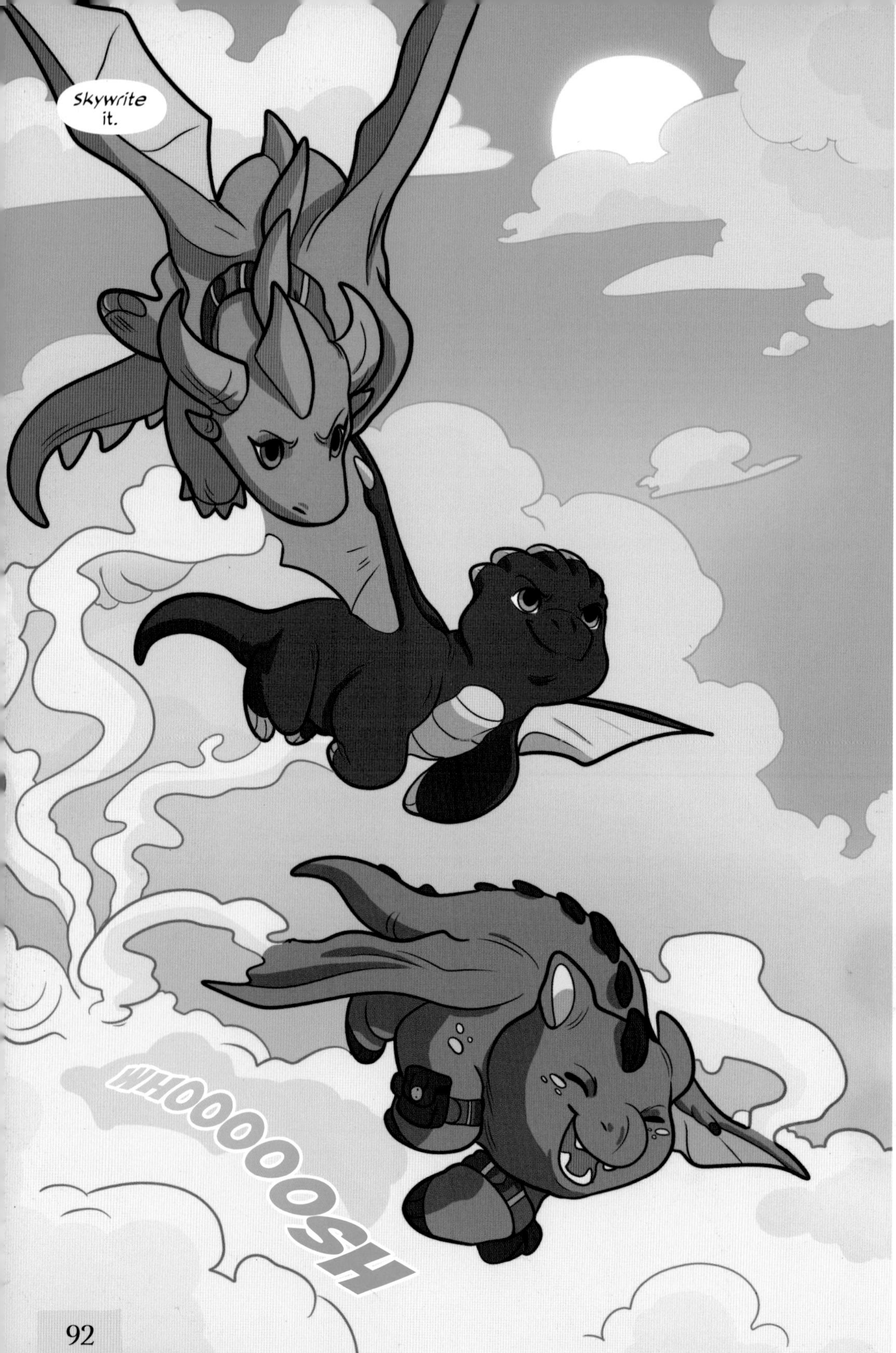
Skywrite it.
WHOOOOOOSH

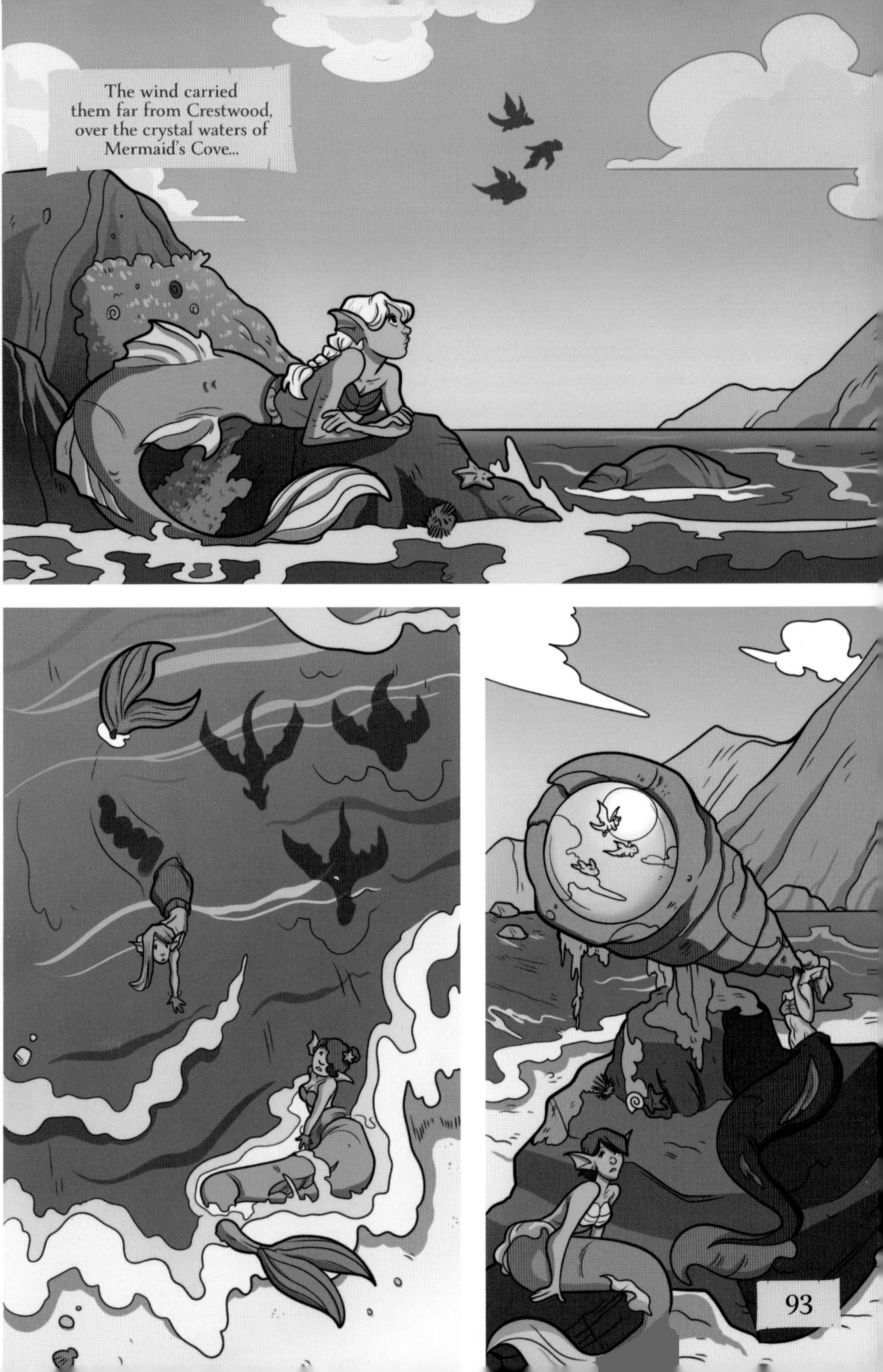
The wind carried them far from Crestwood, over the crystal waters of Mermaid's Cove...

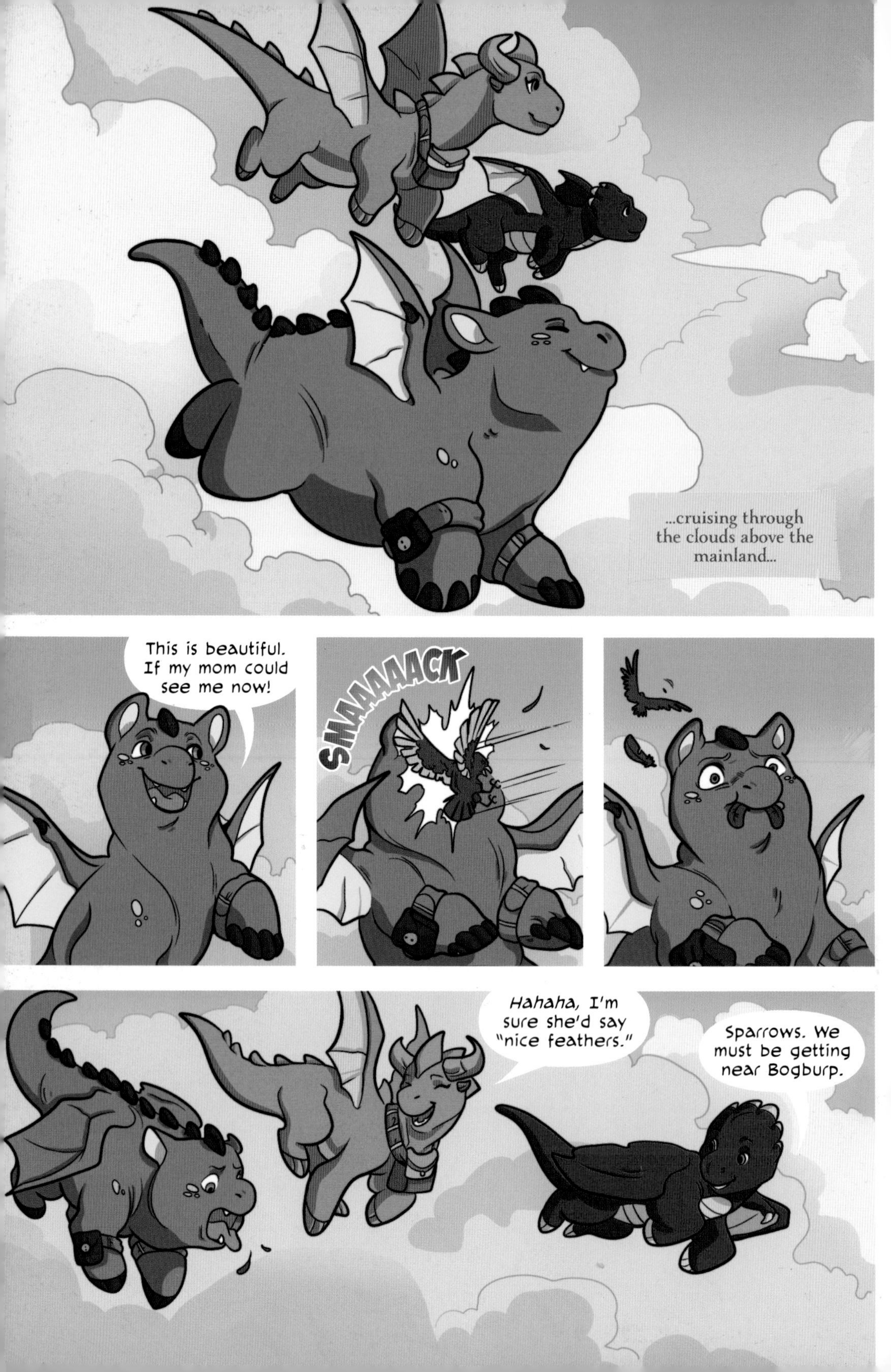
...cruising through the clouds above the mainland...
This is beautiful. If my mom could see me now!
SMAAAAACK
Hahaha, I'm sure she'd say "nice feathers."
Sparrows. We must be getting near Bogburp.

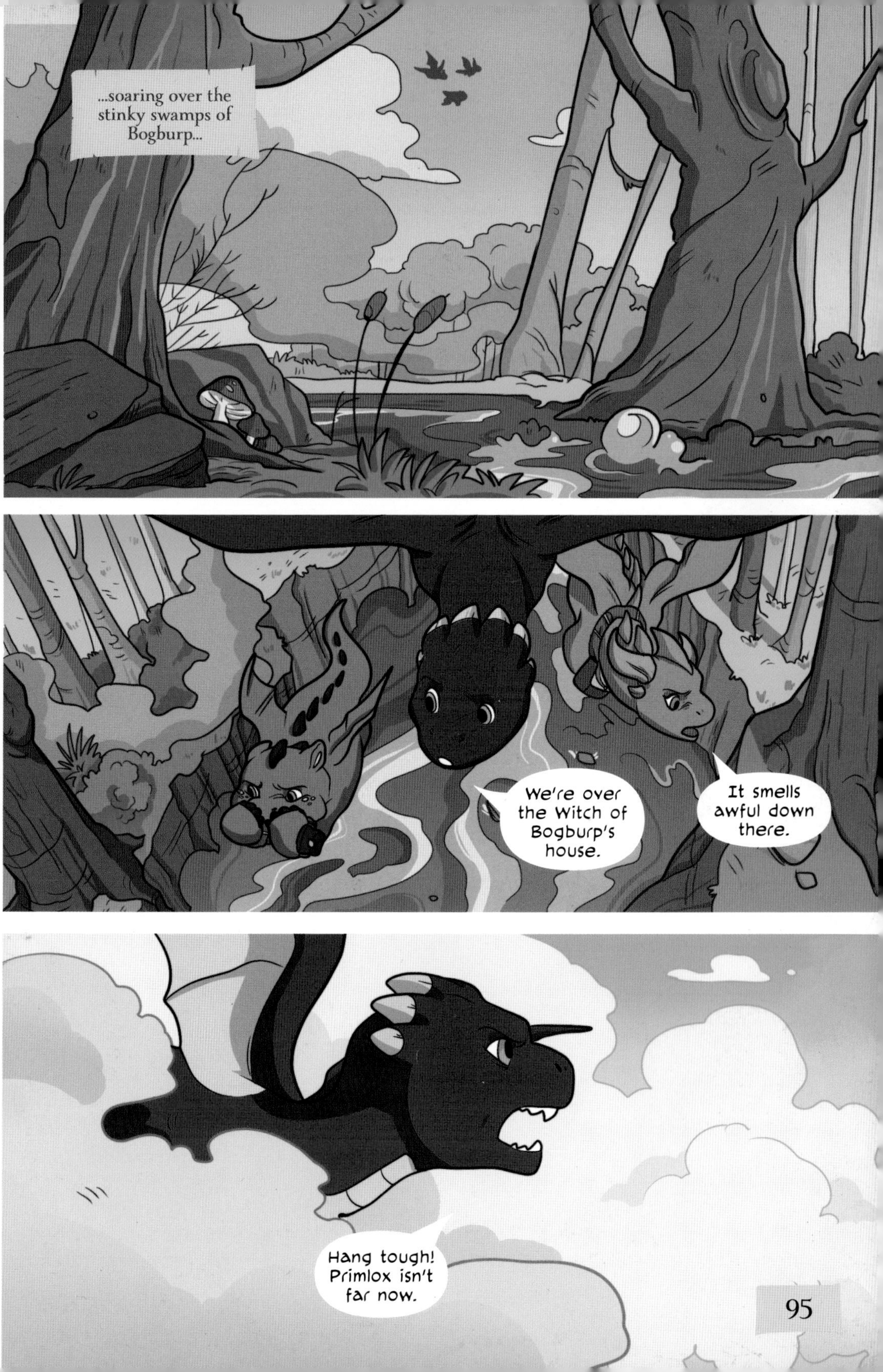

...soaring over the stinky swamps of Bogburp...
We're over the Witch of Bogburp's house.
It smells awful down there.
Hang tough! Primlox isn't far now.

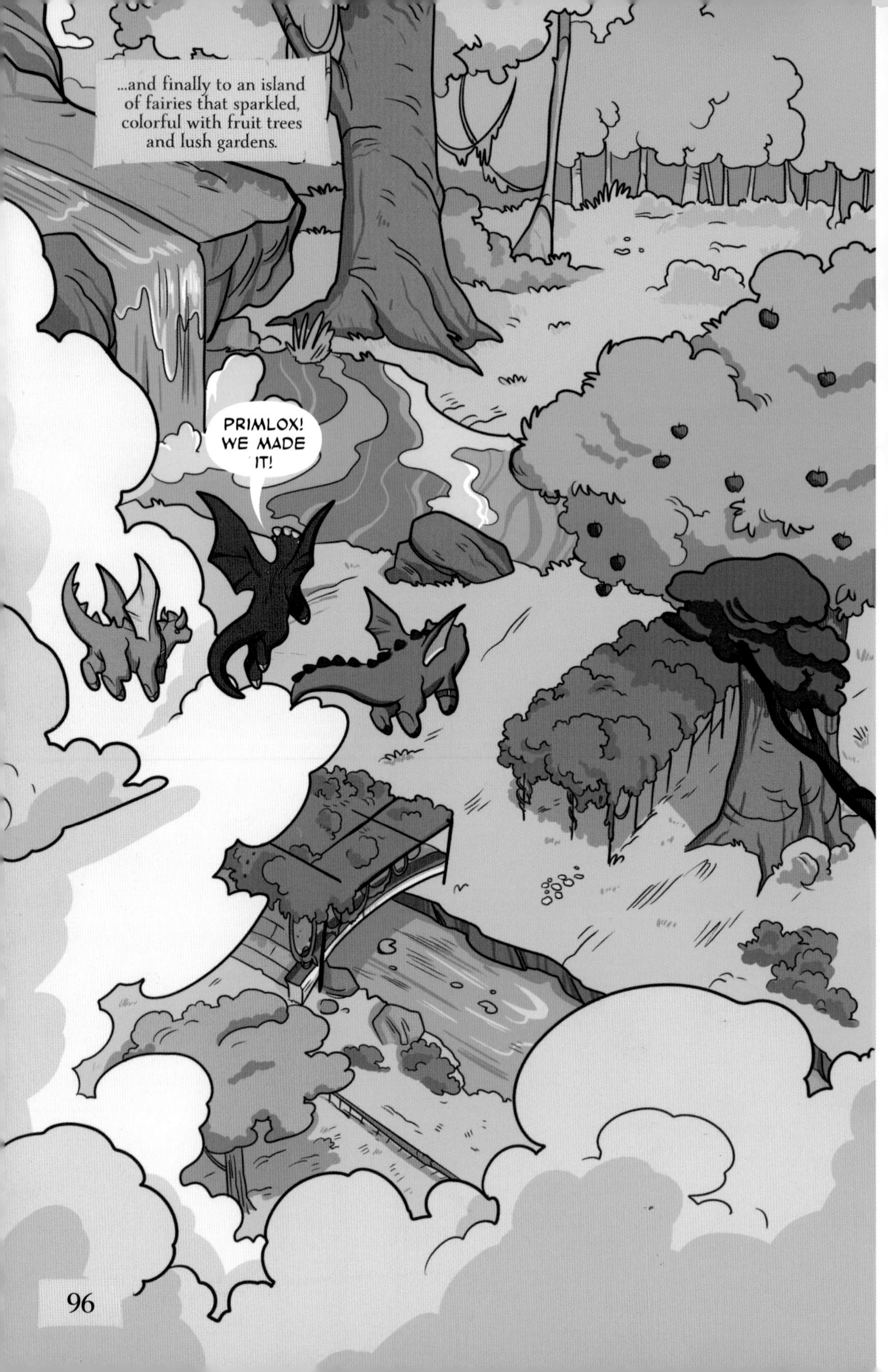
...and finally to an island of fairies that sparkled, colorful with fruit trees and lush gardens.
PRIMLOX! WE MADE IT!

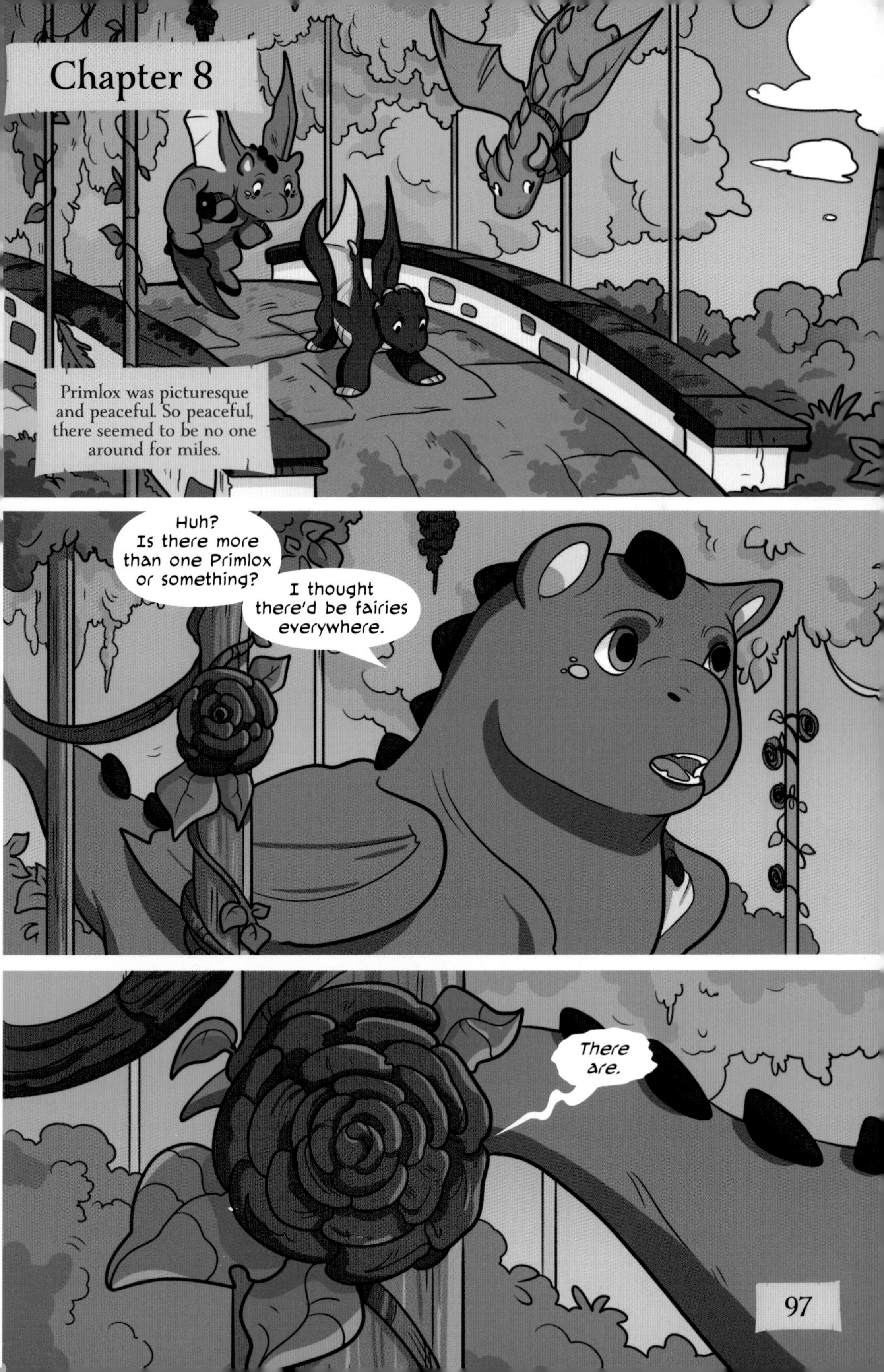
Chapter 8
Primlox was picturesque and peaceful. So peaceful, there seemed to be no one around for miles.
Huh? Is there more than one Primlox or something?
I thought there'd be fairies everywhere.
There are.

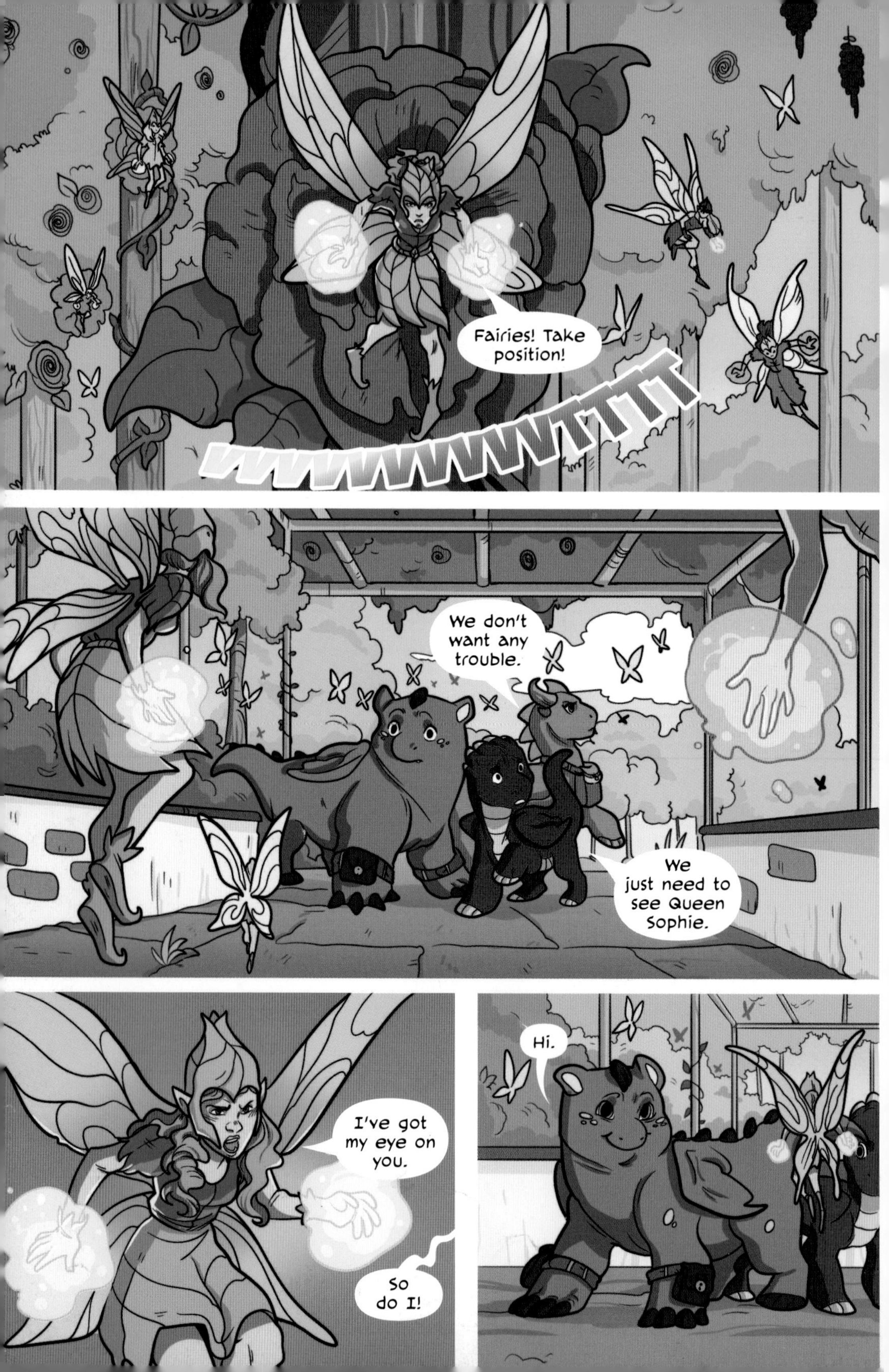
Fairies! Take position!
VVVVVVVVVVTTTTT
We don't want any trouble.
We just need to see Queen Sophie.
I've got my eye on you.
So do I!
Hi.

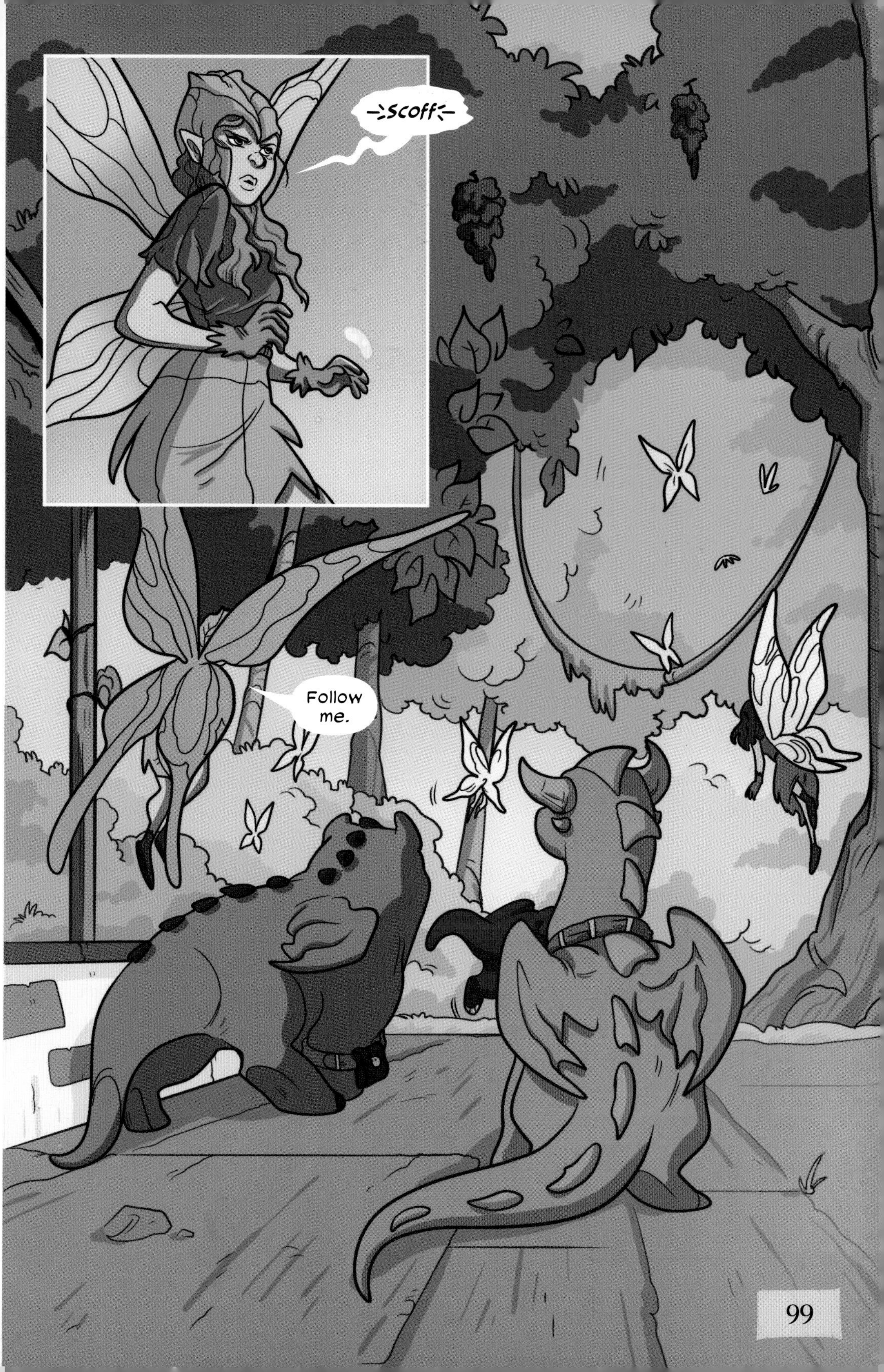

-Scoff-
Follow me.

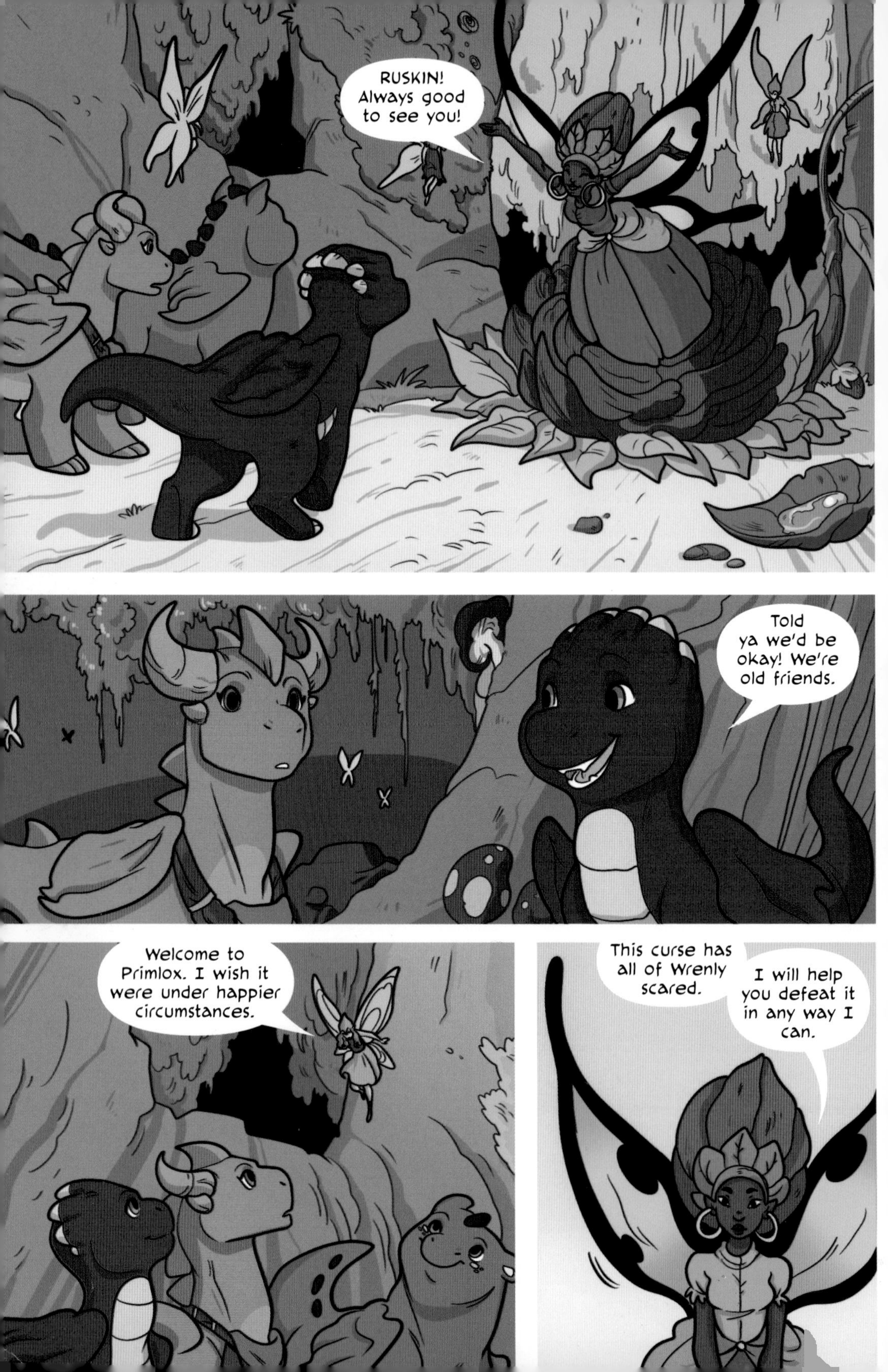
RUSKIN! Always good to see you!
Told ya we'd be okay! We're old friends.
Welcome to Primlox. I wish it were under happier circumstances.
This curse has all of Wrenly scared.
I will help you defeat it in any way I can.

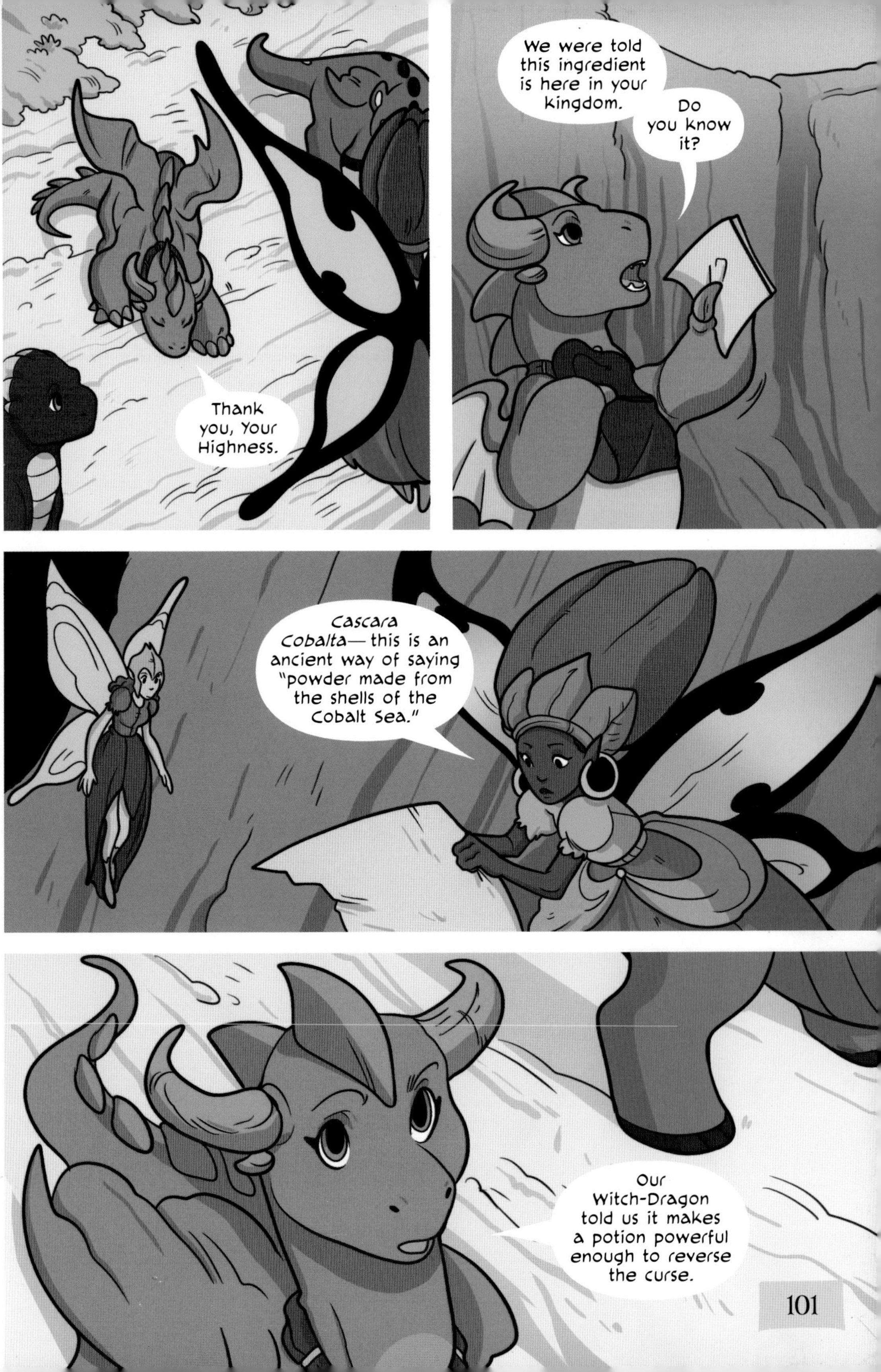
Thank you, Your Highness.
We were told this ingredient is here in your kingdom.
Do you know it?
Cascara Cobalta— this is an ancient way of saying "powder made from the shells of the Cobalt Sea."
Our Witch-Dragon told us it makes a potion powerful enough to reverse the curse.

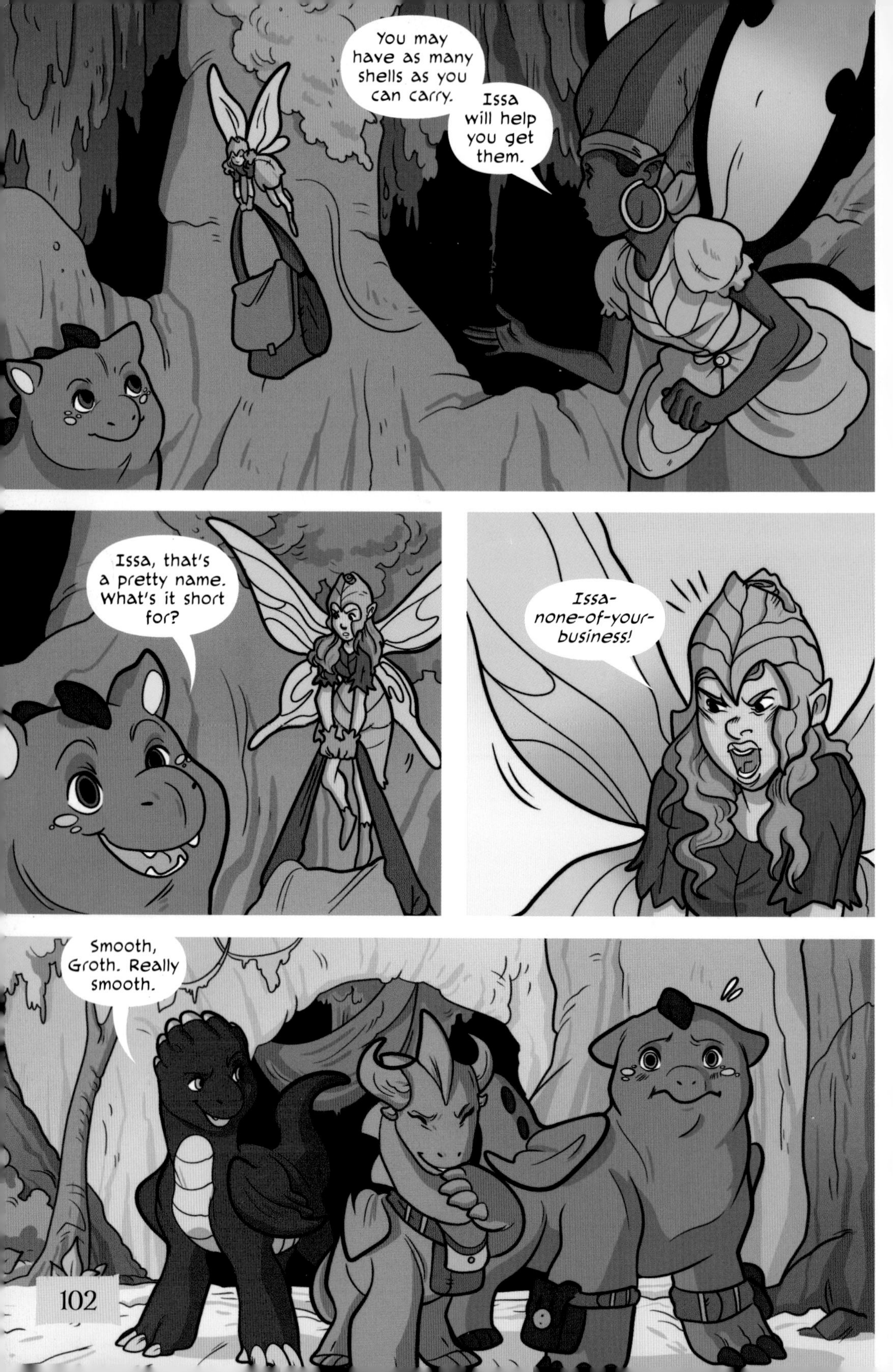
You may have as many shells as you can carry.
Issa will help you get them.
Issa, that's a pretty name. What's it short for?
Issa-none-of-your-business!
Smooth, Groth. Really smooth.

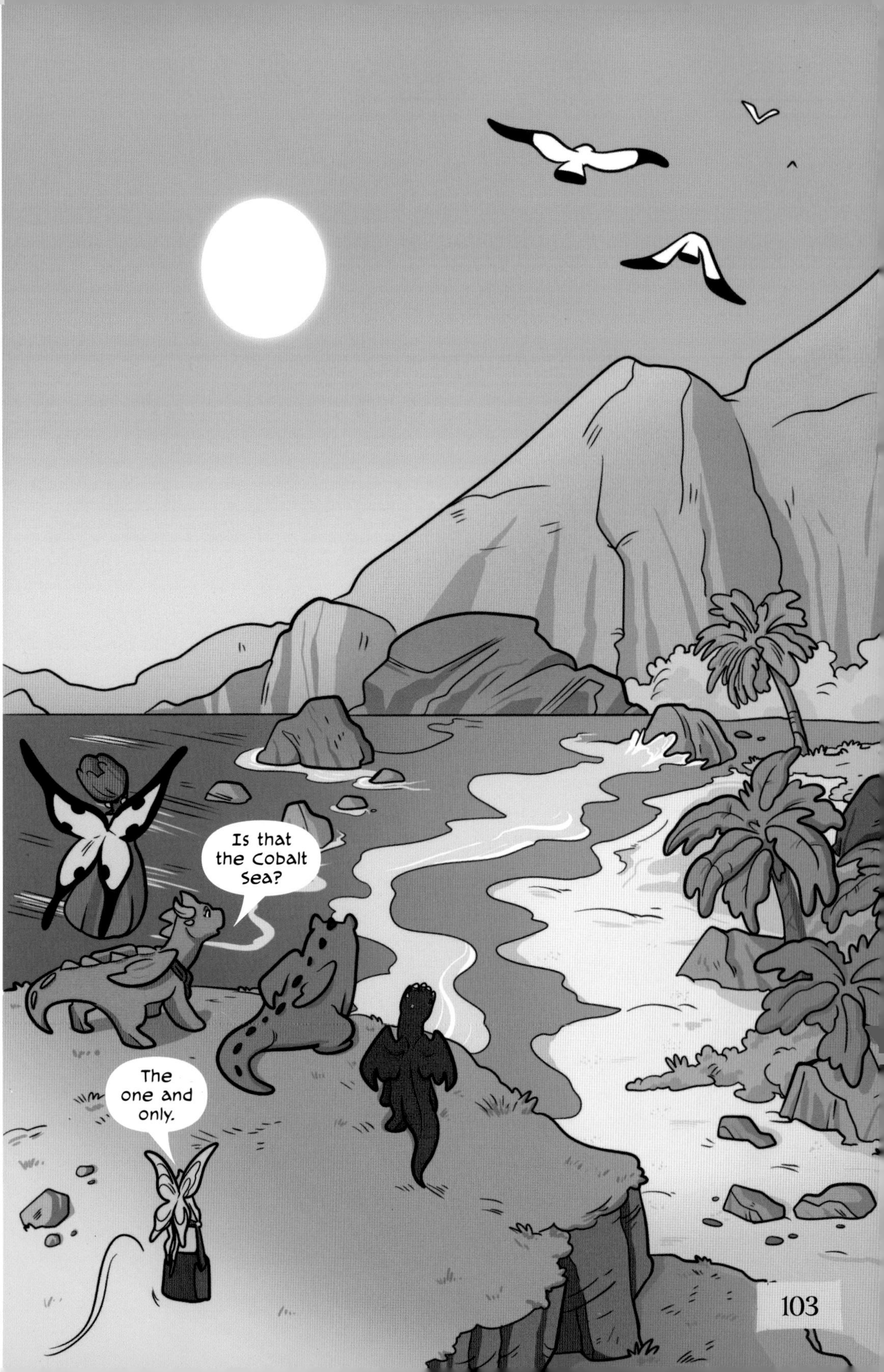
Is that the Cobalt Sea?
The one and only.

KERSPLOOOOOSH
FSHHHHHHHHHHH

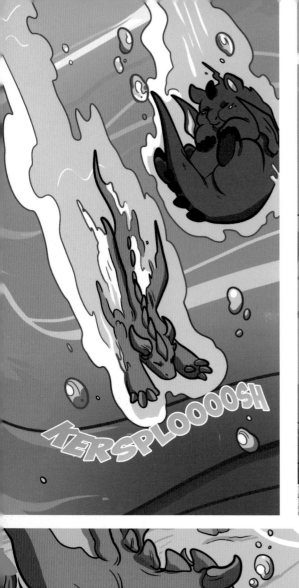

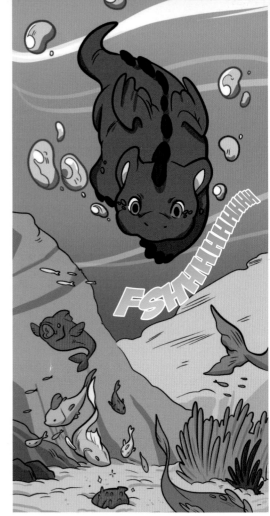

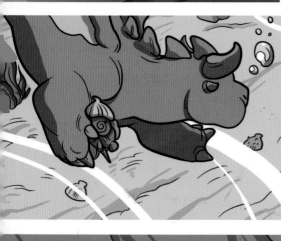

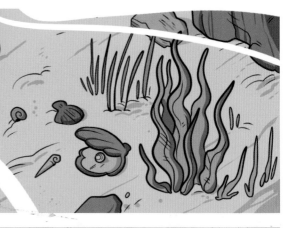

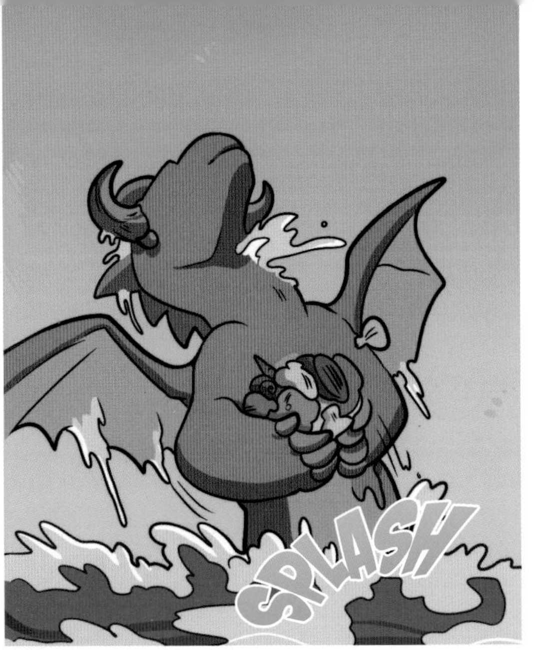
SPLASH

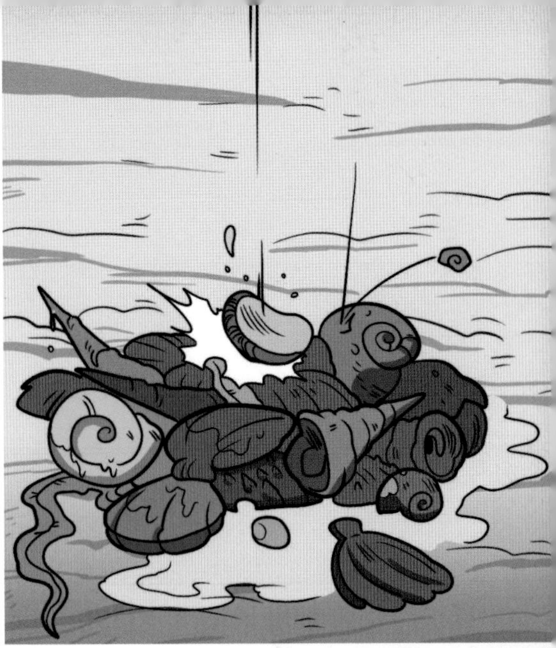

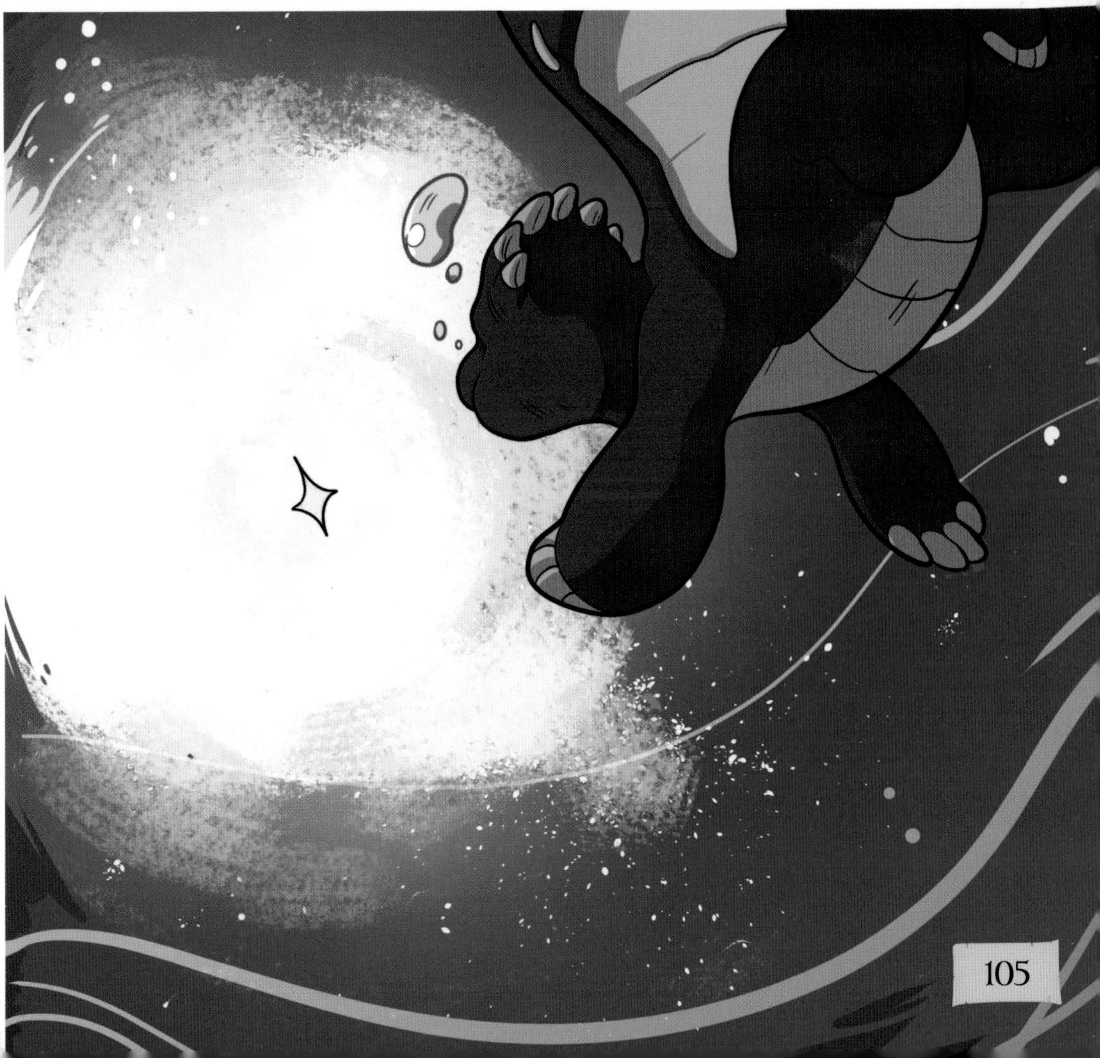

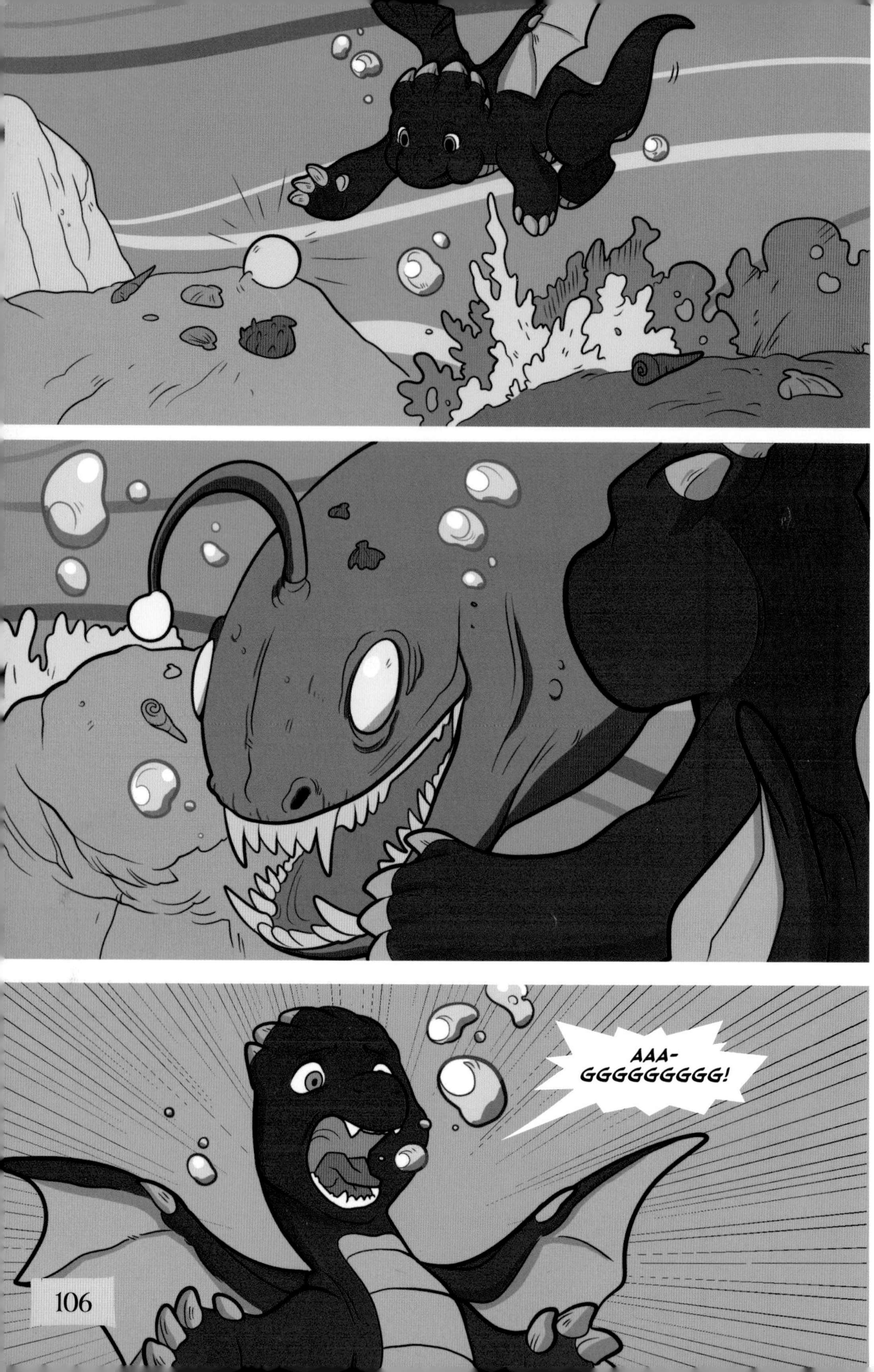
AAA-
GGGGGGGGG!

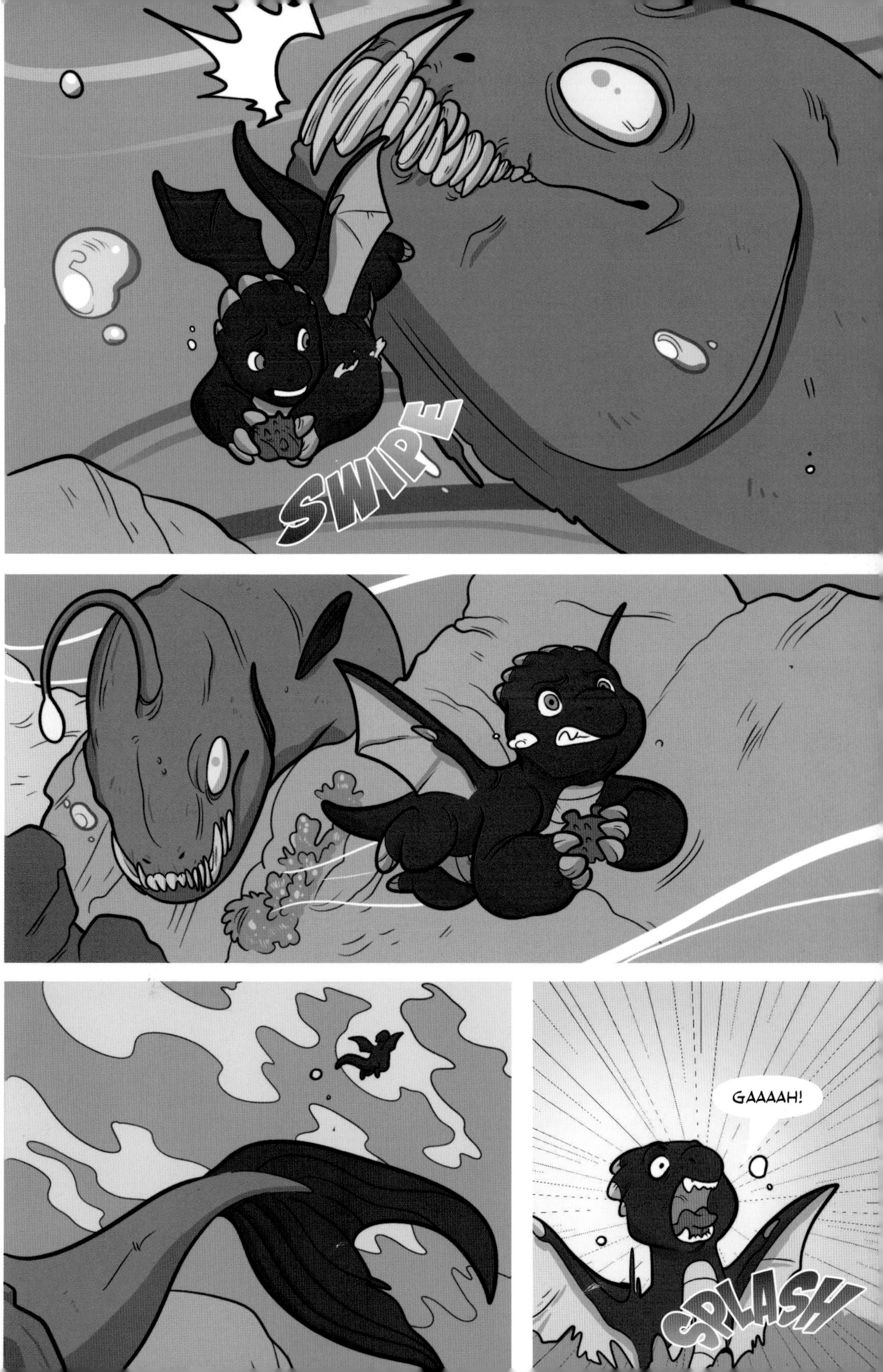
SWIPE
GAAAAH!
SPLASH

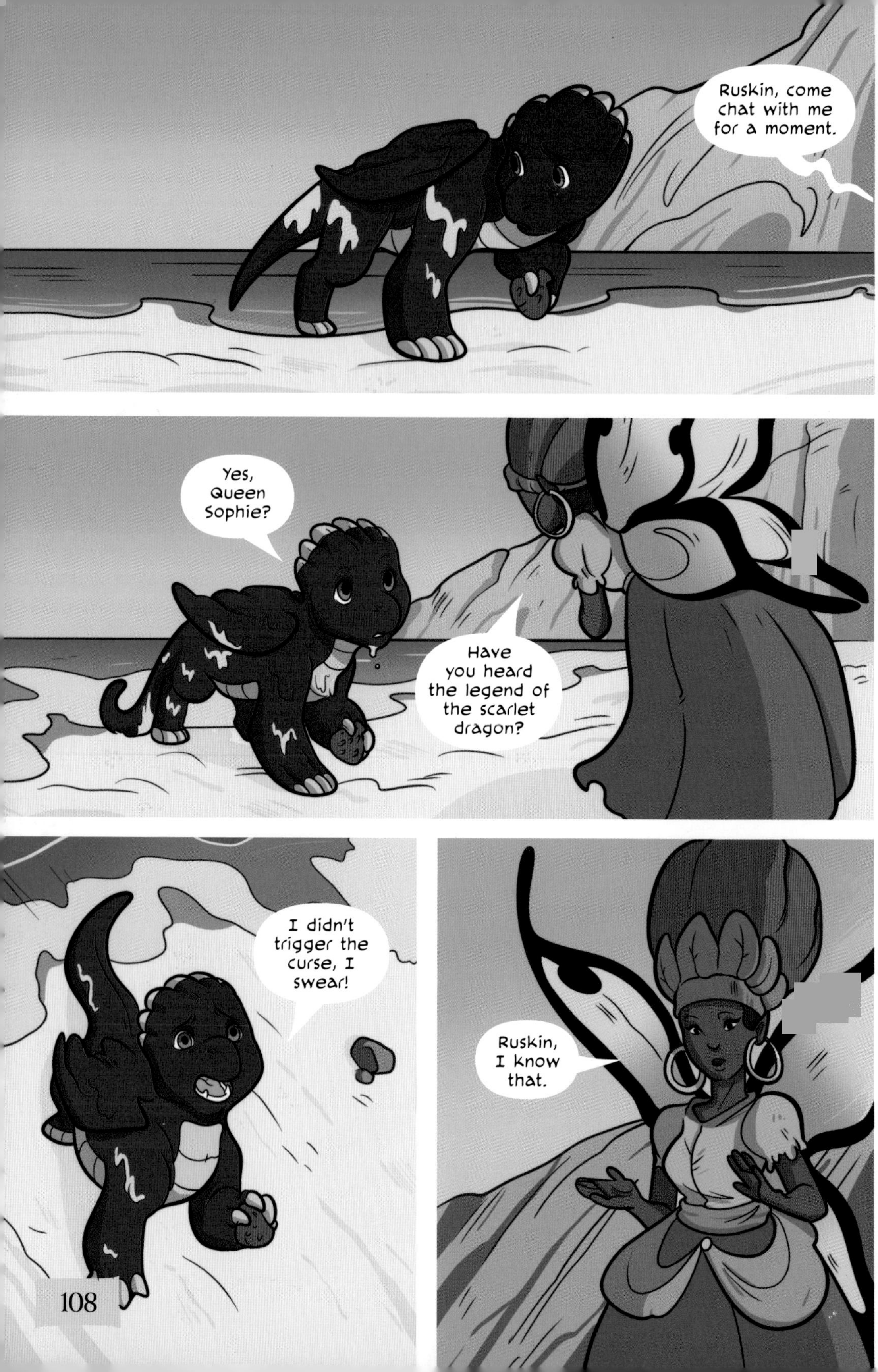
Ruskin, come chat with me for a moment.
Yes, Queen Sophie?
Have you heard the legend of the scarlet dragon?
I didn't trigger the curse, I swear!
Ruskin, I know that.

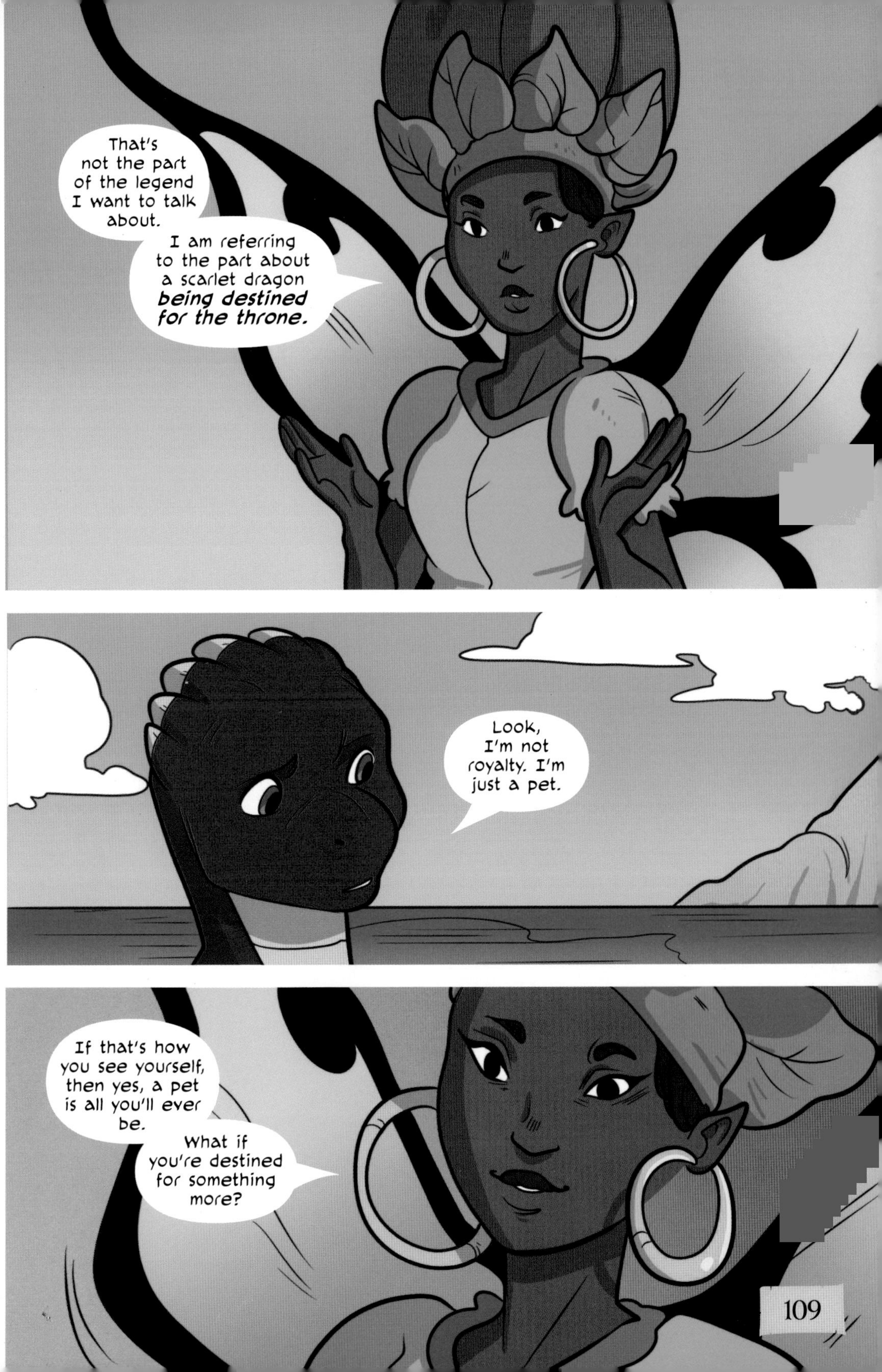
That's not the part of the legend I want to talk about.
I am referring to the part about a scarlet dragon ***being destined for the throne.***
Look, I'm not royalty. I'm just a pet.
If that's how you see yourself, then yes, a pet is all you'll ever be.
What if you're destined for something more?

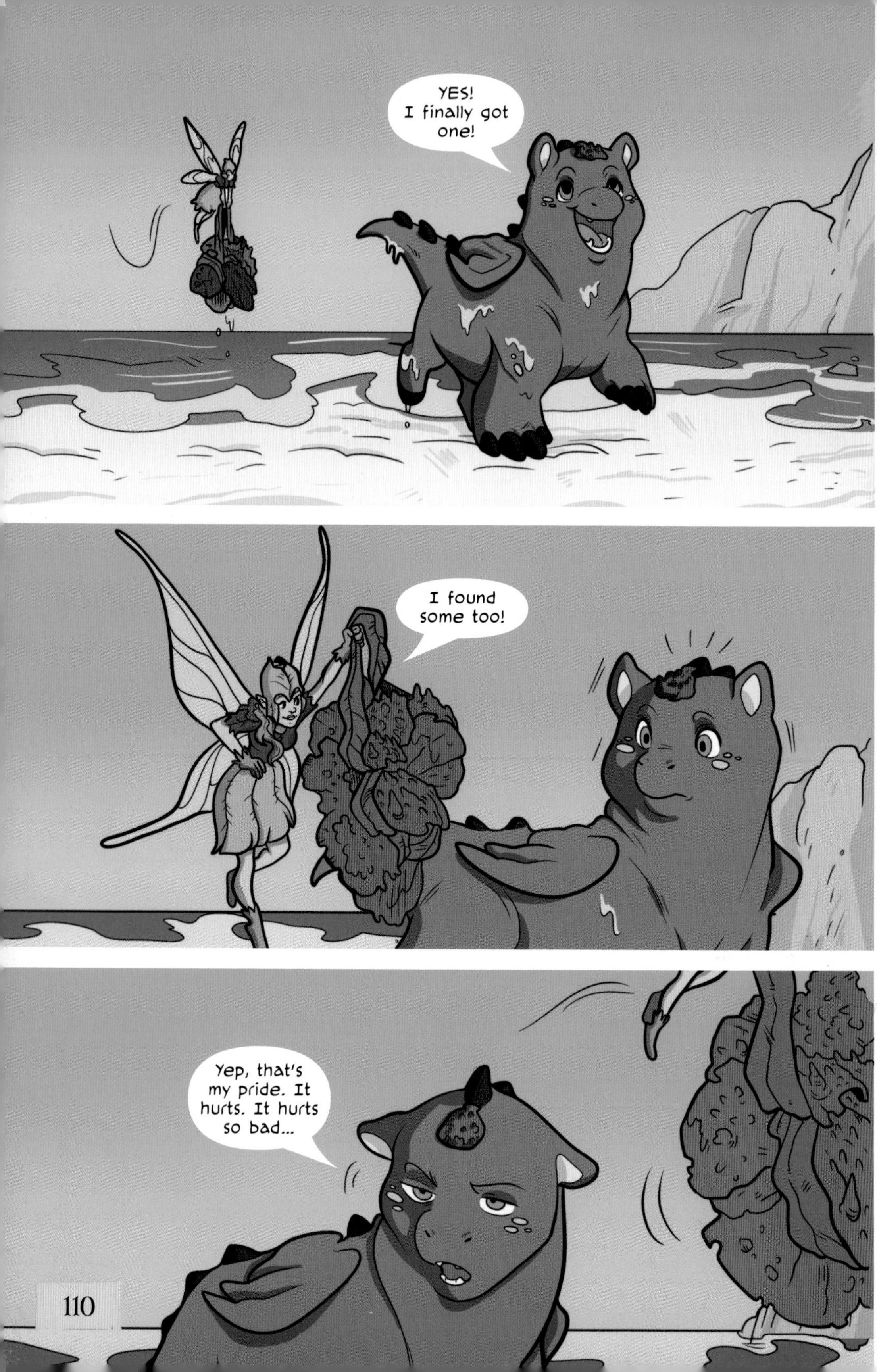
YES! I finally got one!
I found some too!
Yep, that's my pride. It hurts. It hurts so bad...

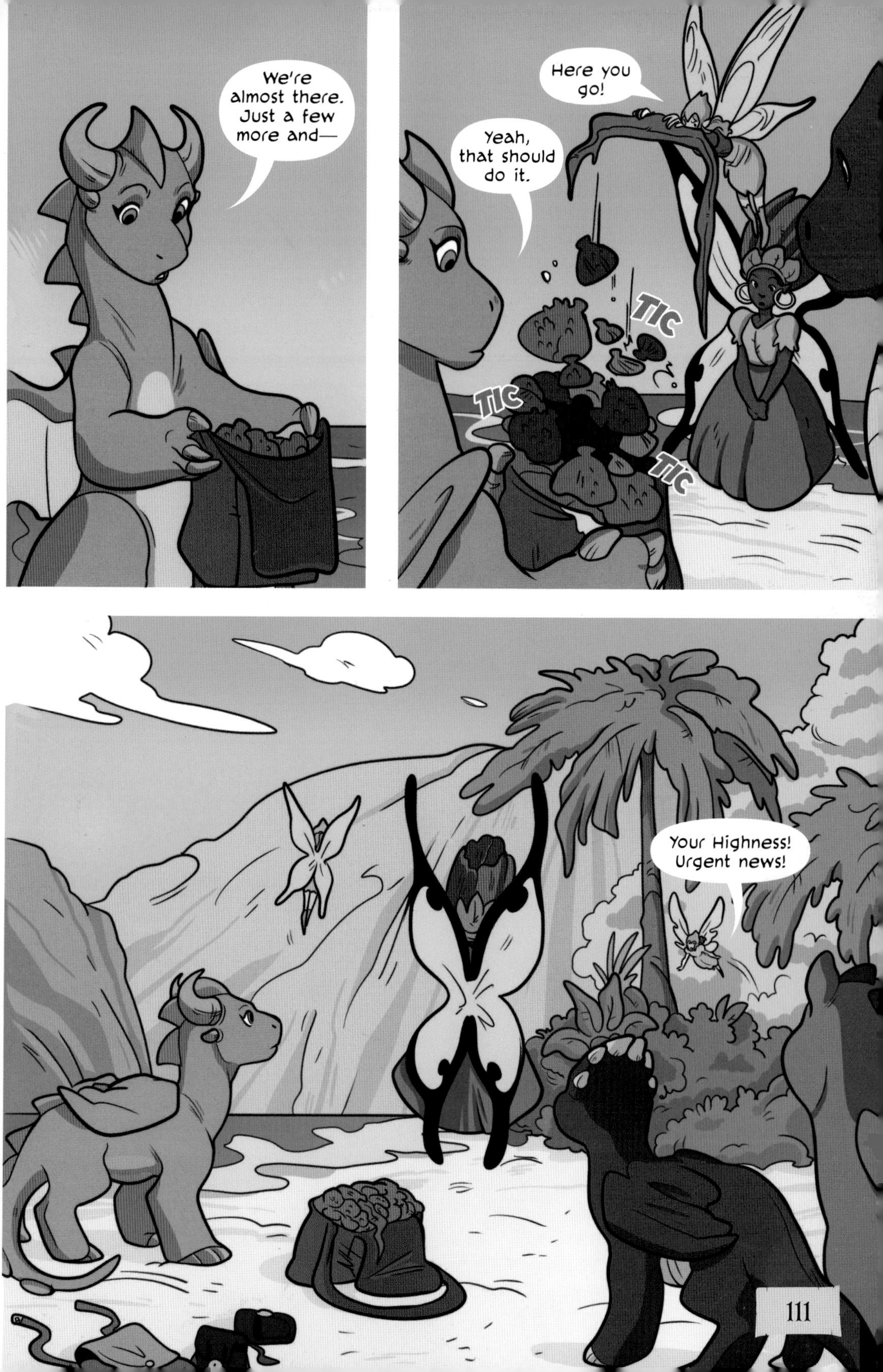
We're almost there. Just a few more and—
Here you go!
Yeah, that should do it.
TIC
TIC
TIC
Your Highness! Urgent news!

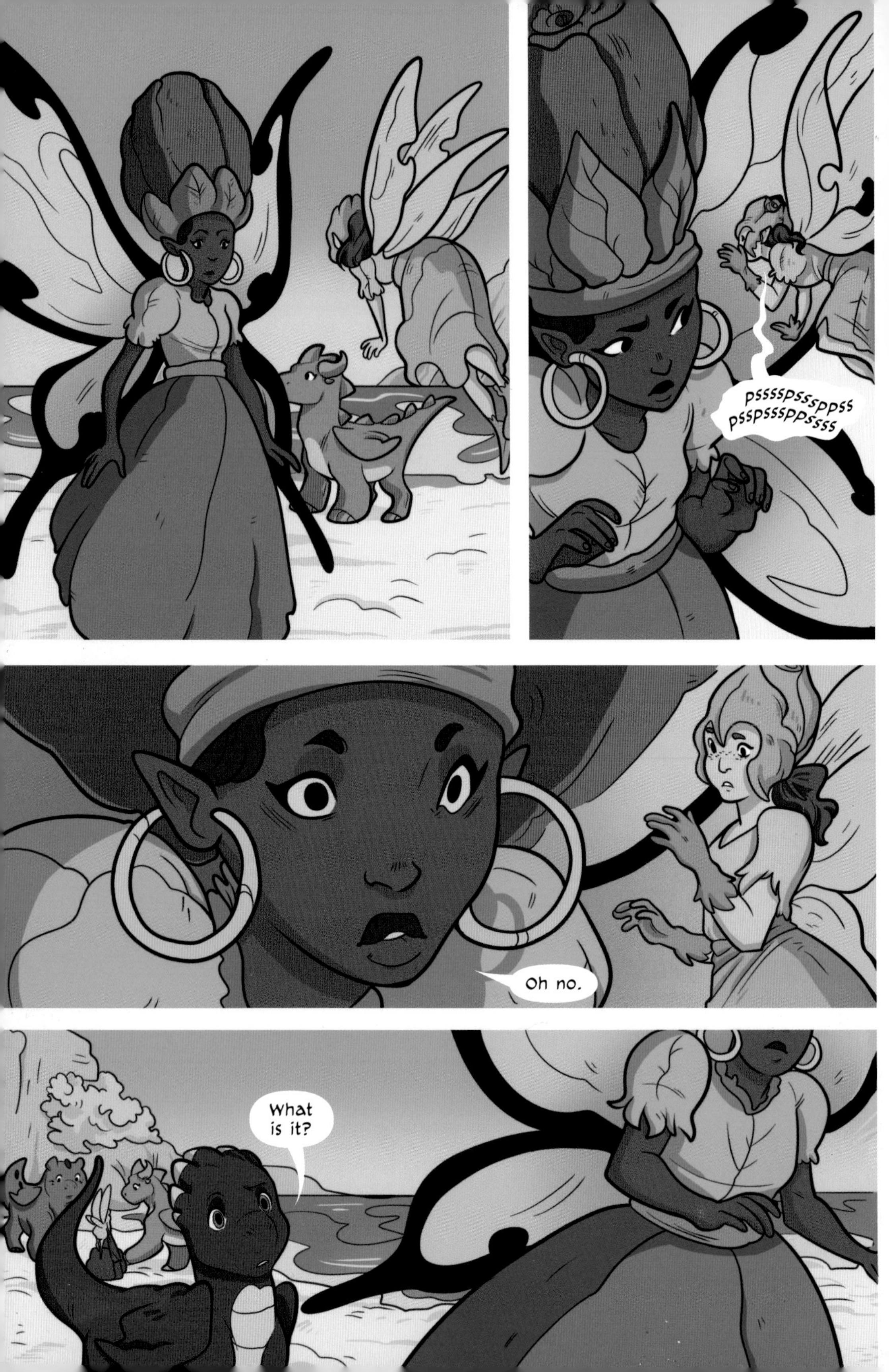
psssspsssppss
psspssspPssss
Oh no.
What is it?

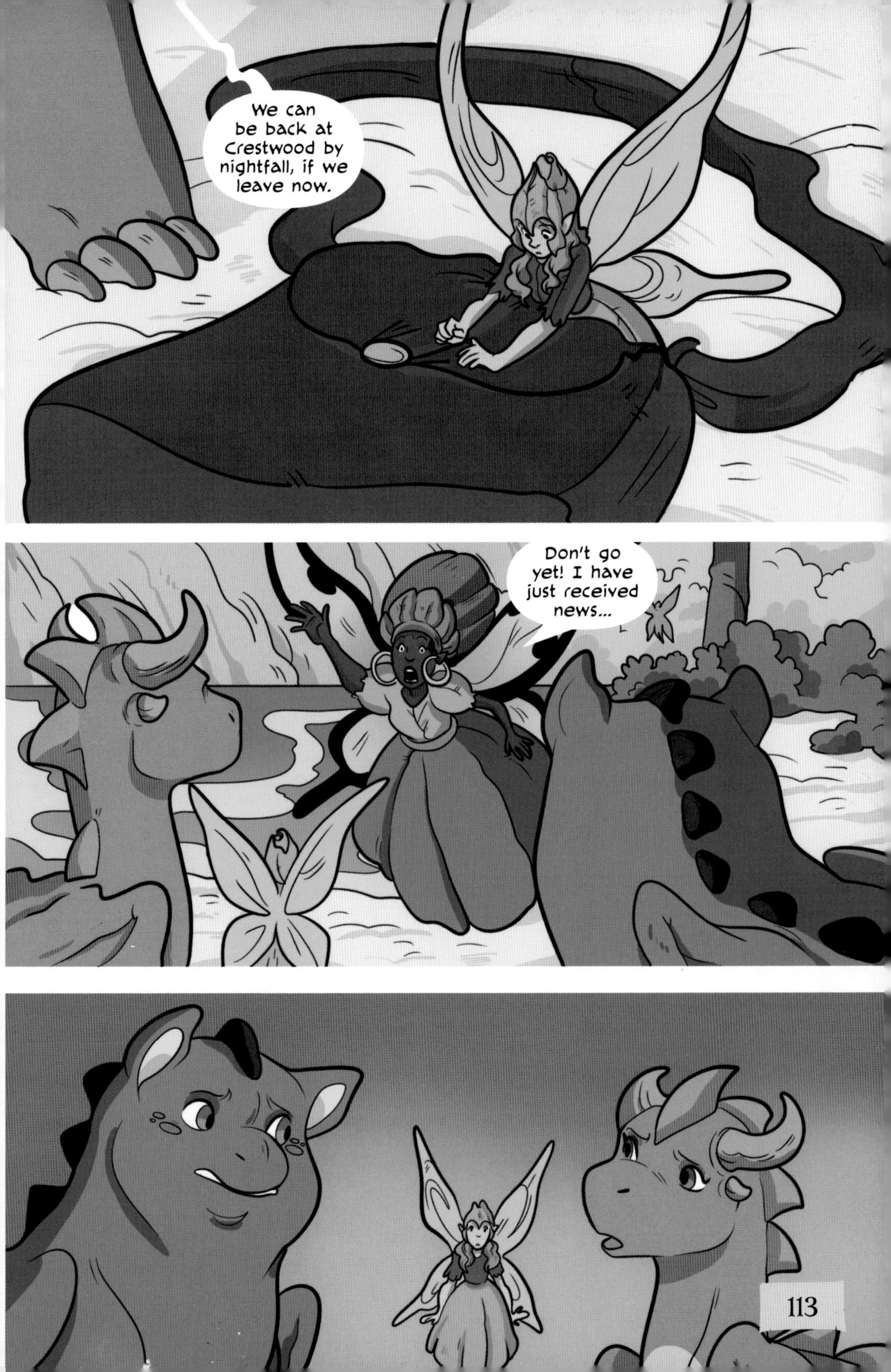
We can be back at Crestwood by nightfall, if we leave now.
Don't go yet! I have just received news...

Chapter 9

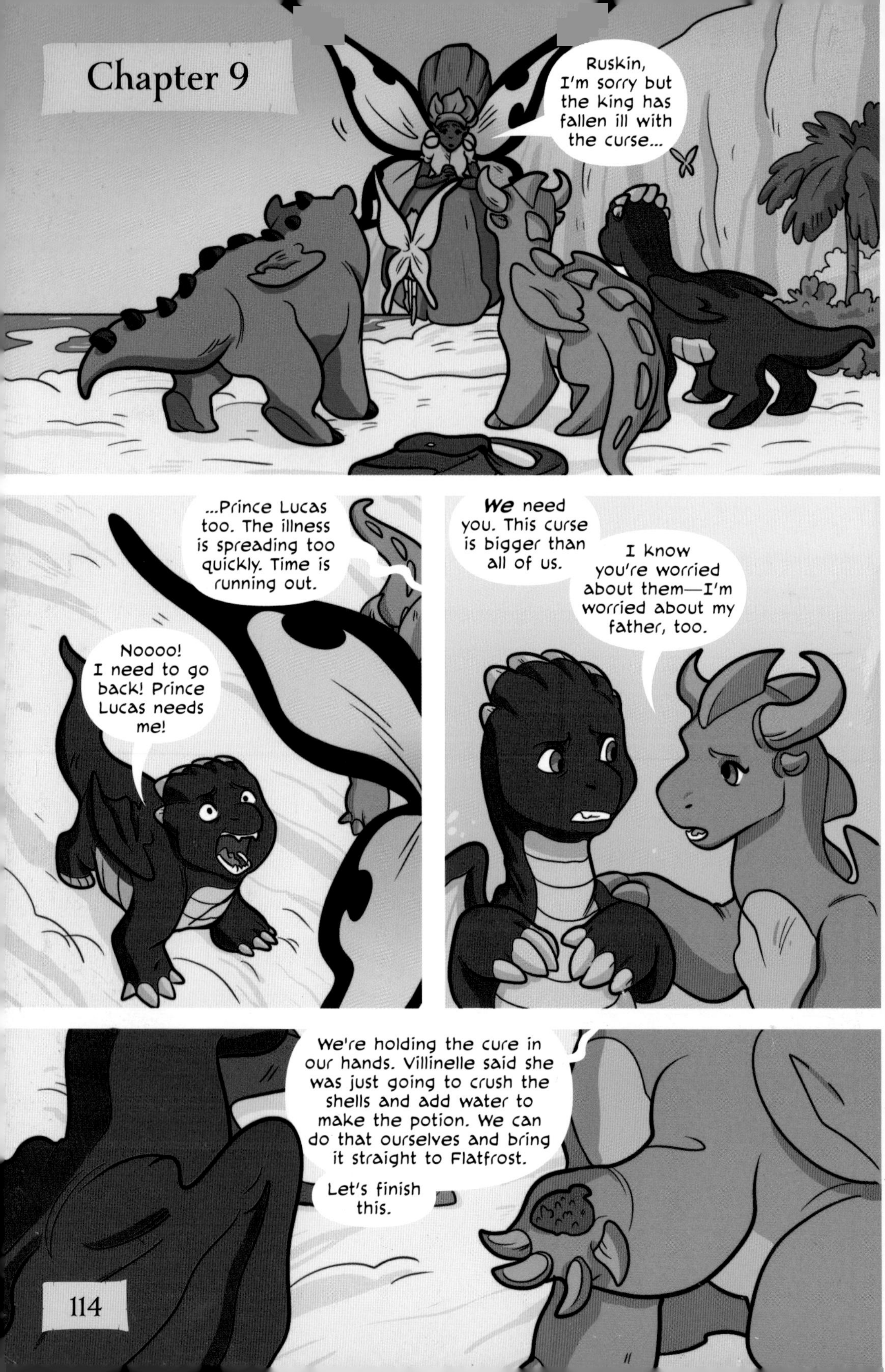
Ruskin, I'm sorry but the king has fallen ill with the curse...
...Prince Lucas too. The illness is spreading too quickly. Time is running out.
Noooo! I need to go back! Prince Lucas needs me!
We need you. This curse is bigger than all of us.
I know you're worried about them—I'm worried about my father, too.
We're holding the cure in our hands. Villinelle said she was just going to crush the shells and add water to make the potion. We can do that ourselves and bring it straight to Flatfrost.
Let's finish this.

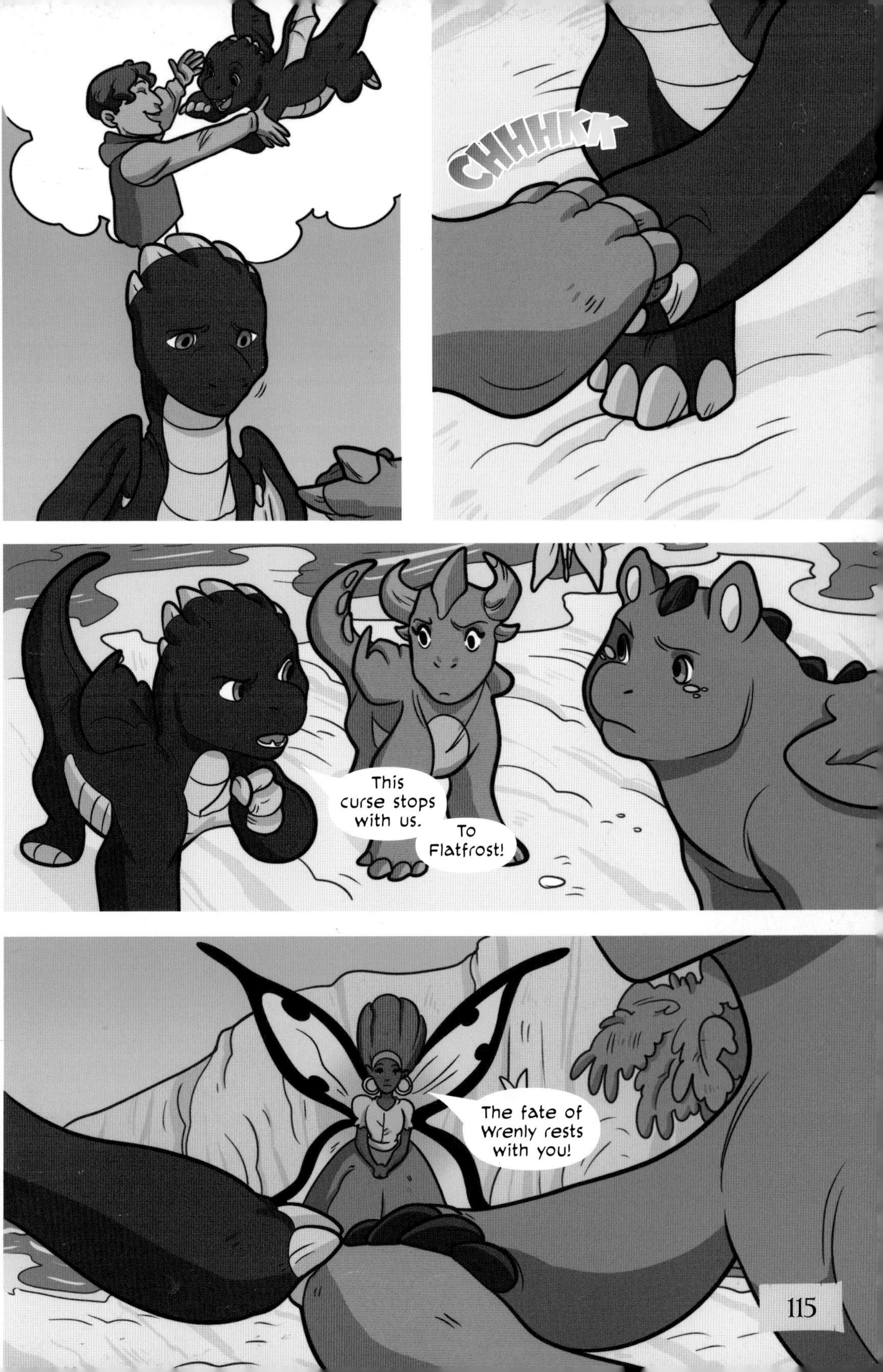
CHHHKK
This curse stops with us.
To Flatfrost!
The fate of Wrenly rests with you!

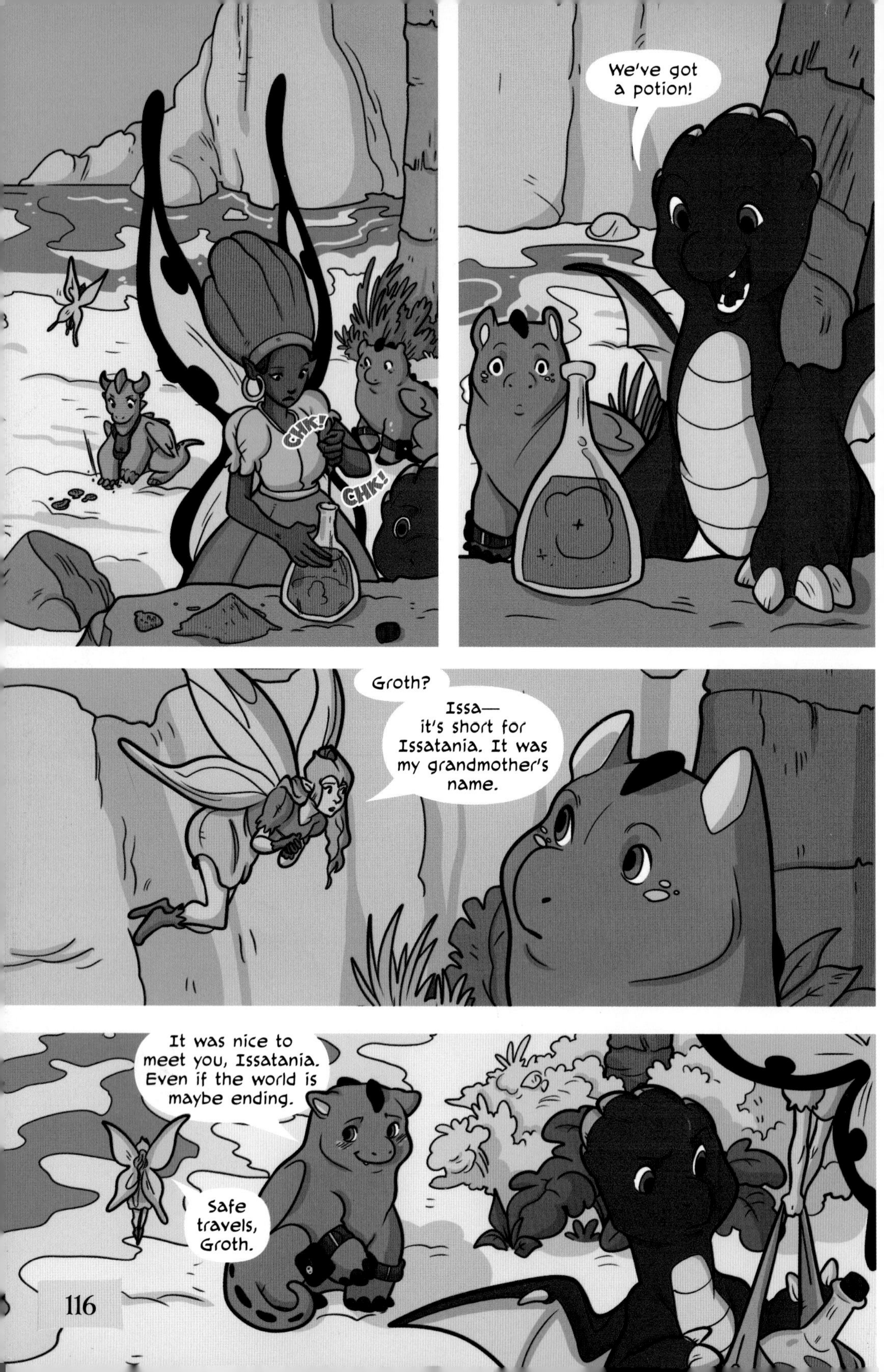
CHK!
CHK!
We've got a potion!
Groth?
Issa— it's short for Issatania. It was my grandmother's name.
It was nice to meet you, Issatania. Even if the world is maybe ending.
Safe travels, Groth.

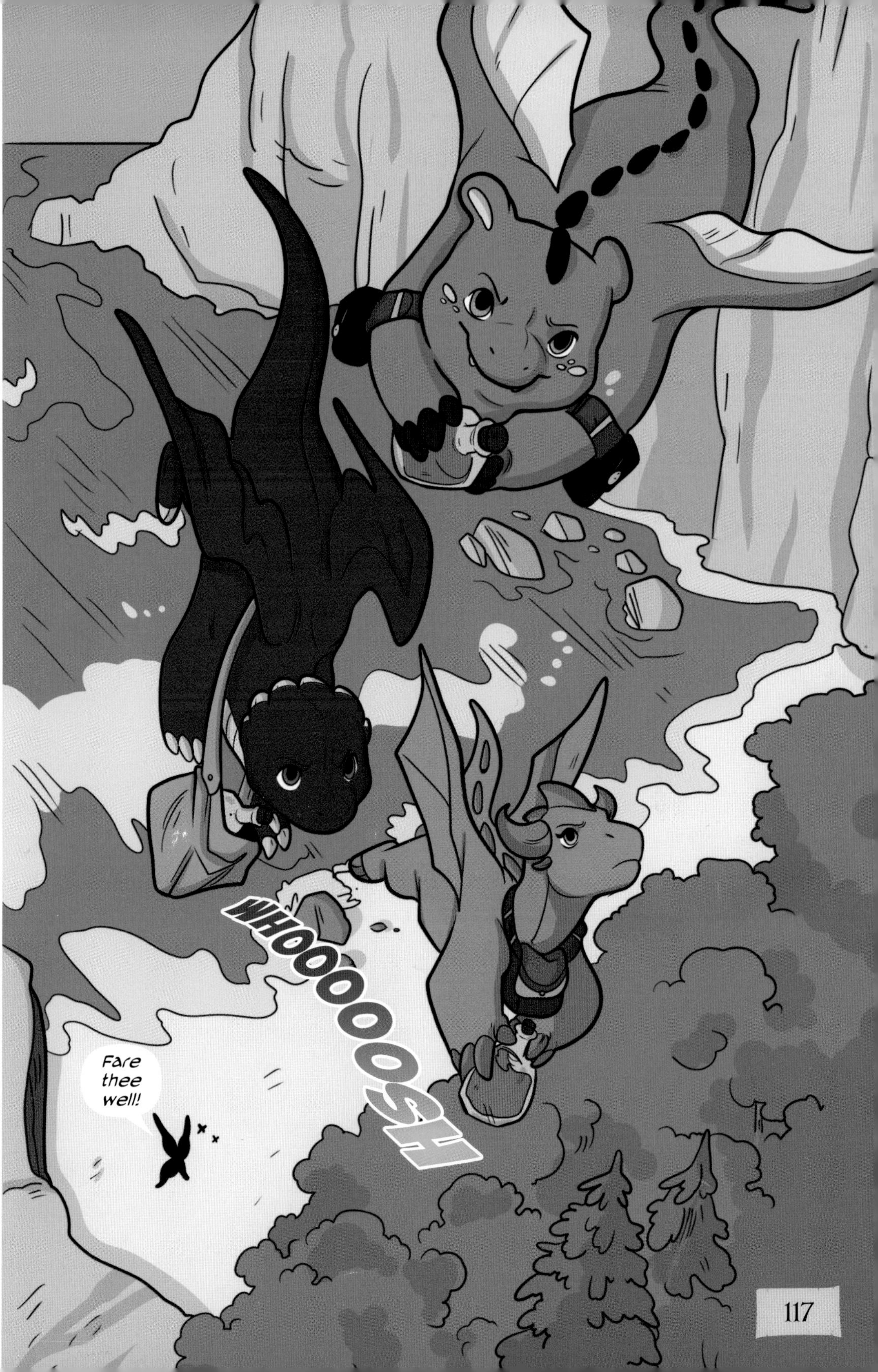
WHOOOOOOSH
Fare thee well!

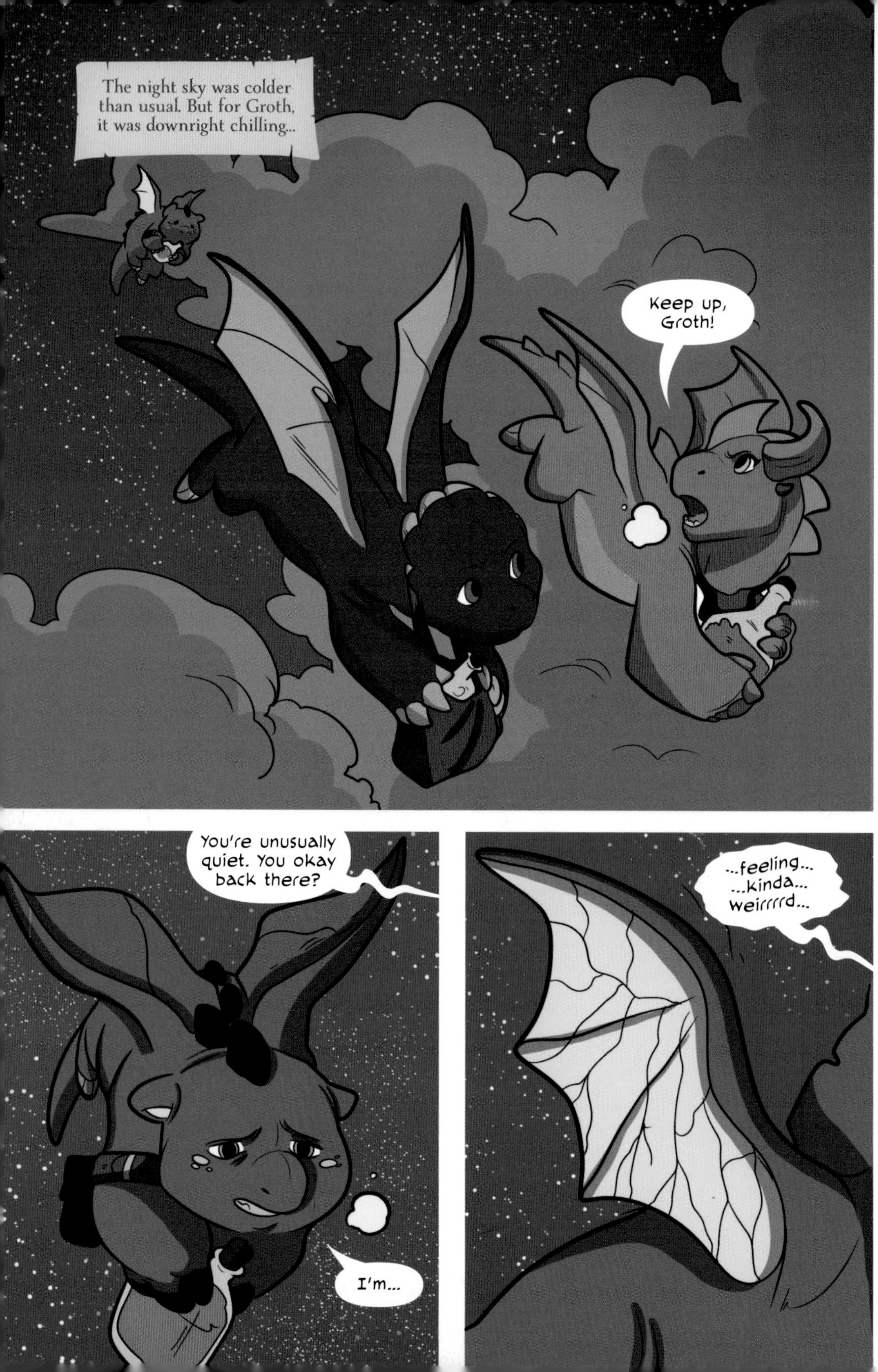
The night sky was colder than usual. But for Groth, it was downright chilling...
Keep up, Groth!
You're unusually quiet. You okay back there?
I'm...
...feeling... ...kinda... weirrrrd...

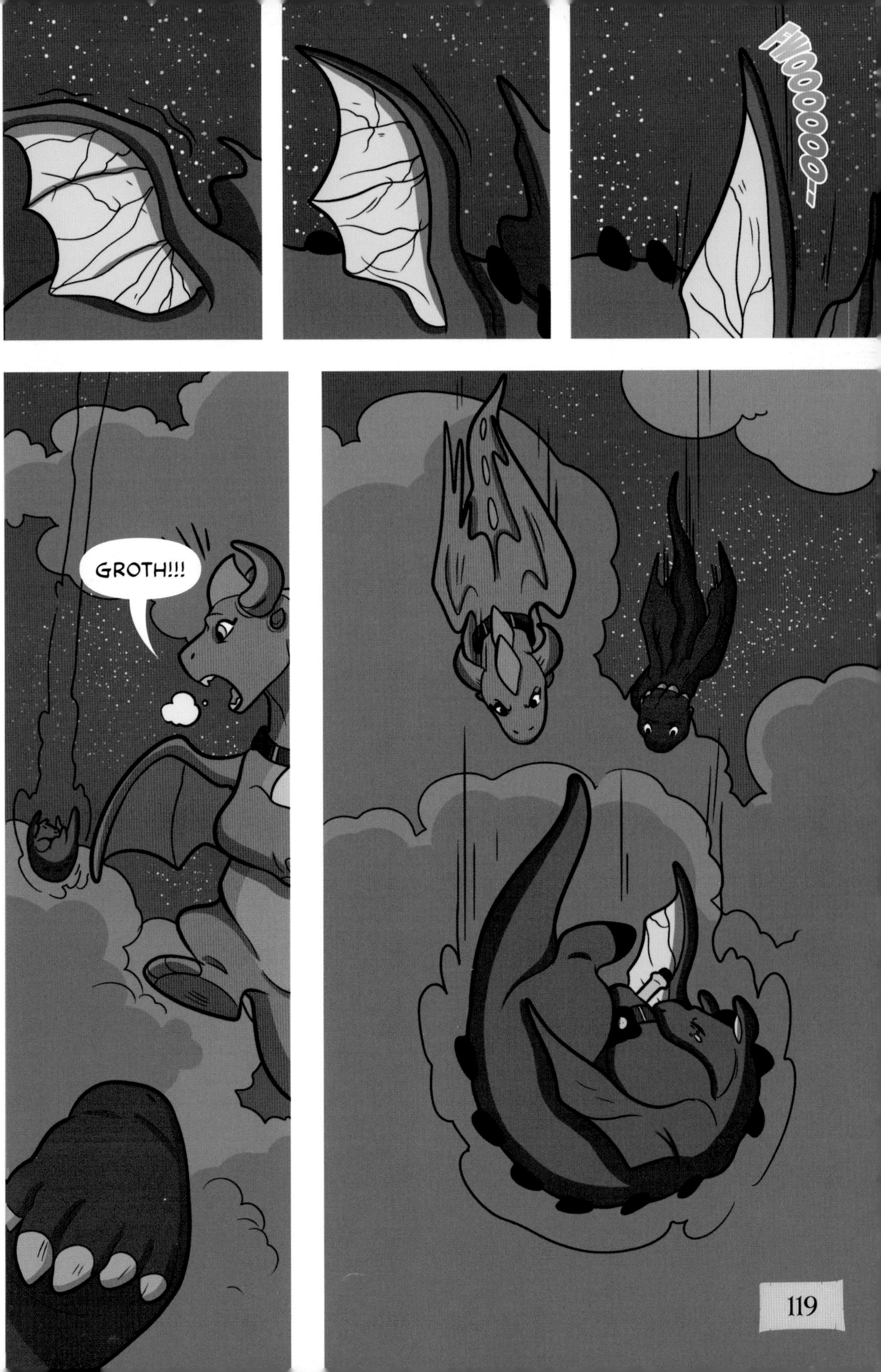
FWOOOOOO...
GROTH!!!

...so tired...

...just need to... rest...

Who turned out the lights?

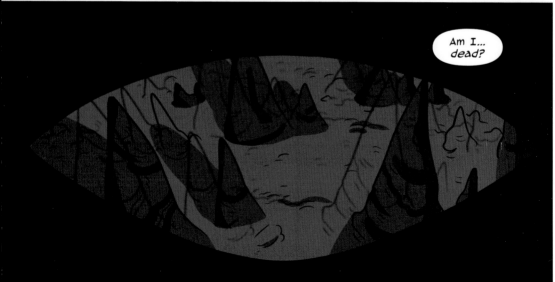

Am I... dead?

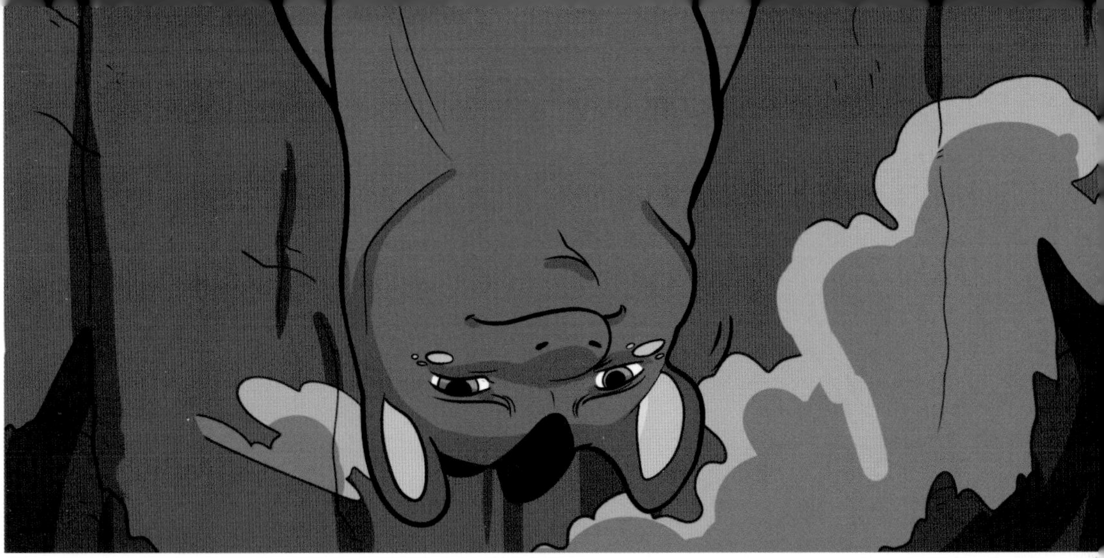

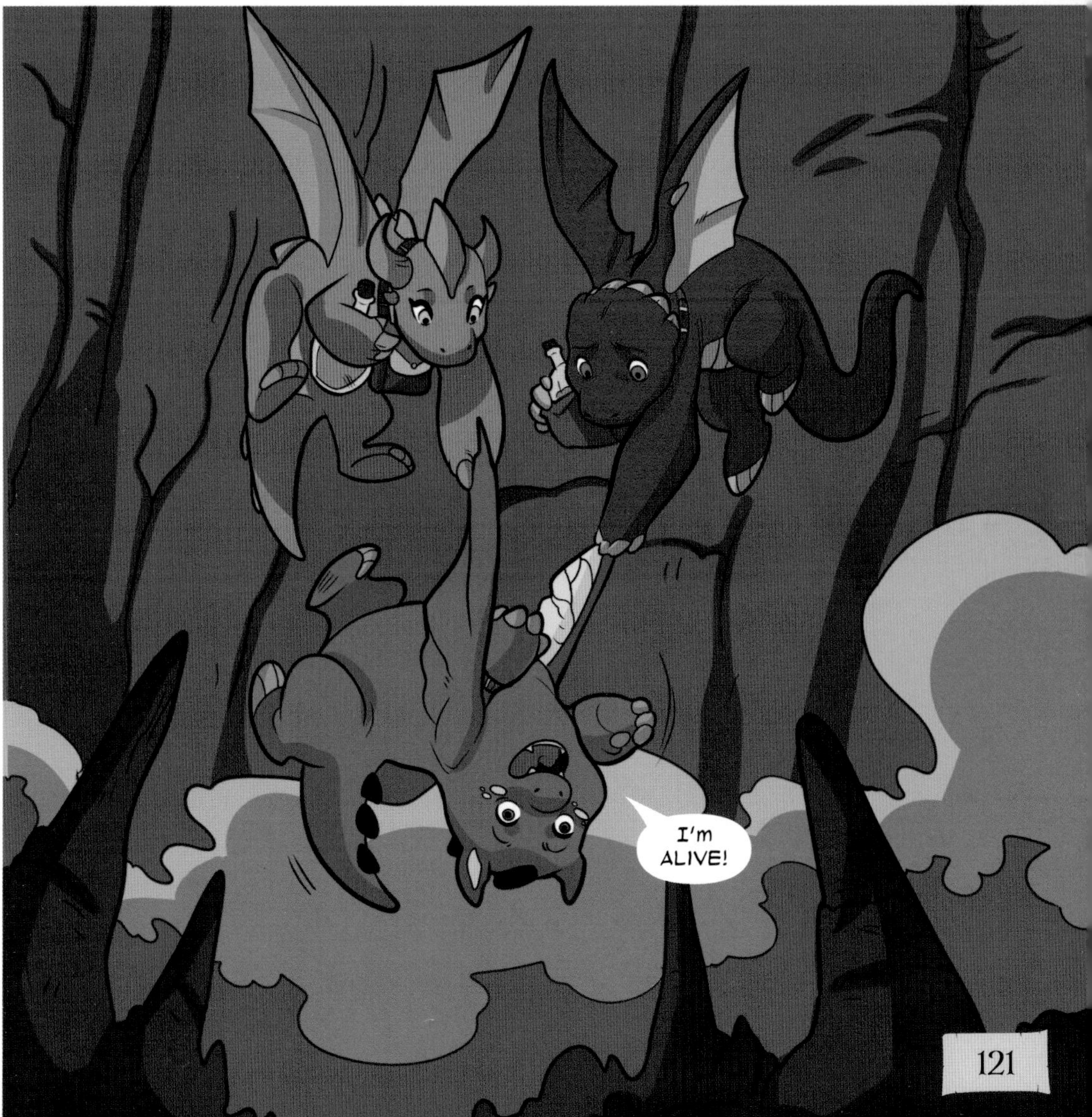
I'm ALIVE!

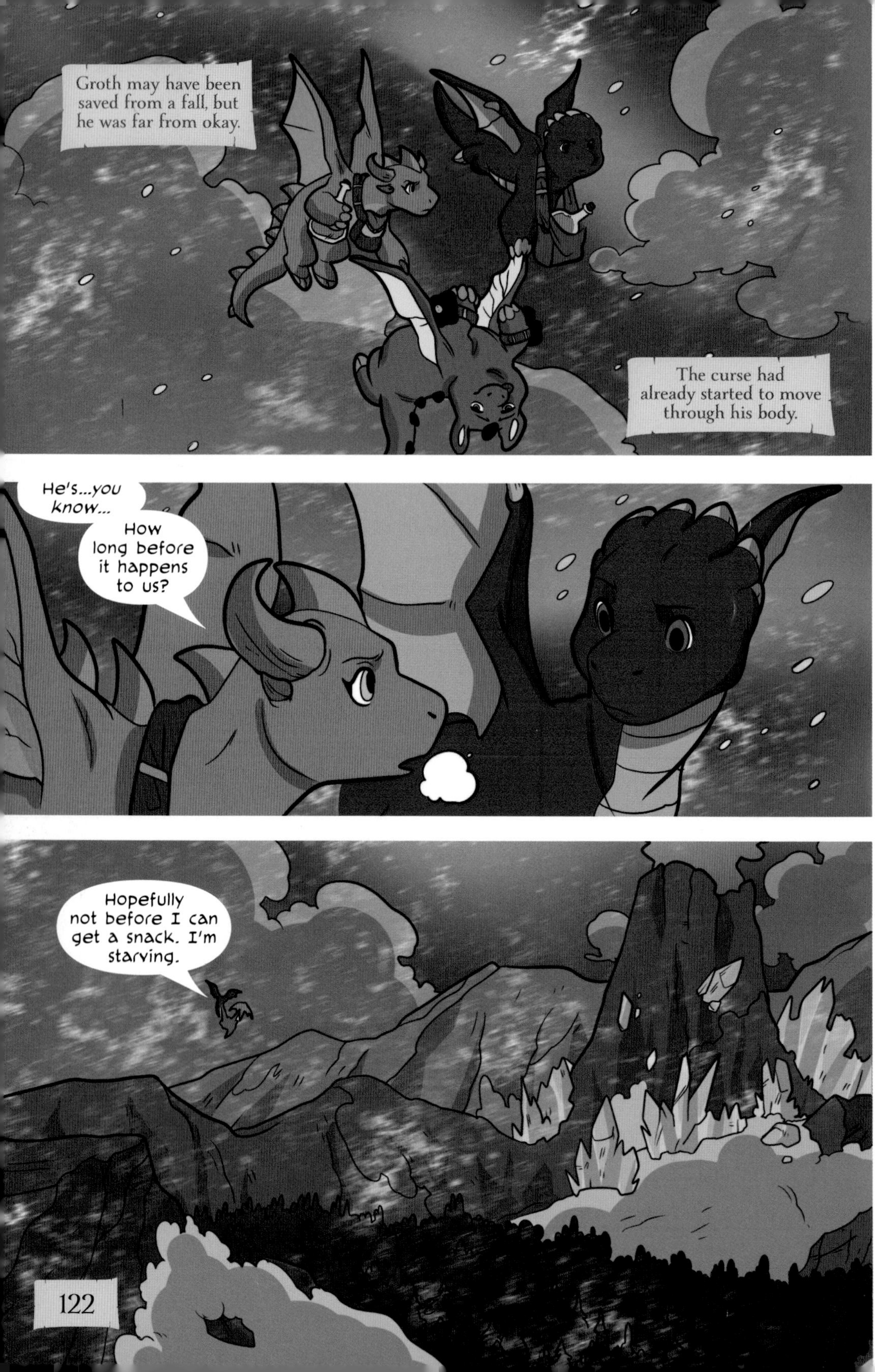

Groth may have been saved from a fall, but he was far from okay.
The curse had already started to move through his body.
He's...you know...
How long before it happens to us?
Hopefully not before I can get a snack. I'm starving.

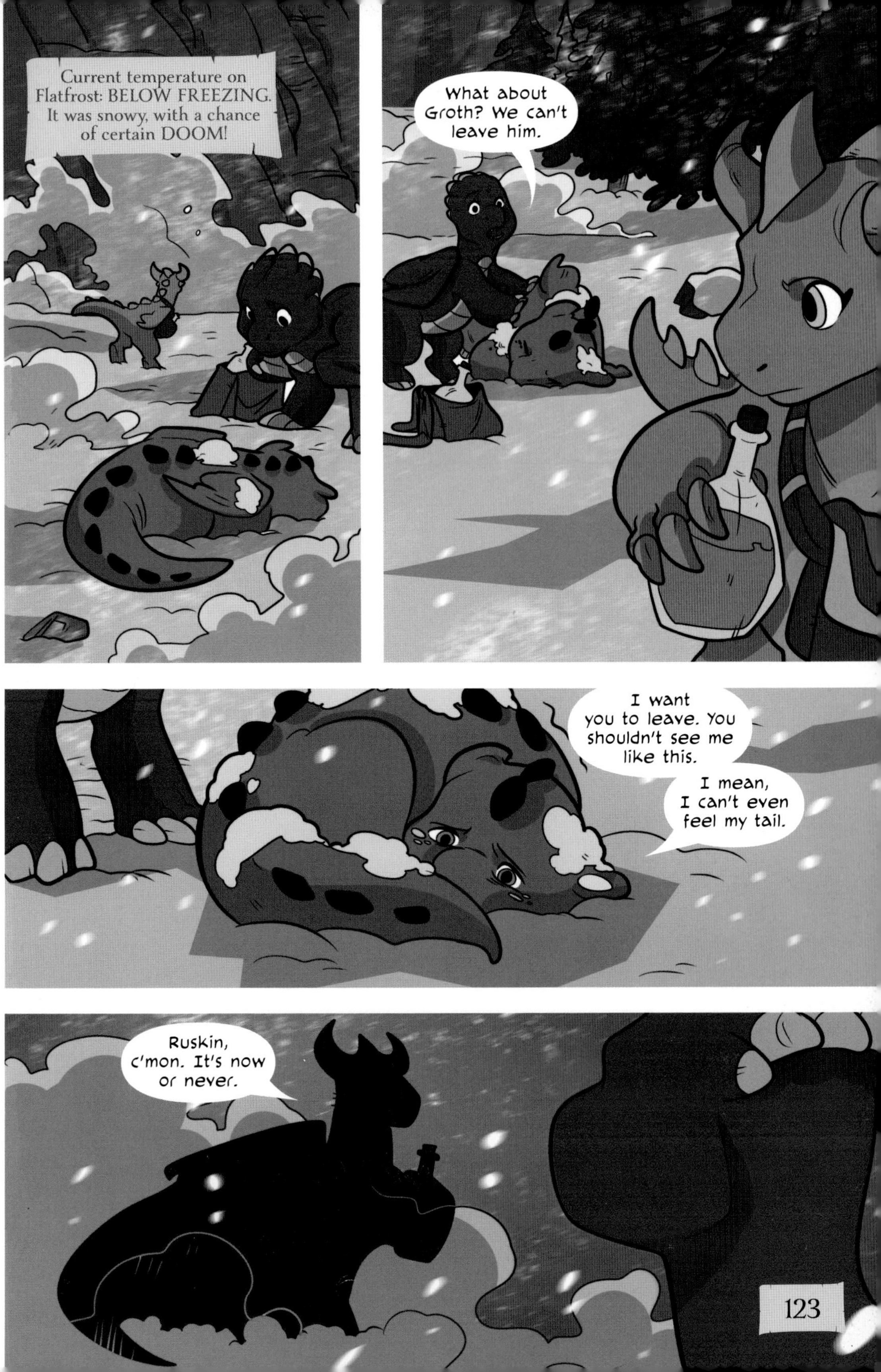
Current temperature on Flatfrost: BELOW FREEZING. It was snowy, with a chance of certain DOOM!
What about Groth? We can't leave him.
I want you to leave. You shouldn't see me like this.
I mean, I can't even feel my tail.
Ruskin, c'mon. It's now or never.

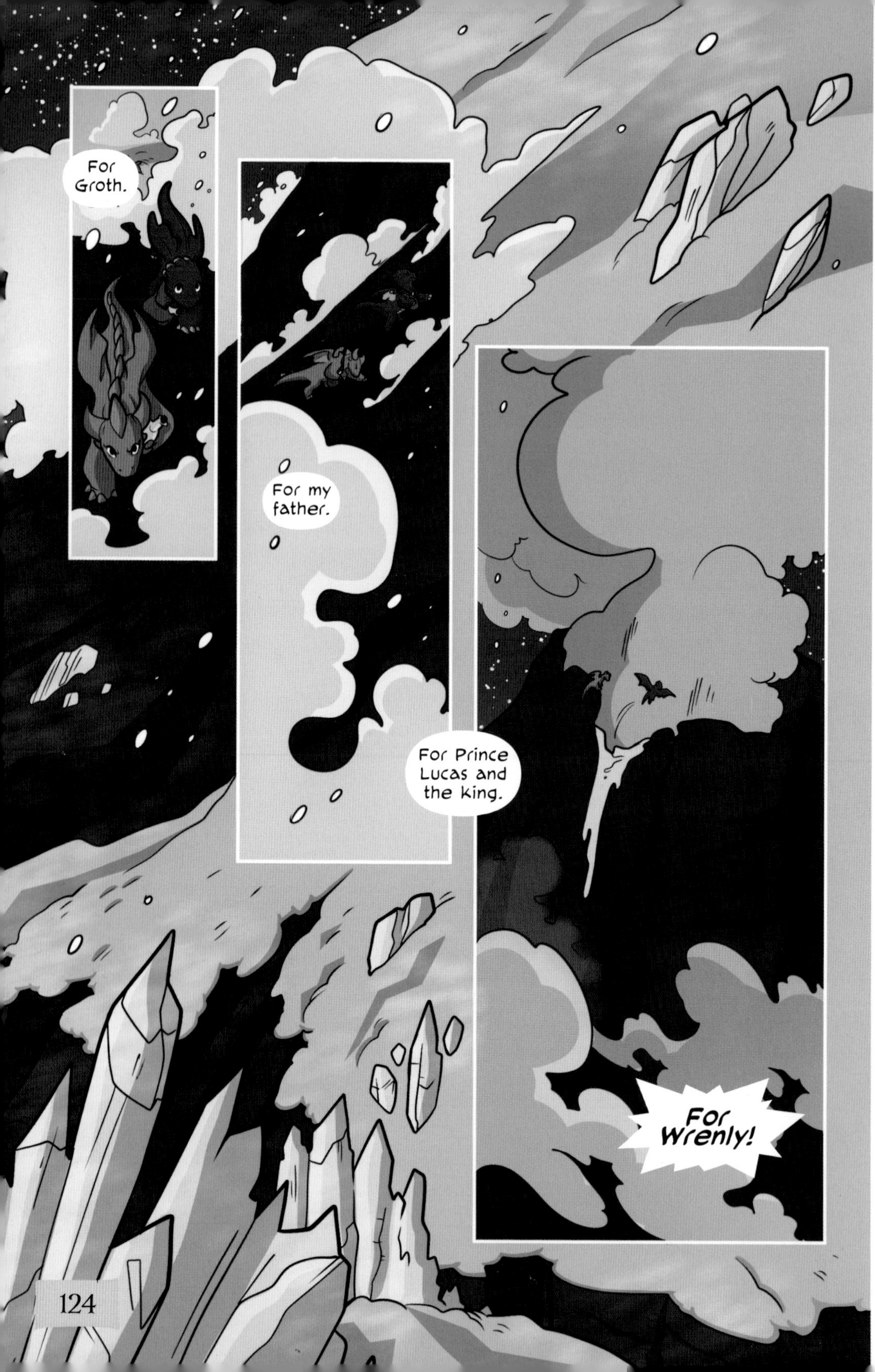
For Groth.
For my father.
For Prince Lucas and the king.
For Wrenly!

Chapter 10

So, we just fly down, drop the potion, hope it's okay that it's just us delivering it, and that's it?

No. *YOU* fly down.

What?

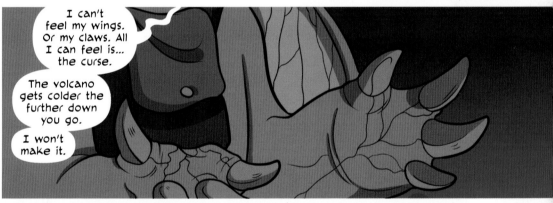

I can't feel my wings. Or my claws. All I can feel is... the curse.

The volcano gets colder the further down you go.

I won't make it.

RUMMMMBLE

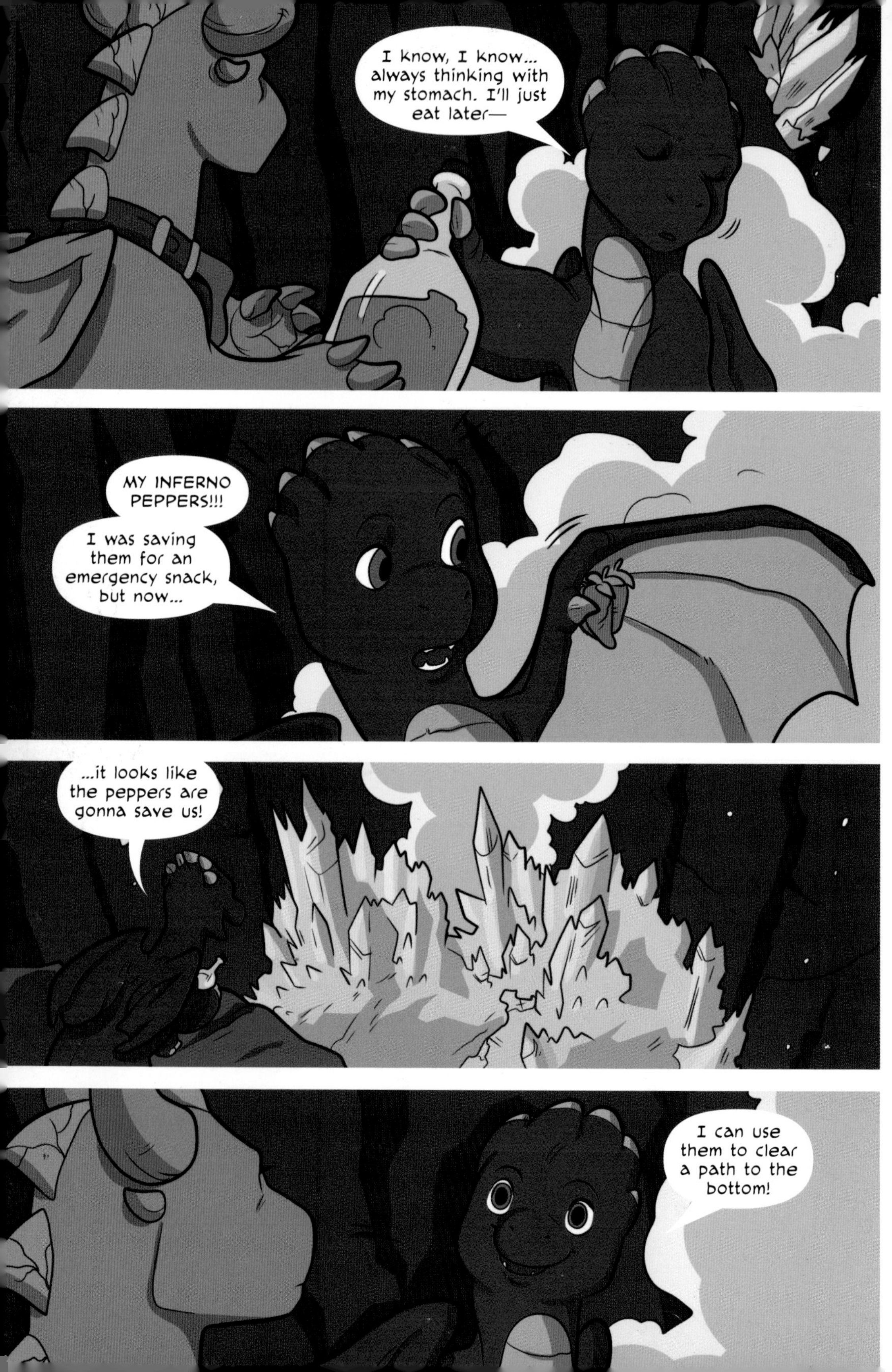
I know, I know... always thinking with my stomach. I'll just eat later—
MY INFERNO PEPPERS!!!
I was saving them for an emergency snack, but now...
...it looks like the peppers are gonna save us!
I can use them to clear a path to the bottom!

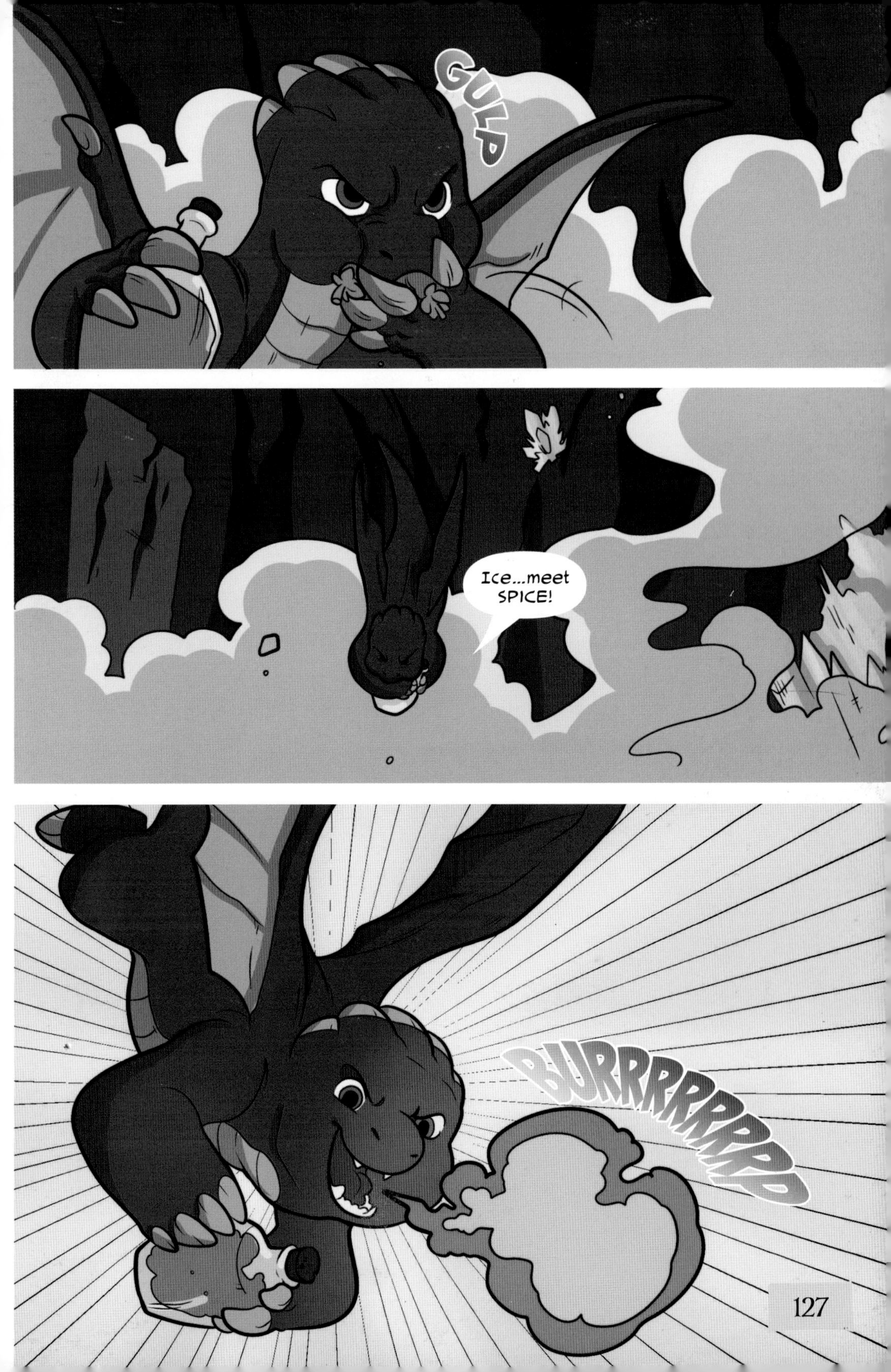
GULP
Ice...meet SPICE!
BURRRRRRRRP

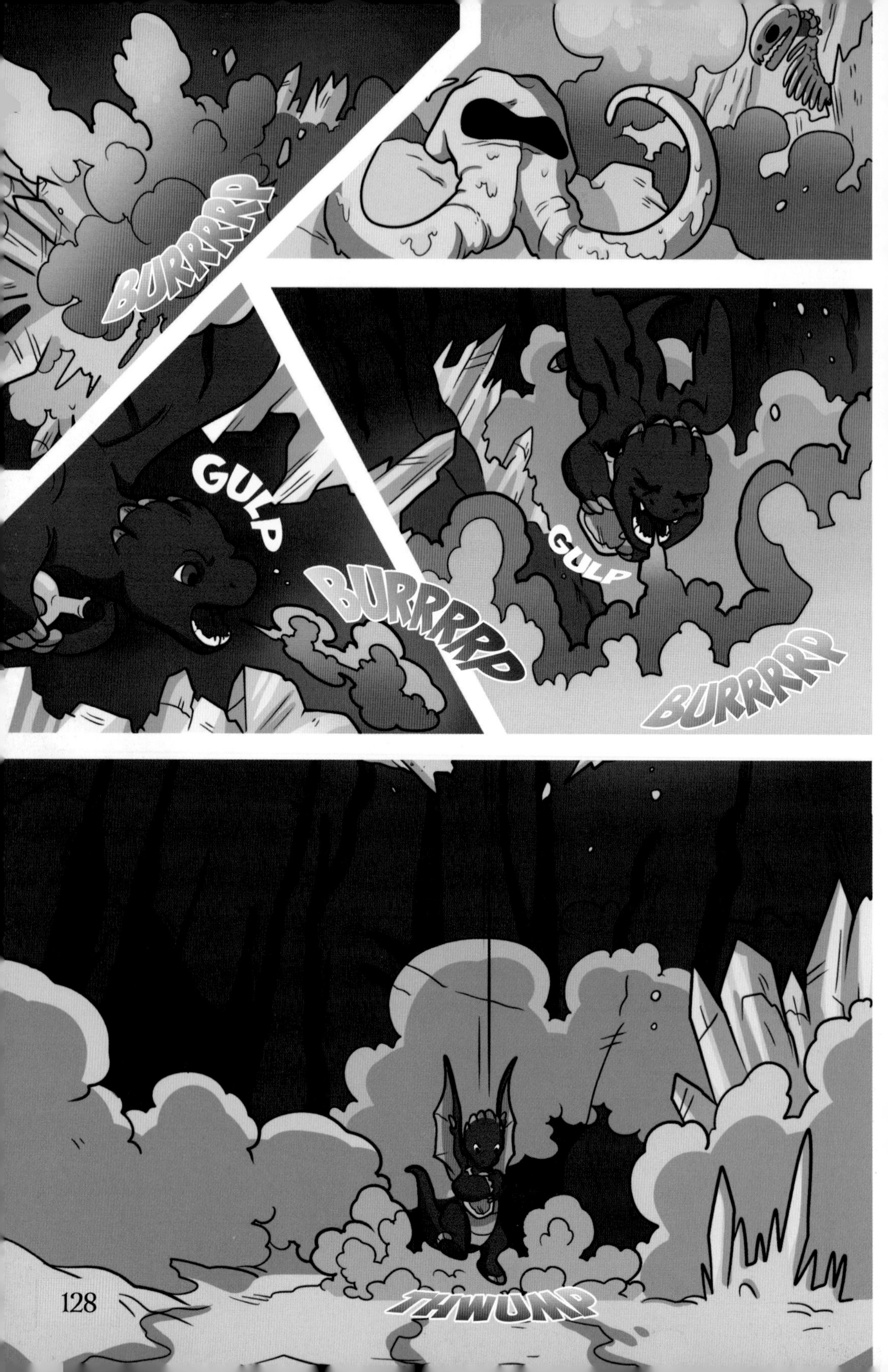
BURRRRP
GULP
BURRRRP
GULP
BURRRRP
THWUMP

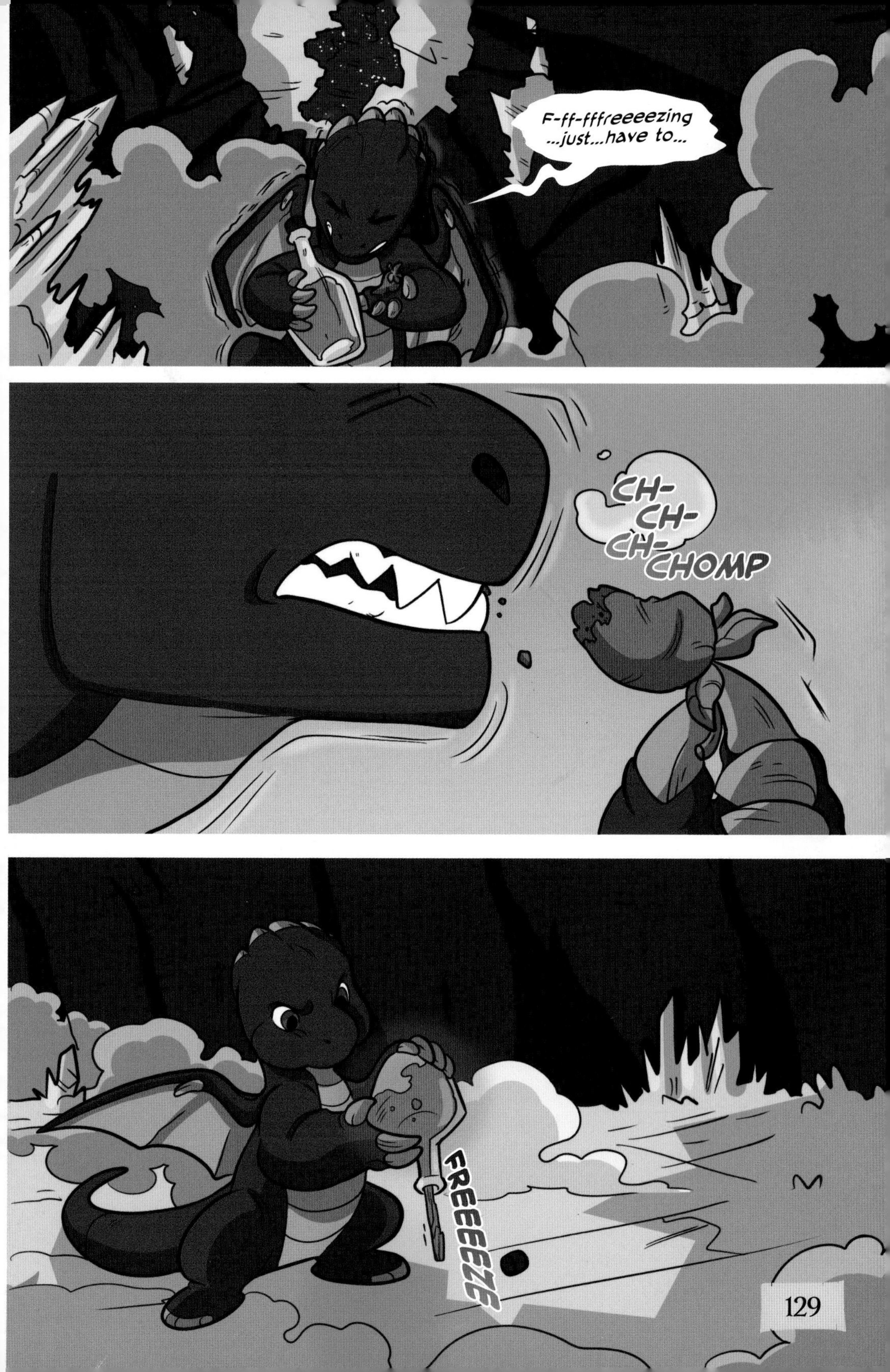
F-ff-fffreeeezing
...just...have to...
CH-CH-CH-CHOMP
FREEEEZE

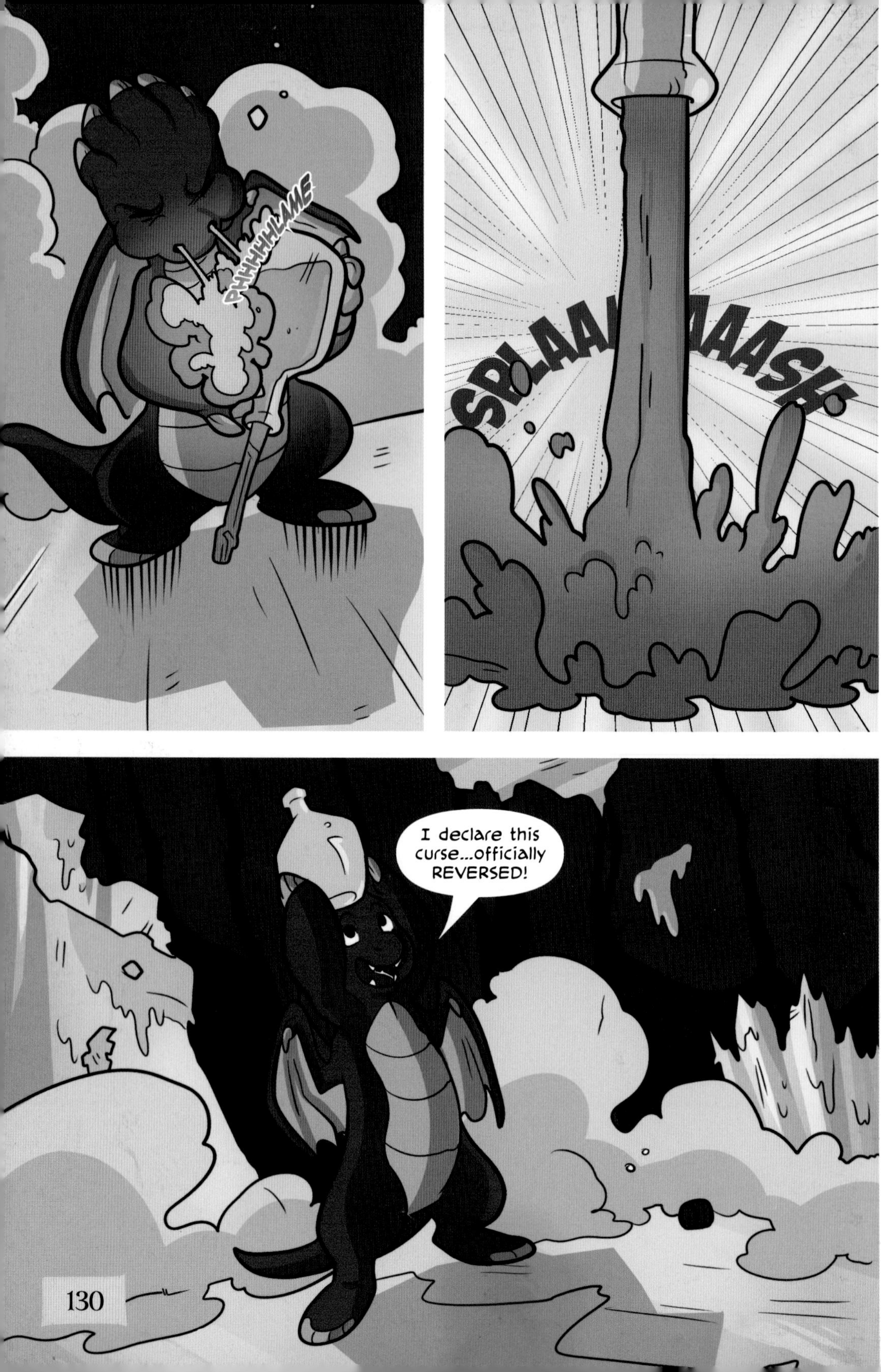
PHHHHLAME
SPLAA AAASH!
I declare this curse...officially REVERSED!

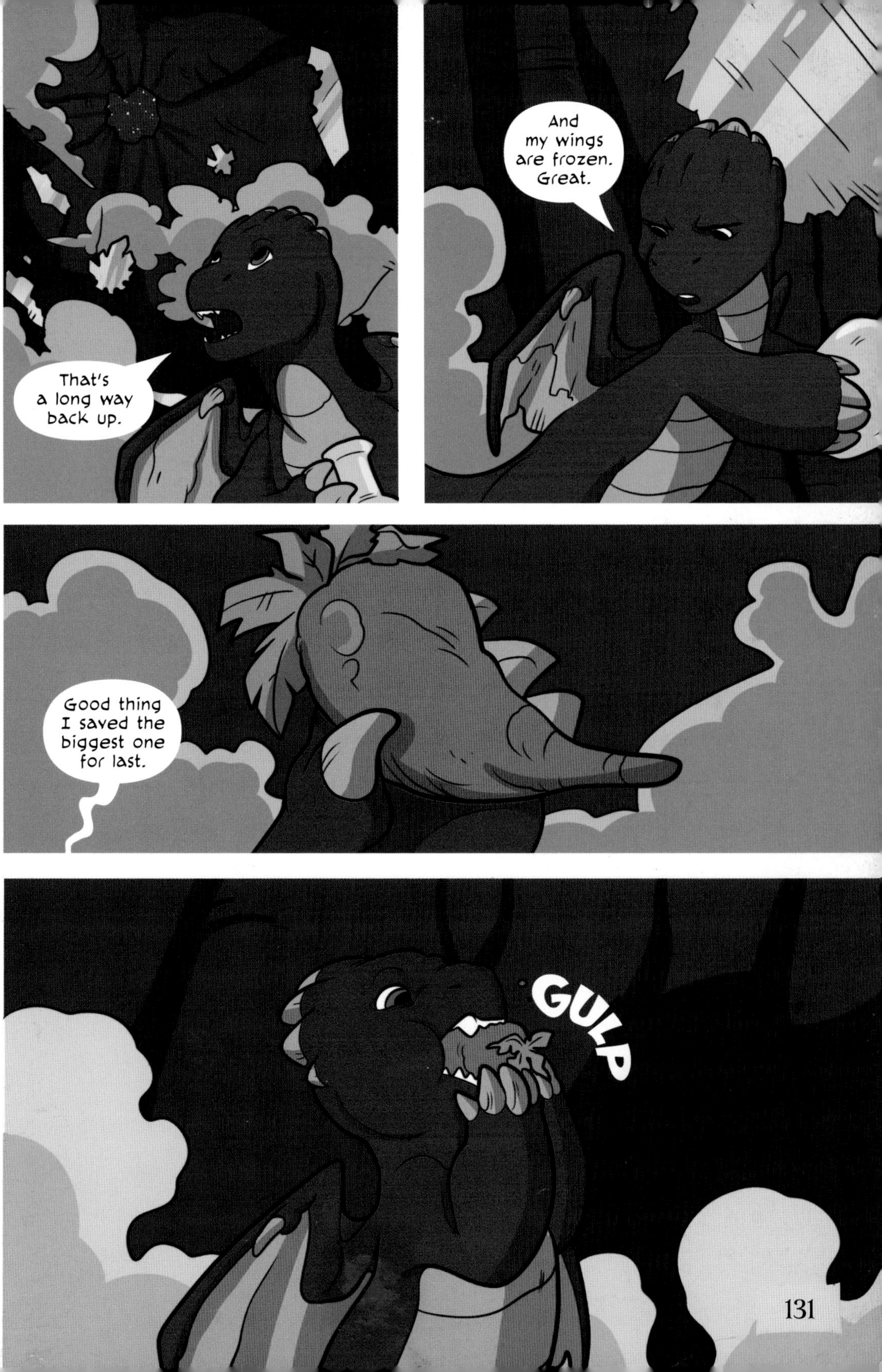
That's a long way back up.
And my wings are frozen. Great.
Good thing I saved the biggest one for last.
GULP

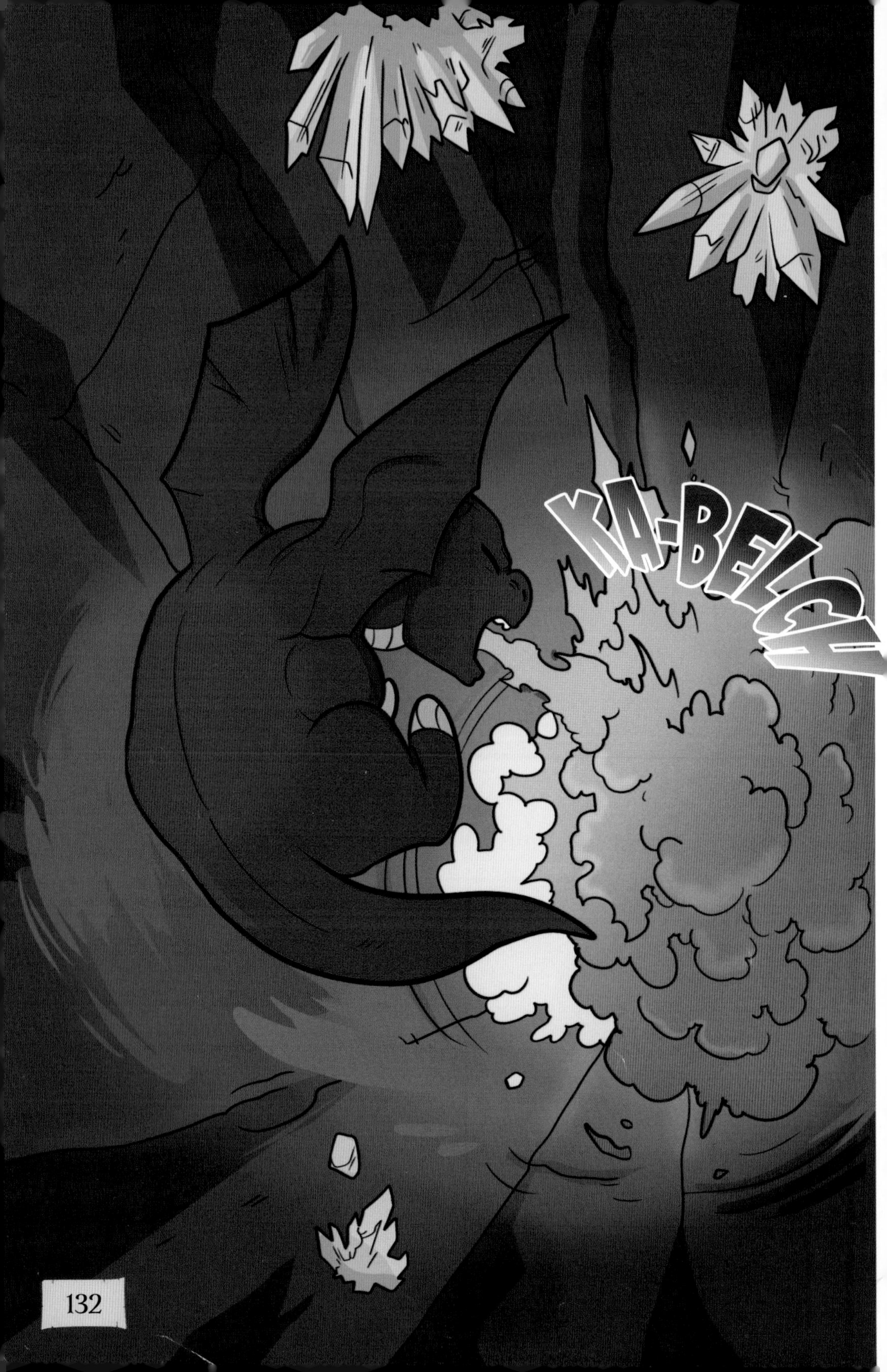
KA-BELCH

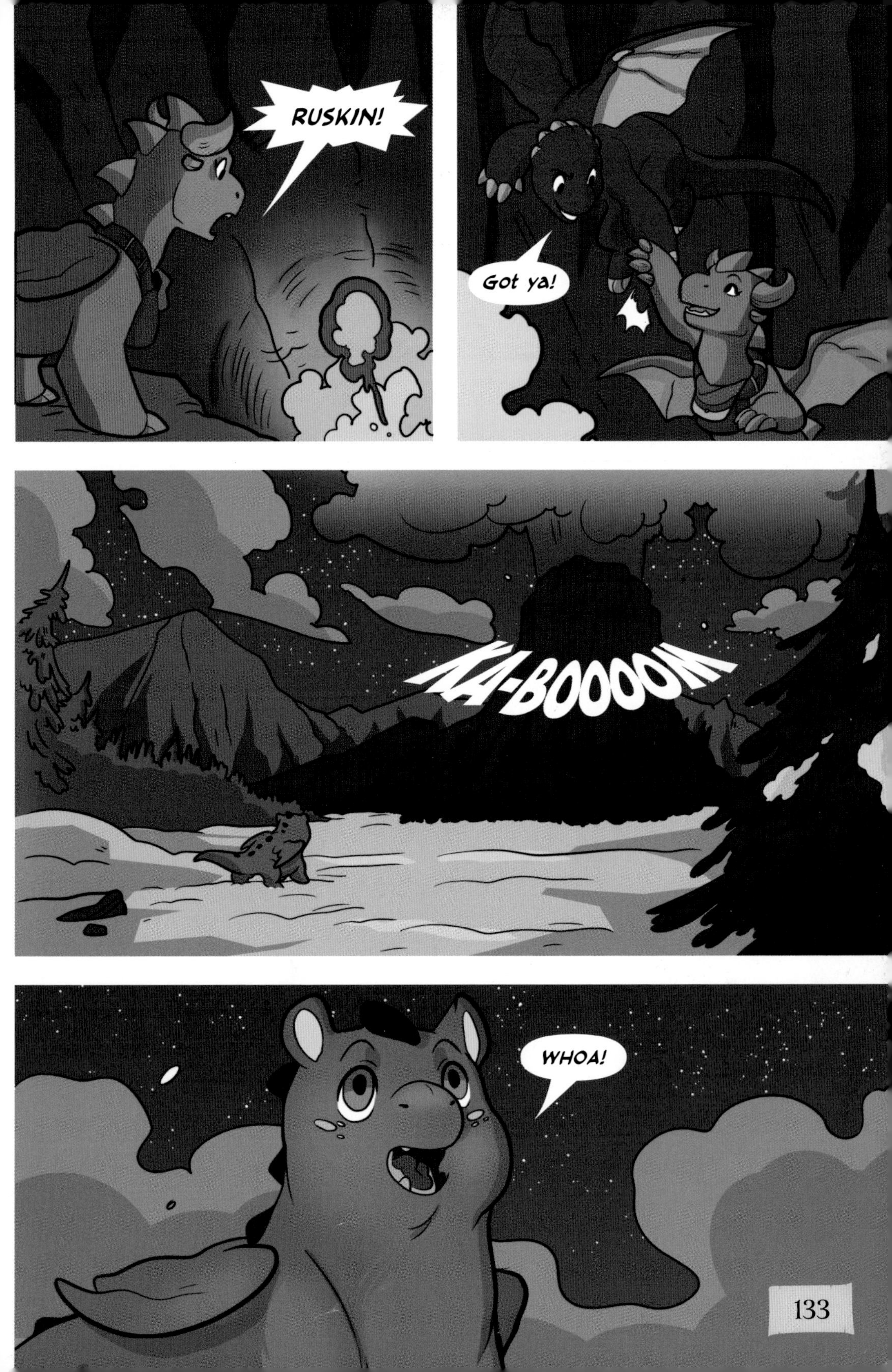
RUSKIN!
Got ya!
KA-BOOOOM
WHOA!

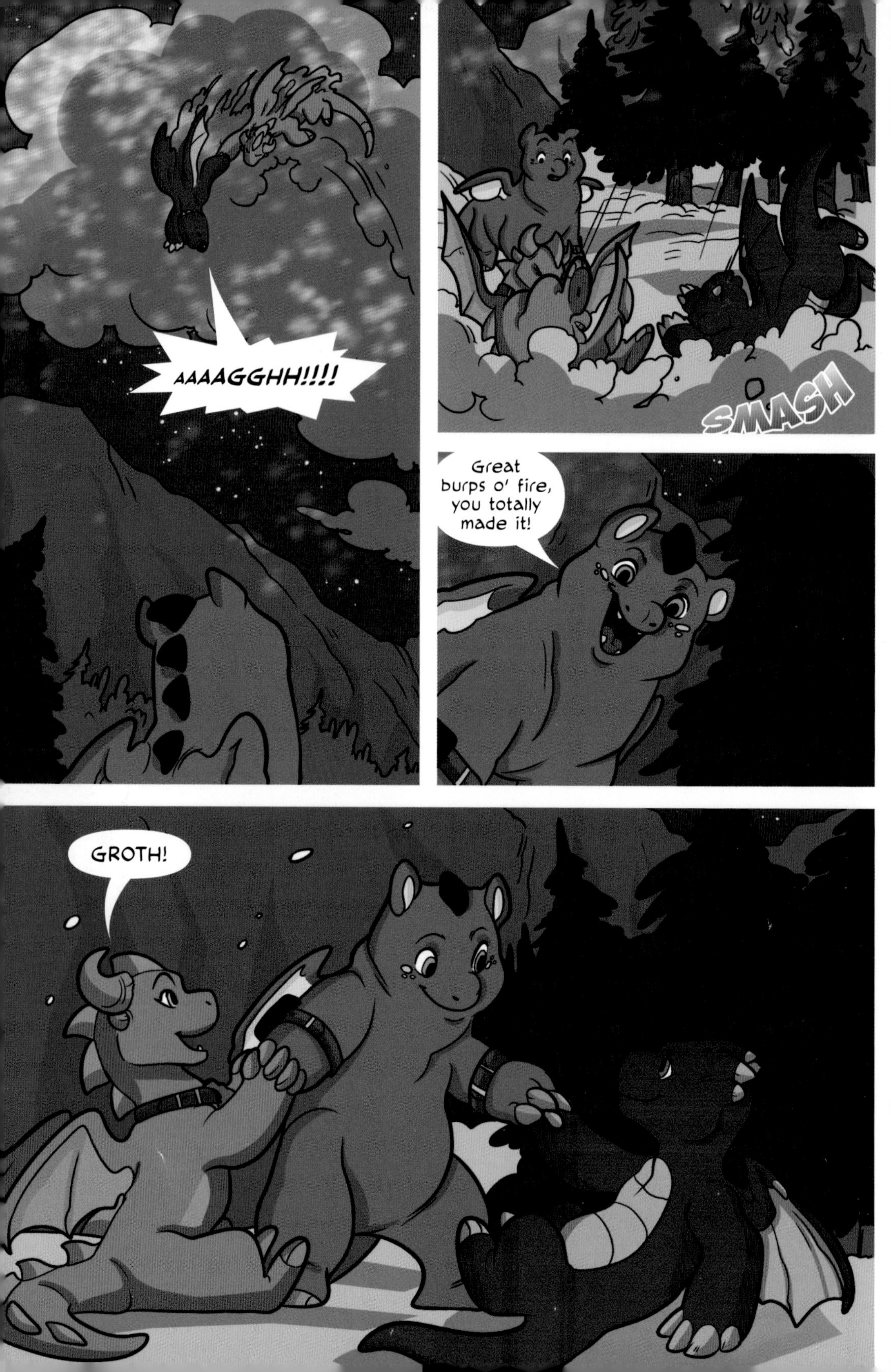
AAAAGGHH!!!!
SMASH
Great burps o' fire, you totally made it!
GROTH!

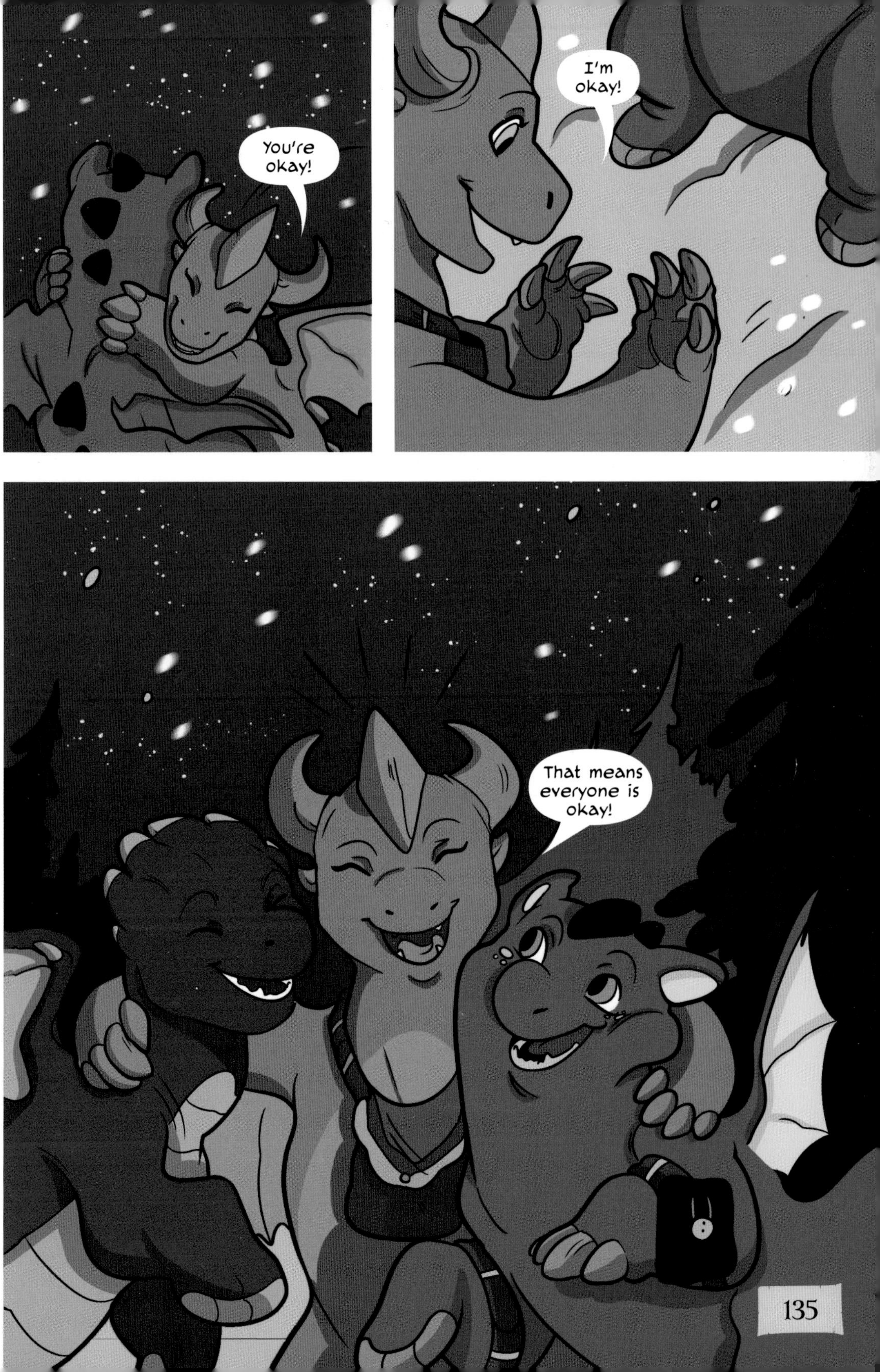
You're okay!
I'm okay!
That means everyone is okay!

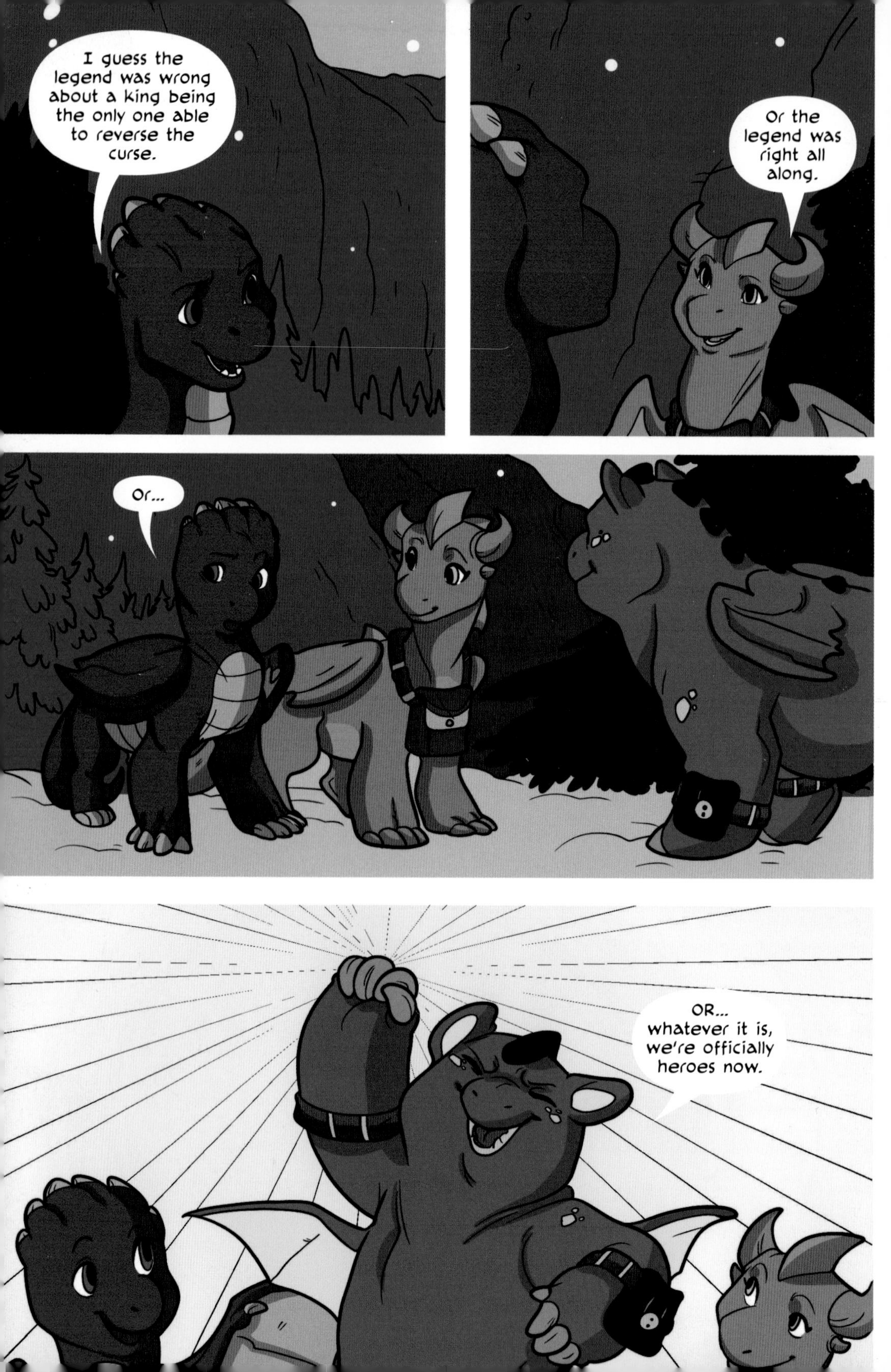
I guess the legend was wrong about a king being the only one able to reverse the curse.
Or the legend was right all along.
Or...
OR... whatever it is, we're officially heroes now.

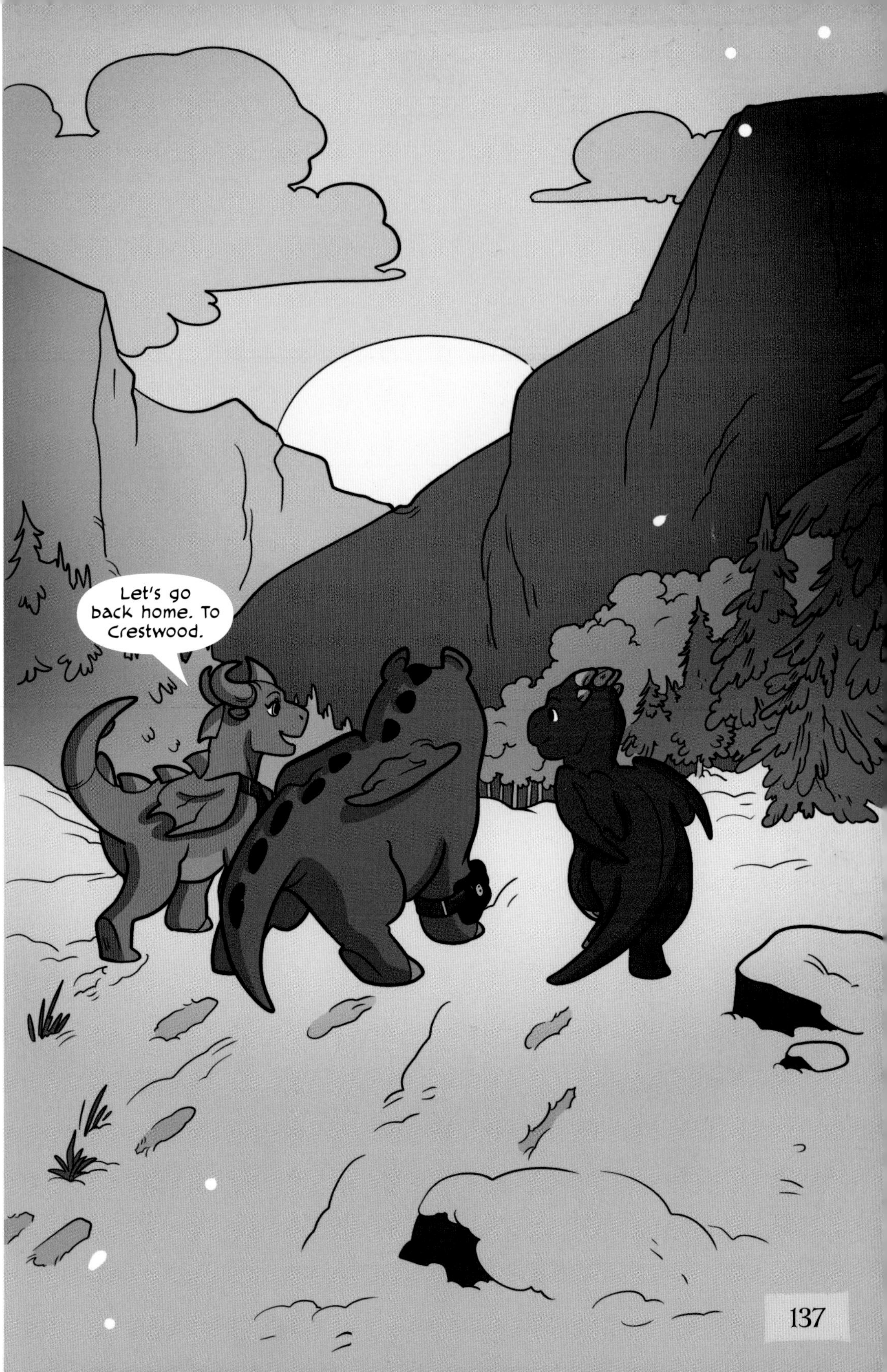
Let's go back home. To Crestwood.

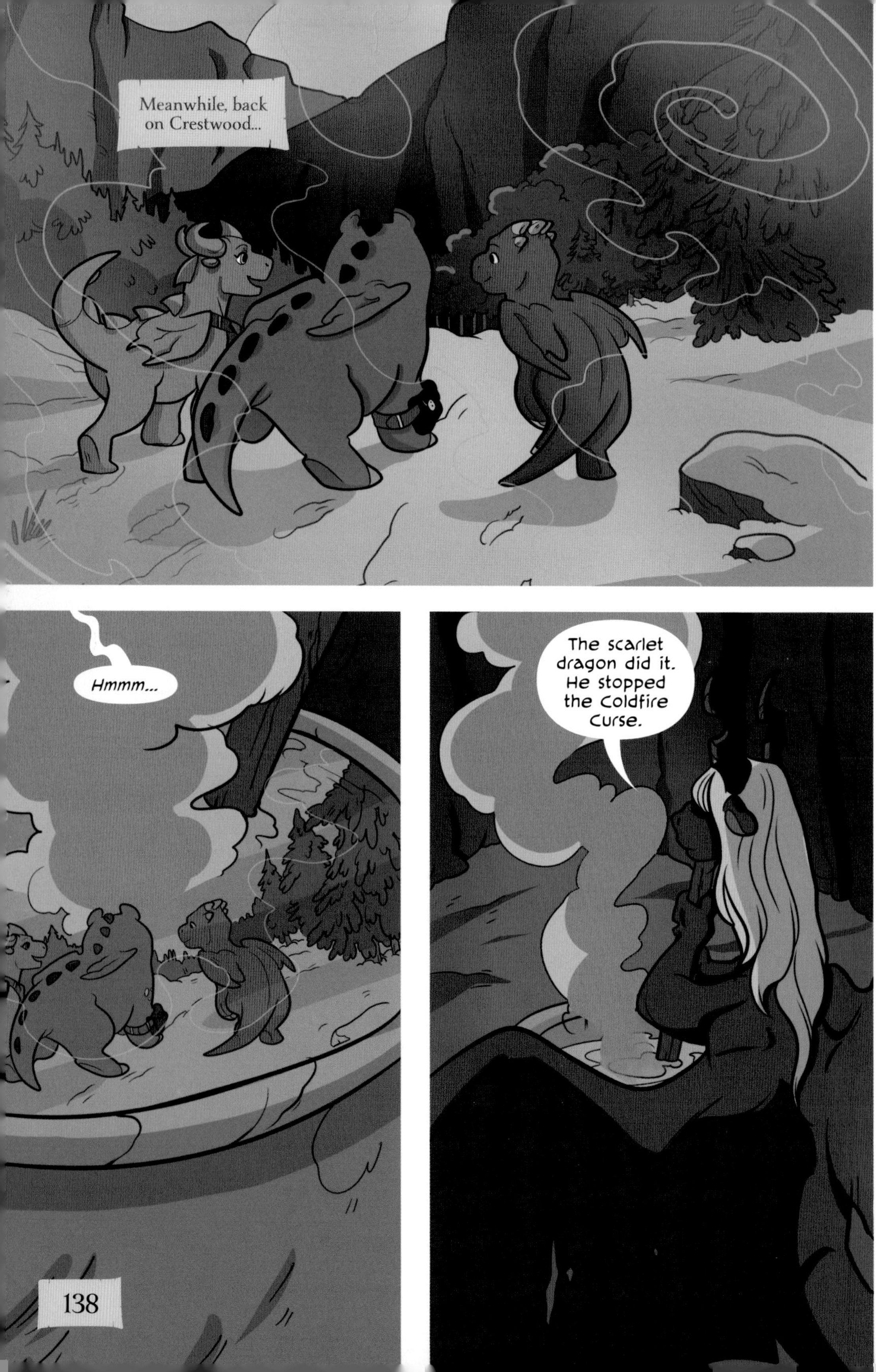

Meanwhile, back on Crestwood...
Hmmm...
The scarlet dragon did it. He stopped the Coldfire Curse.

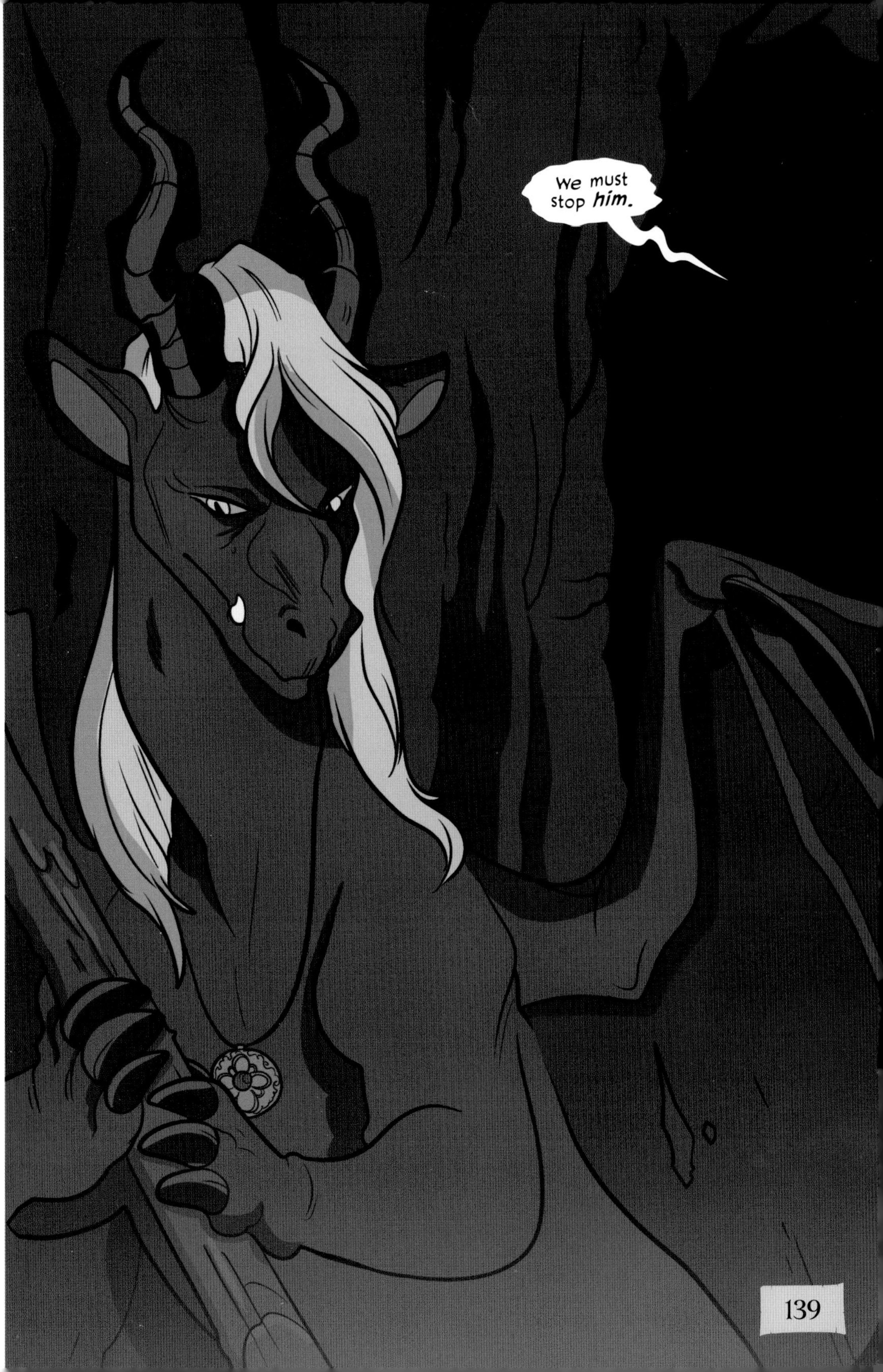
We must stop *him.*

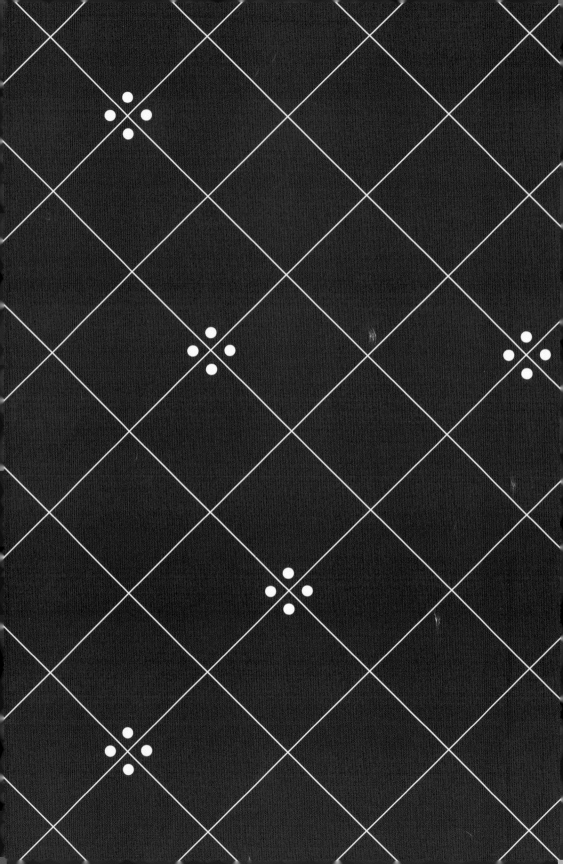

What's in store for Ruskin and his friends next? Find out in . . .

Graphic Novel
Dragon Kingdom
of Wrenly
Shadow Hills

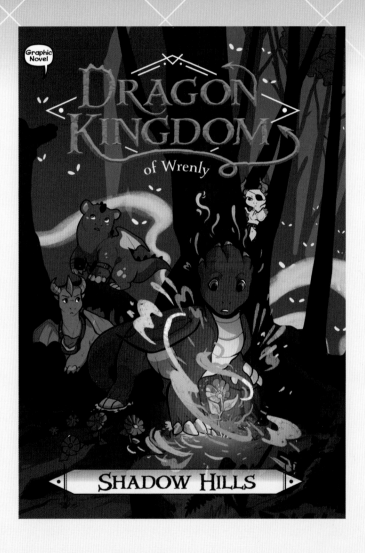

Turn the page for a sneak peek . . .

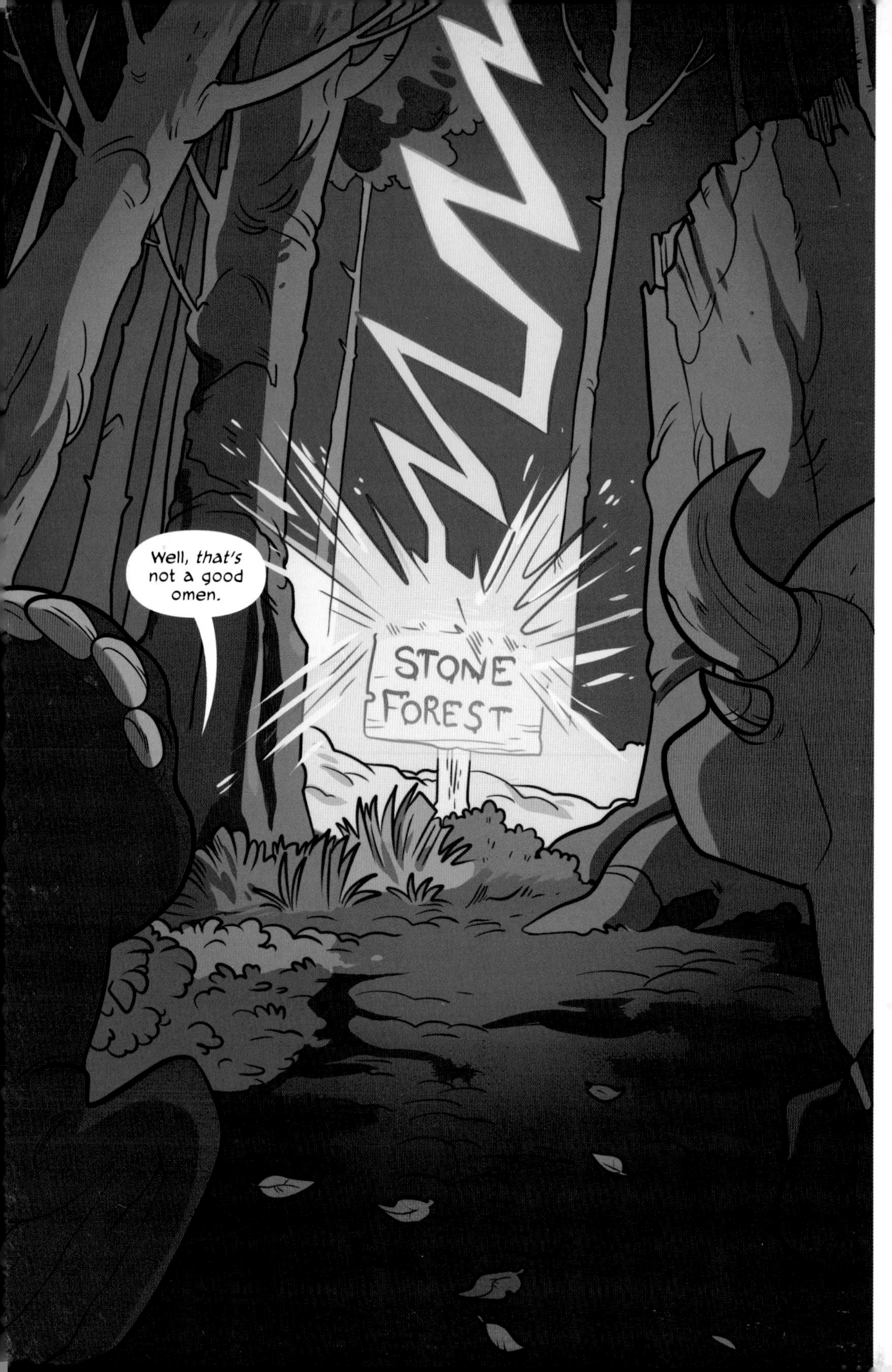
Well, *that's* not a good omen.
STONE FOREST

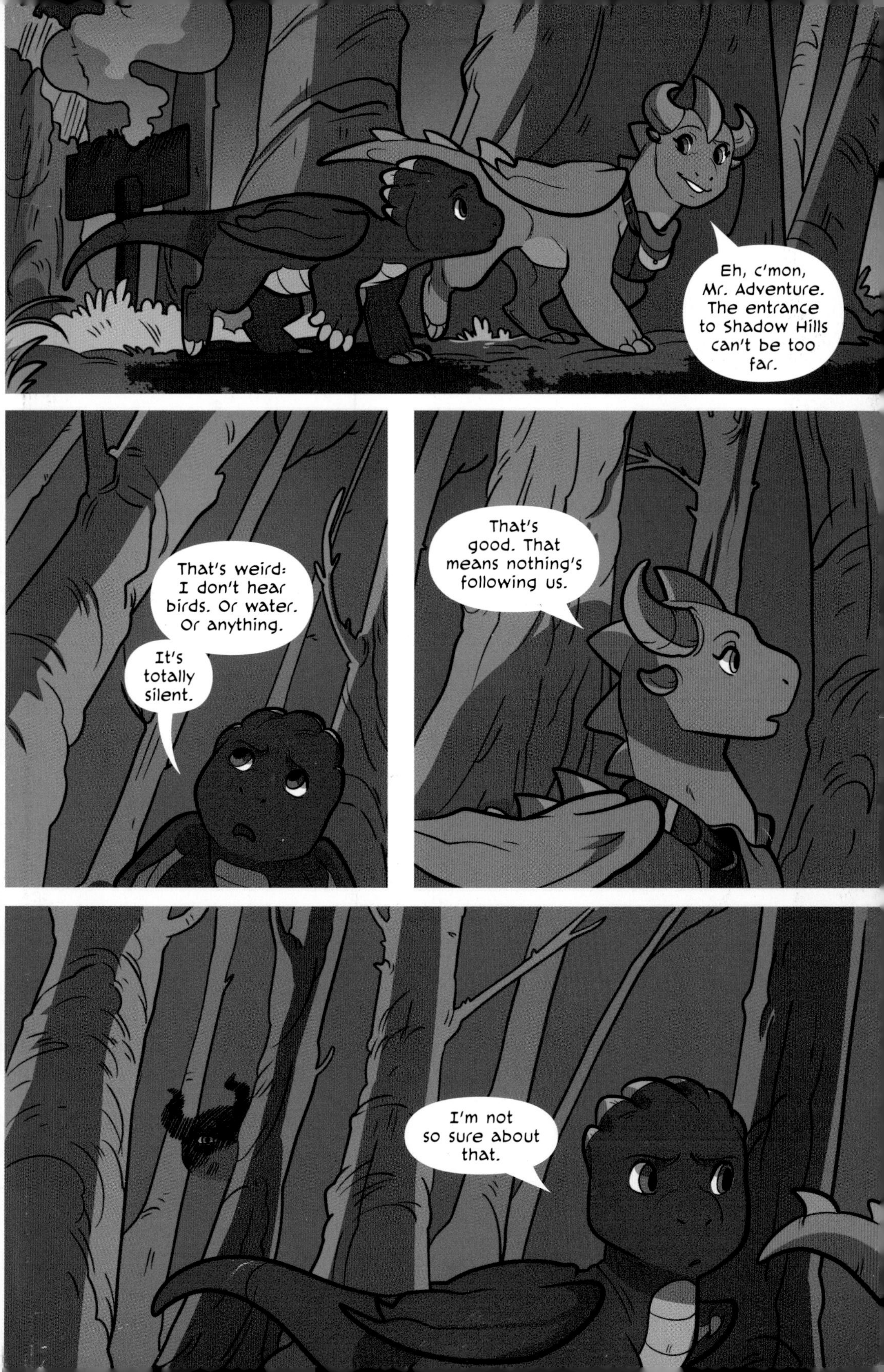

Eh, c'mon, Mr. Adventure. The entrance to Shadow Hills can't be too far.
That's weird: I don't hear birds. Or water. Or anything.
It's totally silent.
That's good. That means nothing's following us.
I'm not so sure about that.

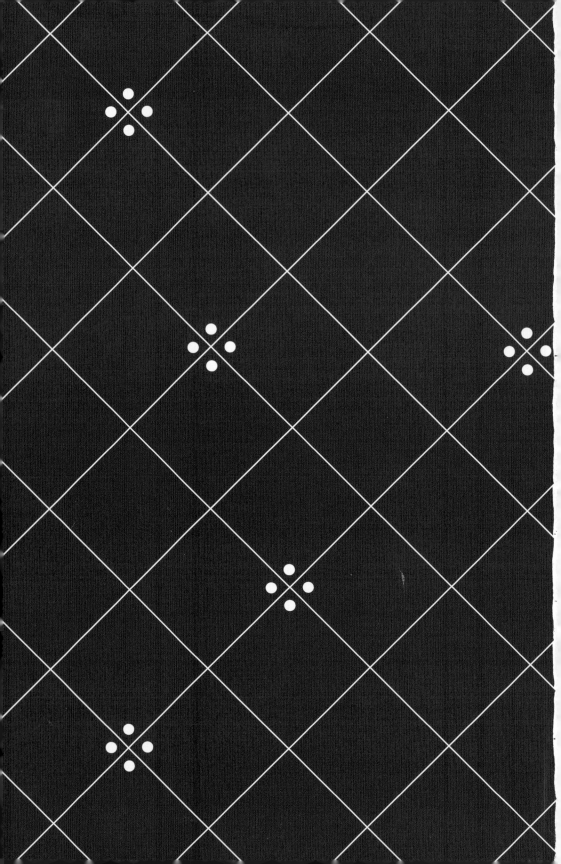